THE TWO WHO BURN

With sudden focus, Ken Jin pressed a hand across Miss Charlotte's mouth. Her eyes flew open in surprise, but she had no time to cry out. His free hand stripped the bed covers away.

He felt her gasp. He would have to act quickly to stop a scream, so he did. He leaned down, his whisper harsh next to her ear. "The Tigress path requires courage even more than secrecy, strength more than desire. Are you brave enough, Miss Charlotte, to walk this path? Are you strong enough to take my yang while your yin gushes like a river?"

She wouldn't understand his words. How could she? Despite her earlier assertions, she was a virginal barbarian, and he had come upon her in the middle of the night.

"Understand this, Miss Charlotte, I am a man who has left the middle path. My weaknesses are legion, and my spirit has splintered into a thousand chaotic pieces. Only one thing keeps my qi strong, only one energy quiets my chaos." He pulled back far enough to look into her wide blue eyes. "Do you wish to know what that one thing is, Miss Charlotte? We call it the Peach of Immortality."

Burning Tigress

JADE LEE

LEISURE BOOKS NEW YORK CITY

A LEISURE BOOK®

June 2006

Published by

Dorchester Publishing Co., Inc.
200 Madison Avenue
New York, NY 10016

ISBN 0-8439-5688-7

The name "Leisure Books" and the stylized "L" with design are
trademarks of Dorchester Publishing Co., Inc.

Printed in the United States of America.

For Staci,
for no reason except that you're amazing.
Thanks for being such a good friend.
I'd say something in basketball-speak
here, but I always sucked at foreign languages.

AUTHOR'S NOTE

The acupressure instructions at the beginning of each chapter are intended for curiosity only. They are taken out of context from a variety of different sources and often shortened for space reasons. Please do not use them as a substitute for qualified medical help.

Each acupressure point is a sensory gateway. When your points are blocked, your senses are not clear, inhibiting your ability to perceive your own feelings, interpret your body's messages, and receive information about the world around you.
Acupressure for Lovers, Michael Reed Gach, Ph.D.

Chapter One

September 10, 1898—Shanghai, China

Charlotte Wicks dashed down the third-floor hallway after her younger brother. Unfortunately, at sixteen William was much too fast to catch, and with a mental age of about seven he was much too strong-willed to listen.

"William!" she called again as she spun into their Chinese servant's room. She skidded to an abrupt stop as she took in the sight before her.

What a large penis! That's all that she could think. *Ken Jin has an immense penis.* She made a valiant attempt to divert her thoughts. Why, for example, was Ken Jin kneeling half naked on the floor in the middle of the afternoon? Why were three very large needles embedded in the flesh right above his very large organ? And why couldn't she look up into the man's face?

She didn't ask any of these questions, of course: All were completely inappropriate. Despite the debauchery that ran rampant in Shanghai—and in this very house sometimes—Charlotte wasn't supposed to know about men's organs or what they did with them. Or that Ken Jin had entertained a good number of her friends with his *very large penis*.

Her brother, of course, had no such restraint. "Mama says not to touch that," he said loudly and pointed at Ken's Jin's dark red erection. "She says you'll go to Hell and burn for eternity with the devil." He frowned. "But she didn't say anything about needles."

Ken Jin didn't respond, except to leap to his feet and hastily drag up his pants. That successfully hid the view, but it probably also drove the needles even deeper into his flesh.

"My goodness," Charlotte breathed, "doesn't that hurt?" She blinked, startled by her own stupid comment. Of course it hurt. Taking hold of her curiosity and her errant brother, she made herself turn away from the blushing Chinaman. Then she addressed her gangly, adolescent sibling.

"You cannot go bursting into people's chambers, William, even if it's a servant's room. It's simply not fair." And who knew what one might see? she added silently. "Come along now. We'll let Ken Jin collect himself and ask him politely to visit us in the library, shall we?"

She tried to lead her brother out, but the boy had been growing again and was larger than she. When William didn't want to leave, she couldn't force him; and right now, William would not be distracted from their father's Chinese First Boy. Truth be told, Charlotte was also intrigued by the handsome young Chinaman. He was desperately intelligent, running her father's extensive business dealings single-handedly while keeping her debauched father and religious mother in opposite corners of the city. With his help, Charlotte was able to keep the house servants in line and manage her rather unusual younger brother. Plus, every one of her friends had commented on how very handsome and skilled he was in a variety of bedroom arts. She couldn't vouch for the latter, of course, but she could attest to his looks.

Ken Jin was tall and muscular, of twenty-eight or twenty-nine years, and had lush black hair pulled back into the most perfect queue. His face was nicely formed, his shoulders were broad, and he had a generous . . . Well, all his physical attributes were built along generous lines. Still, she had no idea that Chinese men—even young healthy ones—were so largely endowed. Or perhaps, she was simply uninformed. After all, her only real experience with men's organs came from assisting her brother with his bath. Perhaps Ken Jin was normal and her brother abnormal. It would stand to reason.

"You shouldn't scratch there either," William said loudly, doing just that. "It makes it worse."

Ken Jin nodded formally to Charlotte's brother. With his trousers back in place, the only indications of anything untoward were the dark flush to his cheeks and the expanding circle of crimson on his tented pants.

"One of your needles has drawn blood," she said, once again proving that she was an utter failure at keeping her attention fixed where it ought to be—on her brother and not on the bleeding servant. So she tried again. "Come along, William. Ken Jin will join us in the library." Assuming he didn't bleed to death first.

"But Nanny said he would take us to the park," William wheedled.

Charlotte nodded. "Yes, yes, of course, dearling, but the park is outside, you know, and we can't get there by staying here."

William blinked in his uncomprehending way, then abruptly turned back to Ken Jin. "Why do you have needles in your stomach?" he asked.

Charlotte sighed. Sometimes her brother could fixate on

the most inappropriate topics. It didn't help matters that she was desperately curious to know the answer as well.

Ken Jin bowed again, no doubt driving the needles deeper. "It is a form of medicine, Master Will," he responded in his low, smooth voice.

"Yes, William," Charlotte agreed. "A Chinese form of medicine. Now let us—"

"I want to see," William interrupted. Then, to her horror, her nearly six-foot-tall brother lumbered forward, his hands going for Ken Jin's pants.

"That is quite enough!" Charlotte cried in her best disciplinarian voice. William stopped his advance, thank God. "Into the library, young man. Now!"

Another long moment went by as the boy hovered, obviously undecided. Then Ken Jin spoke, his manner extremely pleasant. "I should be happy to take you to the park, Master William, but you must let me don the appropriate shoes."

Charlotte's brother frowned at Ken Jin's bare feet. They were nice feet, Charlotte noticed, and wasn't that an odd thing to think about a servant's feet? But they *were* nice: The skin was smooth and not hairy, the toes long and well shaped. They were masculine without being a coolie's hoary feet.

"All right," William finally said, spinning on his heel and abruptly dashing out of the room. Charlotte felt her lips curve into a soft smile. Truly, her brother was a sweet boy even if he was sixteen and slow.

She turned back to Ken Jin. "Thank you for your assistance—"

"My shoes," he interrupted, his voice uncharacteristically tight. "Please, Miss Charlotte, let me put on my shoes."

She frowned, abruptly realizing that she wasn't looking

at his feet but at the dark bloodstains on his pants. There were three circles now, exactly above the three needles, and the tenting fabric wasn't quite so pronounced.

"Miss Charlotte?"

"Shoes. Yes, of course," she babbled. "I'll see you in the library, then?" She didn't know why she was lingering. She couldn't truly ask Ken Jin why he had stuck needles into his . . . She ought to be going. And yet . . .

"Ken Jin . . ."

The muscles of his jaw bulged as he clenched his teeth. "Yes, Miss Charlotte?"

"Do you require any bandages or salves?"

"No, Miss Charlotte."

She swallowed. Of course he didn't. Ken Jin was the most self-sufficient man she'd ever met. "Well then," she snapped, abruptly bringing her thoughts back to order. "I shall just wait for you in the library. After you . . . um . . ."

"After I don my shoes, Miss Charlotte."

"Yes. Your shoes." And with that, she spun around and fled.

Ken Jin waited an eternity for the door to close. When it at last clicked shut behind Miss Charlotte, he hurried to unbuttoned his pants, wincing as he saw how deep the acupuncture needles had pushed. Digging them out was going to burn like hot coals. On the other hand, his dragon thrust forward like a proud beast. Perhaps he had just been too careful in his stimulation before. Perhaps Miss Charlotte's interruption had been fortunate in that it forced him to stab the needles deep into his Sea of Vitality, thereby finally awakening his slumbering yang fires. That was possible, he supposed. He had no other explanation for the return of his suddenly rearing dragon.

A noise came from down the hallway, and Ken Jin applied himself to gently removing the deepest needle, the one planted firmly in the Gate of Origin. The young master was probably becoming impatient. And the young miss . . .

His dragon twitched in interest, the yang fire clearly strengthening, though indiscriminate in its tastes. Ken Jin didn't care. At least there was interest. At least he wasn't completely depleted, as he'd feared.

It had been unwise to perform his exercises in the middle of the day. He had taken the precaution of returning to his own bedchamber, but he'd known the young master had no respect for closed doors—and at sixteen, the child had the strength and speed to outrun his maid and sister. Yet, Ken Jin could not quarrel with the result. Even as he drew out the last of the needles, his yang surged hot and full, his dragon a strong organ once again. It had been over a year now since his dragon had shown such vigor.

He smiled in pleasure despite the knowledge that his new vitality would create more problems. The overly curious Miss Charlotte was going to plague him with oblique questions and veiled stares.

His dragon reared again. Clearly it enjoyed female attention no matter the source. Fortunately, his self-discipline was more than adequate. His employer's daughter would be no more a lure to him than any other grasping, overblown, white woman. Or so he told himself.

Reaching for a change of clothes, he chose the loosest of his white-man trousers. Truthfully, he missed his boyhood coolie pants held up by a rope. A man could do anything in those pants. It was as close to being naked as one could get in public.

But he was a rich First Boy now, a reflection of his employer's status and wealth. Certain things were expected. He slid his pants over his vitals, closing his eyes to appreciate the expanding yang heat as fabric caressed skin. In

6

his mind's eye, he saw the blond miss as she'd burst in on him. Her blue eyes had widened with shock, her skin had flushed, and her lips had reddened. . . . Truly, she was a woman of strong yin.

She had no idea, of course. Though he no longer thought the whites as insubstantial ghost people, he knew they understood nothing of their own passions. The men expressed their lusts without restraint, while the women bottled them up until the yin river dried to dust. Unless, of course, they chose the path of a "slut." He had indeed harvested a great deal of yin from Charlotte's more exploratory friends.

Once when he'd first laid eyes on Miss Charlotte, he had been nearly overcome by the need to stroke her yin fountain to its fullest glory. But he had been busy angling for the position of the family's First Boy while half carrying her drunken father across the threshold. Debauching the daughter of the household would not have helped his cause. Still, the temptation lingered, especially as the girl matured into a frustrated, lonely woman prone to her own fits of impulsive desires.

Sadly, he could not help her. If he lost his job, his entire family would starve. He sighed, already mourning the day when Miss Charlotte lost her dewy spring. She was twenty-five now, and her eventual withering was not long off, especially if her mother had anything to say about it. But such was the way with pure white women, and he did not have the time to teach an entire barbarian race the truth about their energies.

He glanced at the clock on his desk. He had little time to take Master William to the park. Fortunately, they were between shipments. There was no cargo for him to supervise, no inventories to examine. Charlotte's father was at his favorite whorehouse, and her mother at her prayers. All that demanded his attention was the regular correspondence that came with a white man's empire in China. That, and the work required to keep his flagging qi strong.

He donned his white-man's shoes and left the room. Oddly, his dragon had not shrunk away, but remained a thick and heavy presence that he felt with every step down the stairs to the first floor. Ken Jin smiled, pleased with the sensation even though he strove to hide it. How wonderful to feel young and vital again.

"Kin Jin! Ken Jin!" The young master was hopping up and down with eagerness. "Do you have your shoes on?"

"I do, Master William. I will take you and your sister to the park now."

Master William rushed to the door. His sister appeared a moment later, her bonnet appropriately arranged to hide her golden hair. The surging yang in Ken Jin's blood noted that her skin was still flushed, that her eyes kept darting down to his dragon before shying guiltily away. Yin curiosity and a virgin's embarrassment—how his dragon loved the combination.

"Was there a particular park you wished to visit, Miss Charlotte?" he asked, pleased that his voice betrayed none of the thoughts her pert breasts summoned. She had full, ripe mangoes, perfectly weighted for a man's hands, firm enough not to bruise, soft enough to suckle, and juicy enough to yield warm, luscious yin.

"Actually, Ken Jin, I would like you to drop me at the Crane household. I understand Joanna has returned. If you and William stay for an hour at the park, you can return for me directly." Her tone did not disguise the excitement in her voice.

"Miss Joanna has returned home?" he asked stupidly, a sudden fear tightening his vitals.

Miss Charlotte's eyes flashed in excitement. "I heard it from Susan, who learned it from Thomas, who knows the

Chinese man who delivers the vegetables to the Crane chef. Joanna returned yesterday afternoon." Her voice dropped so that it wouldn't carry to William. "With her Chinese husband."

Ken Jin flinched. It couldn't possibly be true. He knew what Charlotte's friend had been doing and where she'd done it. Miss Joanna's activities had nothing to do with marriage. And even if holy unions sometimes did occur between partners, Miss Joanna couldn't possibly marry a Manchurian prince turned Shaolin monk. The idea was unthinkable. Repulsive. And yet, he had discovered the whites' servant network to be eerily reliable.

With sudden inspiration, he turned to the nearest footman. "Go and fetch Mei Li and her son," he ordered. "Tell her she is to escort Master William to the park."

Down the hallway, William spun, his brown eyes liquid with happiness. "Is He Be coming? Can He Be come to the park?"

Ken Jin bowed slightly. "Of course, Master William." That had been his plan all along. At six years old, little He Be was just the right age to play with Master William. The two would have a delightful time, with the added advantage that any onlookers would think William was simply entertaining the child. Meanwhile, Ken Jin would be free to learn all he could at the Crane household.

Miss Charlotte was surprised, of course, but she made no demur. As long as William was happy and she got to visit her longtime friend, she would trust him to accomplish the details. How gullible these ghost people were. Or perhaps her mind was elsewhere, Ken Jin realized with a flush of pleasure. He caught her looking at his pants again, and hastily turning her reddened face away.

All was accomplished quickly enough, and soon he and Miss Charlotte were climbing the steps of the Crane household. Old Mr. Yi met them at the door. In the manner of all whites' butlers, the man bowed politely, then spoke in slow, heavily accented English. "Mistress Joanna is not at home."

Miss Charlotte visibly sagged, but her perception was keen. "*Mistress* Joanna?" she asked, stressing the first word. "Then, she is married?"

"*Dai-ge*." A formal "yes" spoken in Shanghainese. The sound was more of a grunt than an agreement, but it answered the question well enough. Joanna had married—or at least claimed to have. But where was the girl now?

That was apparently the first thing on Miss Charlotte's mind as well, because she pushed into the house, stripping off her bonnet as she went. "I suppose I shall just have to wait for her, then. I'll be in her room. No need to send tea." She was halfway to the stairs before Mr. Yi stopped her. He rushed around to stand before her, his arthritic body amazingly fast.

"*Aie,* no, Miss Charlotte! She is gone."

Charlotte stopped. Even her golden hair tumbling out of its pins seemed to still. "Gone?"

"*Dai-ge*. She and her husband left on horses this morning." Disapproval filled the old man's tone.

"But where could they be going?"

Mr. Li didn't answer. Still, Ken Jin could see that there was more. If only Miss Charlotte would leave them alone, he could find out the truth. Instead, she remained absolutely still, looking at Mr. Yi as if he had sprouted horns.

Abruptly, all changed. Charlotte nodded and more of her hair slipped free to dance about her face. "Very well. Then I shall have to leave her a message for when she returns."

Mr. Yi nodded, gesturing to the library. Charlotte shook her head.

"No, I shall leave my message as I did when we were

children. Yes," she went on, more to herself than to Mr. Yi, "just like when we were little." And with that, she dashed upstairs.

Ken Jin longed to follow. He suspected the two women each had a secret cache somewhere in their rooms. The location would be hidden from parents and servants alike, known only to the two girls who had been best friends since Joanna's arrival in Shanghai ten years ago.

Had Joanna—Shanghai's newest Tigress cub—already left a message for her best friend? What secrets might she reveal? Ken Jin could only pray that the white girl showed some sense and kept private things private. Though when had the ghost people ever been able to restrain their passions? Especially young women? Ken Jin shook his head, fearing the worst, especially since old Mr. Yi was obviously bursting with news.

Taking a cue from the aged butler, Ken Jin accepted an invitation to tea. Charlotte would not take long, he knew. She was not a woman to linger over letters, even one to her closest friend, so he had little time to learn everything.

Like all white monstrosities, the Crane home was built and run in the way of a great English house; so Ken Jin was surprised when Mr. Yi did not lead him to a private butler's sitting room. Instead, they went to the kitchen to sit at a large wooden table while water heated on the great stove. There were servants all around: the English cook, two Shanghai footmen flirting with a scullery maid clearly just in from a country farm. Two parlor maids flitted in and out, their easy manners marking them as low-class Shanghai, barely one step up from nail-shack whores.

All went silent upon Ken Jin's entrance—but only for a minute. Mr. Yi called for tea and then sat down, looking as much like a reclining mandarin as one could while sitting in a hard wooden chair in the middle of an English kitchen.

The water heated while he dropped tea leaves into a teapot on the table, and the gossip began to flow with special animation as soon as the English chef left for the wine cellar.

"I would never take my wife to Peking," said a footman. "It's too dangerous—"

"Too far away," interrupted the other footman as he rearranged the candles on the kitchen altar. "You like things quick and close. And quick."

It was a sexual joke, and it got a predictable response. The maids laughed, while the scullery girl blushed a bright red even as she shooed the two away from the altar.

"These white people are crazy," complained the first man. "Why would any father leave? Simply throw the man out—"

"He's her *husband*," snapped the scullery girl in her thick accent. "A father has no say anymore."

"A man has a say in his own house," replied the footman hotly. "He should have thrown them both out. Any daughter who thinks she can choose her own husband deserves no better."

One of the parlor maids moved close, tweaking the argumentative footman on the cheek. "A smart father opens the doors and learns about his new son-in-law's connections, *then* decides what to do. That's what the master's doing. He may be white, but he isn't stupid. The barbarians know how to use their friends."

"The whites know how to use anything and everything," muttered the second footman, clearly voicing a regular complaint.

The hot water was ready, and Mr. Yi poured according to custom. He said nothing and neither did Ken Jin. They were pretending to have a quiet tea. Obviously, the man wanted to share the newest house gossip, but as butler he couldn't give the information outright. So Ken Jin had to infer what was going on from the talk around him.

Fortunately, he had an advantage. He already knew from

where Miss Crane had come, and with whom. He already knew that she had become a Tigress student, and that her partner was a former Shaolin monk. What he gathered now was that the young miss had returned home and claimed the monk as her husband. Then her father had walked out, disowning them both. Such was hardly a surprise, and certainly what the girl deserved for her disobedient actions. But where were the two lovers now?

"Think the master'll catch them?" the scullery girl asked, her voice quavering with fear. "Will he kill them and eat them?"

The others burst into mocking laughter. They had been around whites long enough to know that the English didn't eat their young as was commonly thought.

"*Hai*," chortled the first footman. "Mr. Crane'll find them. But it's General Kang who'll feast on their vitals." He widened his eyes and dropped his voice. "The Qing Empire has no pity on its enemies."

The girl was appropriately terrified. "But the master . . . What if General Kang catches *him?*"

The footman's answer was as clear as it was graphic. He bared his teeth and pantomimed ripping out a heart and eating it. "The master is as good as dead. Just be grateful the General was too rushed to bother with us."

The room fell into a mournful silence. Apparently, the Crane household had fallen afoul of General Kang, a powerful Manchurian officer. Which meant, of course, that the Cranes would not live long in China. Which meant the servants were all about to be unemployed.

Reality descended hard upon the poor scullery maid. "But I don't have another job!" she wailed.

Neither, apparently, did Mr. Yi, for that was the moment he began to speak, asking after the Wicks family butler. "Tell me, how is the health of Mr. Tseng? I understand he had a terrible cough last month."

Ken Jin nodded sadly. In truth, Mr. Tseng was twenty years younger than Mr. Yi and in excellent health. But who was he to brag about the Wicks family's good fortune? Or to dash Mr. Yi's hopes of a job?

"Ah," he said, "you are correct that Mr. Tseng is not as young as he once was. That cough was terrible and still lingers. The young master hides whenever he hears the hacking sound, and guests shun the house." Ken Jin paused, trying to deliver the truth in his most delicate manner. "But you have worked for the ghost people for years, Mr. Yi. You understand that they are ignorant of the true nature of things. Mr. Wicks cannot comprehend the bad fortune that comes from an ill butler."

"Of course, of course." Mr. Yi nodded, his drawn expression showing he had received the message: There would be no job opening for him in the Wicks household. "The whites are indeed a barbarian people," he rasped. Then he pushed up from his chair. "Perhaps we should see if Miss Charlotte has finished her letter. You would not want to leave her too long. Women should not have so much time alone. It damages their minds."

Ken Jin could not agree more. In his opinion, whites spent too little time controlling their daughters; but it was not his place to comment. It wasn't Mr. Yi's place either, but the old man could be forgiven his grumbling considering that he was about to lose his livelihood. Ken Jin could only pray the man had adequate savings. It would not be easy to find a new job at his age.

They returned to the front parlor, where Miss Charlotte was slowly descending the stairs. Ken Jin waited silently, his head slightly bowed, his manner completely reserved as was appropriate to his position. But he had long since mastered the ability to observe all while keeping his demeanor subservient, and what he saw was nerve-racking. The young miss had obviously figured something out.

Burning Tigress

✦✦✦

(A letter delivered by special courier.)

July 9, 1881
With respect, to Tigress Tan Shi Po:

Honored Tigress, I write in courtesy and with deep shame. I regret to inform you that a great evil has been sent to your home. I did not send it; it comes to you from my mother-in-law, whose age has dulled her mind. It will arrive soon: a demon in the form of a boy. His name is Ken Jin. He will tell you a sad tale with great weeping and gnashing of teeth.

He lies!

I say again, whatever words the demon speaks are ugly lies! Ken Jin is an unnatural demon of no kin this house. Throw him from you! He carries terrible fortune. Do not under any circumstances send him back to us.

In apology,
Wen Qui Xiu

15

*After trauma, many patients remain shaken and
emotionally scattered. This is called "gall-bladder fright."
Points used: GB 34 Yanglingguan [on the outside of the
calf just below the fibular condyle] and LV 3 Taichong
[on the top of the foot in the angle between the first and
second toes].*
The Encyclopaedia of Chinese Medicine, Frank WT
Chung, CA, OMD

Chapter Two

Charlotte felt as if her brain were on fire. Outwardly she
knew she looked composed and quiet, but inside her entire
body crackled with . . . what? She'd found scrolls in
Joanna's room. Scrolls with Chinese writing and paintings
of naked men and women. And their organs! She tried to
take a breath to calm herself, but her mind still crackled.
The images had been large and naked. And painted in
color!

Plus, they looked very similar to Ken Jin's real-life organ she'd seen just an hour ago. She wondered briefly if his
penis could do some of the things she'd seen in the scrolls.
And if she were his partner, would she look as serenely
happy as the women pictured? And how had the painted
woman put that huge thing in her mouth anyway? But she
was drawn so happy—smug even. Something wonderful
definitely came from the man's organ.

The satchel banged hard against her thigh as she descended the stairs, bringing her attention back to the present. Charlotte was excruciatingly aware of the three
silk-wrapped bamboo cases she carried. Indeed, it had

taken her nearly twenty minutes to find a bag that completely covered the naughty picture scrolls. Obviously, Joanna had meant for her to find them, because she'd hidden them in their secret hidey-hole where the two had been sharing diaries, notes, and special bits of ribbon since the beginning of time. Well, since they'd become best friends at the age of ten. It was a child's game perfect for little girls, but no little girl had put these scrolls there. No little girl could possibly understand what was written on them. And no properly bred young woman would ever read them.

Charlotte paused on the last step into the foyer. How lowering it was to realize one was not a proper young woman. She *had* read them. Or rather, she had read what little she could, since the scrolls were written in Chinese on fragile vellum and wrapped in costly silks.

How had Joanna come across what were obviously valuable, ancient texts? And when had Charlotte's most learned and serious friend crossed over to the side of rampant debauchery that filled the rest of Shanghai? Had she been given the scrolls by her husband? If so, why? They couldn't possibly be doing those things. But of course, they could, she admonished herself; they were married after all. And wasn't that what married people did? But was Joanna doing all of that? Everything pictured in that scroll. *Everything?*

For a single horrified moment, Charlotte realized she ought to return the scrolls. After all, Joanna and her husband might need them. The scrolls were clearly reference material meant to teach one how to have marital relations. Therefore, Joanna would need the scrolls, whereas Charlotte did not.

Damn, why hadn't she ever accepted a suitor for her hand? She could be married right now with scrolls of her own. But none of the sycophants and lechers she knew had ever appealed to her. And besides, one mention of

William—because of course he would have to live with her—and they all ran screaming. Which meant she had no man nearby to read scrolls with. Which meant she ought to give them back.

Except Joanna wasn't here to use them, and scrolls as ancient as these shouldn't go to waste. Charlotte was sure that there were some images that did not . . . well, that she could perform without losing her virginity. After all, if Joanna was lost to the realm of sinful indulgences of the flesh, then . . . well, wasn't it time Charlotte did a little exploring on her own? Which meant she was definitely keeping these scrolls.

"Is there something wrong, Miss Charlotte?" asked Ken Jin, his voice further exciting her already jumpy nerves.

She spun back, her voice cracking. "What? Oh no! I just . . . I mean, I thought I'd . . . But of course, I can't now. I mean—" She clapped her jaw shut, forcibly cutting off her words as she gained some measure of control. "I'm fine, Ken Jin, thank you for asking." Did his organ exude a silvery mist like in the pictures? Her friends had never said so, but . . .

She yanked her attention to old Mr. Yi, Joanna's butler. Forcing her lips into as serene a smile as she could manage, she spoke in what she prayed was a calm, collected manner. "I have left a note for Joanna and am most anxious to see her. When will she return?"

Mr. Yi bowed deeply. "I do not know, Miss Charlotte, but I will see she receives your letter the moment she returns."

"Of course, of course," Charlotte murmured. "But where did she go? Perhaps if it is somewhere close, I could join her."

Mr. Yi shook his head. "*Aie,* no, Miss Charlotte, I do not know her location."

"But surely you know when she left."

He bowed again but didn't answer.

"Was she alone?"

Another bow. No answer. Damn, just how did one get answers out of other people's servants? And did all Chinese men have penises that large and red? Even old servant men? Or were the scrolls exaggerated?

"Perhaps I could speak with her father?" Charlotte squeaked out. "When will Mr. Crane return?"

Another bow. No wonder the butler was so bent with age. Were Chinese men's organs heavy? He said, "Mr. Crane is away on business. I do not know when he will return." Was there a funereal tone to that statement? Charlotte didn't know. She couldn't tell which words were significant, what was merely her imagination, and how she could find out what was written on those damned scrolls without Joanna to translate.

"Please, Mr. Yi, I must speak with Joanna right away."

Again, the deep bow. Clearly it was the Chinese version of a shrug and the old man was not going to help her.

"Oh, never mind," she snapped, her irritation getting the best of her. "Let me know the instant she returns, Mr. Yi. The very instant." Then she paused. "I will be in a *most* generous mood the moment I hear of her return." She stared at the old man, trying to read his wrinkled face. Did he understand what she meant—that she would tip him should he bring her any significant news?

"I am desperate for information about Joanna. And I can be generous—"

"Apologies, Miss Charlotte," interrupted Ken Jin, "but we are due to pick up William now."

Charlotte frowned at her father's servant. His penis was the same size as on the scroll. But was he unusual? "Are we supposed to pick up William now? But I thought—"

"You are probably right, Miss Charlotte," he interrupted again, his demeanor solicitous. "We should check on your brother, just to make sure no ill has befallen him."

Charlotte pressed her lips together. She wasn't fooled. Ken Jin didn't like her questioning Mr. Yi, even when she did it subtly. The Chinese were protective of each other. But this was important. She had to get Joanna to translate these scrolls! Which meant she had to make Mr. Yi understand.

Abandoning subtlety altogether, she fished a guinea out of her recticule. It took a moment, and she winced at the expense, but she had to know. She pressed the coin into the old man's hand. "As soon as you know anything, Mr. Yi. I am so desperately worried about my friend."

The butler stared at her, his dark eyes watering. He nodded. "Yes, yes, Miss Charlotte, we are all most worried."

"We are very late, Miss Charlotte," Ken Jin cut in again. "Master William will be anxious."

"Master William is in Heaven right now, running around with He Be," she snapped, unable to control her frustration. Why now of all times did Ken Jin have to voice sudden concern about punctuality? Didn't he see she was trying to accomplish something with Mr. Yi? But as she turned back to the aged butler, all she received a blank expression. She sighed. She'd just wasted a guinea.

"Very well," she said to Ken Jin. His eyes were downcast, his demeanor apologetic. Still, she knew he was not nearly as submissive as he seemed. She had witnessed his management of her drunken father on multiple occasions. Though smaller in statue, Ken Jin often strong-armed her parent to bed—and all without alerting her mother or disturbing William. In truth, she knew of no one—Chinese or English—who so seamlessly kept life's unpleasantness at bay. An extremely attractive asset in a man. Unless, of course, he began managing *her*.

"We may leave now, Ken Jin," she said with as much regal disdain as she could muster, given that she carried three scrolls of questionable moral content.

20

Mr. Yi held out her bonnet, and Charlotte grimaced as she put it on. The humid Shanghai air had already frizzed her hair into a tangled mass. Shoving the annoying knots into a hat was only going to make matters worse. But it was the custom and so she complied; it was important to observe such niceties when one was ferrying pictures of naked male organs. A hysterical giggle rose inside her chest, but she ruthlessly suppressed it. She could not start laughing like a hyena; people would wonder what she was carrying.

Given that particular thought, she took extra care while climbing into the carriage. She was being very casual about the satchel, letting it flop this way and that, because, truly, there was nothing important inside it. Nothing unusual, just silly girl stuff of no importance to anyone. Which is how it hit too hard against the seat, just as she stepped into the carriage, and the whole thing upended.

It wasn't a complete disaster. Nothing spilled *all* the way out. The bag just tipped far enough to half spill and for her to gasp. *Don't gasp!* she ordered herself. *There's nothing important here.* Then she hastily shoved the ancient cases as far down as they would go, and tied the bag closed so hard the cord snapped.

Double damn!

Charlotte looked up at Ken Jin. He was calmly walking around to the other side of the carriage where he would jump up and take the reins, but he had been behind her when the satchel spilled. He might have seen. She narrowed her eyes, trying to read his expression. No change, no indication that he'd seen anything scandalous. Besides, he was a Chinese servant, who would believe what he said anyway? He stuck needles into himself, for goodness' sake. Who would believe him?

21

Everyone, that's who. Servants talked—no matter what race they were—and absolutely everyone believed the nonsense they spewed. She prayed he hadn't seen, but how to be sure?

She didn't know. All she could do was sit calmly beside him while clutching the top of the satchel closed, closed, closed. Lord, she had to relax her grip. Her fingers were going all tingly.

Ken Jin took his seat and gathered the reins just as he always did. His expression remained placid, his demeanor exactly as it always was. Clearly he'd seen nothing untoward. Besides, she realized, what if he had? All he'd know was that she carried bamboo scroll cases wrapped in faded blue silk stitched with a rather hard-to-discern pastoral scene. No one could see the pictures inside. The scrolls could be any of a thousand different Chinese texts. They could be Confucian writings on appropriate female behavior; and a more boring text had never cursed the planet. How she and Joanna had laughed and laughed over those particular dictates.

Charlotte exhaled on a heady release of air. She was safe. No one knew what she carried. Soon she would be home. She could order William into a bath under Mei Li's supervision. She'd even suggest He Be bathe as well, which would keep everyone occupied for at least an hour. Then she would disappear into her bedroom, lock the door, and peruse Joanna's scandalous scrolls at her leisure.

Very soon.

Except, she abruptly noticed, they weren't headed home at all.

Ken Jin's thoughts felt muddy. He couldn't possibly have seen what he had; Miss Charlotte couldn't possibly have those scrolls—a rare and ancient copy of the Yellow Emperor's discourse with the Plain Goddess, the learned responses and instructional materials developed by the first Tigress under the direct tutelage of the Rainbow Goddess? But what other three-thousand-year-old scrolls would have those covers: dark silk embroidered with a simple pastoral scene until one examined closely what the people were doing beneath the trees and in harmony with nature? Where had Miss Charlotte gotten them?

The answer was obvious. Miss Joanna had been in training at the Tigress school, and she must have gotten the scrolls somehow. Indeed, Ken Jin could see the workings of providence. He was one of the few people in Shanghai who would recognize the scrolls, would know to whom they truly belonged. So, of course they had found their way to him.

Yes, Miss Joanna must have taken them when she'd left the Tigress school, but Heaven had intervened with her hasty departure this morning. For whatever reason, she had left the scrolls behind for Miss Charlotte to find. And he would take them from Miss Charlotte and return them to their rightful owner—the school and the Tigress Shi Po. Assuming, of course, he could find an easy way to separate his employer's daughter from her new find.

He glanced sideways at her. Goodness, her yin was flowing strong. Her lips were red, her cheeks flushed, and her breath came in tiny little pants. She'd obviously looked at the scrolls and her impulsive nature had taken hold. She would never willingly surrender them now.

He could simply take them from her. He was quick enough, strong enough—even clever enough perhaps to offer her adequate diversion. But the whites were a volatile race, driven by their passions. He knew more than one First Boy who had been fired without references on a simple whim. Not to mention his employer valued family harmony most of all, and the Wicks family harmony held solely because of Miss Charlotte's stable influence. Upset her, and the entire family would rapidly collapse. In turn that would devastate his own finances. No; Ken Jin had to find a way to separate Miss Charlotte from her scrolls without upsetting her or risking his position. And he had to do it within the twenty minutes it took to drive to the Tigress school.

"Um, Ken Jin?" The young miss's voice was high and tight. "Where are we going?"

"To a school, Miss Charlotte."

"A school? But why—"

"I learned something from the servants, Miss Charlotte. About Miss Joanna."

That got her attention. She straightened in her seat and her hand slackened a little on her satchel. "What is it? Tell me immediately!"

Ken Jin nodded, but he took his time. She had to be tantalized without actually learning very much. "They believe she was a student at a very special school."

"Yes?" she prompted when he fell silent.

"The servants weren't sure which school, of course. Miss Joanna was very secretive about it."

"Of course, of course. Joanna was always going off to study one thing or another." Her gaze dropped to the scrolls, and Charlotte tucked them tighter against her skirt.

"This is the only school I know, Miss Charlotte, that might take in a white student in secret. And where she might meet—"

"Her Chinese husband! Of course! I overheard a maid talking. She said Joanna had a Chinese husband." Charlotte shook her head, emotion coloring her skin a fiery red. "Imagine, marrying a Chinaman. I cannot quite credit it." She sighed. "But if anyone were to do it, it would be Joanna. She has such a passion for Chinese things . . ."

But that wouldn't explain the decision of her Chinese husband, Ken Jin thought. Imagine, being so desperate for milky thighs as to actually marry an Englishwoman. He couldn't credit it either.

Miss Charlotte twisted in her seat to survey their surroundings. "Where is this school? Obviously not in the English territory or any of the foreign concessions. There would be no reason for secrecy if that were true."

Ken Jin didn't respond. For all that she was white and a woman, Miss Charlotte had a quick mind. She was rapidly coming to the conclusion that the school had to be native. And so it was. Soon she would have to hide her face and hair as he bribed their way into the only Chinese territory left inside Shanghai.

Miss Charlotte took a deep breath, as if steeling herself. "Exactly what kind of school are we going to, Ken Jin? What was Joanna studying?"

"You must ask the director of the school," he responded smoothly. Ken Jin had great faith in the Tigress Shi Po. If anyone could handle an overly curious white woman, it would be she.

"But, Ken Jin, you have to know something. What—"

"You must be silent now, Miss Charlotte. We will be in Chinese territory soon."

"But—"

"Unless you wish to remain behind?"

"Of course not, but—"

"Then you must cover your head and remain very quiet."

"I cannot see the reason that our two countries—"

"Please, Miss Charlotte."

She subsided then, though her sigh was so heartfelt is actually rocked the carriage. Ken Jin hid his amusement. How long before her innate life energy forced her to express herself again? To speak or fidget or even to touch him simply because her mortal form could not contain the qi that bounced about inside her? He hoped it would last at least three minutes—long enough for them to pass through the gate and get five houses away from the soldiers.

She was already beginning to stir, so he shot her a warning glare. She immediately stilled, pressing her lips together, and he nodded in approval. He did not want her talking. He would much rather she touched him in her anxiety. The sight of her slender white fingers on his body— even with the protective covering of his shirt and coat—would be enough to stir his yang fire. He did not understand his spirit's love of white hands or long unpainted fingernails, but he had always responded to such a sight.

Perhaps it stemmed from that first night when he looked up and beheld her—a blond goddess in ethereal white— watching as he guided her father across the threshold. In that moment, she had appeared divine to him, and from then on, white women stirred his blood as no others could.

When they were past the gate, he sent her another warning look: Don't speak. She nodded, her jade eyes huge. His dragon stirred in appreciation. Master William had once told him about white people's legends, about dragons who hoarded wealth—gold, diamonds, and emeralds. Never once had the boy mentioned jade. But there was great power in that most precious of Chinese stones, a subtle beauty only revealed when light shone from behind or within it, and such was the way with Miss Charlotte's eyes. Normally, they were a dull, murky green. But sometimes something happened and her internal light sparked. She would come alive and her eyes seemed to glow like jade before a flame.

Ken Jin loved the sight and had made a personal study of what brought the light to her eyes: her brother, when the boy managed to accomplish anything without disaster; her visits to the now absent Joanna; any unusual occurrence. There had been that light when she surprised him this morning during his dragon exercises. And there was light now, as they wended their way through Chinese Shanghai.

She took a breath to speak, and Ken Jin shook his head. He almost laughed at her frustrated sigh. Then, finally, he got his reward. She slipped her hand onto his thigh. She was leaning forward, obviously wanting to talk, and in her need to express herself she'd not only put her hand on his thigh but tightened her hold there, gripping him as firmly as any tigress would its prey. The moment was was so delightful that he closed his eyes to savor the feeling.

It didn't last long, of course. All too soon she began to speak, her voice low and husky in the way of all stimulated women—though he knew she did not understand how a woman's yin automatically responded to a man's yang.

"Tell me about this school, Ken Jin," she whispered. Her voice and hand had his yang fires surging, but he was still driving the carriage. He had to focus on not crashing. Unfortunately, that required some movement, and his leg flexed beneath her hand. He was too late to freeze the muscle twitch, and much too late to stop her from realizing where she'd put her hand. Gasping in horror, she pulled back to sit excruciatingly tall beside him. He suppressed his sigh of regret even as he spoke in a sharp undertone.

"Slump, Miss Charlotte!"

She twisted slightly. "I beg your pardon?"

"Slump," he repeated. "Chinese ladies are not nearly so tall." In truth, no one who looked at her could mistake her for Chinese. Her clothing alone, not to mention the horse and carriage, marked her as an Englishwoman no matter how she covered her face and hair. But if she slumped, then she would need to position herself low in the carriage, low enough, perhaps, to steady herself by gripping him again.

He knew he was depraved to toy with a girl in this way, especially a white girl. What kind of deviant resorted to subterfuge just to have a woman touch his thigh? It was stupid, and she was, after all, his employer's daughter. No man pissed at the dinner table. Yet here he was, stirring his flagging yang fires with an innocent white girl. How much lower could he sink?

Very low, apparently, because he grinned as Miss Charlotte once again leaned forward, slumping in her seat and setting her long white fingers across his thigh. Perhaps if he scooted forward, her hand would slip higher.

"Ken Jin, you must explain where we are going," she whispered.

"Right here," he answered with regret. He pulled back on the reins, simultaneously sliding his hips forward. Unfortunately, his ruse failed. Miss Charlotte was already straightening, her hand lifting to her chest as she looked around.

No matter. His dragon was already well stimulated. So he set the brake and leapt down to the street. Except, he couldn't exactly leap because his dragon had stretched to large and happy life. Ah, what a joy to realize this morning's acupuncture had finally cleared his energy blockage. After more than a year of wilting nothingness, his dragon lived and lusted again. He didn't even care that it made walking difficult. He was a whole man again.

He extended his hand, assisting Miss Charlotte as she descended. Or such was his intent, but she hadn't waited for him. As he rounded the horse, she was already climbing out. Which required him to stand quietly and watch the shift and sway of her full buttocks. Ah, what great yin flowed in his employer's daughter! Her husband would be a lucky man—assuming he had the wit to tap her ample stores. But then she was down, and Ken Jin had to escort her to the door of the famous Tigress Shi Po.

"Ken Jin," she whispered. "Where are we? What shall I say?"

"Perhaps you should leave the satchel in the carriage. I can lock it in the boot—"

"No," she snapped, clutching the sack. "I wish to keep it with me."

"As you wish," he returned. He had to find some way of separating her from the scrolls. They were not for barbarian eyes.

They progressed to the outer gate and banged the gong. The Tigress's home was managed with the grace and style befitting a great leader, so he was sure the summons would be answered immediately.

Except, it wasn't. No one came to open the outer doors, and Ken Jin and his white companion were forced to stand outside and wait while people stared at them from all sides.

Charlotte tucked her shawl more securely about her head and face, but it was a useless gesture. No one could possibly mistake her for a Chinese. Even a blind man would be able to smell the sweet rose and lavender scent that clung to her skin. Only a white woman would choose such floral perfume.

He rang the gong again, his dragon withering from his anxiety. Silently he cursed whatever lazy servant had just cost him a morning's yang fire. With a grunt of disgust, he pushed at the gate. He did not expect it to give; the Tigress household used white men's locks. To his surprise, the large barrier swung open, and Miss Charlotte quickly ducked inside. He followed immediately behind.

Inside, he barely managed to stifle his gasp of dismay. The front courtyard was in shambles. Pottery lay in pieces, and ornamental plants were crushed. His nose twitched as he detected a strong odor.

"What happened here?" Miss Charlotte asked, her voice a bare whisper on the still air. "It smells like . . . like . . ."

"Soldiers. On horses."

She gasped. "But why would the British—"

"Qing soldiers," he snapped. How like a white barbarian to assume that theirs was the only military.

To her credit, she ducked her head in embarrassment. "Of course, of course. I am not thinking clearly." Her gaze settled much too keenly on his face. "But why would your soldiers come here?"

"I don't know," he lied. "Let us see—"

Little Pearl burst through the reception door. Her hair was askew, her eyes wild, and her hands fluttered anxiously even as she skidded to a stop before them. "Ken Jin!" she cried. Her gaze hopped to Miss Charlotte and back. Over and back, over and back; then her expression hardened and her body stilled. "What an unexpected pleasure," she finally drawled.

Ken Jin opened his mouth to respond, but Miss Charlotte never gave him a chance. She stepped forward, extending her hand in a white-man's greeting. "I am so sorry to intrude," she said politely, "but we were—"

"She does not speak English, Miss Charlotte," Ken Jin interrupted. Then, before she could do more than blink in confusion, he rushed on. "Perhaps I could speak for you."

The last thing he wanted was for Miss Charlotte to switch to Shanghainese. In truth, her accent was respectable for a white person, but he knew better than anyone how condescending Little Pearl could act at the smallest offense. He had no wish to expose his employer to such venom.

He pushed forward, trying to walk ahead with Little Pearl—away from Miss Charlotte. He failed. No matter how they moved, Miss Charlotte hovered a bare half inch off his heels. "My gravest apologies for disturbing your day," he said to Little Pearl. "What has happened here? And where is the Tigress?"

He was trying to usher both women through the reception area to the inner courtyard. Once there, he was sure he could slip far enough away from Miss Charlotte to have a private word with Little Pearl. Except neither woman co-operated. Little Pearl stood her ground, her arms folded, her yin clearly poisoned by whatever had happened.

"Please, Little Pearl," he coaxed.

"Why have you brought another white whore here?"

Ken Jin froze. Silence was the only defense against this woman when she was in this mood. Unfortunately, Miss Charlotte stood behind him, clearly shocked into her own silence. But that wouldn't last long. He had to intervene. He had to say something.

"Please allow me to introduce my employer's daughter," he said in icily polite tones. "Miss Charlotte Wicks." Her foreign name seemed to crackle in the air.

Little Pearl put on her most ingratiating smile, bowing respectfully. Her Chinese words were anything but. "I have no time for your playthings. You cannot wallow between the dung slugs here. Not today."

Ken Jin could only pray that Miss Charlotte did not understand that dung slugs referred to white maggots—or fleshy white thighs. He stepped forward, barely keeping his tone polite. "I must speak with Tigress Shi Po. It is urgent."

"She is not here," Little Pearl snapped, already turning away.

And so Ken Jin did the unacceptable. Without conscious thought, he thrust his hand out and grabbed her arm. "Where is Shi Po?"

Little Pearl spun around, using his own force against him to break his hold. "Not here! No one is here! We are scattered to the four winds." She spoke in anger, but her fire quickly petered out. Her last words were spoken on a whisper. "Only I remain. And a few servants."

Ken Jin frowned, trying to sort truth from speculation. "General Kang was here yesterday." He had heard that from his Dragon friend Fu De. "But then the General left, and all was well."

"All was not well," Little Pearl growled. She gestured angrily at the ruined courtyard. "None of this happened yesterday. The General was *most* respectful."

"In the daylight."

Little Pearl nodded, and he saw the sheen of unshed tears in her eyes. "Shi Po and her husband are gone. No one has seen them since evening meal."

So, they had been taken in the middle of the night. And Little Pearl was left to pick up the pieces. Which meant . . . "Was anything else taken?"

Little Pearl threw up her hands in disgust. "Everything was taken! Or desecrated. Or destroyed."

Ken Jin winced. The loss was devastating, but at least he knew some of the sacred scrolls were safe. They were right now clutched in the arms of the conspicuously silent Miss Charlotte, where they would have to remain. Right now the ancient texts were safer in a white woman's hands than at the school. Only the rats survived Imperial scrutiny.

Ken Jin bowed deeply to Little Pearl, trying to offer both respect and support in the one gesture. She would have none of it, of course. She had always become furiously angry when unsettled. He hoped she found peace someday, but for now, he could only offer his meager services. "I will learn what I can about the soldiers."

Little Pearl sneered and spat into the dirt at his feet. "The ghost peoples' stench covers you. Do not meddle where your influence will only bring a quicker death to those *I* love." And with that, she spun on her tiny bound heel and stomped heavily away.

Ken Jin closed his eyes, his blood ice inside his chest. Little Pearl had said "those *I* love"—as if he did not owe equal love and loyalty to the Tan family. But he would get no understanding from Little Pearl. He had forfeited that right long ago.

"My goodness, she's an angry little thing," Miss Charlotte commented from just behind him. Her tone was conversational, completely devoid of blame, and its warmth eased some of the constriction in his chest. Until she added, "Why does she hate you so?"

He shook his head, dropping his gaze in apology. "You misunderstand," he lied. "She hates whites. I should not have brought you here. I beg your forgiveness."

Charlotte waved off his apology with a quick snap of her wrist. "Nonsense. That woman hated you. True, she didn't like me, but I'm just a maggot."

Ken Jin winced. Obviously she had understood the dung slug reference.

"But she spit at your feet," she continued. "And named me as *another* of your whores." The light was back in her green eyes, shining with an intelligence rare in any race, his own included. "Why is that, Ken Jin? Do you often bring white women here to . . . to whore with them?" She sounded intrigued rather than horrified.

Ken Jin lifted his gaze to meet and defy the bright light in hers. "I have no concert with whores, Miss Charlotte— white or yellow. Little Pearl speaks from her own poisoned yin." He carefully did not elaborate on the source of that poison.

Charlotte did not reply at first, and he felt himself squirm under the force of her gaze. In the end, she sighed and turned toward the door. "I suppose you are right," she commented as they stepped out into the street. "I believe, technically, one has to pay for them to be called whores."

His breath thickened enough to choke him. And yet,

somehow, he still managed to hand her up into the carriage. Some of his horror must have shown on his face, for she paused halfway to her seat.

"Men always think they're so clever." She rolled her eyes, and when he didn't respond, she elaborated. "I know you've lain with every white woman in Shanghai." Then she flushed a brilliant scarlet that in no way dimmed the intelligence in her eyes. "All of them, of course, except me."

A letter clutched in Wen Ken Jin's ten-year-old fist and handed to Tan Shi Po.

July 9, 1881
To dearest Tigress sister Tan Shi Po:
   My daughter-in-law is insane. My son is possessed by a demon. Please, for love of the practice we both share, take this boy and protect him. I will send what money I can for his care, but he has no one. Please, I beg you, care for my grandson. He is the cleverest of the lot. He will bring you great fortune.

In wrenching grief,
Wen Ai Men

*To relieve vertigo, apply pressure at the point which is
about 2.5 cm/1 inch below the outer ankle-bone.*
Tong Sing, the Chinese Book of Wisdom, Dr. Charles
Windridge

Chapter Three

She'd done it again; Charlotte had opened her mouth and
something scandalous leapt out. She closed her eyes and
tried to breathe. If only she could keep her mouth shut as
easily, but the urge was too strong: She had to explain herself. But what to say to the servant who sat in stoic silence
beside her? He wasn't even taking up the reins. He just sat
there and stared at the horse's ears.

"I am so sorry," she blurted. "I should not have spoken
so bluntly. And on an open street, no less." She used
Shanghai dialect so as to keep up the pretense that she belonged in this Chinese side of the city. Unfortunately, that
meant the pair of women passing on the street overheard
and understood. As one, they turned and stared, and Charlotte's face heated to a burning crimson. Lord, even her
hands had gone red with embarrassment.

"It's not what it sounds like," she said hastily to the pair.
"He's a modest man, most moral. Well, for a man, I mean.
Not—"

Her words were cut off by a squeal of horror. One of the

women—she was actually more of a girl, really, with a soft moon face and chapped lips—let loose a bizarre sound that was half scream, half Chinese wail.

"Really," Charlotte cried, desperate to end the spectacle. "He's not evil at all. It is only that my friends talk to me. About . . ." She trailed off. Nothing she said could possibly help. Besides, the women weren't listening. They just kept screaming or cursing or praying—it was hard to tell exactly what was happening; the Chinese words ran too fast for her to understand. Charlotte caught the phrase "ghost devil" and "fire tongue." Or maybe it was "fire head." It must have been the latter, because she heard Ken Jin curse before throwing her shawl back over her. She had let it drop in the courtyard and forgotten to hide her reddish blond hair.

"Oh yes," she scrambled to say to the two still-squealing women. "My hair. It is very bright, but—"

"Be silent!" Ken Jin hissed as he snapped the reins. The horse obediently kicked into a stately walk. The women followed, screeching.

"But I'm trying to explain."

"You're not!" he snapped in English.

"But I have damaged your reputation! I cannot—"

"They don't care that I lie with women!" he ground out in English, glaring at the growing crowd of pointing and squealing and jabbering Chinese.

"But then—"

"It is *you!*" he snapped. "An Englishwoman who speaks Chinese. They think you are invading."

She blinked, first at him and then at the pointing crowd. "But I'm not. How—"

He shook his head, clearly struggling with the words. "Not invading. Possessing. They believe you have possessed a Chinese person."

"What?"

"They think you have sucked out her brains. How else could you speak Chinese so well?"

The horse was moving faster now, losing the worst of the crowd, but the shrieks still echoed in Charlotte's head. "They think I sucked out the brains of a Chinese person simply because I can speak Chinese well? That I am a white person who sucked out someone's brain?"

"Yes!"

She shook her head, dumbfounded. "But I learned Chinese with Joanna. From a tutor."

"I know." His words sounded as if they grated his throat. "And they think—"

"That you are a ghost. Miss Charlotte, please, will you please speak English?"

"Oh!" She shifted languages. "But everyone knows I speak Chinese. I am practically famous for it."

"At home, yes, but this is here." *Here* meant a bare mile or two east of where she lived. But they were in Chinese Shanghai, where no white person ever went. Or at least no white people who spoke Shanghai dialect.

Charlotte pressed her lips together, annoyed with her own stupidity. And yet, her mind still struggled. "You mean, they don't care that you . . . that you . . ." Why was it more difficult to say in English? Her father whored. All his friends whored. But she could not say that aloud to Ken Jin in English. It would make it too real, somehow. "That you spend time with white women, but they're terrified I can speak Chinese?"

They were past the commotion now, turning into a street clogged with carts of vegetables and women carrying upside-down chickens. Charlotte stared at one of the poor birds tied by its feet onto a looped line. This particular hen was one of about ten, all still alive, all piled on top of each other as an old woman rushed to market. The chicken didn't move, didn't even cluck, but hung silently upside down like one banana in a bunch, completely unaware that it was destined for the chopping block. Soon it would see stalls that held live scorpions next to a water bin of bulbous squid beneath hanging ducks interspersed with black eels. And in all this chaos, a single white woman speaking Chinese produced screaming horror?

Charlotte sighed. The Chinese made no sense. She turned to Ken Jin. "So, how many white women must you lie with for it to be unusual?"

He stared at her, his normally golden brown skin paling. He opened his mouth to speak, but no sound came out. Then the horse demanded his attention as it shied away from an unusually aggressive rickshaw runner.

While Ken Jin fixed his gaze on the reins, Charlotte could not stop her thoughts from running in a stream from her mouth. For all that she told herself to stop, she simply could not halt the flow. In truth, she had been thinking about this for a long, long time now. It really did not seem fair that Ken Jin would spend so much time teaching her friends about certain forms of man-woman relations without sharing the experience with her. After all, he was *her* servant.

"Would the Chinese be more shocked if you spent your evenings with Chinese women?" she asked. "You are most famous among white ladies, so I know you are unusual to us. But is it common for Chinese men to delight in . . . ? To share company with . . . ? Well, you know what I mean. Do you spend time with Chinese women as often as you do with Europeans? And, my goodness, why aren't you more tired? Of course, Sophie claimed you were indefatigable, but surely she must have exaggerated. You cannot have gone on for as long as she claimed. Unless that is typical for your race. So I want you to show me, too."

She paused to take a breath, barely daring to look at him. But when she did, her breath left her in an embarrassed whoosh. He hadn't moved. His attention was firmly and completely absorbed with driving the cart through the clogged streets. Which meant, she supposed, that he hadn't heard her.

"Ken Jin?" she said a little more forcefully. "I wish you to show me . . ." She swallowed, knowing she needed to be explicit. "I want you to touch me." She looked down, horrified to see that her hands were fluttering about her bodice. She slammed them down hard into her lap. Except, she didn't hit the soft cushion of her thighs; she cracked the back of her hand on the hard end of a scroll. She winced, but even that pain did not stop her words, especially as her servant still did not appear to have heard. And he had to hear, because she would never again get the chance to be alone with him in Chinese Shanghai where no one else could understand what she said.

"I have scrolls," she heard herself say, "with pictures. I don't understand the words; they're written in Chinese. Joanna would have understood, of course. She read all manner of things, but I will need someone to translate them for me. That will prepare me for what I want. For what you will do." She paused. "Or, is there something I need to do first? Sophia didn't mention anything. Well, actually she talked about all sorts of noises which did not sound at all nice; but then she always is making some sort of sound, isn't she? But are they important? She dwelt most particularly on her *hmmm* and a *whee* and a hiccup kind of thing. At the time I thou—*umph*."

Ken Jin clapped his hand over her mouth. It was a large hand, with lovely calluses that tickled her lips. But even more delicious was the way he leaned close and whispered in her ear, his breath warm even as it made her shiver. "The sun has made you ill, Miss Charlotte. When we get home, I will get you a cool glass of lemonade and all this will be over."

She didn't answer. How could she, with his hand still over her mouth? So she sat still, smelling the ink on his skin and a lingering whisper of spicy incense. The smell pervaded his clothing too, she realized, and his thick braid of dark hair that slipped over his shoulder to tease her cheek.

"Do you understand, Miss Charlotte?" he continued. "You have a fever brought on by the heat and tainted Chinese scrolls." She felt him tug at her satchel, trying to remove it from her hands. "Soon you will be home with William. You can take a cool bath and sip a special tea that I will prepare. Then all that has happened today will fade away."

His voice was hypnotic. The heat from his body added to the noise in her mind and soul. There was a crackling, sparking, burning kind of clamor that seemed to grow louder whenever he was near. And right now he was very, very near. Except, he was pulling away, lifting his one hand from her mouth while the other pulled the scrolls away.

She almost did it; she almost gave in to the constraints of moral behavior, to the pressure for obedience and purity and absolute holy ignorance on her wedding night. Ken Jin obviously wanted her to forget everything she had seen and heard this afternoon, to continue as she had been continuing every day of her most boring, moral, sterile life.

"No!" She grabbed the scrolls and hauled them back. "These are mine, and if you will not explain them to me, I will find someone else who will."

He did not release his hold on the satchel, but his brown eyes darkened to pitch, and his words held dangerous authority. "You are not yourself, Miss Charlotte. I believe I shall have your mother call the doctor the moment we return."

She trembled in fear, his threat very real. If her mother discovered these scrolls, she would first burn the parchments, then call the surgeon to bleed the ill humors out of her before paying for a full Mass to pray for Charlotte's tortured young soul. Charlotte could not, not, not have her mother involved.

Charlotte bit her lip then said, "The man is gone."

Ken Jin frowned, obviously confused, so she waved toward the street.

"The man with the bamboo poles," she clarified. "The one who was crossing the street. He's gone. We can keep going."

Ken Jin looked at the street and nodded, slowly refocusing on driving the carriage. Except he did it one-handed. Charlotte had counted on him needing both hands to steer, but he clearly did not. He kept one hand firmly on the satchel while the other steered the horse.

"These are Joanna's scrolls, Ken Jin. I will not give them up to you."

"They are Tigress scrolls, Miss Charlotte, and no barbarian has ever seen them."

She straightened. "*I* have seen them. Joanna has seen them, too. I'd say a great number of barbarians—"

"No!" he snapped, jerking hard on the bag. But he had only one hand on the bag, whereas she had two. She did not release it.

"You will tear them!" she cried. Then she glared up at his hard profile. "If you tell Mother I am ill, I'll say that you took me to a brothel this morning. That I saw your . . . your . . . you know. With needles in it! And then—"

"I'll be fired." He turned to look directly at her, his expression as empty as his tone. "Is that what you want? To have me fired?"

She swallowed. "Of course not." She lifted her chin. "I want to know what Sophia knows, what Joanna knows." She felt tears burn her eyes. "What everyone knows but me."

He sighed. It was a quiet sound, more like the creak of a branch in the wind, but she heard it nonetheless, and it made her wonder what exactly went on in his mind when he acted so very, very Chinese. She was so absorbed in scrutinizing his face that she missed his next words. And then, when she realized he'd spoken, she had to forcibly redirect her thoughts.

"What did you say?" she asked.

They were nearing the gate back into the English concession, so she didn't think he would speak, but he did. He pulled the carriage to a stop and twisted to stare at her.

"I said I will teach you." Then he narrowed his eyes to emphasize his next words. "But there will be no talk of this to anyone—not your parents, not Joanna, not even to Sophia. Do we understand one another?"

She swallowed, nodding her head slowly as she agreed to who-knew-what. But as Ken Jin turned back to guide the carriage, she ripped the satchel from his grasp.

"I'm keeping the scrolls," she said, straightening in her seat. "I have to make sure you're doing things right."

Ken Jin entered his bedchamber and stared at his desk. The old wood was pocked and ink-stained, the drawers stuck, and one corner was frayed to splinters. And yet he had a fondness for the large beast.

For one thing, it was huge. He had lots of space to work, lots of room for papers and ledgers and all manner of clutter; and yet his elbows were never crowded, his abacus was always within reach, and his brushes never dripped on anything vital. Large and serviceable without beauty, that was his desk.

That was Ken Jin too. He was not a handsome man, not by white women's standards, but they certainly seemed to enjoy his size and his serveability. They cared little if he was rough to them; indeed, some seemed to enjoy it. So long as their requirements were met—no penetration—all was well in their eyes. He brought their yin rain to full bloom, drinking up their qi like water, and they got to remain virgins.

An excellent arrangement until the encounters began leaving him exhausted. His yang—so strong at the beginning with Little Pearl—now barely moved despite the stirring perfume of a willing women. Over the last year, his dragon became so weak, he had stopped undressing before Charlotte's friends.

So now Charlotte wished to learn what he had taught her friends. The goddess who had appeared before him so many years ago wished to descend to his chamber and feel what other women felt. He ought to be grateful. His flagging yang responded lustfully to Miss Charlotte. He should be thrilled that she came to him on the very day he regained hope for his weak dragon.

Instead, it made him feel worn, old, and a little sad.

Odd, how this morning had held such hope. His dragon had reawakened, his investments showed promise, and he'd even received an encouraging letter about his nephew's academic progress. But that was this morning. Now, a bare three hours later, his mentors Shi Po and her husband, Kui Yu, were in prison, sacred scrolls were in barbarian hands, and his employer's daughter demanded service that would likely get him fired.

When Heaven turns its back, even the rats perish.

He grimaced in disgust at the reversal in fortunes. He would need to be at his peak to weather the coming storm. Without conscious thought, he stripped off his jacket, shirt,

and tie. Why the whites insisted on so many ridiculous lay-
ers, buttons, and ties, he would never understand; it prevented full breath in skin or lungs. But the master insisted,
and so Ken Jin obeyed. Except, Ken Jin would not accept it
now. At this moment, he needed a boost in vitality, so he
shut and locked his door—or attempted to lock it. This
morning's debacle had proved the mechanism was faulty.
Then he pulled out his tools and knelt bare-chested in the
tiny space between desk and bed.

He knelt on a rug with a dragon design. He placed his
knees on the belly of a cloud dragon, the tops of his feet extending toward the whipping, spiny tail. He had to unbutton
the top of his trousers, as he could not afford to rip another
pair. Then, once the fabric was rolled sufficiently down his
hips, he carefully inserted a great needle into the Sea of Energy point, three finger widths below his navel. Two deep
breaths, and then he raised his hands, pressed both thumbs
and forefingers into the Gates of Consciousness.

*With fire below and openness above, all of Heaven is
within reach.*

This time, his breath had an echo—a depth that told him
his spirit stretched toward the divine. His eyes closed and
he began the internal inventory that was his ritual. His
mind was more scattered than usual, but he carefully
brought it into focus. Starting with his head and flowing
down to his toes, he surveyed his body. It was strong with
no pains. His energy channels flowed clearly with only one
obvious blockage. Wind, fire, water, wood, and metal co-
existed within him at an acceptable balance.

He turned his attention to the energy blockage in his
pelvis at the gate to his dragon. This morning's work had
opened up the channel, allowing some of his carefully
stored yang to flow. His dragon lived and breathed again as
it had not for over a year. In truth, the problem had begun

long ago, perhaps even in early childhood. He did not know the cause, only that as he aged, the blockage became worse and his dragon began to wither.

At first he thought his yang stores were simply weak. He devoted all his attention to purifying his male energies, carefully hoarding and cleansing his masculine power through privations and meditations, special herbs and careful exercises. After two decades, his yang was the rarified substance of the most devout practitioner. Unfortunately, there seemed to be too little of it.

Then he learned that yang responds to yin; that a woman's energies give rise to a man's. So he became a gatherer of women. He teased them, he seduced them, he did whatever was needed so that he could drink of their fluids. And his yang responded . . . for a while.

But three years ago, a blockage had appeared. Though his yang remained pure and strong, it could not flow to his dragon. His organ was slow to rise, quick to withdraw. And in the last year, it could not be woken at all. At least not until this morning. Not until his needles were inadvertently driven deep into his Sea of Vitality.

Had he at last opened the channel to his yang stores? He fervently prayed it was true, even as he began his strengthening meditation. He would have to use all of his resources to build upon this new beginning. He would need special herbs, deep meditations, and yin—lots of female yin—to simulate the renewed growth of his yang and keep the dragon gate open. He would need Miss Charlotte's yin in great quantities.

Odd, how the thought excited him as much as it repulsed him. But he had no room in his mind for doubts. He needed her yin to bolster his yang. She wished to give him her fluids, and he needed to take them. Any other thought had no place in his spirit.

As if summoned by the thought, Miss Charlotte slipped

into his room. He heard the rustle of her skirts, her futile effort to lock the door, and her gasp of surprise when she saw him kneeling on the floor.

Ken Jin's hands slipped down and away, closing off his access to Heaven. He opened his eyes, automatically seeking out his prey. She wore the same burnt-orange clothes as before, including that impossibly tight waist contraption overlain by a cotton dress with sleeves that made her shoulders look like big fat roosters. And yet, for all the ridiculousness of her attire, he could not help but be drawn to the sparkling delight in her eyes. She seemed to bounce with energy before him.

He did not speak. There was no need as he understood her desires. So he occupied himself with pulling the needle out from his Sea of Vitality, twisting it back and forth as he did in order to gain the tiniest bit more stimulation.

"Oh, don't stop," she cried, rushing forward a step. "That is part of what I have come here to learn."

He looked at her, and he felt his entire being—body, energy, and spirit included—focus to a concentrated point, one that could be directed wherever his mind willed. "I am preparing to teach you," he said.

"Ah," she replied, though she obviously did not understand. "So . . . does the foggy stuff come out of there?" She pointed at the needle.

He paused as it slipped free. "The foggy stuff?"

She nodded, her eyes on the tiny welling of blood that seeped free. "The mist," she said in Shanghai dialect. "The cloudlike thing on the scroll. In the pictures, it came from the man's . . . from his . . ." Her face flushed a dark scarlet. "Does it come from there? Do you always have to poke a hole for it to—"

"You misunderstand," he snapped, startled by the break in his control. There was no need for him to explain, and

46

yet he did not stop. "These needles stimulate and enhance. They also release evil energies." He switched into English, using terms her father employed. "Bad humors or sicknesses. But that was not my intention here."

She giggled, the sound high and nervous as she dropped to her knees before him. "Well, *some* evil humor has gotten hold of you. Perhaps you did not stick the right location."

He felt his jaw clench, and had to concentrate to relax. It took so long that his needles were carefully stowed back in his desk before he could speak again. "As I said, that was not my intention today." Then he sighed, his blood cold despite the recent acupuncture. "I gather that you are ready for your instruction?"

She had watched him put away his kit, an interested sparkle in her eyes. At his words, her expression grew somber. "Yes," she said with a nod. "I am ready."

He stalled, knowing the risks outweighed the benefit. "You understand that my lock does not work. We may be interrupted."

She shook her head. "William is in a bath, and I have already arranged for him to eat dinner in the nursery. Mama is handing out pamphlets with the priest, and Papa . . ." She shrugged. "Well, you know that Papa is at his club drinking and will not return home."

"Your father is at the docks checking on his investments," Ken Jin lied.

"Yes, yes, I know you are supposed to say that, but this is me. I know the truth, I have for years."

He doubted she knew the full truth. No woman who called yang emissions "foggy stuff" could truly understand her father's debauchery. But before Ken Jin came to work here, Mr. Wicks had often brought his women home whenever Mrs. Wicks spent a night at the mission. Miss Charlotte had been young then, but never stupid. She would have learned a great deal. Fortunately, Ken Jin was able to convince his employer to take his sexual adventures out of his home, but obviously the damage had been done. Charlotte—and the friends she socialized with—had an undeniable curiosity about sexual relations. It was a testament to her mother's prudish vehemence that Charlotte had not come to his door long ago.

She stepped forward, her expression earnest. "We will not be interrupted."

She was right, and so he sighed as he gestured to the bed. "Very well. Please arrange yourself."

She blinked at him, but did not move from where she knelt on his mat. "Arrange myself? How?"

He looked at her, working his thoughts into the appropriate frame. It wasn't hard; Miss Charlotte was indeed a beautiful woman. Her dress lifted her breasts to just the right height for his hands. Her waist, of course, was impossibly small, due to the strange whalebone contraption all white women wore; and her skirt shifted and flickered about her folded legs like tempting yin flames, drawing the mind to the secrets concealed within.

"You will have to remove your corset. It restricts your breathing."

She flushed, color bursting across her features, but she did not comment. Nor did she move.

He felt his hands clench and realized he was impossibly weary with these white women's games. At least at the Tigress school there was no confusion as to what one was about. No discussion, no illusions; it was simple practice. Except, of course, when it wasn't simply practice. But thoughts of Little Pearl soured his stomach, so he forced his attention back to Charlotte: beautiful Miss Charlotte, the flaming sun in the sky, the whore at his feet.

Whore? The name would not reconcile, and so he grabbed her, startled by his own sudden anger. He took hold of her arms and quickly lifted her up to her feet. She was not a small woman, but he was strong and she was too startled to resist. So he set her on her feet and glared at her. His voice was harsh, his manner cold. And yet his body shook from the heat she generated in his hands where they touched.

"Are you a virgin or a slut?" He spoke in English, making sure that there was no misunderstanding.

She tilted her head, seeming not in the least bit shocked. "Can I not be both?"

He frowned, wondering if he had chosen the wrong words. "How can one be both? Was the Virgin Mary a slut? Was the Whore of Babylon virtuous?"

She didn't answer. Instead, she slowly folded her arms, using the motion to dislodge his hands. She stared at him as she often stared at young William: with a mixture of bafflement and superiority. Finally, she said, "You agreed to teach me, Ken Jin. It won't take my—my maidenhead, will it?"

He shook his head. "Your virginity will remain intact." But her purity would not. Her sweet nature would not. Her very angelic image would fade away like so much dirty smoke. He ought to throw her out, but already his dragon was pushing forward in interest. This was the most virile he'd felt in a very long time. How could he stop?

"Teach me," she insisted.

Pressure built in his chest, an impossible pain that cut off his breath. What did he care what she chose to do with her white-woman virtue? What difference did it make to him if Miss Charlotte Wicks chose to follow her father's example rather than her mother's? Both paths were wrong for her—rampant debauchery or ascetic withering—and yet with no suitor in sight, she had no other choice.

Therefore, he would service her, release some of her stopped-up yin, and not think beyond that. He mentally stopped the pain that clogged his throat and pushed his worries away. It was as simple as slicing off an arm, but he accomplished it even as he took one step backward.

"Very well. Remove your clothing and lie upon the bed." His voice was not quite normal; it was higher in tone, though otherwise calm and detached. She, obviously, did not notice any difference, because she tilted her head and frowned.

"Why should I need to do that? Is it not you who must remove . . ." She waved at his lower parts.

He straightened, surprised. Most white women preferred him to remain clothed while he harvested their yin. He was, after all, simply a servant performing an unusual task, and servants remained clothed. Yet Charlotte obviously wanted the illusion of intimacy, and so he complied, stripping off his trousers with quick motions.

When he was done, he looked up to find her calmly appraising him. Or perhaps not so calmly, for he saw a brightness in her eyes, a slight sheen of perspiration on her lip, and a kind of movement in her whole body but in such small ways that he could not isolate one from another. In short, she was excited and interested and so very alive the air seem to crackle with her energy.

Even stranger, his dragon responded to the call of her yin. Indeed, her essence was so strong, he thought he could detect her scent in the air: musk and white-people flowers: the earthly and the heavenly combined. How strange, and yet how delightful to his dragon, which surged forward enough to poke its head out from its tunnel. Charlotte reached tentatively forward, her hand steady and her eyes focused.

Ken Jin practically leapt onto his desk to get away. "What are you doing?"

She looked into his face, her eyes wide. "Learning?"

He straightened. "That is not how you learn." He dipped

his head slightly in a mocking bow. "Please arrange your-self on the bed."

She looked where he indicated and shrugged. Then she reached down and gathered her skirt, awkwardly climbing onto his small bed. She gasped slightly as she settled onto her knees, probably because her corset had just pushed her breasts up higher than usual. But then she adjusted, shaking her shoulders enough that a tendril of hair slipped down beside her cheek. She blew it away with an irritated huff.

Looking back at him, she arched a single eyebrow and said tartly, "I cannot see how this will serve." Her gaze lowered to his thickening dragon. "You are tall for a Chinese, but really, Ken Jin, no man . . . Wouldn't it be better if I were on the floor?"

She spoke as she often did to young William, her voice high, her tones smooth and coaxing, and Ken Jin's dragon shrank away in horror. "Remove your clothing," he repeated, louder this time, and in the exact manner he used when her brother disobeyed. "And lie on your back."

She frowned and stared at the bed, then turned to face him. "On my back? But whatever for?"

"Instruction!"

"But that is not what was in the scroll!"

He was already stepping forward, prepared to lift her skirts himself to get her to obey. After all, she was the one who had demanded that he do this. She should not make her own debauchery so difficult! But then her words finally penetrated, and he froze. Which scroll had she read? Which text was she studying? "What exactly did the scroll say?"

Charlotte flushed a deeper scarlet, her color exceedingly beautiful. "Well, I couldn't actually *read* it."

"The pictures, then. What—"

"A woman on her knees before a man. She was . . ." She gestured weakly at Ken Jin's dragon.

"Playing the jade flute?" At her look of confusion, he re-phrased in English. "She had her mouth on his dragon? His long John."

Miss Charlotte nodded vigorously.

"*That* is what you wish to learn?" he pressed. "How to steal a man's yang? How to take his vital essence into your-self while he lies gasping and withered in your wake?"

She shifted on his bed, and her breasts bobbled slightly. "I was under the impression that men eagerly sought out ways to . . ." She frowned as she struggled with the Chi-nese words. "To surrender their yang."

"Of course some do. They are the unenlightened, the lewd, and the dissolute." He reached for his trousers. "But I am not such a man."

"Then, what were you going to teach me? If not that, then . . ." Her eyes widened as understanding lit her fea-tures. "You were going to do the same to me, weren't you? You were going to take my yang—"

"Yang is a man's power," he snapped, pulling on his clothing. It was difficult, because his dragon did not wish to be hidden. "A woman has yin."

"Yin," she repeated, testing the word. "You were going to take my yin, weren't you?"

"That is what a slut wants, isn't it?" He made his words deliberately harsh.

"To give up her essence to you? And then would I lie gasping and withered in *your* wake?"

He didn't like the way she was throwing his words back at him. No white person—much less a barbarian woman—had ever demonstrated such cleverness with words. Still, he would not lie to her. "Yes, that is what I thought you wanted."

"Because I am ignorant and lewd."

He shrugged, unable to deny it.

She abruptly pushed off the bed. "You are a pig, Ken Jin, and I would not take your yang if you begged me." She headed for the door, but he was there before her. "Get out of my way," she snapped.

"Give me the scrolls, Miss Charlotte." He matched her threatening tone, but his words were more deliberate.

She was not impressed. She flipped her hair out of her eyes and shifted her weight to step around him. "They are mine until Joanna returns."

He was losing patience with this farce. "They are stolen property, Miss Charlotte. They belong to the Tigress school, and I will see them returned."

She lifted her chin. "I don't believe you. And don't try to find them. I've hidden them where no one will ever guess."

He doubted that, but he did not argue. He could not have her angry with him. His livelihood depended on the Wicks. Plus, he wanted those scrolls. So he switched tactics. No woman could resist a trained Dragon, and his skills were legendary. So he reached out and took hold of the bow tie Charlotte wore. It was a silly female parody of a man's, only serving to emphasize how very feminine she looked, but it was useful to him. He pulled it loose with a single flick of his wrist. Another tug and he held it in his hand.

"What are you doing?" she cried.

"You wished to learn. Indeed, you threatened my employment if I didn't teach you."

"I have changed my mind."

He shook his head. "Sluts are not allowed to change their mind. Indeed," he said as he took a firm step forward. "I believe some sluts particularly desire to be threatened. Pushed." His voice dropped. "Forced."

She was shying backward—away from him, toward his bed. "Stop this immediately! This is most unlike you, Ken Jin."

"I didn't know you were a slut before."

She backed up to the bed. "Let me go!"

"Give me the scrolls."

"I'll scream!"

His hand went to her throat, quickly cutting off her breath. The force of his assault knocked her backward onto his bed, carrying him down on top of her. He was a large man with trained hands. He knew how to make a woman's yin flow like a glowing river, and he knew how to stop it cold, which was exactly what he planned now. He pressed his hand into her throat, restricting her breath but not stopping it. Then he leaned down far enough to whisper his threats into her ears.

The motion brought his dragon full and hard against her skirt, and the bonfire that was her cinnabar cave began to torture his thoughts. Her legs slipped open and he thrust fully against her. Thankfully, the barrier of his thin trousers and her even thinner skirt kept him from slipping inside her heated cave. Still, he could feel her wetness, even smell her scent on the air as their bodies ground together. Once, twice, even a third time he pressed forward, his yang strengthening to a hard rod of glorious power.

"This is what happens to sluts," he said as she gasped beneath his onslaught. "This is what those scrolls teach. This is the life that your Joanna has embraced." He did not add that her friend's choice would probably lead to her death. He wanted to frighten Charlotte, not inflict a pain that would come all too soon. "This life is not for you. Now give me those scrolls."

"But," she gasped. "Ken Jin . . ."

She was struggling. Her face was flushed, her eyes were wide; even her back was rigid with horror. So he thrust one last time, hard, his meaning unmistakable despite the separation of fabric. And then, as a further punishment, he crushed his pelvis against her, round and round in the pleasure circle.

She would not soon forget his meaning or this experience. Her reaction was coming; he could feel it. Her body was rigid beneath him. Charlotte had great pride, but she would give in. It was her female nature to yield, especially when a man showed his superior strength. This was inevitable, and Ken Jin was man enough to relish the moment.

Then she wrapped her legs around him, arched her back in her own sudden thrust, and exploded in a yin rush that made her scream a joyous whoop of victory.

❦

July 16, 1881
To Wen Qui Xiu:
I thank you for your warning. The demon Ken Jin did indeed appear on my doorstep. As you urged, I cast him off. However, as he departed, my heart was most heavy. He did not seem at all demonlike, but quite a normal, resourceful boy. Is it possible that the demon who possessed your son has fled for a better victim? Would you like me to watch this boy? If nothing else, I could learn more about his demonic ways. And if the demon has left, would you not wish the return of your son?
In hope,
Tigress Tan Shi Po

PS—I understand your husband is an acupuncturist. How fortunate for you! I wish my husband had such talent. Alas, we have spent our time in the study of plants. Though my skills are feeble, I do have a recipe to release the fog that clouds many elderly women's minds. Could you pass this on to your mother-in-law? It may help restore peace in your home. And please have her write me to tell if it is effective.

To honored Grandmother Wen Ai Men, Tigress sister,

I recently began using this recipe. The patient stays in my home so I can watch for any ailment or problems. So far, the tea has been most effective.

Sincerely,
Tigress Tan Shi Po

(Attached, a recipe labeled: To Ease Your Mind. In truth, it is a common potion known to all tigresses for the strengthening growth of young dragons.)

To treat Insomnia: Before retiring, take a leisurely walk, self-massage the body all over, and then massage the yung chuan acupoint, which is in the middle of the sole of the foot.
Tong Sing, the Chinese Book of Wisdom, Dr. Charles Windridge

Chapter Four

Charlotte felt her legs go slack as the last of the ripples shivered through her. The sensation dissipated quickly, and if it weren't for Ken Jin's weight upon her, she would already be feeling chill. But he was here, and she found his presence a wonderful addition to the experience. "Now I know why Sophie says it's better with another person," she murmured as much to herself as to him.

"Your yin peaked!" he said, obviously stunned. "But I wasn't trying to . . . Few Tigresses even . . ." He swallowed. "How is this possible? How can you have such responsive yin?"

She blinked, trying to understand his words. She couldn't, of course, but she was feeling so lovely that she didn't really care. "Thank you, Ken Jin. But that wasn't what you were supposed to teach me, you know."

He reared back, then scrambled off her. Once on his feet, he clearly had no idea what to do except gape. "You are supposed to be ignorant!" he accused.

She pushed onto an elbow and frowned. "Is something the matter? This *is* what you expected to do this afternoon, isn't it? This is what you thought my 'lesson' would entail."

He didn't answer. His gaze leapt from her face to her belly and then back again. His mouth was open; then it shut; then it fell open again. So Charlotte sat fully upright. She fussed with her clothing, not because it needed straightening, but because she needed something to do with her hands.

"That was delightful, Ken Jin, truly. But . . ." She glanced up at his blanched face, then quickly down at her skirt. "It wasn't really what I came here to learn. As I was trying to say before, I want to understand about *men's* bodies. I already know all about mine."

"You do?" he squeaked. Then he took a breath and spoke in a steadier tone. "You understand what just happened?"

Charlotte sighed. "Do you truly believe that women in this city are so ignorant? That we know nothing of these things? I'm twenty-five years old!" She set her feet daintily upon the floor. "Think, Ken Jin. My father disappears for hours on end while my mother preaches ceaselessly about the horrors of physical pleasure. Yes, I know there are girls who know nothing of the body's pleasures, but my parents piqued my curiosity when I was still playing with dolls."

"Your mother preaches against such things!"

"My mother said that fun such as this was the devil's trap." She rolled her eyes. "All I heard was fun."

"But how—"

"My friend Stacy has a machine. One to prevent migraines."

He stared, obviously not understanding.

She shook her head, unwilling to give up her friend's secrets. "She taught me."

He took a step forward, anger contorting his usually placid features. "What did she teach you?"

Charlotte stared at him, annoyance beginning to sour her mood. "Why are you angry?"

He blinked and abruptly stiffened his shoulders. "I am not angry!"

Except, of course, he obviously was. Charlotte sighed. Men pursued their pleasures with single-minded abandon, and yet it never occurred to them that women could discover their own ways to enjoy life. How disappointing to find out that Ken Jin was just like other men.

Charlotte abruptly pushed to her feet, her tone prim and authoritative. "Ken Jin, my actions are none of your affair."

He stopped abruptly. So did she. And there they stood, on opposite sides, servant and master, English and Chinese. Except . . .

"You wish to learn more," he said, his voice low and eerily calm. "I wish for a return of the sacred scrolls."

She blinked. "They're sacred?"

He nodded, but the movement was slow, as if he had not intended to reveal so much. Then he abruptly sat down, then gestured to the open space beside him on the bed. "Please, Miss Charlotte, will you sit and listen?"

His manner was so different than from a moment before, she needed to adjust. Then they'd struggled across a great divide; now he seemed to want to be her friend. Or, if not her friend, her equal. The concept was so disorienting that she sat down merely because she could no longer stand. Just what was this Chinaman about?

"Miss Charlotte," he began, "the scrolls you found describe a course of study, a path to Heaven in a most unusual way."

She felt her face and chest flush with embarrassment. "Only the Chinese would make sex a course of study." When he looked at her in confusion, she elaborated: "We English do not write such things down. We simply . . ." How to express her father's lecheries?

"You simply rut," he supplied. She opened her mouth to object to the crude term, but he held up his hand to stop her. "You believe you understand your father's activities?"

She looked away. "We English do not talk of those things either."

"But you know of them."

She nodded. Yes, of course she knew. Shanghai's gossip-mongers made sure of that. Indeed, her father's exploits were discussed among even the most sheltered of her friends.

"What he does is rut," Ken Jin continued, his voice gentle despite his harsh words. "Like a beast in the field, he performs according to instinct without conscious thought, except to meet his most basic desire."

Charlotte felt Ken Jin's fingers touch her chin. She felt the rough brush of his calluses, the cool press of his skin against hers as he drew her around to look at him.

"What he does is not wrong. It is merely ignorant."

"Mama believes it is wrong. She says that's why William is . . . isn't very bright. And that is why she prays so much." She bit her lip, stunned by what she had just admitted. Why would she tell that to a servant? And yet, who else would she talk to about it? Ken Jin was here. He'd lived in their home for the last ten years. He understood what went on in the family; he probably knew better than she did.

His eyes held compassion as he spoke. "I do not understand your white gods."

She shrugged, weary of the conversation. "I'm not sure anyone does."

"That is in the nature of gods." His hand was still on her chin, but now he extended his thumb and drew it across her lips. Charlotte did not move. It was an unconscionable liberty, but she had already allowed a great deal more. Besides, she was too entranced by the tingling pleasure to stop him. How could her lips feel so full, so electrified, by a single caress?

He too gasped, and his eyes widened as his thumb repeated its pass. He moved slowly, and she felt every texture of his thumb, even to the point of imagining how it would taste against her tongue. The tingling became a throb.

"Do you feel that, Miss Charlotte?" His voice held a note of breathless awe. "Do you feel the fire of yin and yang in combustion?" He let his finger slip to the indentation between her lower lip and chin, and abruptly pinched her there. The single quick bite of pain caused the heat in her face to blossom into riotous sensation. She gasped, stunned by the accompanying shiver of warmth in her belly.

Then, before she could speak, he licked his thumb before returning it to that very same location, rubbing in a wet circle. The slide of wet made her belly liquefy; the cold kiss of air made her face feel even more hot. And then he leaned forward, replacing his thumb with his lips.

She should move away. She knew that. This was much too familiar from a servant. But nothing in her wanted to escape. In fact, she extended her chin to give him better access as his tongue swirled in another erotic circle. She shivered and her nipples tightened. And then he finished with a sucking kiss that seemed to draw her out of herself. As he pulled away, she wanted to follow, but she was too stunned to do more than utter a nearly silent whimper.

"I have opened the gate for intimacy, Miss Charlotte. This attunes our spirits, one to another. Do you feel the difference in your body?" He spoke in Chinese, but she understood. And the foreign words made the experience all the more intense.

"Yes," she managed. "Oh yes."

"This is what I study." The cadence of his voice set a kind of rhythm in her blood. It made no sense that a single touch could do so much, and yet she felt aligned to him as had never happened before with anyone. Her heart even seemed to beat to the tempo of his words. "This is the pathway to what is beyond rutting," he continued. "It is what your father has not found and your mother does not understand."

"I want to learn," she said. She had no idea how she formed the thought, much less managed the breath to speak, but her desire was unquestionable.

"Your mother will damn you for it."

Her eyes flew open, but the fire she felt did not dim. "No," she whispered, "she will damn you."

She saw him blanch and he draw back. The loss was so devastating that she grabbed his arm.

"Teach me anyway," she said. "Teach me, and I will protect you. She won't ever know." Her words were rash, possibly lies. There was little she could do if her mother thought a servant had debauched her daughter. But there were ways to avoid discovery.

"Give me the scrolls, Miss Charlotte, and I will show you the first steps."

She shook her head, not willing to compromise. "*All* of the steps."

He smiled, but the expression seemed mocking. "Only the Enlightened know all the steps." A look of longing crossed his features briefly; then it was gone. His hand returned to her face, this time with more than his thumb. This time, he pressed two fingers to her lips. Then slowly, inexorably, he pushed them inside her mouth. At last, she could taste his fingers. She could feel the texture of callus and nail against her tongue. She could purse her lips and suck him deeper inside.

"Give me the scrolls, Miss Charlotte, and I will show you the path."

He was wiggling his fingers, spreading them wide

against her teeth and the roof of her mouth. His movements touched off sparks in the strangest places—the base of her teeth, the underside of her tongue, even the back of her throat though he'd only penetrated to his first knuckle.

She slid her hand up his forearm to his wrist and abruptly pushed his fingers deeper into her mouth. She had no understanding of her actions, only that she wanted to taste more of him. It was disconcerting to feel touched in places that he couldn't possibly reach. If he could do this with just his fingers, how much more wonderful it would be with his whole penis in her mouth? The thought was thrilling beyond belief.

"Give me the scrolls, Miss Charlotte."

She couldn't focus on his words. She wanted to understand how she could tingle in places he hadn't stroked, how there could be heat and power pulsing in the back of her throat. And how that erotic pulse could continue all the way down her body deep into her womb.

He withdrew abruptly, leaving her open and empty. "Give me the scrolls, Miss Charlotte."

She swallowed. It took an act of will, so completely had he tied her to his power. "Or what?" she finally rasped.

"Or I will teach you nothing more."

She struggled to gather her thoughts. "I don't need you. The scrolls will teach me everything," she hedged.

He looked unimpressed. "One or two scrolls that start in the middle? You are not so foolish as to believe that paper can show better than a teacher."

No, it couldn't. She'd already looked at the pictures, even tried to decipher the Chinese characters, but nothing had imparted the tiniest clue about what she had just experienced.

"If I give you the scrolls, you won't teach me anything. It's too dangerous for you. If my mother finds out . . ."

His hands were in his lap, folded neatly. She stared at

them, wondering at the power he possessed. Could he affect her from there? Could he touch her from across the room? How far did his abilities reach? She lifted her gaze to his eyes, only now noticing the sweat beading his upper lip. A quick glance showed that his male organ was large beneath his trousers. He was not unaffected by what he'd done. Perhaps he wanted to teach as much as she wanted to learn.

"Teach me first," she offered. "I'll give you the scrolls afterward." That would give her time to have the text copied and translated.

He waited a moment, looking at her with a steady, flat regard. She might have worried, so cold was his expression, except right beneath his hands she saw his sex twitch. He was quite large; she remembered from her unexpected view this morning. The demands of his organ must be equally huge. He would teach her, she realized with a sudden rush. His organ would demand it.

As expected, he sighed and pushed to his feet. He moved slowly, and she guessed he was protecting himself from accidental jostling. She had learned from caring for her brother that a thickened male organ could be quite sensitive. Indeed, she had learned quite a lot when poor William had hit puberty. He had stimulated himself in the most inappropriate places and times. Rather than slap his hands, their mother had slapped his organ as a form of discipline. Charlotte surmised that Ken Jin was trying to avoid a similarly painful fate.

"We can begin tomorrow," she offered as sweetly as she could manage. "When you are feeling more the thing."

She avoided a gloating smile as he bowed before her. But a moment later, she felt a wash of sadness. He had returned to his place as servant, offering her respect without emotion. Her victory felt hollow.

He straightened and walked to the door. "I regret that we could not come to an understanding, Miss Charlotte. Please allow me to return to my work. Your father will wish to check my progress when he returns."

Charlotte blinked, confused. She had won, hadn't she? She stood up and headed slowly for the door. "So, I shall come back here tomorrow afternoon? We will begin then?"

He shook his head. "No, Miss Charlotte. I regret to inform you that I cannot do as you request."

"But I don't understand. Surely you aren't going to just stop . . . I mean, naturally you wish to continue at another time. Don't you?" Her last words were high-pitched, squeaked as if by a little girl. Appalling, really, since she was no child.

"No, Miss Charlotte, I do not." Again he gave a deep bow. "Good day."

And a moment later, she found herself on the opposite side of his closed door.

Ken Jin stood facing the shut door. His legs were spread, his hands planted firmly on his hips, and his dragon was as hard as a Shantung maple. All in all, an excellent day. So why was he clenching his jaw as if he were about to chew ginger?

He turned to his desk, refocusing his thoughts on work. He had ledger entries to record, bills of lading to reconcile with ship accounts, and hours of letters to write for Mr. Wicks's signature. Nothing was urgent, but all was important. And with nothing else to occupy his time, he knew he would be at his desk well into the night.

Squaring his shoulders, he settled into his chair, making sure his legs were spread wide so as to give his organ room to breathe. He pulled out the ledger, opening it . . . only to stare at the neat columns of barbarian writing. No, he abruptly decided, he would not work on white people's numbers today. His qi was in too much disorder to work in straight lines.

The letters, then. Putting the ledger away beneath the abacas, he drew out Mr. Wicks's special letter paper. He curled his lip in disdain at its scent and feel: too flat, too cold. It never absorbed the ink correctly, not of a good Chinese brush at least. And so he had to use a "fountain pen"—a barbarian creation of metal that was too small and dead to properly control.

No. He would use a brush to write his family, and he owed his brother a letter. That would be an efficient use of his time. And it would be an adequately Chinese pastime, to counteract the other forces in his life.

He set down the pen, but did not take up the brush. Slowly, his hand curled into a fist. Abacas, brush, ink stone. Stationery, ledger, pen. What did he want? What should he do? A balanced man walked the middle path, but when the Dragon played near the Tigress's mouth, the Tigress seized the fallen jade. Ledgers or letter? Balanced path or Tigress play? White or Chinese?

Who was he? Disowned by his Chinese family, he had to learn to be white to work and survive. Now the Chinese would not speak to him unless it was to take his money; the whites used him as translator and manager but still disdained him as a servant. Where was his path?

His dragon wilted away to nothing as thoughts churned in his mind. His qi was weakening by the second. Grabbing his bills of lading, he abruptly strode out of the manor, pretending to head for the docks. In truth, he had no thought as to where he would go. Or rather, he had too many thoughts, too many responsibilities.

Should he return to the Tigress school to help Little Pearl? Should he go to his private rooms for practice? He even considered a more public venue, with a willing woman where he could gather more yin. But no answer was right, nothing settled his disordered spirit.

At last he decided to help the Tans. He would drive the Wicks carriage to the prison. He judged it would take half his money to bribe his way into the Tigress's cell, and the other half to arrange for her release. It would take a good deal longer and a great deal more money to arrange for her husband Kui Yu's freedom, but Ken Jin knew the man's honor; he would want Shi Po released first. And so Ken Jin hefted his tiny purse and prayed he had enough.

Very soon, he realized he didn't have anything close to enough. In several hours, he spent two-thirds of his money just to verify that the Tans were indeed held exactly where he'd guessed, in Shanghai's military compound. The last third went toward the discovery that some guards could not be bribed. He did not even manage a visit to the "whore Shi Po" and her husband, the "barbarian-loving Kui Yu."

In short, his scattered energies doomed him, and he spent everything he had to learn that lesson. He should have remained in his airless room at the Wicks household, where disordered qi reigned and conflicting desires found their own odd form of balance. But where to now?

He did not go back to their home. Nor did go back to the Tigress school. He did not go anywhere for hours and hours; he simply drove around in aimless paths through Shanghai. He did not find true direction until the sun had left the sky when the city readied for sleep. Unfortunately, his final path was more a weakness, a total collapse of his resistance.

He knew before he crossed back into English Shanghai that he would give in to Charlotte. His energies were too weak to resist the lure of her burning qi. Yes, he needed to get the scrolls from her. But even more, he needed to taste her yin, needed to feel her power stroke his yang to full strength. Without her, he seemed to be perpetually limp and withdrawn.

He returned to the Wicks home, quickly grabbing his tools from his bedroom. And then in the quiet of a sleeping home, he crept up the stairs. Slipping easily into Miss Charlotte's room, he made sure to shut the door fast before stepping close to her bed. She had a washstand nearby—a perfect place to rest his tools. He did so quickly, arranging them for easy access. Then he turned to the bed.

She was asleep, the red-gold flames of her hair criss-crossing every which way on her white pillow. He looked at her and his grip shifted on the hard metal implement. A balanced man walked the middle path. But what did an unbalanced man do? When the Dragon plays near the Tigress's mouth, the Tigress seizes the fallen jade.

No! His dragon would not play anywhere near her mouth. She was no tigress to seize his ejaculated yang. And an unbalanced man should strengthen himself any way he could—even with stolen yin.

With sudden focus, Ken Jin pressed a hand across Miss Charlotte's mouth. Her eyes flew open in surprise, but she had no time to cry out. His free hand stripped the bedcovers away.

He felt her gasp. He would have to act quickly to stop a scream. He leaned down, his whisper harsh next to her ear. "The Tigress path requires courage even more than secrecy, strength more than desire. Are you brave enough, Miss Charlotte, to walk this path? Are you strong enough to take my yang while your yin gushes like a river?"

She didn't understand his words. How could she? Despite her easy yin peak this afternoon, she was still a virginal barbarian, and he had come upon her in the middle of the night.

"Understand this, Miss Charlotte, I am a man who has

left the middle path. My weaknesses are legion, and my spirit has splintered into a thousand chaotic pieces. Only one thing keeps my qi strong, only one energy quiets my chaos." He pulled back far enough to look into her wide blue eyes. "Do you wish to know what that one thing is, Miss Charlotte? We call it the Peach of Immortality. Do you wish to know that it is?"

He would not let her move. He barely allowed her to breathe. But to his surprise, she managed a sound. Not a whimper, not a cry, but a firm reply.

"Shir." "Yes," spoken in Chinese.

"It is a woman's rain, Miss Charlotte, the fluid of ecstasy, and I am quite a connoisseur."

Her eyes grew wide, and he felt her breath suspend. He removed his hand to allow her air should she choose to take it; and while she stared at him, he straightened and turned to the wall sconce. With a quick flick of his wrist, he lit the gas lamp, drawing up the flame to cast a soft red glow over her bed. She still said nothing, so he turned back to her and began to slowly, deliberately, strip off his shirt and tie.

"I want your yin, Miss Charlotte. Indeed, I must have it."

"The scrolls?" she whispered. Her voice was hoarse, and she had to clear her throat before she spoke again. "What about the sacred scrolls?"

He dismissed them with a flick of his wrist. "They reveal only isolated stones. I can show you the path."

She lifted her chin. She made no movement to adjust her body or her nightdress. "But you want them."

"I will take them. Tonight, after I am done."

She bit her lip, and he knew she toyed with bargaining. He showed no compromise in tone or stance. In the end, her eyes dropped and she nodded. "What must I do?" she whispered.

"Not scream." Then he reached for his razor.

Sept 10, 1881
To Tigress Tan Shi Po:

Dearest friend, the recipe you sent is most ef-fective. My heart is greatly relieved, and I find my-self much less warlike with my daughter-in-law.

Unfortunately, I seem to have other ailments common to old women. Indeed, I find the cries of the youngest grandchild—a boy with grasping hands and a greedy look—to be most irritating. He is my son's new heir to all our fortune, but I feel as if he has supplanted my best hope. Do you have a recipe to relieve this agony? To reassure an aging heart that all can be well again?

In hope,
Wen Ai Men

Sept 28, 1881
Honored grandmother Wen Ai Men, Tigress sister:

How pleased I am that my poor recipe eased your angry spirit. And of course I understand about the wailing of children. It can be most grat-ing upon elderly nerves.

My newest assistant has copied a perfect recipe for you. He is a clever boy with a beautiful hand for calligraphy. He is the grandson of my sister's sister's sister, but she had a tragedy at home and would not feed him. Thus, he has come to me to live and learn. My sons adore him, and he has brought great order to my chaotic house. I am most pleased with my good fortune, and though I would be happy to return him, I am honored to share my love and fortune with him. Perhaps in time your grandson's wails will fade and he will find his proper place in the family. But until that day, please rest assured that all is well.

Is it not strange that a single misfortune can disharmonize an entire family? In the meantime, please try the attached recipe for soothing the spirit. My assistant finds it most helpful.

Sincerely,
Tigress Tan Shi Po

(Attached, a recipe labeled To Harmonize the Spirit, but in truth is a common recipe—known to all tigresses—for expanding the girth and power of a healthy dragon.)

To relieve excess perspiration, press firmly or massage the acupoint which is three finger-widths from the wrist crease and in line with the thumb.
Tong Sing, the Chinese Book of Wisdom, Dr. Charles Windridge

Chapter Five

Charlotte readied herself to scream. Her mother would expect her to scream; it was important to her virtue, to her immortal soul, that she scream and end this crazed Chinaman's presence in her room. Especially as he took his razor in one hand and the bottom of her gown in the other. Instead, she held her breath as he began to cut a single straight line that split her dress in two.

She should definitely scream. She whimpered instead. Except, it wasn't really a whimper, not like a child or a frightened puppy would make. It was more a nervous crackle of sound, almost a giggle, but she wasn't laughing. And when she lifted herself up slightly on her bed, he pushed her back down with a single touch on her shoulder.

She could have broken away. She could have thrown him off completely, but she didn't. She did nothing except sink down into her pillow. Her gown was tight about her neck, buttoned all the way up to her chin. The lacy sleeves held tight to her arms and her wrists. But down below, all was now open. Ken Jin's blade had slit high enough that her knees were exposed, and air touched a great deal more than was bared to his gaze.

She should really tell him to stop. Her mother would be horrified if she ever saw this gown. Mama would order a full Mass and then send Charlotte to a nunnery. Charlotte had to remember to burn this gown in the morning. Fortunately, she had a dozen more gowns just like it.

Cold air caressed her thighs. Fabric fluttered open higher and higher along her legs. Soon above her hips, and then her belly. Her legs shifted restlessly, but Ken Jin dropped a hand to her knee, stopping her nervous movement. His eyes remained on her face: cold and hard and penetrating, even in the darkness.

"Do not move," he said.

She felt a moment of panic. "I'm going to stay a virgin, aren't I?" Her voice came out a breathless whisper. "And there won't be any blood, will there?"

He took a moment to answer. The light caused her white skin to glow, and she could see a flame reflected on the blade. But her eyes trained on his face, trying to discern his emotion. Though he remained in shadow, he was definitely frowning.

"Are you going to scream?" His voice was low and smooth, and her pulse quickened. Clearly whatever he had done this afternoon still affected her. Their energies were still aligned, which made her feel nearly as powerful as he was dangerous.

She swallowed. He stood above her, his knife working above her belly. She felt the jagged edge of her gown flutter against her hips, and knew that her sex was exposed to him. But his gaze was direct on her face even as each thread strained and broke. Higher and higher the blade cut. It was obviously very sharp. The buttons fell away with barely any resistance at all.

The remaining fabric grew tighter against her chest. He could not lift the gown up very high. Indeed, she felt the cold back of his blade skate, then tickle, then press hard between her breasts. Finally, it stopped. "Are you going to struggle in any way?"

"No," she said. The word came out in a rush, but she said it clearly, and a little too loud.

His lips curved the tiniest fraction. "Then there will be no blood."

She nodded, though she couldn't move her head very far. The neck of her gown was so taut that it was nearly choking her. "And my virginity?" she whispered.

Her belly was completely exposed, and she knew she trembled. She could feel the fabric catch on her tightened nipples, abrading her with each of her soft, panting breaths. But it wouldn't stay that way for long. It was going to fall away, leaving her totally open to Ken Jin. She was going to be completely naked before her servant.

His blade rose higher, neared her throat. The stitching made the fabric thicker there, and the lace tickled her chin. In fact, it tickled exactly the spot that Ken Jin had stroked and sucked this afternoon. The memory set her blood pounding in her face, her chest, her womb.

"Arch your back," he ordered.

She pressed her heels into the mattress to obey. But the moment she did, she realized her problem. She couldn't arch and still watch him. She had to pick one or the other. He paused, clearly sensing her dilemma, but his expression did not change. He would give her no help.

Did she trust him? Could she look at the ceiling and await whatever he wanted to do?

She wetted her lips, the memory of that afternoon vivid in her mind and senses. Her body was already on fire, and he had done nothing more than cut away her gown. She desperately wanted more of those feelings, of those experiences. But did she trust him enough to keep her virginity intact? To not damage her body or soul?

No, a thousand times, no. She didn't trust anyone that far. And yet, even as she decided against him, the lure of what he could teach overwhelmed her reason. She let her head drop back and closed her eyes. The risks be damned; she wanted to feel.

Ken Jin's blade slipped up to her throat. The fabric of her gown strained, pressing against the back of her neck. Then, with a soft whisper, it split. The edges drifted down and Charlotte felt the cloth catch on her nipples before falling away. Except for her arms, she was completely naked, and she felt her lips curve into a smile. How freeing this all was!

He touched her then. He must have set down the blade, because she felt his fingers on her neck, brushing from her jaw to her throat. Two fingers—one on each side—pressed into her flesh, one after the other, moving to just above her voice box.

"This is the spot of welcome," he said. "It will harmonize your qi with Heaven and Earth."

Her back was straining, so she slowly let herself down. The mattress welcomed her, supporting her weight and enfolding her in its softness. But his fingers on her throat were what created the sensation. She could not explain it; she only knew that what he did made everything seem different. Better. She smiled, and he slid his two fingers slightly lower, to just below her voice box.

Again, he touched one side and then the other, but this time his stroke circled. "This is the spot of rushing water. It will increase your yin rain."

Charlotte didn't dare move for fear of dislodging his fingers. He touched only her throat, and yet she felt a tingling response in her entire body. And yes: Perhaps she did feel as if her blood were rushing, as if there was more . . . wetness . . . everywhere.

He moved his hands lower. She licked her lips, watching his eyes as he watched hers. His gaze didn't waver; he didn't even blink, but his hands flowed downward, his touch exquisitely light—like feathers or leaves, barely touching her skin—until he found her breasts. She felt more of him then, his palms extending out to ten fingers as they surrounded her. His hands were larger than she'd expected. They seemed to engulf her breasts. But his skin was cool, certainly cooler than her own flushed body.

He lifted her breasts, but lightly. His touch remained gentle. He flowed around her rather than pushed, and she felt her belly quiver. The distance between his hands narrowed as he drew them toward her nipples; but he moved slowly, twisting slightly, as if he wanted to feel her texture but not change her shape. His hands moved and she remained just as she was, trembling breathlessly beneath his exploration.

He leaned forward. His face came close to hers and she felt her eyes widen. Would he kiss her? Did she want him to? She had no ability to grapple with that question, and no time either—especially as his hands continued to surround and narrow, surround and narrow, never quite reaching her nipples.

Then his face shifted, and she felt his lips against her throat. Odd, how disappointed she felt, and yet what he did was so intriguing. His lips found the places on her neck he'd touched earlier. What were they called? She didn't remember, and she didn't really care. He was sucking, harmonizing her or something, and increasing her water flow. Whatever the purpose, it felt delightful and strange as he methodically worked on each of the four points. She barely had the consciousness to turn her head halfway through the process. But when she managed, she was rewarded by a swirl of his tongue over the left points.

Finally, he lifted himself up. "Do you feel the increased flow?" He might have been asking about the weather. She nodded in silence, not having the control to speak. "Then I will continue."

His head dipped again. His lips closed over her left nipple. His tongue swirled around it before he pressed his lips together and pulled away. She thought her breast would pop out of his mouth, but it did not. Instead, it slipped away in a slow withdrawal.

"Your virginity will remain intact," he murmured into her skin. She had forgotten her question, but felt a relaxation of her fears at his words. She would still be pure enough for marriage when—if—the time came. Then her thoughts scattered as Ken Jin's hands moved down her body. His lips disappeared from her breast. She couldn't see him; her eyes had drifted closed. And yet she could feel his presence by the tingling shift of air on her skin, and knew he would soon circle and nip at her other breast.

The hands that left her chest—one slid to the bed to support his weight; the other caressed downward, lifting slightly so that all she felt was a single digit—his thumb, she thought—tracing a path to her navel. It stopped there, holding in the indentation, and soon the rest of his fingers dropped down—one . . . two . . . three . . . four— and stopped. His lips took her right nipple. She abruptly realized that she had breathed deeply, expanding her chest toward him, anxious for this moment. Now that it was here, she let the air out in a happy sigh.

His thick, luscious queue of black hair slipped forward to land on her sleeve. It was a welcome weight, and she wanted to touch it. Ever since he'd come to work for her family, she'd longed to stroke the silken cord. At last she could. But when she raised her hand, he lifted himself abruptly off her. The pressure on her belly increased, and she had to tighten her stomach at the sudden weight.

"Don't move," he said, his words harsh.

She blinked. "But—"

"This is what you want, isn't it? You want to learn?"

She nodded, disconcerted by his hard tone. How different his words were from his touch.

"Then do nothing. I will direct all the movement I need from you."

Her hand fell back to the mattress. Ken Jin waited a moment, staring hard at her so she understood.

"But why?" she asked, her voice sounding childishly plaintive to her ears.

His expression softened, and she saw a flash of confusion on his face, but then it quickly disappeared. "This is the path of the Tigress, Miss Charlotte. It is not for the faint of heart."

"You don't really know," she accused. "You don't know what—"

Her words were cut off as he pressed a finger to her mouth. "I need your yin," he rasped. "You wish to learn. There is no more and no less than that. Do you now change your mind?"

"No." How quickly she spoke even though she knew she ought to refuse. Ken Jin felt dangerous to her now. Thrillingly, wonderfully, fascinatingly dangerous. "I want to learn."

He nodded and returned to his task, lowering his lips back to her nipple. How bizarre this felt, almost like a visit to a doctor. And yet, it was also very different, especially as he shifted his hold on her. His thumb lifted out of her navel, his fingers as well until only one last finger remained. In fact, all the pressure transferred to that tiny dot, halfway between her navel and her most intimate place.

What was he doing? Was this what he'd done to Sophie? To Marilyn? Was this why he was a favorite among all the girls in her set—because he did this without taking one's virginity? Charlotte felt her lips curve into a smile. Finally, she would know for herself.

Her legs trembled slightly. They had been pressed together, but as Ken Jin's tiniest finger took more of his weight, pressing deeper and deeper into her belly, she felt her muscles release. Her legs went lax, and her thighs rolled slightly open. His finger began massaging a tight, deep circle.

"How often have you felt the yin release?" he asked.

She blinked, struggling to focus on his words rather than his finger.

"What happened this afternoon," he clarified. "The contractions in your womb. How many times have you experienced it?"

She felt her face heat in embarrassment.

"How often?" His demand was harsh and cold.

"Often!" The word burst out of her. There had been stretches where it was a daily ritual, beginning with the time the experience was explained to her with the Migraine Relief machine—the day that her father had gone to his mistress, her mother to church, and even her brother had masturbated during his bath. From that day on, Charlotte had sought opportunities for a pleasurable moment of solitude.

Ken Jin nodded in total acceptance. "That explains why you retain such youthful beauty despite your age." She stared at him in confusion. "Yin fluids keep a woman's body supple. Correct stimulation will preserve your beauty and sweetness."

"I have been keeping myself young?" What odd things the Chinese believed!

He nodded in agreement and dipped his head again. Her nipples had grown cold, but now he heated them again. He took his time, exhaling a long, hot breath across her right peak. Then he took it in his mouth. Again came the swirl of the tongue, this time followed by a sudden sharp suck.

A flash fire expanded across her skin, an exploding circle that she felt all the way down to her toes and up to the crown of her head. But then it was gone, almost before she felt its presence. And he was lifting himself up again, drawing away from her nipple with the slow slide that made her clench the sheets in frustration.

"Ken Jin—" she ground out.

"Stay silent, Miss Charlotte." He directed his attention to her belly and slowly withdrew his finger. "Your yin is strong," he said, "but it is not yet pure enough to draw out. You need to be cleansed."

He reached for his razor and strop cloth. While Charlotte watched, he began to sharpen the blade with quick, fast strokes. She pushed up on the bed, wanting to sit up straight. She felt the strongest urge to cover herself with the cover, but she did not. She knew the moment she did anything to counter him, he would simply pack up and leave. Her lesson would end, and she would learn nothing more. She would *feel* nothing more.

So, she didn't cover herself. Instead, she shrugged out of her sleeves and tossed the torn garment away. He watched her, unmoving except for his rhythmic stroke of blade against leather. She tried to be silent. She wanted to be as stoic like him, but the pressure to speak was undeniable.

"How am I to be cleansed?"

She didn't think he would answer. He simply watched as if measuring her reaction. She tried not to fidget beneath his regard, but her insides felt as if they were bubbling. She couldn't contain it much longer.

"Ken Jin—" she began, but he interrupted her.

"Hair traps disease and vermin. It must be cut away. That will cleanse your outside."

She swallowed. "And the inside?" Her voice was a squeak.

"There are exercises. I will teach them to you."

She nodded, her belly relaxing now that she understood.

"And then I will take your yin. I will draw it from you until you are limp and empty, and your spirit is too dry to even weep for the loss."

She blanched. "Tonight?" She bit her lower lip. "All that tonight?"

He set down the strop cloth. "No, Miss Charlotte. It will take many, many nights."

She didn't know what to say. She knew what she ought to think, but what did she really want?

"Spread your legs."

She started. "What?"

He didn't answer, simply waited for her to obey. She stared at him, at the razor, and then at the juncture of her thighs. He was going to shave her *there?*

She nearly rolled her eyes at her own stupidity. Of course he meant there. After all, his other lovers hadn't been walking around bald-headed. By his own account— and her friends' gossip—he had been with every scandalous white woman in Shanghai and quite a few honorable ones. Which meant that all those other women . . . that they had walked around without . . .

"It's not cold, is it? I mean, doesn't hair keep things warm?"

"Do you feel cold?"

She shook her head. Truthfully, she felt like she'd swallowed an entire sun.

"Then open your thighs, Miss Charlotte."

"So you can shave me." It wasn't a question. It was nervous anxiety, and they both knew it. Migraine Relief was one thing, but shaving? What if her mother noticed? Charlotte could claim that she got hot, she supposed. Besides, no one—not even her mother—had seen her naked since she was a child.

Ken Jin didn't speak, simply stood there waiting. He wouldn't remain for long; she knew that eventually his patience would end and he would turn around and leave. Which would be for the best, right? No decent woman walked around shaved. Charlotte should let him leave. She was a good girl. She went to church. She prayed for her parents and her brother. She even prayed for the Chinese poor.

She should have screamed long ago. But since she hadn't, she ought to just keep her legs closed. He would leave then, and they would both pretend that this little interlude had never happened. She would wake in the morning, finish her toilette, and help William with his. She and her brother would do daily lessons in the nursery, and maybe Joanna would return so they could talk about her adventures. Charlotte would sit on her knees and listen with breathless envy to her best friend's exciting life and never, ever have an adventure to tell of her own.

She looked Ken Jin in the eye, and slowly widened her legs.

He gave no indication of pleasure at the sight. In fact, he gave no sign of any emotion at all. He could have been a dark Chinese tree for all the reaction he gave. And she felt her irritation rise as the cold night air hit her most private parts.

She had assumed he would give her the blade. After all, she'd shaved her brother's face on a few occasions, and was skilled with a straight edge. But he was her servant. If he wanted to stand there looking like some towering god, then she was damn well going to put him in his place.

She lifted her chin and closed her eyes, just as she instructed William to do whenever she shaved him. Of course, Ken Jin wasn't going to scrape her face, was he? And she was never more aware of that fact—and of her vulnerability—than when she felt the bed shift beneath his weight.

She cracked open an eye. He was climbing onto the mattress to kneel between her legs. His expression remained impassive, but there was no disguising the enormous erection that strained his trousers. Especially as it was framed by her open thighs.

Charlotte swallowed and a moment of panic gripped her belly. What was she doing? She closed her eyes, too caught in indecision to watch. Should she scream? But how would she explain her position on the bed? Had she gone too far to stop? Of course not. And yet . . . Something cold and wet hit her belly, and she flinched, releasing a whimper of fear. Her irritation at his attitude fled. It was nothing more than pretense anyway. Anything to cover her fear.

A strange scent permeated the air: cloves, sandalwood, ginger, and other exotic scents. She had smelled them before and in this combination. Her eyes popped open. "That's the oil you use. Your cologne."

He shook his head as he continued to dribble the perfumed oil between her legs. "I do not use your English cologne."

"French, actually—"

"This will make the shaving process easier." His gaze flicked to her face. "And more stirring to your qi."

She blinked, not understanding what he meant. The oil was cold; the irregular drip annoying. She didn't like the feel of slick fluids coating her. It was . . . She blinked. It was *heating*. Wherever oil and skin connected, she felt a slow simmering of warmth expand and grow. The sensation was mildly pleasant at first, but soon it became like fire beneath her skin.

"I will burn up!" she gasped.

Ken Jin frowned and abruptly stopped pouring. "It is just mild stimulation," he said.

Charlotte shook her head. Indeed, her legs were beginning to shake. "No, it's not, Ken Jin. It's . . ." She swallowed. How to explain the pulsing inferno growing between her legs. She was beginning to sweat. Her thighs fell wider and wider open in an effort to cool herself off. She even began to pant. "It's so hot. Get it off! Get it off!"

He fumbled for a moment, obviously thrown by her reaction, but his hands soon steadied—a good thing, actually, as the only way to get the oil totally off her skin was to be shaved clean and to have any residue wiped off.

He quickly began scraping. The rough glide of the razor brought fresh sensation to the bonfire raging beneath her skin. Her buttocks tightened to lift her off the coverlet, but the increased air only intensified the reaction.

Her legs shook harder. Her breath had quickened to the point of dizziness, so she let her head drop backward. She felt her nipples tighten as they jiggled, and she found she liked the sensation. But that wasn't enough. She needed more pressure, more feeling above to counter the power below. Reaching up, she massaged her breasts. She grasped them, pulling at the nipples, drawing herself every which way in search of the best sensation, the most stimulation.

"Your yin is . . . it's boiling over!" Ken Jin said. She heard awe and shock in his voice, but she didn't care.

"Touch me," she ordered. "Touch me or I'll scream." She might scream anyway, but at least this way she could focus on something—on the glide of the razor, on the touch of his hands, on anything but the building pressure to cry out, to explode.

"Try to direct the energy," he coaxed.

"Where?" she gasped.

Then she felt him. A single finger found her core and pushed inside. She straightened up on a gasp, half shocked and half relieved. She needed to see what he was doing. Like before, when he put his finger in her mouth, he only pressed in to his first knuckle; but she felt the sensation all the way to her spine.

She tried to pull away. Nothing had ever invaded her like that. Nothing had ever expanded her like this. He pushed deeper. She moaned and arched her hips. But not away; she wanted him deeper. She wanted to know just how powerful he was, just how much he could make her feel.

"Draw your energy down, Miss Charlotte. Send it to me. I will catch it."

"How?" she gasped. "I don't understand."

"Move your hands in circles on your breasts."

Her whole body was shaking; her buttocks tightened and released against the bed. She recognized the build to climax, and yet . . . this was different. This was with *him,* and this was so much more than ever before.

"Circles, Miss Charlotte." When she didn't obey, he shifted slightly. "Mimic me, Miss Charlotte, do what I do."

She didn't understand. Her entire lower body was on fire, and he wanted her to . . .

She felt his finger. No, not his finger—his thumb—on her private parts. It slid forward, higher than where his finger was embedded deep within her. It flowed upward, slipping under and around her most sensitive spot.

"Your hands, Miss Charlotte. Move them around your nipples exactly as I am moving around the yin pearl." His thumb roved a long circle counterclockwise.

"No," she growled. "You're missing—"

"I am not missing anything, Miss Charlotte! Do what I

say." Again came the long slow circle that sent shock waves of heat across her skin. And not just her skin; the heat—the *energy*—went deeper, through her belly and up her spine, every direction but inward, every place but where she most wanted it.

"Miss Charlotte!" His voice held an unsettling note of panic.

"Yes, yes." She tried to focus. Her hands lay on her breasts, so it took little effort for her to push them into motion. She couldn't manage a single direction, so she moved both hands together, toward her breastbone, then circled inward and up, over the tops before coming down again. But it wasn't what she wanted. "I need more, Ken Jin."

Her legs were spread wide. She was half sitting, half reclining, but her entire body was pushing toward him, toward his hand and the circles. His voice was like distant thunder in her ears—barely heard and yet still powerful.

"Your yin is chaotic. You must focus it, Miss Charlotte. You must—"

"I can't!" It was a wail.

"Hush! You will wake the entire household!"

She swallowed and nodded. But her breath was in gasps, her body usurped by this overwhelming heat.

"Focus!" he ordered, and she saw the sweat bead on his brow before his head dropped between her thighs. "I will draw out the yin, but you must send it to me." Then he dropped to lie flat on the mattress, his wide shoulders spreading her legs even farther.

His fingers withdrew, and she whimpered at the loss. But then she felt his hands cup her buttocks as he lifted her up. His fingers burrowed along the sides of her tailbone. Four pressure points on either side, digging down toward him in a rhythmic pull. Wonderful, but too little.

She began to whimper, not in desire but in frustration.

Her hands jerked off her breasts. She had to stabilize her position on the mattress or fall. Random eruptions of heat burned her skin—on her neck, around her left hip, down by her shin—but none of it made any sense and the whole experience served to confuse her even more.

"What are you doing?" she gasped. Would there never be an end to this heat?

Then she felt something. Wet and cool—yet another sensation her disordered thoughts could not comprehend. What was it? She forced her thoughts to organize. She needed to gain some measure of control, and she used the sensation as her focal point. It took a moment for her to realize Ken Jin was stroking her with his tongue. He used the same pattern his thumb: around and up. Circles. No, more like a figure eight.

The air, wetness, and knowledge of what he was doing combined to cool the flash fire, but not put it out. "Ken Jin, this cannot be right—" She ended on a gasp as he stopped his figure eight. The point of his tongue stayed just where she wanted it, spiraling into a glorious pressure point. One moment . . . One moment more . . . But then he stopped and lifted himself away.

"Send your yin to me now, Miss Charlotte."

She nearly growled in frustration. She didn't even understand what this "yin" was.

"The *heat*," he pressed. "Send the fire to me."

The fire? The pulsating waves of flame that rolled not only through her skin, but in her belly, neck, and fingertips.

"Put a pillow over your face."

She blinked and lifted her head. The sight was most alarming. She was wide open. Ken Jin lay between her legs. And though his entire demeanor seemed distant—almost casual—his face showed something different. His eyes were dark and calm, and in this light, his expression seemed to contain something more: a secret knowledge, a wisdom that pervaded his every action. And so she obeyed him without comment.

She grabbed a pillow, but could not stop looking at him. She did not want to break eye contact.

"I will open the gate now," he said, glancing meaningfully at the pillow. She felt his thumbs pulling her open. "When the yin rushes, you might scream. You do not wish to wake William, do you?"

She shook her head.

"Then lie back and cover your mouth—and send your yin fire to me."

She did as she was told. She let her head drop back. The pillow smelled of lilac and starch, and the weight was hot upon her face. Ken Jin's tongue was circling around and around in the most amazing way. She tried to gather her thoughts. She mentally catalogued each little flame that seared her body. Was that yin? How was she supposed to send it to him?

It made no sense. In truth, she felt silly doing it. But his orders were too compelling to refuse, so she mentally commanded each little locus of heat to where he . . .

He began to suck, right at the top of his figure eight. His lips encircled all of the flesh and pulled. She felt a blockage there. She didn't understand any of it, and yet she knew there was something preventing the fire from crossing to the cool wetness of his tongue.

He pulled again. The heat was building exponentially behind the dam. Especially since she was trying to send all the other fires to it. Her neck tensed with steam. She ordered it to his mouth. Her shoulders burned. She sent it to his lips. Her belly caved to her spine as flames compressed her insides. She sent it to his tongue . . .

He sucked again. Harder this time. Charlotte clenched the sheets, drawing the cotton into crumpled knots that became torches in her fevered imagination. She sent the blazes down to him as well. She had to break through the barrier. She had to sear and burn and destroy all that separated her from him.

It worked! The barrier burst into flames and disappeared. Power flowed.

There was no warning trickle, no small flow that became large. The change was enormous: silent one moment, electrifying the next. A current pulled from the top of her hair, from the farthest reaches of her fingertips, her mouth, and her nipples—roaring through her. It sizzled and cracked through each restriction until there was nothing in its way.

Her belly contracted in orgasm, but it was more than just that. Her entire consciousness pulsed and pushed and poured. She became a river of lava. She was the crackle and fire of electrical current. And Ken Jin was the well into which she poured.

More and more, the river grew, the current shining brighter and hotter, until he suddenly stopped. She felt him collapse against her thigh, his breath heavy, his body trembling.

She whimpered in protest. Without him to take it, the heat continued to build without release. Her legs quivered and her belly clenched, but there was no outlet so the power began to curl in on itself.

"No," she sobbed into her pillow. "Ken Jin, please . . ."

She felt him against her thigh, still gasping for breath. "There is so much," he murmured, awe in his tone.

Her body was still shaking, and not with release. The energy was churning inside her, and she was beginning to feel ill from the heat.

"Take it away, Ken Jin. There is so much, I cannot contain it. You must take it!"

If she had the strength, she would have forced him. She lifted the pillow off her face to order him, but her hands were trembling with untapped power, and the cooling streak of air against her wet face confused her even more. How could she be crying? Her body was a torch that was consuming itself. There was no moisture left in her. Only fire.

"Ken Jin!"

She felt him move; his hand this time. She pressed forward, groaning slightly as his fingers pushed deep inside her. She had no idea how many fingers, only that the pressure added to her heat. Wood to the flame.

"No," she whispered.

But then she felt it: another opening of the floodgates. His thumb once again rolled across her most sensitive spot. In her mind, he just brushed the blockage aside. She didn't understand how, but she didn't truly care. She knew only that the power began to flow again to his thumb; not into him, but around him. Her body pulsed around his fingers, and the power flowed across his hand.

Thank God, it flowed. Bit by bit, the heat dissipated. Soon she could breathe again; so long as it continued to flow. On and on and on, in rhythmic contraction.

Finally, it stopped.

She released a sigh of exhausted delight and fell deeply asleep.

Feb 9, 1889
To honored Grandmother Wen Ai Men, Tigress sister:
    I am pleased the gui zhi I sent benefitted your morning pains. How unfortunate that you cannot find such a useful herb in Peking. I also would have difficulty buying such things if it were not for my thrice-blessed assistant.

Did I tell you that he has left my service? Yes, he was beginning to feel caged in my little school. Too many beautiful women to distract him, I suppose. So he chose to avoid temptation and spends more and more time at the docks where he makes a great deal of money helping to unload barbarian cargo ships.

His ability with English—the barbarian language—serves him well, and he thrives. He now has enough money to buy his own residence and live in a comfortable style. Plus, he is also able to procure the best foreign herbs and teas for me. He does this out of respect because of the love between us, and I count myself most fortunate that he lived with us for so long.

Even more happily, he told me yesterday that he wants to become a Dragon student! I already know the perfect partner for him: a girl his own age named Little Pearl. She comes to me from a troubled path as well, and I think they will work very well together.

The only sadness in his young life is his wish for his family. He was tragically lost to his parents, you recall; but I know that if some magician were to discover their location, he would abandon all to reclaim those who once loved him. Oh, how I wish that were possible for this most excellent young man. Do you perhaps know if his parents can be restored to him?

Most Sincerely,
Tigress Tan Shi Po

QUICKIE TECHNIQUE FOR EMERGENCY HAN-
DLING OF TENSION: Reach back to the base of your
skull. Place the third finger of each hand into the hollow at
the base of your skull. Rotate them around. Note the pain.
Now move to the right of this hollow. Note the bump. It
too will be tender. It may be downright painful on pres-
sure. Give it Acupressure, USA. Repeat on the other side
of the hollow. Now with your head bowed forward, run
each hand firmly down the back of your neck toward the
shoulders. Repeat five times.
Acupuncture Without Needles, JV Cerney

Chapter Six

Charlotte woke slowly. She could hear William in his room.
The whole house could probably hear William. He was
throwing a tantrum, complete with kicking and screaming.
She had long since told the staff to just leave him to his fits,
shut him in his room until he found a way to control himself. All breakables had been removed, and in time, he
would learn. Except after ten years, he still hadn't learned.

She heard her mother's hurried footsteps rush down the
hall. Her brother's door opened and the volume increased
tenfold. He might not be bright, but William knew when to
throw his whole soul into a tantrum. It would be a long
twenty minutes before he settled enough to let Mama hold
him. Then another long hour as she prayed and sobbed
over her poor boy.

Usually Charlotte would be at her mother's side, reassuring both woman and boy that they were loved and all
would eventually pass. It never seemed to make a difference. Indeed, nothing ever seemed to change in the unending tedium of her life.

Rolling over, she groaned at the pull of sore muscles. She winced at the pain even as she smiled. The feel of being completely naked beneath her covers was scandalously delightful. Her smile widened into a grin. Nothing had changed until last night.

"Mits Charet! Mits Charet!"

Charlotte blinked, then stared blearily at the family's newest maid. The woman was young, her English deplorable, but after fourteen years in Shanghai, Charlotte knew how to translate broken English.

"Good morning, Mei Su." At least she hoped that was the girl's name. There was a rather large number of Mei-somethings in China. "What—"

"Peas, Mits Charet. Te bo."

Te bo? The boy. "William?"

"*Aie, aie. Aie!*" The girl was tugging on Charlotte's arm to get her out of bed. Which was exactly when Charlotte remembered her ruined nightgown. She couldn't get out of bed naked. She couldn't show anyone the state of her undress. But if William were truly in trouble . . .

She listened intently. Her room was positioned right next to the nursery so that she could hear disasters, but there was nothing, no sounds at all. Was that good or bad? Truly, by his very nature, William created commotions wherever he went. And new young maids were most subject to needless alarm. Yet . . .

"Go find Ken Jin," she abruptly ordered. "I will be there directly."

"*Aie,* no!" the girl wailed, obviously distraught. "Te bo—"

Frustrated, Charlotte pushed up on an elbow. Her nudity be damned. "Fetch my robe and tell me what exactly occurred," she said in Shanghai dialect, hoping to distract the girl. It worked. The girl spun to fetch her housedress while Charlotte jumped out of bed and kicked her ruined gown into the cold fire grate. Mei Su whipped back with the robe in hand and finally answered the most pressing question.

"The boy," she said in her native tongue. "He is not moving. The mama just cries and prays. We do not know—"

"Go get Ken Jin. He has knowledge of medicine." Why she thought he could help, she didn't know. Except, of course, that just yesterday she had seen him with needles in his flesh for some medicinal purpose, and last night he had created the most amazing sensations in her body. Most important, in a crisis Ken Jin possessed the most level head in the entire household. She had always called for him at times like this. From the moment he began working as their First Boy, he had been the rock upon whom she relied. But Mei Su was shaking her head, her wail increasing.

"Not home! Left early this morning."

Charlotte didn't pause. Pulling on her housedress, sans corset, she felt her insides churn into cold knots. "Where did he go?" she asked as casually as she could manage.

"Nobody knows," the girl responded. "Miss, te boy. Please."

Charlotte was already heading out the door, but she paused long enough to grab a match off the mantel to toss at the maid. "Please burn my nightdress, Mei Su. It irritated me last night, and I think I tore it." Then she was out the door.

Two steps inside her brother's room, she knew what had happened and roundly damned herself for it. Her brother lay on the cold floor, curled into himself, and she saw he'd bruised a leg and bloodied his knuckles, and probably a lot more, too. When William threw himself into a fit, he pulled out all the stops. His clothes were torn and dispersed across the room, though one shoe had miraculously stayed on. Apparently he'd been almost fully dressed when temper had taken hold.

Now he lay still and silent on the floor. As always, Charlotte checked first for signs of life. He was obviously breathing, and nothing appeared to be bleeding or broken. Mostly he appeared cold, so she grabbed his favorite dark blue blanket and settled it around him.

Next, she turned to her mother. Mama was kneeling in prayer near the wardrobe, her rosary beads in her hands as she meticulously cycled through them, her lips moving without sound. Charlotte knew from experience that she would not speak to anyone until she was done with her prayers.

So Charlotte set to the task of straightening the nursery. Nanny hovered nearby, half hidden in shadow. Fortunately, she had seen many William fits before and had already accomplished the bulk of the work. Which left Charlotte with little to do but sit in the only chair, a large cushioned contraption that was bolted to the floor, and wait for her mother.

Unfortunately, Mama was only halfway through her rosary, so Charlotte had ample time to dwell. She could see from the sunlight that the morning was well advanced. William must have woken at his usual time and, without Charlotte to keep his temper in check, descended into some fit. It didn't truly matter why; William always had his own reasons. One day, he'd begun kicking because the curtains weren't drawn. The next day's fit was because the blanket was blue. Mama had spent a month driving the staff to distraction making sure the curtains were pulled just right, every fabric was to William's taste, and even the walls repainted to his choice.

Except, William constantly changed his mind, and that

produced more fits. In the end, Charlotte had ended it all. She decided the walls would be a soft blue. The carpet was stripped away to a bare wood floor. The furniture, including bookshelves and window treatments, all were removed. His bedroom became bare except for the mattress and white sheets that now lay on the floor. Even his clothing was stored in a separate room.

And William's fits had lessened.

Bit by bit, they had introduced new things. The chair came first, even though it had to be bolted to the floor for fear he'd grow stronger and throw it out the window. He now had a bookcase—also bolted down—with three soft toys on it and two books. And a dozen or more blankets of a variety of colors were scattered about the room.

Nanny was taking the blankets away. She had already collected the books and toys. After a fit of this magnitude— one that ended in unconsciousness—William's environment had to be stripped down to nothing. It would take at least a week before he'd be able to build back up to tolerating anything beyond his one blanket and the bare floor. She only prayed they didn't have to remove his bed. Sleeping on the floor always made her brother cranky. Still, it was better than endless days of tantrums.

She sighed and stared at her brother. Was this latest debacle her fault? She knew with absolute certainty that she could have avoided it. Years of trial and error had given her a sixth sense when it came to her brother. She knew the signs of oncoming breakdowns and was usually able to stop them before they began. Minimal light, no stimulation, and silence had prevented numerous disasters.

But she hadn't been around this morning. She had chosen to sleep and leave things to her mother and Nanny. She had, in fact, slept through a major disaster because she was exhausted from her nocturnal adventure. And now William had regressed—again—to near infancy. She would spend months restoring him to some semblance of normalcy, and all hope of real progress was completely gone.

Why hadn't she gotten up? Why wasn't William better able to handle life? Was it her fault? Was she doing things wrong?

"This is all your father's fault."

Charlotte looked up. Her mother had spoken in low tones, not wishing to disturb William. The boy would likely not wake for hours yet, but just in case, they continued in near whispers. William never reacted well to being startled.

"What did Papa do?"

"He didn't come home last night."

Drinking and carousing, then. The usual.

"God punishes the wicked," her mother continued.

"But William isn't wicked." The response was automatic; she and her mother had this argument every time William had a fit.

"God chooses the nature of his punishments. It is not for us to say."

"What if God doesn't work that way, Mama? What if—"

"I will order another Mass. Maybe it will speed William's recovery." The woman crawled the few feet to her son's side. She didn't dare touch him for fear of waking him, but she obviously wanted to hold him. Her hand hovered over William's shoulder, over his head, then finally settled back into her lap. "I am so very sorry, my little boy. So very, very sorry."

The agony in her mother's voice tore at Charlotte's heart, and Charlotte couldn't remain silent. "You have atoned, Mama, for whatever ill you did. I am sure God has forgiven you."

Her mother pushed to her feet, and Charlotte could see the sheen of unshed tears in her eyes. "Only God can say when I have atoned. I was a drunken slattern when I was pregnant, and God visited my sins upon my son."

"That is over, Mama. You are forgiven." Charlotte could only repeat the words over and over and pray that one day Mama would believe them.

Obviously, that day wasn't today. Her mother turned back to William and said, "His slowness is my fault. This fit . . ." She shook her head. "That is your father's." She sighed and headed for the door. "Nanny will stay with him until he wakes. You, Charlotte, need to tend to your hair. Cleanliness is next to godliness." She glanced back at William still immobile on the floor. "Learn from my sins, Charlotte. Do not hurt your own children."

She left then, abandoning Charlotte to the weight of guilt. After all, her father had spent many nights carousing through the whole of Shanghai's foreign concessions. William didn't suffer a relapse every night Papa was gone. She could think of at least ten instances when William had suffered no ill effects whatsoever from their father's debauchery. But how often had Charlotte spent the night in a world of corruption? And not more than fifteen feet away!

The thought was chilling. Could it be God? Could William's current state be her fault? After all, he wouldn't be like this now if she had simply gotten out of bed when it started. But she'd slept in because she'd been exhausted. Because she'd chosen her own path of wanton sin.

Charlotte pushed to her feet, horrified to discover she was trembling. It couldn't possibly be true; William's difficulties were not directly tied to anyone's moral behavior. If so, then there would be a lot more unconscious, half-naked children like her brother. And yet, the coincidence was difficult to stomach. Perhaps she should go to Mass with Mama. It couldn't hurt, could it? She could pray for her sins, ask for enlightenment, maybe even search the Bible for guidance.

Unfortunately, she had pursued that course a million

times before; her mother as well. If prayer or Bible study truly gave answers, William would be normal by now. Charlotte had no faith in those particular paths. Which left . . . what exactly? Where could she turn?

Nanny returned, but Charlotte sent her away, wanting to be alone with William. Then she sat with her brother for the rest of the day while the same questions boiled uselessly in her mind.

Ken Jin muttered as he rubbed down the carriage horse. Like all things barbarian, the beast was large and ill-tempered—at least until its needs were met. Then it became placid, cooperative even, and life could proceed as it was meant to. Too bad things Chinese worked on a different level. And worse, because he had been working for the barbarians most of his life, he had become used to acting in the barbarian fashion. That meant whenever he was forced to be Chinese, the task became ten times more difficult.

The whites in China had simple requirements: money and sex. Both were easily provided, given his employer's wealth and his own sexual resources. Therefore, living among the barbarians, Ken Jin had built himself an easy life.

The Chinese, on the other hand, dealt in different coin: money or power. Unfortunately, Ken Jin had exhausted the first and possessed none of the second. Which meant that in all things Chinese, Ken Jin was useless.

He had spent the day trying to be Chinese. He had tried to bribe, threaten, or exploit anyone he could into gaining the Tans' release from prison; and he had failed utterly. That meant the two people he loved more than anyone— the Tigress Shi Po and her husband, Kui Yu—would rot in jail, probably for the rest of their short lives. And there was nothing he could do about it.

Cursing under his breath, Ken Jin tossed the tack into its bin and stomped to the Wicks mansion. He had worn Chinese clothing today, even allowed his Manchu queue to hang down his back like a damned tail, but to no avail. Chinese or English, no one was allowed in to see the prisoners. And now his best silk jacket smelled of horse.

He was halfway up the stairs before a maid spotted him. She was a new girl, hired as a favor to his fellow Dragon Fu De, pretty in her own way but still somewhat lost in an English house. Her curtsey showed more fear than respect, her speech had more awkwardness than style. And in an Englishman's house, style was paramount. That requirement, at least, the English had in common with the Chinese.

"What is it?" he snapped, startled by his show of ill temper.

"Miss Charlotte has asked for you. Many times. All day."

Ken Jin nodded and moved past the girl. "I was already on my way."

He was on the top step before he realized what he had said: He was already on the way to see Miss Charlotte. In fact, he had spent the last hour speeding home in anticipation of seeing the woman. But why? She was a white girl, no more interesting or different than any other. She had given him her yin, and he had been satisfied. That was all.

He swallowed, recognizing his own lies. Last night had not been like any other night, and Miss Charlotte's yin was nothing like anyone else's.

He had been satisfied. That alone left him stunned, especially as he had been satiated to the point of drowning and still her yin had flowed like a river of golden sunlight. His hands had actually tingled as she pulsed around him. Even now his dragon pushed forward, seeking her cinnabar cave, and his mouth salivated for another taste of her yin dew.

Never before had he felt such power. Never before had a woman—white or Chinese—infused him with such hunger. Was it any wonder that he sought her now? Especially after a day as frustrating and humbling as today? Of course not; and yet he did wonder. Something was wrong with this attraction, something was not as it should not be. But he had no focus to understand his vague misgivings.

He paused, intending to head for the back stairs, to his room and desk so that he could puzzle out this situation logically, but his body did not obey. All too soon he stood at the door of Master William's nursery.

It was evening, long after the sun had set, and dinner had been served and cleared. He knew that Mr. Wicks would be at his club and soon afterward with his mistress. Mrs. Wicks would be at prayers in her room and then would retire. Master William would be fighting the maid and the nightly press to bed, and Miss Charlotte would be attending some party.

Except, he knew that she would not be out tonight, not after last night. She would be too unsettled to depart and too hungry to miss a chance to see him again. Therefore, Miss Charlotte would be at home; and when she was at home, she was with William.

He knocked politely on the door, then entered quietly. If the boy was asleep, she wouldn't want to call out.

He stopped a bare six inches into the room and his heart dropped into his stomach. The boy must have had a fit. The room was stripped bare. Charlotte sat with her back against the far wall, her arms and a navy blanket wrapped around William. She sang to him, a monotonous tune that soothed. The boy's eyes were shut, and he appeared to be sleeping. Unfortunately, at sixteen he was much too large for her to carry to bed.

Ken Jin stepped to her side and crouched down. Easy enough to work his hands beneath the boy. She helped him, lifting as best she could, but the work remained his as he burrowed his fingers between child and woman. He lifted the boy. It took all his strength. Worse, it took all of his will not to keep his hands deep against Charlotte's thighs, close to her warmth, an inch away from her cinnabar cave.

"Thank you," she whispered, and her voice woke his dragon.

He stood, the boy in his arms. Charlotte did the same. It took some moments for her to straighten; she had obviously been sitting for a long time. He watched her movements because he could not stop himself. Her slow undulations as she returned blood to her limbs tortured his dragon, filling it with insatiable lust.

After a moment, Charlotte moved through the nursery to William's bedroom. Ken Jin followed, then stood behind her, watching as she bent over to pull back the covers of William's bed. The mattress was on the floor, and she dropped to her knees to arrange the covers just so for the boy. Which meant her bottom was raised as she worked. Ken Jin stood behind her, the boy in his arms, watching her present the Stepping Tigress position.

Lust slammed through him, stiffening his dragon to the point of pain. Vague embarrassment filtered through his consciousness, but he could not deny the joy he experienced, too. She finished her task and slid out of his way. He gently set the boy in bed, but as he moved, he realized he was not acting normally. At this moment, his every task was suffused with awe. His tasks were worship, his every moment in her presence filled with reverence. To him, Charlotte was a yin goddess, and he could not wait to continue their practice.

Eventually, the boy was settled to Charlotte's satisfaction. The blanket was arranged just right, the door moved to the correct angle. And then, finally, Ken Jin and Charlotte withdrew to the hallway.

As expected, she glanced around before canting her eyes to her sitting room. "Could I have a word with you, Ken Jin?"

He bowed with deepest respect. "Of course, Miss Charlotte."

They moved as one to her sitting room door, which he held open for her. She crossed to her favorite chair by the fire while he stared hypnotized by her smallest action. How had he missed it before? How had he not seen that yin power saturated her every breath, the smallest of her most feminine movements? Whatever the reason for his earlier ignorance, he saw it now and lauded her for it.

He waited until she was situated. He would have gone to his knees before her if that were the custom. As it was, he remained standing until she urged him to sit. He did not. Instead, he knelt before the coal fire and started a blaze. She remained silent as he worked, though he knew she fiddled with some stitching. She was embroidering a beautiful waistcoat for her brother—an odd gift for a boy who still stripped off his trousers whenever and wherever he became hot. But such was the nature of families. Even barbarians held dreams for their eldest sons regardless of reality.

"Tell me about Chinese medicine, Ken Jin."

Her voice jolted him out of his thoughts. He'd been staring into the fire to make sure it flamed just right—neither too hot nor too cold—but her lilting words made him rise to her side. He didn't dare touch her yet. Virgins had to come to you.

"What do you wish to know, Miss Charlotte?"

His dragon was straining against his trousers, and his blood ran hot with yang. He had no idea how long the condition would last. Even his practice with Little Pearl had never been this intense. But did that mean her power over him would burn out all the more quickly?

"Well," she began, then stopped. Her pink tongue darted out to wet her lips, then disappeared behind her white teeth as she bit her lower lip. "I don't see many . . . many . . . The Chinese don't seem to have any slow children. I wondered if Chinese medicine held some secret that we English—"

"Boys such as William are hidden away, Miss Charlotte." Or worse. "You would not see them."

"Oh," she said. Her entire body seemed to deflate. "So, what you were doing with the needles the other day when you poked them into . . . well, when you . . ."

"I was opening and strengthening energy channels."

She nodded as if she understood, though he knew she did not. "I have seen people on the street sometimes with needles in their necks or arms. Even their feet."

He nodded to cover his surprise. He had not thought her so observant. "Acupuncture is used for a wide variety of ailments. I learned the technique from my parents. As a boy, I saw them treat infected limbs, stomach weaknesses, even brain fevers."

She looked up and he saw hope shine in her eyes. "So, perhaps there is something to be done for William, something we English don't know . . ." Her voice trailed away as he shook his head.

"You love your brother and so you search for an answer where there is none. Your brother's energies are different from ours. He must grow as he grows without the burden of inaccurate expectations."

She obviously struggled with his words. Indeed, such thoughts were difficult for him as well. So he sat down in a chair across from her and leaned forward to explain. "The Chinese believe every child has a large number of influences upon them: the year, date, and time of birth, the

legacy of parent and grandparent, even birth order as compared to siblings—all these things contribute to a child's
basic nature."

She nodded. "There are those in English society who believe that as well."

He nodded. "So you understand. It is every child's responsibility to make the best of what he is born with, to
bring honor to family and ancestor." He spoke without in-
flection, stating simple fact; and yet, his blood cooled with
his words and parts of his body went numb.

"But what if a child can't make the best of it? William
can't . . ." She looked into the fire, unable to finish. "Do
you know he's heir to a baronetcy? He'll never inherit, of
course. Uncle Phillip will eventually have something other
than daughters. But still . . . what if he did? He can't possibly be a baron. He can't even tie his own shoes."

"Your brother has a path, but every time he tries to walk
it, he is hemmed in by your expectations."

She stared at him, stricken. "Mine?"

He shrugged. "All of you. To your mother, William is a
punishment. To your father, he is . . ."

"An embarrassment."

He nodded. "And to you—"

"I just want him to be my brother," she whispered.

He didn't answer. They both knew she wanted more, and
in time she dropped her gaze. "Is it wrong for me to want
him to dress himself? To grow like other boys?"

"Of course not." He wanted to touch her, but he could
not; she held herself too far apart. "Have you not noticed
that William takes off his clothes when he is hot? That he
sings when he is happy? That he dances and sits whenever
he wants?"

"That he kicks and screams when he wants," she added
dryly.

"But only when his natural desires are stopped."

She looked at him, completely appalled. "You cannot be suggesting we allow him to run wild."

He shook his head. "No, of course not. Compromises must always be made. A child must learn discipline."

She nodded. "But you think we are instilling too much?"

He looked at his hands, wondering why they were so cold. The fire in the hearth was hot, the room pleasant, but his hands felt shrunken and chill. "I believe," he finally said, "that the weight of everyone's hopes distorts William's qi—his energies—and distorted qi brings on fits."

"Can his energies—his qi—can it be balanced? With those needles?"

"Not by an acupuncturist. The problem is too scattered." Her expression became tormented, so he rushed forward to clasp her hands. The heat from her fingers was painfully intense, especially when compared to his own chilled flesh, but he pressed tightly so that she would listen.

"William's qi is very strong." She shook her head, ready to argue, but he spoke firmly. "Qi is energy, not intelligence. Sometimes the lowest beast has the strongest qi. The boy's energy presence . . . believe me when I say it is very strong."

Her eyes narrowed. "How do you know this?"

He shrugged. "I feel it. I have purified my energy to the extent that I can feel very strong fields." He did not admit that the reason he was so sensitive was that his energy was so very weak. Instead, he focused on her. "You also are very strong."

"And my parents?"

He sighed. "Your father is very weak. You should not be surprised by that."

She nodded, and her words came out on a sigh. "Weak in will, weak in discipline."

"But your mother is very strong. Her prayers make her very powerful."

Charlotte tilted her head. "So, I should pray to make William better? Just like my mother . . ."

Her voice trailed away as he shook his head. How to explain an entire philosophy in one moment? "Your mother's qi is strong, but she focuses that energy on making William into her punishment."

"But she is praying to make him better!"

He shook his head. "She is praying to absolve her sins, which she believes will make William better. She does not support him, Miss Charlotte. She makes him into a divine tool to beat herself."

"And that's why he has episodes?"

"What happened just before his last fit?"

"My mother . . ." She swallowed and looked away. "My mother went in to comfort him. But she was probably angry. My father was gone all night. She said . . ." Charlotte pushed out of her chair. "She said William's fit was God's punishment because father was gone all night."

"And her energy would have pushed exactly that thought onto William."

"Creating the fit?"

Ken Jin nodded. "I believe so."

She stared at him. She stood before the fire, the hot coals creating visible waves of heat and light about her body, and yet the energy went nowhere. It was like the energy of many barbarians: all-enveloping but chaotic. It usually dissipated without direction or focus.

"Where did you learn this, Ken Jin? It sounds very odd."

He looked down at his hands. He should have known better than to expect a white person to grasp this concept, especially a woman. And yet, he desperately wished her to understand. A yin goddess should know what she was.

"You have such power, Miss Charlotte. You should learn to direct it."

"I thought we were supposed to 'grow naturally, without interference.'"

He pushed to his feet, irritated with himself for trying so hard. The barbarians did not understand the nature of things, they would not even try. Why was he wasting his breath? "Your qi has grown, Miss Charlotte. It has grown to the size of a great river of molten gold, but it is not refined and it is not directed. It can do no good for anyone in that state."

She folded her arms, no doubt responding to his angry tone. "I want to help William, not—"

"William must be left in peace, to grow as his energies direct, but your mother will not allow that."

She growled in frustration. "I cannot change my mother. I am not even sure I should." She reached up and toyed with the crucifix that hung just above the mantel. There was at least one in every room, four in the nursery. "My people put a great deal of faith in our God."

"Does your God direct that a child should be a punishment to the parents?"

She bit her lip. He knew she and her priest argued the point constantly. "Father Peter believes in vengeance, that sin is punished."

He nodded. "I believe our energies create our punishments." He waited for her to make a decision. When she did not, he pushed her. "What do *you* believe, Miss Charlotte?"

She turned back to the fire, gazing deep into the coals as if the answer was written in the shifting patterns of light and heat. Finally she spoke, her voice a low crackle of sound. "I believe that my mother's prayers have not worked."

She abruptly straightened. She had been so drawn to the

flame, so connected to it, for a moment it seemed to Ken Jin that she had stepped out from the hearth, growing from the flames into a living, breathing woman of fire. Her energy infused the room and tingled against his skin. "What must I do?" she asked.

He straightened, doing his best not to smile. "You must take off all your clothes."

She didn't react at first; she simply stared at him. But he knew white women. He had spent many years harvesting yin from virgins and trollops alike. All they needed was a reason. Usually he talked about pleasure, explained away their fears, whatever they were, and eventually they all surrendered to him. Miss Charlotte would be no different. Especially since she now had the best reason of all to surrender: She needed to purify her yin. She needed to understand how to use the power she possessed.

None of his thoughts showed on his face. Virgins, he knew, were especially skittish. But in time Charlotte released a soft exhale, surrender expressed in the most feminine of sounds. Ken Jin took a step forward to assist her with her clothing.

"I thought you were different, Ken Jin. I thought . . ." Her voice broke on the last word, and he frowned at her in confusion. Then she took a deep breath and focused. Her next words were delivered with strength and the heady power of full qi.

"Go pack your bags, Ken Jin. You're fired."

❦

March 1, 1889
To Tigress Tan Shi Po:
   Your assistant does indeed seem a most excellent young man. I envy you his strength and influence. Alas, I know of no magician who can aid

him in reclaiming all that was lost to him. As much as he may wish to reunite with his family, other forces conspire against him.

I understand the difficulty of an insane family. You recall that my son and daughter-in-law are acupuncturists. They daily cleanse and strengthen their patients' qi energies, and yet they have the hardest hearts and most clogged energies of all. Even their last remaining son—the new heir— learns to close his ears to all I might teach them.

Evil indeed befalls all when the young refuse to listen to the wisdom of their elders.

In great pain,
Wen Ai Men

SPIRITUAL PRACTICES FOR TRANSFORMING ANGER: Press B10 (Heavenly Pillar, located on the back of your upper neck one finger-width below your skull and one finger-width out from the center of the spine on both sides.) . . . Press CV17 (Sea of Tranquility, located on the center of the breastbone, four finger-widths up from the bone's base).
Acupressure for Emotional Healing, Michael Gach, Ph.D, Beth Henning, Dipl, ABT

Chapter Seven

Charlotte smiled as her pronouncement finally made it through Ken Jin's thick head.

"I'm fired?" He gaped at her. Clearly he had expected her to just strip bare on his say-so. She was just a woman, after all, and he had a great deal of experience with women of easy virtue.

Well, he was an idiot if he put her in the same category as all the others. She was not so easily duped. Or at least she wasn't now. Last night she'd been sleepy and surprised, or so she told herself. She was past her moment of feverish curiosity.

A day's reflection brought the certain understanding that something had to change with William. They could not go on this way: living from fit to fit, praying for a change but seeing no real results. She had spoken to Ken Jin in all seriousness about a way to help William. But rather than offer her an answer, he turned it into another sexual game. Did he really think she was that stupid? That desperate?

"M-Miss Charlotte," he stammered, unsuccessfully trying to both step forward and rear back. "I cannot . . . You couldn't . . ."

"I can and I have." She stared at him while disappointment crushed the breath from her lungs. "I thought you were different, Ken Jin. I thought I could talk to you about something serious." She straightened slowly and deliberately turned her back on him. "You are fired. Go collect your things and leave. I shall inform my father—"

"Your father will have your head!" he snapped. He sounded very English. Much like her father, come to think of it.

She spun around, undaunted. "I very much doubt that."

"He knows nothing about his business. If I leave, your family will end in disaster!"

His words sent a cold chill down her spine, but that only made her angrier. Her hands clenched as she leaned forward. "My father may be a lecherous beast, but he is not stupid," she hissed. "He understands his business. I know he does."

Ken Jin's color darkened; his body stilled. She could tell he was furious, and the sight was disconcerting. He was so unlike the explosive tempers to which she was accustomed. Her father blustered, her mother wailed; William threw fits, and even Charlotte herself had been known to kick things. Ken Jin just stood there and froze her with a stare.

"I tell you," he said coldly, "your father knows nothing of what I do on your behalf. Without me, you will soon be impoverished."

"And with you, I shall be debauched by morning!" She gasped and clapped her mouth shut. That wasn't at all what she'd meant to say. Especially since Ken Jin seemed amused by her words. He began to smile, and it wasn't a nice expression.

"You think I play games," he said. "You think I am a . . .

a . . ." He could not find the right English, so he switched to Chinese. "That I am a whoremonger." He sneered. "Why do you English judge everyone by your own immorality?"

"You told me to take off my clothes!"

"I do not do this for my pleasure!" He made a gesture with his hand, fast and lethal like a branch whipped about in a strong wind. "You are the one who plays, Miss Charlotte. You are the bored one who steals sacred scrolls and plays with herself in the darkness, never knowing that it could be more." He shook his head, his disgust clear. "You cannot fire me, Miss Charlotte, and you cannot drag me into your emptiness." He sighed. "I thought to teach you."

"And I believed you!" she cried. "But I am not talking about last night. I want to help William." She released a hiss of disgust at her own gullibility. "But all you want is more . . ." She stopped, the memory of what they'd done last night fresh, too mortifying for words.

"What, Miss Charlotte? What do I want? To bury my dragon between your milky thighs?" He grunted. "That is what *you* want, not me."

She gasped at his audacity, even as her belly quivered. What would it feel like to have him there? "I want nothing from you," she snapped. She meant to turn her back on him. She was already pivoting, but suddenly he had her. His hand was large and powerful where it gripped her arm. He pulled her back around with such force that she would have stumbled had he not been holding her.

"Never lie, Miss Charlotte. Not to anyone, and most certainly never to yourself. It poisons your yin, it poisons the air, it—"

"Poisons. I understand." She kept her voice excruciatingly dry as she glared at him. They both knew she had enjoyed what he'd done last night, so instead she spoke clearly and with a great deal of force. "I want to help my brother." She lifted her chin. "I have no interest in games of any kind."

He nodded. "Then we are in agreement." She frowned, but he gave her no more time to question. "What I do is not play, Miss Charlotte. It is serious work—harder than anything you have ever done, harder than anything you will ever do."

She narrowed her eyes and canted her gaze in the direction of her brother's room, then returned it to Ken Jin.

He answered her unspoken question. "No, I do not know that this will help your brother. I only know how to refine qi. What you do with that power is up to you." Then he fell silent.

It took a moment for her to realize he was waiting for her to speak. But what did he want her to say? In the end, she shook her head, using body and tone to show her disbelief.

"And refinement requires me to be naked?"

"A sheathed sword cannot be sharpened."

She spent a moment on that image, but couldn't make it fit. "I am not a sword—"

Once again, he moved faster than expected. He gripped her chin and pulled so that she looked him in the eye. He was tall for a Chinese, so she had to tilt slightly upward. When had he moved so near? She stared at the reflected firelight in his eyes.

"Listen closely, barbarian, and try to understand. I will only explain this once more." She shivered at the threat in his tone. He was at the end of his patience. "Qi—energy— is a force, a powerful, awesome weapon. Refined, it can even kill." He moderated his tone. "Or defend."

"Can it heal?"

He nodded, though the motion was hesitant.

"You don't really know," she accused.

"No one knows all. Qi is a thing of mystery. We can only know some aspects of it."

She didn't know whether any of what he said was real or not, but she could tell Ken Jin believed. He believed with a passion that made his entire body tremble. Her skin tingled. She hesitated, trying to understand. "And I have this energy? This qi?"

"Yes, though it is composed of much more yin—the female energy—than the male yang." His voice softened to include a note of awe. "You have a great deal of yin, Miss Charlotte. More than anyone I have ever met."

"I have qi?" She felt her knees weakening beneath an onslaught of power. She had no other word for it; she felt his intensity—his qi?—and it literally weakened her knees.

"You have *yin*," he emphasized even as he adjusted his grip on her arm. Soon he was guiding her to her seat.

She shook her head. This was all too much. "I don't understand." Soon she was once again staring into the fire and feeling lost. How to help her brother? Was Ken Jin a liar and a cad? Or was he her last hope? "I just don't know."

He sank to his knees before her. The action was surprising enough that her attention riveted back on him. She'd never seen him on his knees. He almost looked like a supplicant. "I can teach you, Miss Charlotte. I know how to strengthen and refine qi." He took a deep breath and his fingers fluttered before her, but he did not touch. Instead, he withdrew, folding his hands tight to his belly. "I know a great deal, Miss Charlotte, but I cannot tell you how to wield your power once it is pure. And I do not know if it can heal William or divert your mother."

She sighed. "This is so strange. How do you know it is real?"

"I have seen a qi master use one finger to throw a man across a room. I have watched a Tigress bring a man to yang release with just the power of her eyes."

She blinked. "A tiger?"

"A Tigress," he repeated. "A woman who studies yin refinement. I am a Dragon."

She lifted her chin, but caught herself in time. She had almost looked at her hiding place where his precious scrolls were hidden. She had promised them to him last night, but had fallen asleep before she could give them to him. "There were tigers stitched in the silk. The ones that covered—"

"The scrolls. Yes, Joanna Crane was . . . She is studying to become a tigress."

It took a while for understanding to sink in. It took several long moments, but eventually her own stupidity became clear. "You are a Dragon?" He nodded. "And Joanna is a Tigress?"

He nodded again, though the motion was slower.

"That's why she has the scrolls. Because she was studying them like you study."

He shook his head. "Not like I study. I am a Dragon. My exercises are different."

"But you . . ." Her voice grew stronger, her tone higher. "You have known all along."

He frowned, clearly not following.

"All this time, I have been sick with worry about where she was, and you knew." This time, she was the one who reached out. She gripped his arms. "Where is she? Where is Joanna? Is she still at that place, that school where you took me? With that woman who hates you? Is she there?"

He was staring at her. His body was still, and he obviously did not understand why she was furious.

"Damn it, Ken Jin, how can I trust anything you say?" She shoved him away from her and stood, not caring that he had to scramble backward to get out of her way. "You've been lying to me from the beginning. Where is Joanna?"

He stood slowly, his voice cold. "She has left the Tigress school, she and her monk. I do not know where she has gone. Her servants believe she is dead—or will be soon."

Charlotte spun around. "Dead?"

He folded his arms. "She and her monk fled from a powerful general, the most powerful in China." He shook his head. "No man or woman can stand long against such a force."

"She's dead?"

"Most likely. With her monk."

Charlotte gripped the mantel to keep herself upright. "My God . . ."

"There is more."

She looked up at him and trembled. "Worse?" she whispered, afraid of his answer, but more afraid of not knowing.

"Her father followed them, so he will likely suffer the same fate."

"Mr. Crane?" She liked Mr. Crane. He had always treated her decently. He spoke politely, and he never smelled of opium or drank to excess. "Dead?"

"Most likely. Mr. Yi asked me for a job."

She closed her eyes. Her head was spinning.

"Such is the power of unrefined qi, Miss Charlotte. Miss Joanna's flew out every which way, leaving devastation in its wake."

"Joanna?"

"Her passions purified her qi, making it an awesome power. She was learning to direct it when she ran from the school." He shook his head. "She was a foolish, foolish girl." His gaze grew hard. "Many will die because of her."

Charlotte's legs would not support her. She sank to her knees beside the fire, her skirt pooling about her. "Dead?"

"Miss Joanna and her father, her monk, and now the Tigress who thought to teach her and the Tigress's husband

117

who sheltered them." Charlotte didn't know the people, but clearly Ken Jin did. And just as clearly, he was furious. "So you see," he continued, his every word like a thrown rock. "Refining qi is a dangerous process for both student and teacher. Mishandle it and devastation occurs. Treat it without respect—as a game—and you will bring disaster upon yourself and your family. Better to die than do such a thing to those you love."

Intentional or not, his words held a note of challenge, and she felt her spirit blaze in response. "But you are doing it," she shot back. "Playing games. With your needles and naked . . . naked . . ." She glanced down at his groin.

"Dragon. Or jade stalk." He spoke in Chinese, which somehow made the words poetic rather than graphic, exotic rather than sinful. "Yes, I refine my qi. But it is practice, not play."

It was too much to comprehend; the concepts too foreign. She pushed away thoughts of her best friend and focused on the meaning beneath the story. Could one person's actions become a devastating force? Of course. That was exactly what her mother thought and the priest taught. They said one's actions resulted in divine reward or punishment.

Ken Jin claimed that Joanna's scattered qi rained havoc on her entire household. Mama believed her own lewdness had caused William's disability. All revolved around sex—Joanna's explorations and Mama's drunken exploits. Were they saying the same thing in different ways? Could sex in the right way—in a concentrated, focused manner—create energy for good and not evil?

She looked at Ken Jin, not daring to hope. "Do you think refined qi can heal William?"

He cursed under his breath, clearly exasperated. "I do not know whether William can be healed. But as you said before, your mother's prayers are not helping."

She lifted her chin. "I said they don't *seem* to be working." She was splitting hairs and she knew it.

"Intention is everything, Miss Charlotte. Do not embark on this path without clear and focused intention. If you want to help your brother, keep that thought foremost in your mind. Do not allow it to waver. That is your only hope."

She nodded, her thoughts still scattered. "Joanna . . ." She refused to think of her best friend as dead—in grave danger, perhaps, but not dead. She looked at Ken Jin. "Is there anything I can do to help Joanna? Anything—"

He shook his head. "I cannot even help the Tans, and they are not the cause of the whole disturbance."

She frowned, trying to remember the Tans—the Tigress teacher and her husband, she recalled. "But if we can find Joanna—"

"We cannot. They are running, Miss Charlotte, from a powerful enemy." Ken Jin stepped forward, towering over her. "She made her choice and now walks her path. It is time, Miss Charlotte, for you to choose yours."

"But I don't understand any of this!" She was crying now, not with tears on her face, but inside, like a little child lost in a grown-up world. Her head seemed too large for her body, and her thoughts sizzled and popped, but in no order, with no coherence.

"Focus!" he ordered.

"On what?" she snapped back. But she knew what; he had already told her. "On healing my brother," she whispered.

Ken Jin just stood there, backlit by the fire but not warmed by it. Indeed, there was nothing warm or giving about him. Which meant she would have to choose her path without further guidance. Would she pursue what he offered, his strange qi energies and naked madness—or did she throw it all away?

If Ken Jin was a cad, she still believed she could get rid of him. A few well-phrased half-truths to her father, and Ken Jin would be tossed out on his ear. But that was the path of a liar.

She had already tried the Christian devotion her mother embraced. She abandoned that years ago. She still went to Mass, she still supported her mother's good works, but she could not throw herself into endless prayers and hours of castigation for past sins. That was her mother's road, not hers.

Which left what? Modern science hadn't helped William; neither had practical discipline or any number of other discourses on child rearing. What was left?

She shuddered at the thought of embracing something so completely alien as Ken Jin's teachings. Not that she feared the sexual, but she knew there would be no turning back once begun. Ken Jin would require total dedication or nothing, and she had no idea where this path would take her.

There was some consolation. It seemed her friend Joanna had already embraced the Tigress teachings, and she was the smartest person Charlotte knew. She read and discussed ad infinitum all the classics—Chinese, American, British or French. If Joanna had embraced this path enough to disappear for a week and then run off . . . Charlotte's thoughts stopped there. She could not speculate on Joanna's fate. Except—

"How do you know that I won't destroy everything around me like Joanna?"

Ken Jin slowly lowered himself until he crouched on his heels before her. "I do not know the details of Miss Crane's introduction to the practice. It is possible that she did not begin in the best way."

There was something there, something unpleasant. "How wasn't it the best? What happened?"

"I do not know. I was not there, and one does not question the Tigress Shi Po. She has her reasons and has already guided one couple to Immortality."

"Immortality? They're dead?" Charlotte gasped.

He took a moment, then grimaced. "When the Chinese say Immortal, we refer to living people who walk both on Earth and in Heaven."

"So, Immortals are alive?"

He nodded.

"But Joanna . . . She's running for her life—"

Again, the heavy sigh. "I do not know the details. I will not speculate."

Charlotte huffed. She recognized the tone of a man who would not be pushed, so she tried a different tack. "How do you know we won't make the same mistakes, end the same way?"

"I am well trained, Miss Charlotte. I have seen many introduced successfully into the practice."

She stared into his eyes, suspicious. "But have you done it?"

He nodded. "Once."

She did not like his flat tone. "How did that end?"

He shrugged. "Badly. As you said, Little Pearl hates me."

She blinked. "Little Pearl? The woman at the school?"

"Yes."

"What happened?"

His gaze did not waver from her face, but in his lap, his hands whitened into fists. "I was too young, too eager. Little Pearl grows angry when pushed." He lifted his chin. "I will not make the same mistake."

"You think you are the best teacher for me?" She wasn't sure how she felt about that.

He snorted with impatience. "I am the only teacher for you. The Tigress and her husband are in jail. I cannot even see them, much less manage their release. Little Pearl will not accept a white woman, nor will any other Tigress in the whole of China." He paused long enough to make sure she looked directly into his eyes. "And I will not turn you over to another Dragon partner, some stranger who will not understand your goals and will not like your white yin." He spoke with a force fueled by anger. He clearly did not like her questioning his choices. But this was a significant choice—a life-altering choice. He would have to understand that she would not walk any path blindly.

Except, how could this be anything but blind? She had only his words to guide her, only his faith and his passion. She couldn't even ask anyone else for direction. At best, the questions would brand her a bluestocking. The worse and much more likely outcome was that she would be ruined.

No, she could not ask anyone else for advice. She had only Ken Jin's words and her own powers of reason, and the knowledge that Joanna had sought this training as well. And that was the tipping point she used to finally make her decision. If she wanted to find her friend—as she did—she would embrace this learning. True, Joanna might be dead, but Charlotte wouldn't give up. Besides, she was much more levelheaded than her friend. Joanna often got caught up in intellectual fervor, whereas Charlotte had never had such inclinations. She would be able to remain focused where Joanna probably wandered off into the quagmire.

Charlotte had one other advantage: She had Ken Jin. As far as she could tell, despite all the bizarre things he believed, he had never, ever lied to her. He had never dismissed her, nor had he ever forced her.

Yes, she was starting in a much safer place than her friend. She would not end up destroying everything around her with rampant, uncontrolled qi. She would be careful. She had a goal: to refine her yin in order to make William better. She could stay focused on that. And if she ever wandered from that path, then she would simply abandon the practice. She could stop at any time and would trust that she could make Ken Jin obey. He was, after all, her servant. If she changed her mind, she would make sure he had no choice but to accept her decision.

She lifted her chin. Ken Jin remained crouched before her, his gaze level, his attitude patient.

"Very well," she said, appalled to hear her voice shake. It wasn't fear, but excitement. "Shall I undress here? Or in my bedroom?"

Jan 2, 1892
To honored Father, honored Mother:

Many years have passed since I left your gracious presence. In that time, I have often yearned for knowledge of your health. As your hands are skilled and your knowledge vast, I am sure that your business thrives and all in Peking are in a state of great health due to your work. How I wish we had acupuncturists of your ability in Shanghai.

The New Year fast approaches, and I find I long to see the soaring temples of Peking again. Plus, I miss the smell of red peony root tincture and the low moans of patients benefiting from your vast experience.

Please accept these humble gifts as a token of my esteem, my most respected parents. Though I am sure none of it compares to what can be found in Peking, I have poured all my skills into purchasing the finest objects in Shanghai. As I did not know your sizes, I have sent seven bolts of silk for fabric and taels of silver to pay the tailor. And because the measurement process would be most tedious, I have included a jade toy elephant for my younger brother to pass the time.

Of course, he must be a tall, handsome figure now, since he always favored our father. Perhaps he is too old to play with such a meager thing. If so, please give it to a young cousin. My brother can enjoy the scroll of Tang poetry I have included instead.

I will be traveling to Peking soon on business for my employer. It would bring such happiness to my heart if I could see what work the Peking tailors accomplished with such average material.

In fervent prayer for your continued good health,

your son,

Ken Jin

Jan 13, 1892
Dear Sir:

Do not visit; we do not know you. We have only two sons. One, Gao Jin, lives inside the Forbidden City, and is the Emperor's most valued eunuch. The other, Feng Jin, grows daily in studious application of the family craft. Both are filial, devoted children. We would accept nothing less from those we call our own.

Wen Geng Zi

FOR FAINTING: *Apply the fingernail to stimulate the acupoint on the midline two-thirds of the way up between the upper lip and the nose. If a person faints frequently for no apparent reason, medical advice should be sought.*
Tong Sing, the Chinese Book of Wisdom, Dr. Charles Windridge

Chapter Eight

Ken Jin tried to not tremble in the face of Miss Charlotte's decision. She wished to train as a Tigress, and he had agreed to teach her—not just the beginning, a few exercises while he absorbed her yin tide—but the true path of a Tigress. What arrogance he showed to think he could do this. But she had no other instructor, and he needed her yin. No other woman had ever brought his yang surging to the fore like she did. In short, it was an equitable arrangement; plus, he was well trained in what they would do.

And yet he still quivered in fear. There were risks, even with the most experienced teacher. He had only been the tiniest bit too aggressive with Little Pearl, and she'd wound up hating him for the last decade. Partners lost control all the time. What if he accidentally took Charlotte's virginity? Made her pregnant? What then? How would he feel if Charlotte despised him? What would happen to his job and his family should her parents discover what they did?

The risks terrified him. Yet he knew his path was already set. He had committed to Charlotte yesterday. It had begun the moment he crept into her room last night to shave her as every Tigress shaved. He knew then—though he hadn't admitted it to himself—that she would be his partner in the practice. They would reach Heaven together or fall exhausted and useless back to Earth.

So it would be. He looked at her, his resolution firm. "We will begin tonight," he said. "We need only decide where."

She frowned. "Why not here?"

He looked about the sitting room and shook his head. This space was too open, too available to servant and family member alike. Nor was Charlotte's bedroom appropriate. That was where the girl took her ease, where she relaxed and rested. The location for study had to be different, focused, and uncontaminated by the energies of brother and mother. Typically, the place would be the Tigress school, but with Little Pearl in charge, Ken Jin would not be welcome there. Besides, Charlotte would not leave her brother just yet. So, if they were to begin practice tonight, it would have to be somewhere in or near the house.

"We will go to the library," he finally said. What better place to impress serious discipline than in a room filled with scholarship?

She hesitated. "Ken Jin, we don't have a library."

He smiled. "But you do have a place of books. A place removed from the business of servants and family, where no one would think to search for you."

She shook her head. "No, Ken Jin, we don't."

He sighed. "I refer to the place where your summer gowns are stored. If someone were to discover us, you could simply claim you were looking for some dress or another."

Her brow wrinkled. "But where exactly is that?"

"Behind the house, Miss Charlotte."

She blinked, and then suddenly her eyes widened. "In the *gardener's shed?*"

"There is a second story and a window that looks toward the house."

"There is not!"

He shrugged. "There is a board that is easily removed. I call it a window."

She turned to stare out of a real window at the back of the estate. "It appears you have made quite a study of this library."

He shrugged. "It has been useful at times. And at night, one can easily monitor what goes on in the house simply by watching the lights."

She nodded slowly, her agile mind catching up. "If William wakes, the maid will increase the gaslight. We will be able to see that?"

He nodded. "Quite brightly."

"Papa will not be a problem. If Mama wakes, her bedroom light will come on."

"Your love of the back garden is well known."

"I could claim to be taking a walk."

"Today has been most disturbing for you, has it not?"

She pushed to her feet. "Most disturbing. Very well, let us go."

He said nothing, merely waited for her to lead the way as was her custom even when she had little idea where she was headed. They moved silently through the house and out the back door, and then he had to guide her from behind as they wended their way to the small shed. Small by English standards, of course; a home for seven by Chinese standards.

She was not accustomed to climbing ladders, but managed it well enough in the dark. Soon Charlotte stood in the center of the tiny second-floor storage room while he found and lit a candle that barely illuminated anything beyond dark shadowy trunks, stacked one on top of the other, and an array of pillows and blankets that he quickly arranged.

"You have done this before," she said. Her voice was hushed, and yet it still held a note of accusation.

"The Dragon path requires a great deal of practice. I cannot always be in my rooms in town, nor is my room here adequately locked." He could not help the dry note in his voice.

She tilted her head, her hair slipping across one shoulder. "But you weren't here yesterday when . . . when . . ."

"When William interrupted my practice?"

Red tinged her cheeks. "You were using those needles, and your trousers—"

"I remember. Perhaps you do not recall that the gardeners were quite busy that day. Plus, you and William were supposed to be closeted in lessons all morning. I should not have been interrupted."

She looked away, surveying the room. "No," she agreed with a sigh, "you should not have. But William can be fast when he wishes."

"Of course."

The candle was burning, the bedding arranged. Ken Jin had even propped open the loose board in such a way that they could see out but their candlelight was shielded from outsiders. In short, the room was set. Now was the time that he would test her true willingness. After all, many a virgin had balked at the very last moment.

He straightened and turned around. She was already naked. Or rather, not fully naked, but very close. She had removed her dress, and stood before him in corset and stockings. Her shoes were set neatly beside her folded gown, and she was distracting herself by wiggling her toes up and down. Her arms were crossed over her belly, but seemingly more out of cold than modesty. Ken Jin could only stare.

She met his shocked gaze with a lifted chin, followed by a raised eyebrow. "Did you think me inconstant or cowardly?"

Unable to find footing with this bizarre woman, he resorted to his servant persona. He bowed slightly to her and queried, "My lady?"

"Oh, stubble it, Ken Jin. You thought I might walk all the way out here and have second thoughts. That, when it came right down to it, I would not be willing to follow through."

He didn't answer, because that was exactly what he had thought.

She flung her arms wide, all ribboned corset and lacy stockings, creamy white flesh and long well-shaped legs. "But how could you imagine such a thing after last night?"

She clearly meant to bluster her way through. She was not as sanguine as she appeared. He could tell by the way her hands would not stop moving. First they spread wide, and then they fluttered back to her sides, only to again twist together as she folded her arms across her belly. Despite the bravado, she was nervous. Not surprising, really. For all her innocence, she knew that she was about to take a momentous step. On some level, she understood nothing would ever be the same again.

He smiled, though he covered the motion with another bow. "My apologies, Miss Charlotte, but I asked you to remove *all* your clothing."

She was a silent a moment. He chanced a glance at her face. Her cheeks were flaming, and she bit her lower lip. "But it is so very cold in here."

In truth, it was nothing of the kind; but he did not argue. "You will not be chilled for long."

She didn't answer, and he felt the weight of her stare. Indeed, it was heavy enough that he felt himself straightening in reaction. She was watching him, her eyes narrowed in thought as she idly twirled her hair. "You understand that I want to remain a virgin? I still want to marry someday. After William is settled, and assuming the right gentleman offers . . ."

He stiffened, insulted. "Were you not safe last night? My restraint is legendary, Miss Charlotte, even among Dragons."

"Of course, of course," she hurried to say. "I meant no insult."

He nodded. "No, Miss Charlotte, you only mean to delay. But it is already late. Like you, I have had a difficult day. So if you do not intend to proceed with the lesson, perhaps . . ."

That was all the spurring she needed. Her fluttering hands went to her corset and she began to strip it off. But her fingers were too unsteady to complete the task. Fumbled, she grimaced. The ribbons knotted, and she cursed. In the end, he had to help her.

Batting away her hands with a quick flick, he set to work on her ties. He'd had a great deal of practice with underclothing, and so anticipated no trouble. But perhaps it was colder than he'd thought, for his hands were nearly as unsteady as hers.

She was of average height for a white woman, so her breasts were chest-high to him. The corset's hooks marched down the center of the garment, so they were in easy reach, and yet he had to stand nearly atop her to manage the unbinding. Unfortunately, the close proximity flooded his senses with her yin power. Her scent became a foglike smoke around his brain, and the short gasps she released as he tugged seemed to echo in his ears. By necessity, his knuckles brushed across her collarbone and the flesh beneath. And when he tugged at the topmost clasp, her knees bumped into his. Worse, her hips surged forward to briefly jostle his fully wakened dragon.

"Hold still!" he ordered.

"I'm trying!"

Threads from the lace had caught on the top hook, holding the corset closed, though a tiny gap of rounded flesh peeked through. She was looking down as well, and her hands fluttered around his. "Let me—"

"Hold my hips," he ordered.

She stiffened. "I beg your pardon?"

"To hold you still," he practically growled. And to keep her hands and yin-filled scent away from his nose.

"Oh. Of course." He felt her hands on his hips: small palms, long fingers with surprising strength, and a feminine heat that felt like a brand. Ten years from now, he would still be able to feel the exact outline of her fingers and know where Charlotte's power had seared through him.

The clasp finally released. He felt her exhale hot air into his face. Normally that would irritate him; after all, he felt flushed enough. But her breath was different. It smelled of the mint leaves she chewed after meals, and it blew the hair from his eyes. Plus, it distracted him from the soft mounds pressed against the back of his hands as he dug deeper down her corset.

Her breath stopped as she tried to shrink backward to give him more room. Her hands tightened on his hips, and her head dipped forward. But without the release of her breath, the energy built and built until he felt as if his fingers were pressed against living flame.

"Breathe!" he ordered, but his voice came out as a soft whisper of fear. If she burned him now, what would happened after she was purified?

The second corset hook released at the same moment she took a breath. He waited, completely still, for her next exhale. He even closed his eyes to better experience the air passing across his face. When it came, it was like lightning—hot power there and gone in an instant.

He glanced up at her face. She was panting—soft shallow breaths of rising yin. He had to say something to distract her, anything that would slow the yin tide.

"The first time I saw a corset, it was in a shipment to my master's house." He watched her face for a reaction, but instead fixed on the wet, red sheen of her lips. "Mr. Lewis was a thin man, you understand, with bony hips and a gaunt face, but I thought the corset was for him."

Charlotte's lips pressed together into a frown, but she did not hold the expression long. Her curiosity got the better of her. "Why ever would you think that? The shape, the ribbons, even the colors are all designed for women."

He nodded. "Of course, of course, but I had just begun working for the English. I knew nothing of what you women wore. Mr. Lewis did not bother much with them."

"Then why did he have a corset?"

The third latch released and her breasts dropped into a fuller, more natural position. Ken Jin could not help but smile at the sight. "I thought—mistakenly, of course—that it was a man's cure for impotence." He felt her start in reaction, and he belatedly realized that she might not understand the masculine ailment. "It is a difficulty with a man's dragon. When he has insufficient yang to draw it out, or sometimes it is because of a weak jade stalk."

He heard her tsk, and looked up from the quivering expanse of her belly. "I know what the word means, Ken Jin. But I don't understand why a corset—"

"It presses upon the Sea of Vitality. Here and here." He shifted his hands around her narrow waist to her lower back. Then he pressed two fingers deep into her flesh, about three finger-widths out on both sides of her spine. He felt her gasp at the sudden pressure, but it soon shifted to a sigh as he massaged in tight circles. Then he shifted his hands lower, delving to the tops of her buttocks. "These points on a man relieve impotency, and the corset rests here."

She arched back slightly, forcing him to press deeper.

He waited a moment, then pulled away, sliding his hands back around her waist to her belly.

He should have moved quickly. After all, he was trying to distract her. But the seat of her vitality pulsed with power and he was loath to leave it. Indeed, without conscious thought, he found himself probing deeper into her energy points. Both his thumbs delved into the Sea of Energy, three inches below her navel.

"And when you move," he breathed, his whole focus on the shifting soft skin beneath his fingers, on the pulse of power that beat just beneath the surface, "the edges dig in here."

She moaned slightly, and he was startled enough to look into her face. Without even realizing it, he had stimulated her yin to the point of cloud creation. Already, she produced a rumble of thunder in her chest.

He stopped kneading, and her eyes opened. She blinked as she struggled against the rising tide.

"All that is left," he heard himself say, "would be to activate the Rushing Door and Mansion Cottage points, and impotency should fade away."

"But most men don't wear corsets," she murmured.

He nodded. "But you understand my confusion. It took me some time to understand why you English created such a thing for women."

She frowned and slowly withdrew her hands from his hips. With a quick snap, she undid the last clasp, then tossed the contraption away. "Because we want to fit into our dresses?"

He shrugged. "Naturally. But why are your dresses designed in such a manner?"

She took a deep breath. Her breasts lifted and bobbed with the movement. "Because men like tiny waists and big breasts, of course."

133

"But the pressure of the corset rests on the back and belly."

"And the ribs." She tilted her head. "I don't understand what you're saying."

"The pressure points, Miss Charlotte. When stimulated, those points increase sexual potency—in a man *or* a woman."

She shook her head. "I have never thought a corset increased anything, Ken Jin. It cuts off the breath and squeezes the belly. It is not a pleasant device, and I long for the moment each day when I can discard the horrid thing."

"Of course. Because too much pressure for too long stimulates too much. In the end, it cuts off all energy."

"Are you are saying my corset is designed to cut off desire?"

"And then to allow it to flood back through you the moment the device is released."

She stared at him as his meaning sank in. "So, women are to be suppressed during the day, and then incredibly active at night?" She looked at the discarded corset, her brow tightened in thought. "How very clever of you men."

He grinned. She had surprising intellect, especially for a virginal woman. "Unfortunately," he said, "use of this device is not restricted to married women. Indeed, I would think it would induce madness in the young ones or the widows."

"Those who have no one to . . ." She looked back up at him, and he had to force himself to meet her gaze. Her breasts and wide hips were much too enticing a view. "No one to help them."

He could not stop himself; he reached out and cupped her breasts. They were full in his hands, a weight that made his dragon rear with hunger. "I have found that, once released from their corset, all white women—virginal or otherwise—have need of extensive yin release." He shook his head. "Truly, I do not think your English corset is a healthy device."

He was manipulating her nipples. Without thought, he was twisting and pulling at those rosy peaks, and she arched into his hands, a low purr of appreciation rolling through her body. He needed to stop. This was not what he had intended when he brought her here. And yet, her skin was so soft, the yin flowed so freely. One tweak of his thumb and the power poured into him like hot lava— potent, powerful, and oh-so-needed by his often-cold dragon.

"How do you . . . know about this?" Her eyes were closed, and the words came in an uneven rhythm as if she too struggled to maintain focus on anything other than his touch.

"I learned in the way of all children—at my parents' knee. I listened, I learned."

Her eyes popped open. "Surely they did not teach you this." She looked down at his hands on her breasts.

He stopped, abruptly recalled to himself, and he let his hands fall away. "No, Miss Charlotte," he said. "I did not learn this from them." Or at least, his mother had not meant to teach him these things. "My parents—my father most especially—are acupuncturists. He has a life-sized doll in our home that shows the lines and points, the secret gates and the open channels. I studied that when I was bored. And I would watch from behind a screen when he treated someone."

Charlotte straightened, her hands retracting to her chest as if she, too, suddenly realized what she had allowed. "You watched him stick needles into people?"

He smiled in memory. "I knew all the hiding places in my home. A boy can learn much if he knows how to be small and quiet."

She looked at him, her expression lightening. "I had not

thought of you as a boy," she said. "But of course you must have been one." She stared at his face, and her head tilted to one side. "So you learned this religion from them. This energy—"

He shook his head and stepped away from her, away from her drugging yin. "I learned some understanding of acupuncture from them. The rest came from another source."

She pursued him, at first with a single step, and then with her eyes as he pivoted in the tiny space. "How did you learn this, Ken Jin—about yin and yang energy?"

"I learned from the Tigress Shi Po." His words were sharp, and he was startled by his own unbalance. Was her unpurified yin so potent that its loss so easily unsettled him?

"The woman who is in jail?"

He nodded.

"I'm sorry."

He did not want her sympathy, and so he glared at her. Yet her softly spoken words still found him, still created a warm center in his chest where a woman's yin would be found. He sighed.

"Your unpurified yin is highly distracting," he said. "Please, arrange yourself for cleansing."

She stilled. All her body froze, except her hands, which once again fluttered idly near her belly. "I do not know what that means, Ken Jin," she admitted. "Do you mean for shaving?"

Her voice broke, reminding him that this could not be easy for her. How simple it was for him to forget that she was no practiced courtesan as he usually frequented. Nor was she even a Tigress cub, partially trained from classes and lectures. She was a virgin barbarian with uncommonly strong yin.

Forcibly reining in his lust, he focused his thoughts on his task. "My apologies, Miss Charlotte. We are here to strengthen your yin." The very thought left him reeling. Wasn't she powerful enough? "My task is to teach you."

"So, there will be no more . . . shaving?"

He smiled. He couldn't help it. Of course she wanted a repeat of last night's performance; her yin had been dammed up so tight that its release had nearly knocked him unconscious. How he longed to return to that moment as well.

"Not tonight," he forced himself to say. Though one look told him that he had done a despicably poor job of shaving her. Which meant, of course, he would have to try again soon. "Tonight we shall purify your yin. You are not to release it; we are cleansing."

She squared her shoulders, and her breasts bobbed as if in agreement. "What should I do?"

"Sit on those pillows, with your right leg bent toward your red lotus. Your heel should press deeply into your cinnabar cave."

She frowned. "My what?"

"The centermost point between your legs. Where a child would emerge were you to give birth."

She nodded, heading for the blankets. He turned to give her a little more privacy. Little Pearl had once commented that it was difficult to begin this task with someone staring at her, so he busied himself with lighting the incense he kept stored here for his own exercises. He lingered over the task, even closed his eyes to absorb the strengthening scent of cinnamon, ginger, and ginseng. He let the aroma filter into his consciousness and open his sluggish yang centers. They responded, of course. Yang always responds to strong yin. He had cause to be grateful for that fact.

When he turned around, she had seated herself as he indicated. Her right leg was bent and pressed deeply into her pleasure grotto, which he could see was slick with yin dew. She was looking at him with an air of expectation—a student awaiting further instruction—but he found he could not speak. Indeed, he was completely robbed of all strength.

He had been prepared to instruct her, to talk her through her exercises as one would teach a child to use an abacus or braid a queue. Instead, he had turned to find a deity. There was no other word for it.

She had discarded her shoes, but her stockings remained on, attached to her thighs by dainty rose bows. Except, both had come undone. The ribbons dangled across her legs like a goddess's trailing ribbons of glory. Her skin was white, her breasts full and shapely. And the color of her moist lips matched the dusky rose of her nipples, her ribbons, her barely hidden cinnabar cave.

Ken Jin licked his lips, tasting her yin scent on the air despite the incense. His hands itched to touch, to take, to worship, and his dragon flushed with unaccustomed power. Never before had he ever encountered such a potent woman. He longed to drink from her fountain again. How would he ever look at her again without thinking of this moment? Without seeing the yin well inside her?

Her hands began to flutter about her belly again. She was becoming nervous as he continued to stare, for she did not know what was happening. But he understood: The more he watched, the more his yang called to her yin— and the reverse—and the hotter the fire between them blazed.

"Yang is like wood," he said, his voice thick. "It fuels the fire that makes the yin boil." He reached out, unable to stop himself from stroking the top of her breast. A single caress, but his dragon surged in response, nearly taking him to his knees.

She looked up at him, her shoulders shifting with her soft, shallow breaths. "This feels terribly strange."

He knelt, unable to stop himself. "You must remove your stockings."

Her cheeks turned an even darker rose. "But then . . ." She stopped and looked away. "Yes, of course. I am being silly."

He touched her chin to bring her gaze back to him. "Qi requires absolute honesty. If we are to purify your yin, do not pollute it by hiding your thoughts." She didn't answer, and he could tell he would have to press further. "Why didn't you take off your stockings?"

She tried to turn away, but he did not allow it. "I told you I was being silly. I will take them off—"

"Answer my question, Charlotte."

She paused, her lips pressing tightly together. But in the end, her entire body sagged on a sigh. "I didn't want to be completely naked. I don't know why. You have . . . we have done . . ." Again the heavy sigh. "I don't understand myself."

"Clothing is a covering. Even when it hides only the feet, our spirit can cower behind it."

"I am not cowering."

"I know." He released her chin and was gratified to see that she did not look away. She met his gaze with an angry flash.

"I will take off my stockings."

"And as you do, you will shed the petty thoughts and dishonest acts that pollute your spirit."

She bent her knee to bring her leg closer to her hands, flashing him a look of irritation. "I am not dishonest or impure." Her voice broke on the last word, and he knew she was worried on that account.

"All people have done wrong at one time or another." He moved backward to allow her more room. "And all people think that—"

"You're a servant!" Then she gasped, frozen with shock. "Oh, Ken Jin! Oh Lord, I didn't mean . . ."

But of course she had meant it, and that stung. Though why he let it hurt, he had no idea.

"Ken Jin—" she began, but she obviously had no idea what she meant to say.

He stopped her with a single press of his fingers on her lips. "I *am* a servant," he said, the words coarse in his throat. "And you are embarrassed to be completely naked before me. *Why?*" It made little sense, especially considering what she had allowed him to do earlier.

She didn't answer, but she didn't look away either. She simply stared at him as she rolled down one stocking. And he suddenly understood.

"It is not that I'm a servant," he said softly, "but that I'm Chinese. All the maids who help you dress and bathe are English." Her right stocking was off. She shifted her weight and bent her other leg, but Ken Jin stopped her. He put his hand on her knee and waited until she looked at him. "What we do is not English, *xiao jie.*" He used the Chinese word for little girl, and she flinched at the term. He wanted her to understand that in this she was just beginning as a young Chinese girl would.

"I am not a child," she said, her tone flat.

"You are not a woman yet either."

Her gaze rose to meet his, but it was not easy for her. Charlotte's movements were jerky, her voice even more so. "And this . . . *this* will make me a woman?"

Was she sneering? Probably. Which meant that she didn't understand. "Not in the fashion you mean. Not in the way of little boys giggling as they peer through peepholes. Not in the way of a whore who spreads her legs and calls herself a divine creature." They were both excruciatingly aware of her position on the floor, one leg bent, the other extended, her pleasure grotto disconcertingly exposed.

"Then how?"

"We make your qi pure and strong. A woman's qi is one of the most powerful forces on this earth."

She took a deep breath, clearly trying to understand. "In England, a girl becomes a woman when her virginity is taken."

"In China, a girl becomes a woman when her inner strength is powerful enough to manage a home and raise her children."

"I am already managing a household."

True enough. "But you cannot defend William yet. Not from your mother's energies."

Tired of the delay, Ken Jin began to roll her other stocking down her leg. She made no demur, though he felt her leg twitch beneath his fingertips. He meant to move quickly. The less time spent bathed in her yin heat, the better for his clarity of purpose. But once again, her energies defeated him. He lingered as he worked, making the simple removal of her stocking into a seduction, a sensuous slide of fabric intermixed with the deeper stroke of his fingers.

He ached to touch her; and indeed, as the cotton cleared her knee, his hands shifted. While his left continued to slide her stocking free, his right cupped the back of her thigh. He massaged deeply, pressing his fingers into the Commanding Activity point before pulling the energy higher, toward the Rushing Door. And when her stocking was at last lifted away, he set her leg away from him rather than back to her cinnabar cave. In short, he opened her to him.

"It is time, *xiao jie,* to become a woman. Will you accept this?"

She nodded. The only indication of her nervousness came from the quick dart of her tongue against her lips.

"Put your hands on your breasts. Press your fingers just inside your nipples."

Her eyes widened, but she obeyed.

"Move them in ever-expanding circles. In your mind, repeat these words: *I dispurse the pollutants. I remove the blockages.*"

He said the words first in Chinese, then again in English, to be sure she understood. Then he watched as she closed her eyes and began the circles. Her lips moved as she repeated his words, and he felt a smile curve his lips when he realized she spoke in Chinese. Whether she realized it or not, she was becoming a proper Chinese Tigress.

"Excellent," he said. Then, without even thinking, he betrayed them both. He shifted his right hand to rest palm-side up. Then he slipped the tip of his finger inside her.

She gasped and reared backward, but he pursued. He pushed his index finger all the way in. "Move your hands!" he ordered. "You are throwing off pollutants. You are—"

"I am purifying my yin," she said in Chinese.

"Yes." And he could feel that she truly was. As she closed her eyes and repeated his words, her yin circled his finger, matching the movement of her hands. It was growing stronger. The dissonance in her energy was fading, and pure, beautiful yin flowed out and around him. Her cinnabar cave was like a furnace, filled to bursting with female heat.

He slowly, carefully, worked a second finger inside her. He wanted her desperately. Oh, to drink of her strength, to fill his body with the heat of her furnace! He began to curl his fingers slightly, stroking against the roof of her cinnabar cave. His other hand pressed against her belly such that her Gate of Origin was engaged from both outside and in.

"Reverse direction," he ordered. "Move your hands in circles *toward* your nipples."

He looked up at her. Her skin was flushed, her breasts large and beautiful as she stroked them; but it was her eyes that caught him. Normally a light blue, they now pierced him with the force of her determination. She continued to murmur and chant, but it was the wrong one now.

" 'I stoke the fire. The yin builds and builds,' " he growled. When she didn't understand, he repeated it. "Say it! 'I stoke the fire. The yin builds and builds!' "

She matched his words, and as she spoke she leaned forward. She echoed his sounds as well, growling and hissing as he had. And all the while, her hands circled her breasts ever tighter.

Without being told, she pulled at her nipples. Without his order, her thighs fell open and trembled, pushing against his hand even as he thrust his fingers inside her.

"More yin," he ordered. "Focus!"

She gasped as he braced himself, using his knees to shove her legs farther apart. He had two fingers fully inside her now. Could he manage a third? She was slick, but small. And yet, even as he hovered in uncertainty, she arched against him. She pushed herself down onto his hand and he spread his hand to catch her. Two fingers delved deep inside to fully stroke her cave roof. His thumb slid up to circle her yin pearl, and his other two fingers slid backward to press into the place of Inner Meeting. All throbbed with the force of her yin.

"Such power," he breathed. "Do you feel it?"

"Is it pure, Ken Jin?" she gasped. "Is it enough?"

"No," he lied. "Focus, Charlotte. Build the power until your entire body sings with it."

"I stoke the fire," she chanted. "The yin builds and builds. I stoke the fire. The yin builds and builds."

Her yin had long since drawn into his arm and blood. He felt it swirl around and through him. He watched her hands on her beautiful breasts: circling, circling, tighter and tighter. He echoed her movements with his fingers, his hand, and power followed their movements. It built in both of them. He felt it push to her nipples just as it roared through his body straight to his mind. It burned in his blood and the smoke fogged his mind.

"I stoke the fire," she chanted, her words throbbing in his veins. "The yin builds and builds," she cried, and both their thighs began to pulse. The energy was rising, drawing up from her toes. Without looking, he knew her feet were clenched. His body mirrored hers, and his entire body was pulling together.

Her knees were rising as the power curled inward; his hips were arching forward. Her hands were narrowing, drawing close to her nipples again. And his thumb extended, poised to open the gate with a single flick.

What he did was insanity. Purified yin could enslave a man. Touch it once, and you craved it forever. And yet, it was too late for him. He felt it. He touched it. He had plunged his hand deep inside it.

"I stoke the fire," she said.

He withdrew slightly, sliding his thumb between her lotus petals. Then he pushed deeper, rolling his thumb in a long, wide circle around her yin pearl. All the while, he watched the movement of her hands.

"The yin builds!" he said.

Another circle. She was almost there.

"And builds!"

She pinched her nipples. He rolled his finger across her pearl, and finally, at the right moment, he pushed.

Fire roared through him. Yang leaped from his belly and dragon to pour into her. The energy flew from him while his dragon tried to span the distance between their bodies. And while his seed was gone forever, lost to the inside of his trousers, the power made the leap. His yang essence wasn't contained only in the dragon cloud; that energy had bridged the distance, flowing through his hand into her cauldron.

He emptied himself in moments, his body and spirit depleted of all his yang storage. Charlotte expanded. Inside, her energy built, her power intensified. On and on and on, her body contracted around his hand. Her head flew back in ecstasy while her internal pump pushed the energy upward, ever higher. She let out a cry of stunned amazement, and then she stilled. Her body became lax as her spirit left her.

Ken Jin stared at her in shock, his release leaving him hollow and cold as he realized the hideous truth. His yang, purified and strengthened through years of devoted study, had just taken Charlotte Wicks to Heaven.

❦

March 18, 1895
Dearest younger brother Feng Jin:

I tear my heart and beat my breast at the most wretched news I heard today. Truly, can both our parents and our most cherished grandmother be dead? It is not possible, and yet I am told that the Wen family acupuncturists are almost all gone. Only one practitioner remains—namely, yourself.

I shall come to Peking next week to pay my respects.

In great wretchedness,
Your brother,
Ken Jin

March 24, 1895
Kind Stranger,

Acupuncturist Wen Feng Jin spoke about your letter. Pray do not distress yourself on behalf of his family. Grieve instead for China and the curse that haunts our great land.

It is true that the Wen family has suffered

greatly of late, but only recently has Mr. Wen dis-
covered the true cause of their misfortune. The
Wen grandmother, steeped in the confusion of old
age, wrote often to an evil sorcerer. He is a young
man, once of Chinese descent, who early showed
his deceptive ways in a crime of great magnitude.
He now works for the barbarians, aiding them in
their depravity as they poison all of China.

The Wen family elders died because of this as-
sociation with the sorcerer. Grandmother Wen
corresponded with this evil man, and in response,
Heaven cursed the family with a sickness that
claimed her life and the lives of her son and
daughter-in-law. Late at night, neighbors still
hear her ghostly wails of despair. I can only pray
that the evil sorcerer does as well.

Fortunately, Mr. Wen was untainted by her de-
ception and so escaped death, as did Mr. Wen's
other brother. Indeed it is believed that the eunuch
Wen's devotion to the Emperor is all that prevents
total disaster for the family. His service to the Em-
peror balances out the evil perpetrated by the sor-
cerer.

Perhaps one day the sorcerer will understand
the horror he does. Perhaps he will recall the hon-
ored traditions of his ancestors. All the Wen fam-
ily prays earnestly that he returns to the
appropriate relationship with his elders and Em-
peror.

In the Wen family, of course, that means the
second son must devote himself to the Emperor's
service. Indeed, eunuch Wen tells us that the
medics outside the Forbidden City are most effec-
tive, and few die of castration. Such an act of de-

*votion would most certainly dispel the evil cloud
that darkens the Wen family home.*

*If only the evil sorcerer Ken Jin would forsake
his cursed ways and devote himself to his proper
place. They say castration is not nearly as painful
as most believe. A single stroke removing stalk
and pearls, and then the agony fades. We pray
nightly that this evil man repents and visits the
surgeons. That is the only way to reverse the family curse.*

Sincerely,
Lo Xin Si
Assistant to the Wen family patriarch

When an anxiety attack occurs, Sea of Tranquility (on the center of your breastbone) is the single best point to use for relief. Find the indentation in the breastbone, four finger-widths up from its base, to hold with your fingertips.
Acupressure for Emotional Healing, Michael Gach, Ph.D., and Beth Henning, Dipl, ABT

Chapter Nine

Ken Jin's power flooded Charlotte's belly. Heat and strength and something incredibly wonderful filled her, mixing with her essence and becoming exponentially more fabulous. She wanted to ask what he'd done, wanted to pause just for a moment to orient herself, to see and feel and categorize, but there was no stopping the sensations. And she had no breath to ask.

So she gave up. She released her consciousness to the experience and allowed herself to fly.

Was she really flying? It was more like floating, but terribly fast. And she was warm—beautifully warm, as if she were swimming in the most perfect water in the most perfect place. But it wasn't water; it was air, because she could breathe. She saw lights as well: thousands of different balls of shimmering color dancing in the perfect dark air that felt sensuously like water.

There was sound too. She couldn't hear it, but she felt it. Music slid through the waterlike air right into her soul. She was floating in sound, immersed in beauty, and filled with such love that she began to giggle—which bizarrely made her soar even higher, right up to the colored lights.

So close! And so beautiful! If she reached out her hand she could touch . . .

William? One of the lights was her brother?

He was dressed all in white. No, he was the one who shone. And he was so bright that his raiment appeared white, but in truth, he was glowing with all colors. And he was smiling. He reached out a hand for her, and she grasped it without thought.

This was her brother! This was the man he would become: handsome, strong, with every piece of his attire in place—no stains, no rips, no untied laces. Better still, he looked at her with such intelligence. He understood her. More than that, he understood everything about everything.

"You're an angel!" She had meant that he *looked* like an angel, but as the words shimmered through the air between them, she realized it was the literal truth. Her brother was an angel.

But how was that possible? Even as she phrased the thought, she understood the answer. She was in Heaven, brought here to speak with her brother, the angel. She frowned, trying to sort through her thoughts. She was in Heaven with William. But if William was here in *Heaven,* if her brother was an *angel,* then . . .

"Oh God, you're dead!"

Panic formed, a dark cold knot in her chest. As it formed, it drew all the rest of her into it. Heart, lungs, ribs, skin—all of her chilled and tightened. Worst of all, the bits of her became heavy. *She* became heavy. She began to sink.

"William!" she cried, stretching out to him. He extended his hand as well. First one arm, then the other, he tried to hold her to him. She heard her name tremble in the air. William's mouth was open, as if he were trying to talk to her, but she couldn't hear. The icy hole in the center of her chest had expanded to include her ears. All she heard was a dull rumble.

But she still felt him. His left hand managed to connect with hers. He couldn't hold on, but she touched him nonetheless. Strength, gentleness, and a love that was all William passed into her from her brother's spirit—her dead brother's spirit. She knew he had something to say to her, something she needed desperately to hear, but there was no time. She was sinking like an iron weight.

She fought, stretching, she screamed and ran, but that only made things worse. She seemed to fall faster, grow colder, and all that she was became ugly and heavy. All that surrounded her became even worse.

She didn't want to be here. She wanted to be back with her brother. She had to know: Was he dead?

She landed. She hit bottom in the darkest place, the coldest location, in the most horrid of ways: sprawled on a floor, her flesh so heavy that she couldn't lift a finger.

She opened her eyes. Even before she pried her lids open, she knew where she was: in the gardener's shed with Ken Jin. She could feel the lumpy pillows and the hard floor beneath her. She smelled his strange incense and felt the scratch of a blanket over her body, a blanket that did nothing to alleviate the chill.

Swallowing, she tasted bitterness in her dry mouth. Across from her, Ken Jin was drawing on his trousers, a dark stain in front. His movements were jerky, as if he suppressed great anger, but she had no ability to understand his frustration.

So what if his pants were wet? Her brother was dead!

The thought spurred her to action. She sprang from the

150

floor and ran out the door—or so she intended. Except, when next she focused her distraught mind on her surroundings, she realized she'd done no more than lift her head.

"Ken Jin . . ." she rasped.

His head snapped up. "You are awake."

She tried to speak. Her brother was dead. She'd seen him in Heaven as an angel, which meant he was dead here on Earth. She couldn't form the words. Instead, she felt tears slip from her eyes and trail into her hair. Her brother was dead.

"William," she finally managed. As she spoke, a great anger welled up inside her. Her brother was dead. She would not lie naked in the gardener's shed when she should be with her family. Her mother would need her. Her father would have to be found. And William . . . sweet William. Charlotte swallowed and grabbed hold of her fury. It warmed her and stiffened her spine. It gave her the power to roll onto her side and try to push herself upright.

"You should not move so soon after ascending," Ken Jin said, his voice tight.

"William's dead," she rasped. "I must go."

He put his hands on her shoulders. She tried to draw away from him; the last thing she needed was more weight, more resistance to plow through. But strangely, his hands did not hold her back. If anything, they seemed to ground her so that she could coordinate herself. She no longer moved a finger here, an elbow there, but her entire body with direction and purpose. She straightened her arms and lifted her head.

He meant to stop her. She could see it in his eyes, but he must have recognized her determination. He ended up helping her—to a point. He supported her until she sat upright on the floor, her legs spread and the blanket pooling at her waist. His grip had shifted to her upper arms as she moved, but now he released her and dropped back onto his heels. He crouched before her.

"Tell me what happened."

She had not stopped crying. Her face was wet, her eyes felt swollen, and her lips were thick and hot. She raised a hand to push the hair from her eyes, only to stare in stupefied shock at her arm. It was bare.

Well, of course it was bare! She was completely naked except for the blanket, and that could hardly be deemed clothing.

"I must get dressed," she managed. "Where are my clothes?" They were right beside her, easily within reach, but she could only glare at them while grief dragged at her thoughts.

"Charlotte . . ."

"Oh, sweet William," she whispered; and then fresh tears burned in her eyes. "I must go. Mother will need me."

"William is fine. He is sleeping."

She shook her head. It wobbled and felt five times too large.

"He is sleeping," Ken Jin repeated. Then he huffed with obvious frustration as he crawled to the loose board in the wall and dragged it to one side so she could see more clearly. "The house is dark. William sleeps."

"No," she whispered. "They don't know yet. He's d—" She couldn't say the word, but she would have to now. She would have to tell everyone. "He's dead."

"No, Miss Charlotte—"

"Damn it, Ken Jin, he's gone!" Then the reality of what she'd just bellowed hit her, and she all but collapsed into herself. Her hand flew to her mouth and she curled into her knees in an effort to stop the sobs. It didn't work, of course, and she ended up breathing wet wool as she gasped and strained for control.

She didn't know how long she stayed there, wrapped around her knees, but in time consciousness returned. It came in the form of a large hand that rested upon her back. Ken Jin, his hands gentle, quietly touched her. It was no attempt at a sexual caress, or even to gain her attention; he merely placed his hand upon her back and waited. In truth, it was very servantlike, a quiet presence available if needed, ignorable if unwanted.

Except Charlotte found she didn't want a servant just then. She wanted a person—a man, to be exact. She wanted Ken Jin. Without questioning the urge, she turned into his arms. He had no choice but to hold her. She knew that; and yet, this was her first real warmth since returning from . . . the other place. She relished it, especially as his hands found her back and she was enfolded in his arms.

"Tell me what you experienced," he said into her hair.

"William. Dead." She spoke into his shirt, only now noticing that the starch had long since wilted. What she felt was a fine, soft linen that was rapidly becoming sodden from her tears.

"You saw his body?"

"No." She felt renewed awe slip into her consciousness, but only barely. There was still too much grief to leave room for much else.

"Then what?" he pressed.

"An angel." She swallowed and forced herself to explain. "I saw William as an angel. I was in Heaven." She looked up, knowing how crazy she sounded, but she knew it was true. "I was in Heaven, and I spoke with my brother's spirit. I was brought there to speak to my brother one last time."

He did not answer, and she felt her grief overwhelm her once again. "Let us go see," he said.

She nodded. She would dress; then she would see to her family's needs.

Thankfully, Ken Jin helped her. She was still a little weak, and she wanted to appear excruciatingly correct. It wasn't guilt over what she'd been doing; this was out of respect for her brother. The least she could do when she found his body was to appear like a proper sister and not a tavern wench. Once she felt more composed, Ken Jin restored the room to order and together they walked silently through the back garden to the house, then up the servant staircase to the nursery. But then, she couldn't make herself step through the door.

"A Tigress only hides when stalking," Ken Jin murmured in her ear. "You are an Immor—" He swallowed, cutting himself off. "You have gone far, Miss Charlotte, further than anyone I know after a single night. Shall you abandon that? Shall you forsake the Tigress to once again become a rabbit?"

She turned to him, her heart beating painfully in her throat. "I've never understood half of what you say."

"And the other half?" he challenged. "What of the part you do comprehend?"

Charlotte sighed and put her hand against the nursery door. "That half is scary, Ken Jin." Then she pushed inside.

A maid sat dozing in a chair near a fire. The coals gave an infernal glow to the room, painting everything in tones of red and black. As Charlotte entered, the girl started, then rose quickly to her feet. Charlotte shook her head and gestured for her to remain seated. There would be plenty to do soon enough.

Her heart began to race as she walked to William's bedroom. Even through the doorway, she could see the dark lump of his body, still in death. Odd, how it took little effort for her to cross into his room, to kneel beside his bed, and to stroke his cooling brow. He was her brother, and she loved him. Indeed, she felt lost without him. What would she do with her days if not care for him? What would she do with her thoughts if not spend them in the endless search for ways to instruct him?

He stirred beneath her fingers. His eyes fluttered open to stare in bleary irritation. "Chary?" he asked.

She gasped, surprised enough to fall backward onto her bottom.

Her brother pushed up and rubbed his eyes. When he was finished with that, he scratched his groin and stared at her. She stared back, unable to reconcile her memory of William's angel with William alive in his bed. Had she been mistaken? But she had been so certain.

Huffing with the effort, her brother climbed out bed, dragging his blanket with him. He dropped down on his knees beside her and plopped his head in her lap, just as he'd done as a small boy. He snuggled close to her. He shifted and fidgeted until finally she did what he wanted; she wrapped her arms around him and dropped her chin on his forehead. The words came by rote, not because she willed them but because this was what she always said.

"Sweet dreams, sweet William. Sweet dreams, my sweet."

He smiled, though his eyes were closed. Moments later, his breathing had steadied and deepened. He was asleep. And he was alive.

She didn't understand. She'd seen his angel. She'd *touched* it. And yet . . . She looked up at Ken Jin. "He's alive."

"Yes."

"But I saw . . . I . . ." She straightened. "It wasn't a dream, Ken Jin. It was real. It felt so real . . ." Her voice trailed away as she looked down at her brother.

"I will go make some tea, Miss Charlotte," he said softly. "And when it is ready, I will return to help lift him back to bed. And then . . ." He paused until she looked up at him. His expression was firm as any tutor's to his student. "You will tell me everything that happened."

She nodded. What else could she do? Especially as William was so obviously warm and happy and very, very much alive in her lap.

Ken Jin despised English tea. It was a sterile brew with water strained through leaves and kept separate, as if knowing the source of one's food was terrible. In truth, it was very English in that every aspect was held apart from the others with no thought to the whole. Did they not realize that qi infused the leaves and therefore the water, but only when kept inside the teacup? Did they not know that a hint of flower or citrus, of ginger root or ginseng, brought body to the tea leaves and wholeness to the taste?

Of course not. They were barbarians, and they knew nothing of such things. But Ken Jin did, and yet he chose day after day, at all hours, to drink English tea. Why? Had he indeed become what his mother accused? Was he more barbarian than Han, more English than Chinese? Or was his fate more subtle than that? Was he doomed to spill all his skills upon the whites?

His family called him ill fortune; and yet whatever he touched for his white employers turned to gold. His Chinese lovers despised him, and yet white ladies sang his praises. Now, most damning of all, a white girl had taken his yang—carefully purified and stored—and with it, she had gone to Heaven. He had remained behind on the dirty shed floor.

How he hated his life! How he despised what he had become! And yet, what could he change? Would he choose Chinese poverty over English wealth? Would he want Chinese impotence over English debauchery?

No, a thousand times no! And yes, a thousand times yes.

His heart ached to be Chinese, but basic survival required him to be English. Was there no place he could simply be himself, neither Chinese nor white, neither rich nor poor, neither impotent nor debauched?

The answer was clear, as always. He longed for Heaven, where all souls were equal, where Immortals were revered. He strove for a fulfillment that could only be reached by the perfect combination of purified yin and yang. The Celestial Real was his destination, immortality his goal.

Except, Charlotte had just taken his yang. She had used it to go to Heaven in his place, and all his dedicated study for the last decade had led to nothing. She was launched; he was bereft. And now he had to go lift and carry her brother just as he fixed her tea and made her father money. He was a prop to the whites, his only power in servicing them.

Looking down at his still-wet pants in disgust, he resolved to burn them. He could ill afford to lose his best trousers, but he knew he'd never be able to look at them again without remembering his shame, without knowing he had accidentally poured years of refined energy into a white girl.

Abruptly pushing through the kitchen door, he abandoned the heating water in his haste to tear off his clothing. Moments later, he rushed back, this time in dry clothing, finished preparing the tea, and then climbed the stairs to assist Miss Charlotte. If fortune decreed he was nothing but a white man's aide, he would be the best aide the world over. Some piece of that fortune would eventually spill back to him and flow to his family. If nothing else, it would buy him a wife and put his name back on the family altar.

His knees creaked as he climbed the stairs. Indeed, a great deal of his body felt cold and stiff as he assisted with the large boy. It was the loss of yang, he knew, and he had trouble keeping his anger tucked away. But in the end, he did as he had to. The boy was settled, the tea was finished, and Miss Charlotte was seated before him at the downstairs dining table.

He stood beside her, his feet numb from the day's labors, while he watched her sip the tea he'd made. He knew she would talk. She often spoke to her servants as one would a family pet. Indeed, the maids gossiped that with Joanna away, Charlotte confessed her thoughts and feelings to the plant in her bedroom. All Ken Jin needed to do was become as still as her fern, and eventually he would hear all.

True enough, after a moment she blinked, glanced up at him, and spoke. "Sit down, Ken Jin, you're glaring."

He bowed slightly, using the opportunity to smooth out his expression. "My apologies, Miss Charlotte."

She stared at him, then frowned as he refilled her teacup. "Where's yours?"

He returned the pot to the sideboard. "My what, Miss Charlotte?"

"Your teacup," she snapped. Then she abruptly dug the heels of her hands into her eyes. "Lord, I'm tired. How do you do it, Ken Jin? You've been working all day and still you look . . ." She lifted a palm off her face to wave at him without actually seeing. "Like you."

He didn't know how to answer. She wasn't sounding at all like herself. But then, he supposed, that was only to be expected. After all, she had ascended to the Immortal Realm this day.

She abruptly lifted her head and frowned at him. "Ken Jin?"

He bowed. "Miss?"

"Talk with me."

He frowned, thinking back to her previous question. "I changed my clothes. The others were soiled."

She blinked, uncomprehending, so he explained further.

"That is how I look . . . like me."

She rolled her eyes. "Sit down. Get some tea. Talk with me."

He hesitated, uncertain how to proceed. "You are the one who needs to talk, Miss Charlotte. You must explain what happened."

She glared at him. "I know, but I'm not going to do it to a damned servant. Sit down. Get some tea. Lord," she moaned, "I wish Joanna was here."

He felt awkward settling into a chair across the table from her. Indeed, he had the strongest urge to deny her request and stand against the wall like a plant. But Miss Charlotte had always known her own mind, so if she thought she could talk better to a seated person, then he would sit.

He perched on the edge of the seat, his legs an even distance apart, his hands folded neatly before him. It was a pose he had often disdained as a boy, and now here he was—a full-grown man and a jade Dragon—perched like a child before a girl. Except, of course, Charlotte wasn't a girl. Barbarian or not, she was an ascended Immortal.

"Tell me what happened, Miss Charlotte," he said, his voice a whisper.

She raised her eyes to his, and he saw the sheen of tears sparkling there. "I don't know what happened, Ken Jin. I don't understand any of it. What did you see?"

"Nothing."

She blinked. "Nothing?"

He looked down and saw that his fingertips were white where his hands clenched. "You were ascending. I know that. I felt it." He would never forget that outrush of power. "Then . . . you left."

Her head tilted sideways, even as her whole body strained toward him. "Left?" she asked.

"Your body was still, your eyes closed. You appeared to

be sleeping, but so deeply that I knew your spirit was not within your body."

"Like I was dead."

He studied her. She was not looking at him anymore. Her gaze was trained on her right index finger as she traced the tiny handle of her English-style teacup.

"You were not dead. Your spirit was visiting the Immortal realm." His voice was rough and exhaustion pulled at him. Even his skin felt heavy. So he abruptly matched her position. He leaned forward, put both hands down on the white tablecloth, and peered into her haunted blue eyes. "What did you feel?"

"Light. As if I was filled with sunlight, and yet I was in a dark place. But it wasn't scary; it was beautiful. And there were other lights moving."

"The Chamber of a Thousand Swinging Lanterns. It is the antechamber to Heaven. It is immortal, holy, but only the beginning."

Her gaze leapt to his face. "There is more?"

"There is always more. You did not go farther? To a temple? A garden?" He tried to think of all the texts he had studied, all the descriptions of the Celestial Realm that were written down through the ages.

She shook her head. "There was nothing like that. Just the darkness and the swinging lights. One of them was William."

He studied her face. She appeared stunned and confused, but also radiant with the trailing ribbons of glory. When she spoke of her experience, he felt her power rise. Her skin flushed, her eyes sparkled, and his own body tingled just from being near her. Indeed, he wanted to draw back, to settle his hands into his lap again, but he could not bear to leave her energy. Her qi was so strong that his palms actually itched. He had to keep her talking. He had to see how much power she still held, but he dared not touch her for fear that she would draw out the last of his yang.

"I went closer to one of the swinging lights. I don't know how; I just did. And as I reached it, I knew it was William. His spirit. And he was so . . ." Her voice broke and she could not continue.

He could see that she fought tears, and he could not understand why. "He was a shining light?"

"He was *normal*." She bit her lip as if she fought her words, but they came out anyway. "He was smart and handsome and mature and . . . so perfect."

He frowned. "Are you sure—"

"It was William!"

He looked back down at his hands. Her power was buffeting him, pulsing against his fingers with a heat that warmed this cold, dark room. Then it faded, and he was left with the faint echo of a tingle that carried no heat.

"He wanted to talk to me. He had something to say." She sighed. "But I thought he was an angel. Which meant . . ."

"That William was dead?"

She nodded, her eyes searching his face. "How could his soul be in Heaven when he is still here on Earth?"

Ken Jin shook his head. "I do not know, Miss Charlotte."

She abruptly pushed up from the table to pace about the room. Her energy followed, spiking across his skin when she was near, fading to almost nothing when she moved away. Then she stopped just behind him, forcing him to turn to feel her radiance on his face.

"Don't lie to me, Ken Jin."

He blinked. "I am not lying."

"But you're not telling the whole truth, are you? You're being a servant again."

He blinked again. "I do not understand."

"But you do understand!" Her voice rose in accusation. "You see and hear everything, and you know what I'm talking about. You just won't explain."

Her radiance had grown, and so he stood to face her, to feel it against his entire body. Except, as he straightened, he realized he had a problem. His jade stalk had grown. Indeed, his dragon was thick and heavy against his trousers when he should not have had the yang to do anything. It was clearly her leftover glory affecting him. He needed to stay with her longer, perhaps reabsorb some of what he had lost.

"Ken Jin!"

His focus snapped back. "Miss?"

She flounced back into a chair, this time the one beside him. From there she simply stared at him. "I think we're well beyond the 'miss' stage, don't you?"

He frowned. Sometimes the English language could have extra meanings. Perhaps—

"Call me Charlotte. Not Miss Charlotte, not miss, just Charlotte. Or better yet, Char."

"Char?"

She grabbed his hand. He hadn't even realized she'd moved, but suddenly her warmth surrounded his wrist, her power penetrating through his arm, and his dragon reared up even farther. She drew him closer, back down into his seat, and he had no choice but to comply though his heart raced to understand this strange white woman. What did she want from him?

"I do not have your answers," he said. "You have ascended beyond my understanding."

"Damn it, Ken Jin!" she exploded, her hand tightening around his. *"Stop being a servant!"*

"But I am a servant!"

"Not anymore!" She threw his hand away. She exploded

out of her chair again, only to spin around as if searching for something to do, somewhere to go.

"I have never been to Heaven, Miss . . . Char. I have never even gone to the Antechamber as you did tonight. If the Tigress Shi Po were here, I would take you straight to her. I would have her counsel you, but she is in prison, locked up with her husband so that we cannot even see her." His voice deepened as he spoke those words, and he rushed to cover the pain he felt. "I do not know what you want me to do."

She turned back to him, her shoulders slumped in defeat. "You cannot tell me why my brother's spirit is both in Heaven and here on Earth?"

He shook his head.

"You have no idea at all?"

He hesitated, and she pounced. She rushed forward and dropped back into her seat, but only the closest edge of it. The rest of her was leaning into him, grabbing his hands, and peering into his eyes. "Tell me, Ken Jin. Tell me what you think."

He could not deny her, not with her qi pressing into every pore of his body. "Could that not be the explanation?" She frowned, so he rushed to explain. "Could that be the reason William is the way he is?"

"Slow?"

He nodded. "If part of his spirit is in Heaven and part . . ."

"Here in his body . . ."

"Such a split spirit would be incomplete in both places."

She blinked, and he watched comprehension flow through her body. Never one to remain still, she widened her eyes as her shoulders dropped and her spine straightened. Then her hips and feet shifted as well. "All we have to do is reunite them, then. We must get the rest of his spirit into his body, and he will be normal!"

Ken Jin didn't move. He didn't dare. Though the idea sounded logical, he felt a dissonance, as if they had a piece of the answer but not the whole. But Charlotte had no such restraint. She widened her feet, preparing to leap up again, then apparently changed her mind. Her hands tightened on his.

"How do we do it?" she asked. "Can I just bring his soul back and take it to my brother? Or does William have to do what I did—rejoin himself up there?" A shudder went through her. "No, we can't do that to William. I can't see him . . . well, I just can't do that with my brother." She frowned. "But if it's the only way . . ." She bit her lip. "But I can't."

"He cannot ascend," Ken Jin said. His voice was hard, which snapped her wandering attention back to him.

"He can't?"

Ken Jin shook his head. "I have studied for over a decade and have never once ascended. It takes a great deal of discipline and focus."

"But all I had to do was . . ." She trailed off, and her skin flushed a dark rose.

"It is different for women, and you had a great deal of help." All of his yang, in fact; but he did not say that aloud. "A man must withhold his seed for many years. He must cultivate his yang power through mediation and discipline." He stared hard at her, willing her to understand. "He must hold in his yang power, Miss Charlotte. He cannot release it."

Her eyes abruptly widened. "Ohhhh." Her voice trailed away. Thankfully, she had already been educated on the mechanics of a man's dragon. Indeed, young master William had lately been caught releasing his yang on a regular basis.

"Years?" she whispered. "No, he could never hold off that long." She abruptly frowned, looking down at him. "You changed your pants."

He pressed his lips together, but she had already guessed the truth. Nothing would stop her from saying it aloud now.

"You didn't hold off. I saw the wetness. You released your yang."

"Yes." His throat closed up after that one word.

"After years? How many years?"

He couldn't speak. He could only look down at their entwined hands as he tried to pull free.

"Ken Jin—"

"Fourteen years of practice. Eight years of purifying restraint."

"Eight years? You have held off for eight years, and then I manage it on my first night?" She suddenly gasped. "Oh my God, you *gave* it to me. All that yang—eight years' worth—you gave it to me. Oh God, Ken Jin, why? Why would you—"

"It was not a gift!"

But she would not be interrupted. "You said you would teach me, that you would make me stronger to fight my mother, so you gave me all that power. Eight years' worth. Oh, Ken Jin . . ." She stopped, and he could see that his words had finally reached her consciousness.

"It was not a gift?" she whispered.

He shook his head.

"But . . . I didn't steal it, Ken Jin. I wouldn't know how!"

He had no response to that. He didn't know what to think.

Bit by bit, he watched the light fade from her eyes.

"That's why you hate me now. That's why you're acting like a servant again. Because I took your yang." She bit her lip in dismay. "Eight years, Ken Jin. All gone."

He felt his jaw clench. He knew what had happened. Did she have to keep repeating it?

"But I didn't mean to. You understand that, don't you? You know it wasn't on purpose."

He didn't answer, even though he knew it was true. Other women might have stolen it, if they'd known how. Other women would have taken all he had and more, if he'd allowed them. But not Charlotte. She would never be so cruel.

"Ken Jin!"

"It doesn't matter how it left, my yang power is gone." He kept the anger from his voice. Still, his despair slipped through as he dropped his gaze away.

"But you can get it back, right? You can get more?"

He thought of the hours of meditation, the thousands of needles he had pressed into his flesh, and the accumulated yin from countless women. Could he do it again? Could he gather such power again?

"No," he whispered. The very thought left him weak and cold. Perhaps another day he would think differently. After a night's rest, perhaps he would have the strength to try again. But now, after a long and fruitless day, he felt too much a failure to even contemplate hope.

"Don't be ridiculous," she snapped. "Of course you can."

He felt a surge of humor at her forceful words. "You would instruct me, Miss Charlotte?"

"Yes, I would—Kenny."

His gaze narrowed at the Anglicization of his name. Why did she insist on this bizarre familiarity between them? She suddenly smiled at him, decision written in every line of her straightening body.

"You're tired. I'm tired. Neither of us is thinking straight."

True enough. But . . .

"We will sleep tonight and attack this problem again tomorrow. You'll feel differently, I'm sure. We'll renew your yang, and then we'll do things again. Both of us together. We'll both go to Heaven this time and talk to William

GET UP TO 4 FREE BOOKS!

You can have the best romance delivered to your door for less than what you'd pay in a bookstore or online. Sign up for one of our book clubs today, and we'll send you **FREE* BOOKS** just for trying it out...with no obligation to buy, ever!

HISTORICAL ROMANCE BOOK CLUB

Travel from the Scottish Highlands to the American West, the decadent ballrooms of Regency England to Viking ships. Your shipments will include authors such as CONNIE MASON, SANDRA HILL, CASSIE EDWARDS, JENNIFER ASHLEY, LEIGH GREENWOOD, and many, many more.

LOVE SPELL BOOK CLUB

Bring a little magic into your life with the romances of Love Spell—fun contemporaries, paranormals, time-travels, futuristics, and more. Your shipments will include authors such as LYNSAY SANDS, CJ BARRY, COLLEEN THOMPSON, NINA BANGS, MARJORIE LIU and more.

As a book club member you also receive the following special benefits:

- **30% OFF all orders through our website & telecenter!**
- **Exclusive access to special discounts!**
- **Convenient home delivery and 10 day examination period to return any books you don't want to keep.**

There is no minimum number of books to buy, and you may cancel membership at any time. See back to sign up!

*Please include $2.00 for shipping and handling.

YES! ☐

Sign me up for the **Historical Romance Book Club** and send my TWO FREE BOOKS! If I choose to stay in the club, I will pay only $8.50* each month, a savings of $5.48!

YES! ☐

Sign me up for the **Love Spell Book Club** and send my TWO FREE BOOKS! If I choose to stay in the club, I will pay only $8.50* each month, a savings of $5.48!

NAME: _____

ADDRESS: _____

_____

TELEPHONE: _____

E-MAIL: _____

☐ **I WANT TO PAY BY CREDIT CARD.**

☐ VISA   ☐ MasterCard.   ☐ DISCOVER

ACCOUNT #: _____

EXPIRATION DATE: _____

SIGNATURE: _____

Send this card along with $2.00 shipping & handling for each club you wish to join, to:

**Romance Book Clubs
20 Academy Street
Norwalk, CT 06850-4032**

Or fax (must include credit card information!) to: 610.995.9274.
You can also sign up online at www.dorchesterpub.com.

*Plus $2.00 for shipping. Offer open to residents of the U.S. and Canada only.
Canadian residents please call 1.800.481.9191 for pricing information.
If under 18, a parent or guardian must sign. Terms, prices and conditions subject to change. Subscription subject
to acceptance. Dorchester Publishing reserves the right to reject any order or cancel any subscription.

JOIN NOW!

there." She frowned. "He'll know how to do it, won't he? How to rejoin his body on Earth?"

Ken Jin opened his mouth to answer, but no words came forth. He had no idea what the angelic William knew or didn't know.

"Of course, he will," she continued. "He'll know, and he'll tell us, and then we'll do it. Then my brother will be normal, and everything will be just perfect."

"Miss Charlotte—" he began.

"Char!" she snapped, a flash of anger pushing through her determined cheer. "We are compatriots now, Kenny. Coconspirators, so to speak, with a joint mission."

He stared at her. He looked hard and waited while her false cheer withered. When he spoke, it was to a subdued but still determined Charlotte.

"My name is not Kenny, Miss Charlotte, and we are not compatriots in anything. My yang is gone, and I will not get it back again ever. I cannot free the Tigress or her husband from prison, and I will never ascend to Heaven with you or anyone else." With a supreme act of will, he pushed up from his chair, stepped away from her, and crossed to the door. "We are done, Miss Charlotte. It was an ill-conceived idea from the beginning, and I regret ever attempting this course."

"Ken Jin—"

"Good night, Miss Charlotte." He bowed to her, then turned to exit.

"Ken Jin!" she called, and he froze at her tone. He was too good a servant not to. He looked back at her.

"You are angry, and you have every right to be. You are tired and frustrated and . . . and I don't know what else, but I'm sure you're it." She huffed as she stood and folded her arms. "But you're completely off if you think we can stop. You're not just my servant, and I'm not just your employer. Not anymore."

167

"We are not lovers," he said, his voice harsh. "We are not friends. We are not even partners as a Tigress and Dragon should be. I taught, and you learned. I gave, and you soared." His voice caught, and his chest caved in slightly from the pain. "I am one man, Miss Charlotte, and a tired one at that. I can do no more."

She crossed the room to his side. He expected to see determination in her stride, or maybe fury at being denied. He saw compassion instead: a stunning softness in her eyes and a gentleness in her face. She stood before him, so close that she had to tilt her head upward to look into his eyes. He didn't want to be this close. He didn't want to shift his gaze down to her, but the wall prevented his retreat, and his dragon urged him forward.

"I see I have handled this very badly," Charlotte whispered. "I am sorry for that, Ken Jin. But it is all so new to me, and you have always been strong. I'd begun to think you could do anything."

He opened his mouth to speak, though he had no idea what to say. She didn't give him the chance; she pressed her finger to his lips.

"I don't want you to do anything, Ken Jin. It's my turn to do the doing." She frowned at her own awkward wording. "I've seen Joanna's scrolls. I will learn whatever needs to be done. I can—"

"No." He shook his head, dislodging her finger from his mouth, though the imprint lingered. "It is not so easy—"

She kissed him. She surged up onto her toes and pressed her mouth to his.

The sacred texts spoke at length about kissing. Over the years, he had studied a great deal about the art of lips and tongues. Miss Charlotte had obviously read none of them. Her approach was too rushed, her force too strong. She knew to open her mouth, but had no idea why. In the end he had to catch her about the waist to prevent them both from toppling over. And yet, as his arm wrapped around her, he felt her yin power sear his skin like a brand. Not even Little Pearl had such energy.

He meant to set her away from him. He meant to end this disaster with some dignity, and with the cold firmness he had developed for whenever a white woman became too demanding. He did not. Instead, he drew her lush body flush against him, surrounding himself with her power. And when it was not enough, he dove deeper. He pushed his tongue into her mouth.

He had read the sacred scrolls, so he knew how to kiss. He knew how to begin with a single brush of his tongue, how to coax with a wet caress, how to entice with a little suction. All these skills came into play, and she responded with such yin that his body grew hot and hard.

How wondrous was her mouth. How full were her breasts. How yielding were her thighs. He bent forward, arching her back over his arm. His tongue twisted with hers and her hands delved into his hair, drawing him down into her. Deeper. Fuller.

He took her breast in his free hand, shaping it to a tight point even through fabric and corset restraints. His knee pressed between her legs, working her skirt higher as she shifted and moaned. But mostly, he kissed her mouth. He plunged his tongue into her and tasted her yin. He drank of her unending power, using it to refill his own empty well.

She gave to him without complaint. She poured energy into him as a goddess into a supplicant. Her yin called to his yang, and his male energy surged forward to match her feminine power. And when he could drink no more—when he had to stop for breath—she pulled him back and gave him more.

How long did they merge in this manner? How long did

he plunge into her mouth and drink from her stores? He didn't know. He had no idea except that it went on until he was satisfied, though his thirst had been overwhelming. Their kiss continued until his spirit was refilled and his dragon stretched high and proud.

He straightened, pulling back from her in a daze. She was pressed against the wall, and her dress had become completely disheveled. How they had come there, he didn't know. He had only pulled back because he needed more attention to release her gown and untie her corset. But now that he had drawn away, now that his mind was focusing on more than just her mouth, he knew what he had done, what they were doing.

"Ken Jin?" Her voice was a throaty rasp that fired the yang in his blood.

"I cannot," he whispered. "I cannot practice more tonight. I haven't the strength." It had been an exhausting day and night. And yet, new yang pulsed hot and free in his blood. Could he practice again? Was she powerful enough for the two of them?

Impossible! And yet, his dragon swelled with her power.

She blinked, and her tiny tongue wet her lips. She lifted a hand to her hair, brushing it down where the wall had tangled it. "You're right, of course," she said on a weak laugh. "I don't know what I was thinking."

He straightened away from her; gave a groan of mixed pleasure and pain. How long had it been since his dragon throbbed as it did now? How long since he had felt drugged with the heady potion of yin and yang in combination?

A few hours, only. But before Charlotte? A long, long time.

"So your yang is returning?" she asked as she looked at his jutting dragon.

He nodded dumbly. The evidence thrust proudly between them.

She smiled, and he felt the radiance of the sun in the simple gesture. "Then it won't take eight years this time. We can replenish your yang quickly." She lifted her gaze to his. "I swear, Ken Jin, I will work very hard at this. Night and day, whenever we can. We will replace what was lost, and then we will try again."

He stared at her, his mouth slack. What could he say against such determination? How could he deny either of them the hope that it was true, that she could indeed restore the work of eight years? With her, his yang was more powerful, his energy more potent, the experience more heavenly than ever before. With a single kiss, she had given him the one thing he hadn't felt in so long: hope. With her, he believed he could be filled with qi, Heaven was attainable, and immortality was within reach. But only with her.

"My father said he had a business trip tomorrow."

"What?" Ken Jin blinked, his mind reeling as he tried to understand her words.

"My father is leaving on a business trip."

Ken Jin nodded. Mr. Wicks headed to Canton and his current favorite mistress.

"Mama intends to help with a prayer vigil tomorrow. I will convince her to stay at the mission. She'll be gone at least a day."

He knew this, too. He had to remember to check Mrs. Wicks's luggage in the morning. She often forgot her perfumed lotion when she went to the mission. Then she would send a messenger in the middle of the night to bring a bottle to her. There was also a special cushion for when she prayed.

"We must be sure to take William to the park again," Charlotte continued. "Add in a bath and a nap, and he will be occupied for hours!" She leaned forward, her eyes sparkling. "We can spend hours alone together!"

Except, Ken Jin had appointments all day on the docks.

A shipment for three of the Wicks tobacco shops was due in tomorrow. It wasn't the opium that made most of the Wicks money, but it was vital nonetheless. There would be customs taxes to pay, bills of lading to sort, and cargo to transport. Plus, Ken Jin suspected the dockmaster was extorting goods from the ship's captain, which often meant that the Wicks goods were just slightly underweight. Ken Jin meant to catch the man in the act and extort a refund for what had gone missing.

And on top of all that was the extra shipment of lace ordered under the Wicks name, but paid for from Ken Jin's own coffers. After taxes and transport, he ought to see a good profit from the transaction. But all of it had to be watched closely.

"Hours, Ken Jin. I can hardly wait for what we will study next." Charlotte's eyes sparkled with delight. "Could you finally show me how to play your jade flute, like in the pictures?"

Ken Jin didn't answer. Hope was such a fleeting thing, he realized. Now that their kiss was over, reality began to intrude. He recalled all the obstacles they faced, all the risks that remained. "Miss Charlotte, I cannot lose my job." All of his money was invested under her father's name. If he lost his job, he would lose everything.

"There's nothing to worry about," she promised happily. "Everything will work out perfectly." Then she pushed up on her toes. The movement was so quick, he had no time to stop her and no time to think. She pressed a kiss to his lips, then danced away. Then she gave a happy sashay and a hop before she dashed up the stairs to her bedroom.

He could have followed, of course. He could have run after her and told her this was impossible. No First Boy could partner with the daughter of the house, not if he expected to keep his life, much less his job. But he couldn't stop himself or her.

Nothing had changed, he suddenly realized. He had lost all his yang, and yet he would not leave this path. He toyed with his entire financial future, but he would not be swayed. She was his Tigress, and he was her Dragon. Despite the risks, they would see this through to the end.

Still, he could not shake a sense of doom. He turned away from the stairs to collect the cold teapot and cup, his thoughts caught in this intuition of disaster. Surely his fortune could not withstand this risk. Heaven would not bless practice with a white woman.

Then he understood. The answer came as a blinding flash through his mind. The grip of inspiration was so powerful, it dropped him to his knees. He had not been blessed this night. Heaven had not reversed his fortunes or kissed his spirit. Indeed, it was merely continuing his curse, but in the most cruel of ways.

Not only were his labors doomed to make the white men rich, but now his devotion was fated to make a white woman immortal. Just as his work had not brought money to his coffers, this practice would not take him to Heaven. His work would profit the white master, his yang the white daughter.

And for him? Nothing but toil and emptiness. And the cruel, taunting illusion of hope.

❧

(To Wen Ken Jin from one who serves the Imperial Dragon throne: Eunuch Wen Gao Jin.)

September 20, 1895
Kind Sir,
Have you visited Peking lately? The Wen Acu-

puncturist shop has fallen in reputation of late. The remaining son, Feng Jin, is the only acupuncturist left. He works night and day seeing patients, and has no time to mend the benches or clean the basins. His wife is a lazy shrew who gives no supervision to the many children that run screaming through the building. Newly arrived cousins give no relief, having descended like locusts at last New Year's holiday. All waited for them to leave, but the latest shift of the Yellow River has ruined their family. Their farm is destroyed and so they never left Peking. They remain underfoot, demanding food and giving no thought to the expense.

Even I am not immune to the Wen despair. Not two days ago, water flooded the eunuchs' room of sacred treasure. Every one of our manhoods suffered taint, but mine worst of all. I arrived barely in time to rescue it from the ravages of a rat. Such sorrow, such a devastating curse for a once prosperous family!

Wen Feng Jin searches desperately for an end to the family's misfortune. I visited the Empress Cixi's fortune-teller, who told me the curse could only be lifted by an act of great charity. It is the only hope for this once prosperous family.

There is a solution. The Wen family has a cousin who resides in the shop with them. Yan Wan is aptly named for her beauty and peaceful nature. Though not yet nine years old, she already has many admirers. Unfortunately, all fear that she will grow sick for lack of proper food and clothing.

If only a husband would apply for her. If she were betrothed, no one would look askance if the husband-to-be paid for her maintenance, and the health and growth of her entire family. Such a man would be prized above all for his charity. The two could be wed immediately upon her sixteenth birthday. Then, perhaps, the Wen family curse would lift. Indeed, I am sure Feng Jin would hire the greatest calligrapher in Peking to inscribe the man's name on the family altar.

Sincerely,
Eunuch Wen Gao Jin

June 17, 1895
To Wen patriarch Feng Jin,
    Please accept this humble gift as a token of the esteem I hold for Wen Jan Wan. Tales of her virtue and beauty have reached as far as Shanghai. I know she is of a young age, but such is her glory that I would be honored to bear the burden of her education and growth in anticipation of our joyous union.

In hope,
Wen Ken Jin

(Attached, two bolts of the finest Shanghai silk and two bolts of fine cotton. The first silk bolt is celebration red, with embroidered images of happiness and good luck such as would be worn on holidays. The second is a rich blue, the design of a thousand cranes soaring in the sky, to be worn on special occasions, but not during weddings or New Year's celebrations. The two cotton bolts show a variety of bird and flower designs as appropriate for daily use.)

The tongue is the sense organ of the fire element and the energetic extension of the heart. To exercise the tongue, bring the tip of the tongue in front of the upper teeth inside the lips. Circle the tongue down to the inside lower lip. Continue to circle in front of the teeth and inside the lips about thirty-six times and then switch directions.
Sexual Reflexology, Chia, Wei

Chapter Ten

The Tigress Shi Po had an excellent gardener. Charlotte looked about the front courtyard and allowed herself to relax into the beauty of the place. Ken Jin had brought her here two days earlier, but at the time, this entire front area had been in broken disarray. Now everything was in order. Beauty was restored, and peace reigned. If only her heart would stop racing, she could thoroughly enjoy it. Instead, she could only glare at the huge expanse of green and damn Ken Jin for disappearing on her.

Four days. Four days ago, he had left the house to work away from home. "Hide" was more like it. Why would he do that—especially when both her mother and father were out of the house? Charlotte didn't know. Men were unfathomable, and Chinese men were even more so. Whatever the reason, Ken Jin had been completely unavailable to her. So she was no closer to returning to Heaven, which meant she had made no progress on reuniting her brother with his full spirit. Where was the man? Didn't he want his yang restored? Wasn't that what all men lived for?

Left alone, she had tried to study the Tigress scrolls,

struggling with the strange characters, memorizing each and every picture, even trying to practice. Indeed, because of those exercises, her breasts had spent the last four days in achy fullness and her groin in a wet heat. But Ken Jin had not returned to her. He left early in the morning and returned long after she'd fallen into a frustrated, restless sleep.

She knew he had work to do. Apparently multiple shipments had arrived, and there was something about a corrupt dock person. She realized his work took a great deal of time. But he hadn't even answered the messages she'd placed carefully under his pillow. Indeed, if not for the instructions he'd left the staff, she would have wondered if he came home at all.

Then yesterday, she'd made the greatest sacrifice of all. She'd left the Tigress scrolls on his bed. When she'd woken this morning, she'd found a present on her pillow—a bottle of Ken Jin's oil and a razor. Thinking he meant to come to her today to assist her in the task, she had dressed with special care. But when she'd descended the stairs, she'd learned that he was gone and would return before nightfall.

That was the last straw. If he would not teach her, she would have to find direction elsewhere. Moments later, she'd changed into her Chinese clothes. She'd covered her head in a coolie hat, grabbed an inordinate amount of Chinese money, and set off for Chinese Shanghai. Thank God she and Joanna had done this enough that it wasn't a problem. She'd left notice with the staff where she was going. If Ken Jin wanted to find her, he could.

A short hour later, a rickshaw had deposited her in front of the Tigress school and now she paced about the immaculate front courtyard waiting for Little Pearl. What she hoped to gain wasn't exactly clear in her mind. Information, mostly, anything that would help her understand her experience. She couldn't stop thinking about that night.

From Ken Jin's caresses, to the Antechamber, to Heaven, to William's angel and Ken Jin's kisses—it was all too much to understand. She needed someone to talk to, someone who understood what had happened, what was to come, and what it all meant.

"And what does Ken Jin's newest pet want with me?" drawled a familiar voice in Shanghai dialect.

Charlotte spun around, startled once again not only by Little Pearl's obvious acrimony, but by the woman's overwhelming beauty. "Teach me how to stimulate Ken Jin's yang." She spoke without thought, because Little Pearl had demanded an answer. But as she heard her own Chinese words, Charlotte gasped and slapped her hands over her mouth. This was not at all how she'd intended to approach this woman.

Little Pearl's lip curled in disgust. "So, he has thrown you over for someone else and you want him back."

"No, of course not!" Charlotte snapped. Then she felt her face heat in shame. The fastest way to reveal a lie was to vehemently deny it. "I mean . . ." She bit her lip. She didn't know what she meant because, of course, Little Pearl had voiced exactly what she feared: that Ken Jin was disgusted by her, that he loathed her forward ways and had gone looking for a more virtuous woman.

"Go home, ghost girl," Little Pearl growled. "I have no time for Ken Jin's games."

"This isn't a game!" Charlotte cried, but Little Pearl didn't respond. She was already walking away, her tiny steps covering ground with alarming speed. Charlotte rushed after her. "He has been teaching me. I . . . I have been doing exercises."

Nothing. Little Pearl reached the door and pulled it open.

"I have gone to the Chamber. The one with swinging lights."

Little Pearl stopped, her hand on the open door. She turned, and her eyes narrowed. "I do not believe you."

Charlotte reared back and her hands clenched into fists. "I have been there."

"Describe it."

Charlotte hesitated. How to describe the indescribable? "It was wonderful: dark and scary. There was a song, but it was velvety and quiet. I was terrified, and I met my brother." She raised her hands in confusion. She knew she wasn't making sense, but then again, wasn't that why she was here—to try to understand? "It was terribly confusing. I will do anything to go back."

Little Pearl didn't speak, and dismay chilled Charlotte's belly. Clearly this woman didn't understand, or if she did, she had no desire to help a ghost woman. Charlotte sighed. Why were best friends so hard to find? Very well, she would just have to find another way. She lowered her head in a respectful bow. "My apologies for inconveniencing you. I can see that there are no answers for me here." Then she turned and headed for the street.

"Come inside."

Charlotte was halfway through the courtyard before she heard Little Pearl's words, repeated with some force.

"Ghost woman! Come inside!"

Charlotte barely understood the meaning at first. Looking back over her shoulder, she saw Little Pearl inside a fully open doorway. The woman's head was lowered, her hand turned palm-side up as she gestured to the interior. It was a formal sign of welcome.

Charlotte didn't trust it. No one changed that radically, that fast. But she was so desperate to discuss her experiences with someone else—anyone else—that she quickly crossed back to the woman.

"Please to follow me," Little Pearl said in awkward English.

"I speak Shanghai dialect quite comfortably," Charlotte replied in that language. Indeed, they had been talking in Chinese, so why the woman suddenly wished to change to English was beyond her. But there was no time to discuss more, as Little Pearl led her into the compound.

They moved quickly through the reception hallway, past papered windows and elegant black lacquered furniture. Then they entered the inner garden, and Charlotte glimpsed crystal ponds and ornamental shrubs. A caged songbird dangled from a gingko tree above a very old turtle hidden inside its shell.

"This is stunning," Charlotte breathed. But as she slowed her steps, Little Pearl grabbed her arm. The woman had a tiny hand with long fingernails, and gripped with surprising strength.

"Please to walk fast." English again, in a terrible accent.

Charlotte speeded up. "Where are we going?" she asked in Chinese.

No answer. In fact, the woman didn't speak again until they made it to a building in the very back of the inner courtyard. Pushing open a door to a darkened interior, she wrinkled her nose, clearly sniffing the air before nodding in satisfaction.

"Please to enter."

Charlotte slowed, then eventually stopped. She couldn't see a single thing inside that dark building. Who knew what lurked there? The woman could have henchmen in there ready to lock her in chains before selling her into white slavery. Such things did happen. So she folded her arms across her chest. "I have no wish to offend," she said in her most polite Chinese, "but I do not have much time."

"You, you! Come!" Little Pearl abruptly cried in Chinese. It took Charlotte a moment to realize the comment wasn't addressed to her, but to a male servant crossing the courtyard. At Little Pearl's call, the man abruptly changed direction and rushed over.

He bowed deeply. "How may I serve, Tigress Pearl?"

"Bring candles, tea, cakes. We have a guest." She gestured to Charlotte, and then she clapped her tiny hands. "Immediately!"

The man bowed and ran off. Little Pearl frowned at him, then gestured to a different building. "We wait here," she said in English. Then she half led, half pulled Charlotte to a sitting room in the same building, but with a separate entrance. This room, however, had two large windows over elaborate wood designs. They were papered, to prevent flies, but at least some light came through to illuminate a minimal sitting room with a low couch, fragrant cushions, and a serving table.

"Please to sit," Little Pearl said as she firmly shut the door behind them.

Charlotte complied, still feeling uneasy but reassuring herself that now they could speak. "Can you explain to me," she asked in Shanghai dialect, "exactly what is taught in this school?"

Little Pearl shook her head. "*Aie, aie!* Too hard!" Clearly the woman would not budge from her broken English. Perhaps she thought it would be rude to speak to a guest in anything other than the guest's native tongue, even though her command of English was tenuous at best.

Charlotte sighed and pressed on in Chinese. Eventually, she prayed, the woman would see how fluent Charlotte was and give in to simple practicality. They obviously could not carry on a substantial conversation in English.

"I have studied the scrolls, but I cannot read Chinese well," she said, flushing. Truthfully, she couldn't read it at all. "But I understood the pictures. Indeed, they are quite detailed." She stared at the suddenly pale Little Pearl. "Is that what you teach here? The exercises shown on those scrolls?"

"What pictures?" the woman said in English. "Show me!"

Charlotte shook her head. "I don't have them with me. They are at home in a safe place."

"Not for you!" Little Pearl snapped. Then she descended into a long muttered curse that likened Ken Jin to a diseased dog. Truly, it was quite alarming. Charlotte would have gotten up to leave, except right then the servant returned with tea and sticky rice cakes enfolded in dark bamboo leaves.

"*Aie aie!*" cried Little Pearl to the servant. "No good for our guest! She is Eeenglish!" She drew out the last word with a sneer. "Take it away!"

"No, no!" cried Charlotte, feeling bad for the shamed servant. "No, I love sticky rice. This is fine. Truly, don't take it away."

The man started, his eyes huge as he realized she spoke Chinese. Charlotte smiled, then quickly grabbed chopsticks and plate, deftly plucking up the delicacy and flipping open the leaves. Sickly sweet steam rose from the patty, but Charlotte ignored it. In truth, this was not her favorite food, but she had no wish to prolong her visit. She certainly didn't want to sit while the kitchen struggled to find English food for her.

Both Little Pearl and the servant continued to stare as she ate small bites of the rice. "Ken Jin teach you this?" Little Pearl asked in English.

Charlotte frowned and shook her head. "How to use chopsticks? No, no. My best friend taught me. We used to have tea parties and teach our dolls how to use them, too."

The servant goggled as if he had never heard of anything so strange. Little Pearl, too, seemed stunned, but then she busied herself by dropping tea leaves into the two teacups.

There were a variety of different dried leaves on the tray, each in its own little china container. Charlotte had no understanding of any of them, but Little Pearl obviously did. She was quick as she selected the exact brew—different leaves for each of them—then poured hot water into both cups.

It wasn't what Charlotte was used to. Who brewed tea in the cups and left the leaves swirling in the water? The Chinese, obviously, so she smiled in false appreciation. When in Rome, and all that.

So when Little Pearl handed her the cup, urging her to drink, Charlotte was true to her upbringing; she sipped whenever Little Pearl sipped, drank whenever Little Pearl drank. And before long, two cups of the stuff were gone, and the sticky rice as well. It was frustrating, really. Whenever she asked a question, Little Pearl's answer was to urge her to take more food. Even the blandest inquiry was deflected into the niceties of afternoon tea. Indeed, Charlotte was disgusted to realize that, despite the woman's sudden friendliness, Little Pearl would still not give up any information. And so, Charlotte set down her chopsticks with a hard click.

"This has been a lovely meal, Little Pearl, and I thank you, but I came here with questions. I need . . ." She swallowed, startled to realize how hot her tongue felt. The food had been spicier than she thought. "I want to learn."

Little Pearl looked hard at her. Charlotte returned the look in equal measure. Indeed, she felt a fire building within her, a heat that fueled her anger. She spoke harshly, though the words were difficult to form with a mouth suddenly on fire.

"You said you had no time for Ken Jin's games. I have little time for yours. Will you teach me or not?" Charlotte flushed in embarrassment. She had been raised to be more polite, but it was unbearably hot in here, and she was beginning to sweat. Her temper had been frayed to begin with, and now she barely kept it contained. Arching her eyebrow, Charlotte glared at her hostess. "Well?"

"Very well," Little Pearl said in surprisingly smooth English. "The room is prepared. We will learn what you experienced now."

Charlotte blinked. She had been hearing noise from the other room for some time: bumps and shuffles from what sounded like an army of servants. But all was quiet now. So at Little Pearl's prompting, Charlotte stood, feeling a flash fire of heat skate across her skin. She frowned and took a step, then gasped at the feel of her trousers brushing against her suddenly raw thighs. Good Lord, how had the day turned so beastly hot? Thank goodness she was wearing a Chinese tunic rather than her own corset and gown; all that English fabric would be unbearable! Meanwhile, she had to follow Little Pearl back outside and then around the corner to the first door, the one that led to a darkened, henchman-containing interior.

"Why can't we just talk where we were?" Charlotte asked.

Little Pearl shook her head. "That room for talk; this room for practice." And with that, she opened the door onto a strangely small chamber.

It was dark inside, though several candles had been lit and an exotic scent perfumed the air. Still, there was enough light to see heavy tapestries hanging from all four walls. In the center of the room a knee-high table doubled as a bed. It was covered with a coarse sheet and cushioned by several pillows.

"Please to remove clothing and lie down."

The air was thick with perfume, but the scent wasn't cloying. It tingled in Charlotte's nostrils and brought warmth to her lungs. "What is that scent?" she asked, stepping to the door.

"Perfume. Please to remove clothing and lie down."

"Speak in Chinese, damn it! Your English is atrocious!"

Little Pearl reared back in shock. Charlotte chided herself. What was the matter with her? She was sweating, for God's sake, and a vague discomfort crawled beneath her skin, making her short and irritable.

"I will speak better," Little Pearl returned smoothly, still in English. Then she gripped Charlotte's arm and pulled her inside the room.

Charlotte rolled her eyes. "I'm not going to undress." The heat in her body was increasing, and she leaned her thigh against the low table to stabilize herself. It didn't really help, but she appreciated the hard pressure. "I came to talk to you about Ken Jin. About what's happening—"

Little Pearl slashed her hand sideways. "Ken Jin is unimportant. I wish to see your Heaven."

Charlotte frowned as she pushed a drooping lank of hair out of her eyes. "You can't see my Heaven. I was only there for a moment, and it wasn't even Heaven. Ken Jin said it was the antechamber. It was all dark and had lights." Meanwhile the sunlight disappeared as the door slipped shut.

Little Pearl stepped closer. There was little space to maneuver, and Charlotte found herself backing up so that both her thighs pressed against the table. "We will repeat the experience," the Chinese woman said. Then she reached out and unfastened two of the frogs along Charlotte's right shoulder.

Charlotte reared back, trying to avoid Little Pearl's grasping hands, but the movement unbalanced her. With her legs pressed hard against the table, she ended up falling backward. She managed to catch herself with her hands, but even so, the candle flames danced for a moment. Then, before she could reorient herself, she felt her tunic slip open. Little Pearl had it completely unfastened and was now pulling it away. And as Charlotte sat in her coolie pants and shift, the woman's tiny hands began tugging at those, too.

The disrobing was irritating enough, but what truly shocked Charlotte was the tingling heat that flew across her skin whenever anything touched her. Fingertips, fabric, even the wondrous kiss of air—all of it created waves of heat that rolled at random across her body. She hadn't felt anything like it since a desperate illness as a child. She'd had a terribly high fever then, and her parents had feared for her life. She felt like that now, except there was no coughing, no aching pain, just waves of dry heat as if she were becoming the sun.

How was it that her shift had been removed? But oh, the breath of air on her breasts was lovely.

She took a deep breath and focused. This had to stop. With great effort, she reached down and grabbed Little Pearl's wrists. The woman was tugging at her trousers with single-minded determination, but Charlotte's hands were larger and stronger.

"Stop," she said rather loudly. Indeed, she winced as the word echoed in her head.

Little Pearl looked up in surprise. "You wanted answers, yes?"

"Not this way. Ken Jin . . . Ken Jin is my partner."

Little Pearl shook her head. "Not anymore. *I* will taste your yin."

Charlotte frowned, not understanding. "You? But . . . but you're a girl."

"*Shr.* Yes. I am your partner now."

"No!" Charlotte shoved hard, throwing the woman away from her. Little Pearl stumbled backward. She would have fallen completely, except she managed to grab a huge fistful of a tapestry to keep herself upright.

Meanwhile, Charlotte tried to pull on her shift. She had

no interest in a female partner. The very thought disgusted her. And even if she were interested, she certainly would not choose this arrogant, pushy shrew. How appalling to realize she had actually sought out Little Pearl, that she had struggled against her better judgment to be polite to this woman. To . . .

Why could she not get her shift on? Her hands were shaking, and her body was on fire. And her legs were not moving properly. Her legs were . . .

Her legs were *bound?*

She stared dumbfounded as two rather large women pulled leather straps around her ankles. Charlotte did not know these women, didn't know where they had come from, but they were clearly working under Little Pearl's direction.

"Stop that!" Charlotte bellowed. "Release me!" Then she began to kick, but it was too late. While she had been struggling with her shift, her ankles had been restrained. And now those other ladies were walking up the table. Their hands caressed her legs despite everything Charlotte did to push them away.

"Be at peace, little pet," they murmured in Chinese. They spoke as if she were bad-tempered dog. "Peace, peace. You will like it."

"I will not!" she cried, but they weren't listening. And with their hands—plus Little Pearl's—on her shoulders, there was little she could do to stop them. She fought. She pushed. She shoved. She screamed and cried, but they were stronger than she, and her legs were bound. Her head banged down hard against the cushion, and her arms were spread wide as straps were latched around her wrists. She clawed at the women. She even bit one of them, but the end was inevitable.

Her hands were tied above her head, her shift was torn away, and they were touching her naked breasts. It was clearly meant as a soothing stroke, one to relax a terrified animal. Truthfully, it worked to some extent. There was nothing threatening in their touch, and yet the sense of violation was so overwhelming that Charlotte could only scream until there were no more screams in her, only sobs. And even then, she pleaded, "Stop. Please, stop."

Eventually, they did. Their hands melted away, and the two women slipped backward into the darkness. Charlotte tried to see where they went, but Little Pearl moved closer. She stepped up to the side of the bed to look down at her victim, for that's what Charlotte was: a helpless, restrained, furious victim.

"Why are you doing this?" Charlotte demanded.

"How did get our scrolls? Did Ken Jin give them to you?"

It took a moment for Charlotte to understand the questions. The words seemed to crackle and hiss in her head.

"Did you steal them from Ken Jin?" Little Pearl continued. "Is that why he won't see you anymore?"

"What? No! Untie me!"

"Is that how you learned about the Chamber of a Thousand Swinging Lanterns? From the scrolls you stole?"

"I didn't steal anything!"

Little Pearl nodded, as if Charlotte had just confirmed her suspicions. "Then Ken Jin gave them to you." She sighed. "He is more lost than I thought."

"He did no such thing!"

"Then, he didn't practice with you? He didn't act as your partner?"

"What? No. Yes. I mean . . ." Charlotte had been straining forward, lifting her head as much as possible in this position, but she was exhausted. Her shoulders were aching and her ankles were slick with sweat. She just wanted this to be over. Whatever was to happen, she wanted it done. "What do you want?"

"Our scrolls."

"They're not yours. They're Joanna's." She didn't know why she was arguing. Joanna would be the first to give them over if she knew the trouble they'd caused.

"Joanna Crane's?" Little Pearl's voice was sharp enough to make Charlotte lift her head again.

"Yes. I don't know how she got them, but they are hers."

Little Pearl curled her lip in disgust. "You will return them to me."

"Untie me, and I'll go get them."

The horrible woman didn't move. "That is how you know about Heaven's antechamber? Because you read it in the scrolls?"

Charlotte felt tears sting her eyes. "Fine. Yes. Whatever."

"Where did Joanna Crane get these scrolls?"

Charlotte actually growled in frustration. It was a mean, animalistic sound, but such was her frustration that she could not contain it. "I don't know!" she bellowed. "Ask Joanna!"

"The monk and his pet have disappeared. The Tigress and her husband are imprisoned. Mobs and soldiers stomp through my door. And now you come to me asking about the Chamber of Swinging Lanterns. How do you know of this place?"

Charlotte kicked her feet. It was a useless gesture; the straps bit into her flesh and she screamed at the pain. The leather held fast.

"How do you know?" Little Pearl repeated, this time in Chinese.

"I already told you! I went there. I saw my brother. I went there." She was crying now, her words as much chanted as spoken. Then she fell silent. She realized that Little Pearl was looking at her as a person would look at a strange toy or an unfathomable animal. In fact, William had used the same expression the first time he'd seen a picture of an Australian platypus.

"What do you want?" Charlotte asked again.

"I do not believe you," Little Pearl answered.

Charlotte stared up at the dark ceiling. She couldn't see it. She couldn't see much of anything except Little Pearl, and Charlotte had no interest in staring at the woman. "I cannot prove I was there," she finally said. "I'm not sure I believe it myself. Maybe I was dreaming." Except she hadn't been. It *was* real. Heaven was real. Everything was very, very real.

"I can prove it," Little Pearl said, her voice dark and heavy.

Charlotte strained upward. She couldn't possibly have heard correctly. "You can prove it?"

Little Pearl nodded.

"So, do it already!"

Her tormentor sighed. It was a sound that came from deep within, as if her soul were shrinking into the tiniest of little balls. "To do so, I will have to taste you." Her voice was heavy with disgust.

Charlotte stared. She couldn't possibly mean . . . She couldn't intend . . .

Little Pearl reached into a pocket and pulled out a long, slender knife. "I will remove your pants now."

"What? Wait! No!" Charlotte was babbling in horror. She was trying to squirm away, to slip out of her bonds, anything. But she was caught fast. And despite the woman's obvious disgust, Little Pearl was quite resolved. The cold tip of her knife pressed against Charlotte's belly.

The door burst open. It slammed against the wall with an explosion of power as Ken Jen rushed in. Charlotte didn't even have time to cry out as his gaze swept the scene. He didn't pause, simply rushed over, grabbed Little Pearl's wrist, and wrenched it up and away from Charlotte's thighs. Unfortunately, the knife was already inside Charlotte's trousers and slit the fabric.

Little Pearl grunted as she fought, but Ken Jin was obviously furious. With a quick twist of his wrist, he bent her hand down. Her fingers loosened, but did not release the knife, so he slapped it away with his other hand. The blade clattered against the floor and skittered underneath a tapestry, which abruptly gasped and fluttered with the sound of shuffling feet.

Charlotte lifted her gaze to the heavy drapes, horror creeping over her as she realized the truth. There were people behind those tapestries. She spun her head around. She was surrounded on all sides by the damn things. Which meant . . .

"Get out!" Ken Jin bellowed. And for emphasis, he took two huge fistfuls of tapestry and yanked, tearing the heavy fabric away. Startled women stared back at him. Two. Three. Five. How many had been watching? "Get out!" he bellowed again, and the women rushed for the door.

Seven? More and more filed out while Ken Jin turned to Charlotte. He quickly released the straps on her right ankle, cursing in dark tones as he worked.

"Blood," he spat as he shifted to her other ankle. He kept working but he glared at Little Pearl. "Are you insane? Have you lost all sense of reality?"

"I did what was necessary," answered Little Pearl, her voice devoid of all emotion.

"Do you hate me so much?"

"Ha!" Little Pearl's laugh chilled the air. "You can ask me that? You, who have perverted our teaching to your own lascivious ends. You, who have debauched and debased all of us with your behavior. Yes, I hate you! I hate everything you do!"

He released her other ankle, and Charlotte quickly drew her legs together. Ken Jin shoved Little Pearl out of the way as he stalked to her wrist bindings. "My perversions? I'm not the one taking a knife to a helpless woman."

"She's a barbarian animal! Your pet!"

He stilled. Charlotte couldn't see him because he stood behind her head, but she felt his hand against hers as he released the straps. Except, he wasn't releasing anything. He was frozen in place, and when he spoke, his voice was low and filled with deep sadness. "I forget that I once thought like you, that people still believe such stupidity." He shifted and freed Charlotte's right arm. She moved it immediately, gritting her teeth against the needles of pain that burned through her fingertips.

Little Pearl curled her lip. "*I* do not consort with animals. The barbarians are stupid beasts and deserve what they get!"

Ken Jin was working on the last binding. His fingers worked quickly, but Charlotte could still feel the anger boiling inside him. His voice was hard. "They are not animals, Little Pearl. And even if they were, would you tie up your dog like this? Would you bring your students to watch while you did it?"

"I have to know!" Little Pearl cried. "I have to understand!"

"I told her about Heaven," Charlotte interrupted.

Ken Jin turned to Charlotte, his expression unreadable in the dark. Then he looked back at Little Pearl. "She went to the Chamber of a Thousand Swinging Lanterns," he confirmed. "I was there. I saw."

With a scream of fury, Little Pearl launched herself at Ken Jin. Her fingers were curled like claws, and her face contorted with such rage that she did not even look human. Ken Jin barely flinched. He caught her easily, gripping her forearms and holding her still until her scream ended on a gasp. She fought him. She kicked and screeched and even tried to bite him, but he spun her around, pinning her against the wall with his body. And when she had to stop screeching to breathe, when she finally grew silent as she dragged air into her lungs, only then did Ken Jin speak.

"Shi Po is gone, Little Pearl. I have begged and bribed and railed, but General Kang will not give her up. That means you lead the temple now."

Little Pearl's breath released in an angry hiss.

"Think hard," he continued. "Think hard what your actions do to the temple, to all of us." He pushed away from her, disgust in every word. "You shame us all."

She crumpled without his support. There were no tears, just a complete loss of strength. She fell to her knees on top of the ruined tapestry, her shoulders quivering with some great emotion. Staring at her, Charlotte could hardly believe this was the same woman who had tormented her so cruelly.

"Can you walk?" Ken Jin asked.

Charlotte blinked. He was beside her, gently easing her shift over her head. She looked at him, her mind still reeling from all that had happened.

"The fire will ease soon," he continued. "How much of her tea did you drink?"

Fire? All too soon she remembered the burning on her skin, the churning heat just below the surface. It was still there, flaring to life as she pulled on her clothing, weakening her legs as she tugged on her tunic. "I don't know," she finally managed. "But it's getting better," she lied.

He looked hard at her face, his gaze dropping to her taut nipples. She could tell he didn't believe her, so she tucked her arms close and pretended she was cold. "We will go to my rooms nearby," he said. "I have some herbs that will help."

She nodded and allowed him to help her off the bed. He didn't even look at Little Pearl as they moved toward the door. But Charlotte did. "What happens now?" she asked.

The woman hadn't moved; she just sat in the middle of the torn tapestry and stared at the floor.

"We all choose our own paths according to our natures. Hers is a cruel nature filled with much anger. It makes her way very difficult." As he spoke, he led them out the door, only to pull up short as a large white man with dark reddish hair came running across the compound.

Ken Jin paused, a frown on his face. "Captain Jonas? I am pleased to see you. I had heard things about a mob and soldiers." He leaned forward. "Are you well?"

The man paused, a hand pressed to his side as he gasped for breath. Truly, he did not look so good, but he nodded. "Well enough," he grunted. Then his eyes slid past them to the dark room. "Little Pearl?"

Charlotte could feel Ken Jin stiffen. "She has a poisoned heart. I will not speak with her . . ." His voice trailed away as the captain pushed past them, obviously not listening as he rushed inside. Charlotte gasped as the man brushed her arm, sending sparks of reaction through her body.

"You should go," the man called from the interior. "It is not safe here."

"This way," Ken Jin said as he gently guided her away. She wanted to ask about the large captain. She noticed other things, too: White sailors slipped past upper-story windows, a little girl watched from behind an ornamental bush. Clearly something very strange was happening at the Tigress school. But Charlotte had no chance to ask as Ken Jin took an unexpected turn and rushed her out a side gate to where his horse waited.

He mounted first, then drew her up into his lap. She clenched her teeth as he adjusted her. It took all her strength to tolerate the brush of fabric across her skin, the press of his body, the rhythm of the horse as they moved through the streets. All those sensations contributed to a frightening hunger that ate at her control. She wanted to be naked. She wanted to be stroked. She wanted to move and scream and convulse all at once.

Ken Jin's arm wrapped around her belly, pulling her tight against him. It felt wonderful—the hard press of bone, the heated musk that filled her nostrils and fogged her mind—and yet it was too little and too much. She wanted to scream with frustration at her own body grown alien.

"Try to hold still," he said against her neck, and she arched back just to press harder against him.

"I can't control it," she confessed.

"I know," he answered. "Only a few streets more. Hold on until then."

"Then what?" she gasped. She had not thought these feelings could get worse. She had not thought the sensation of a hard pommel against her flesh could make her insane. She could not think, she could only grit her teeth and endure. And want. And ache.

"Then I will be able to help you."

❧

June 21, 1893
Honored Sir, Wen Ken Jin:

We are pleased to entertain your suit for Wen Jan Wan. Indeed, upon hearing of your suit, she gifted me with one of her most rare smiles.

Alas, the mood did not last. So great is the purity of her heart and so tender her spirit that she weeps at the pitiful state of her family. How can she wear finery when her cousins wear rags? How can she dine on pork and thousand-year-old eggs, when her parents share one bowl of rice?

If such a state continues, I fear the goodness

*within her will force her to refuse your suit. Such
a burden it is to raise a virtuous daughter.*

> *In grave fear,*
> *Wen Feng Jin*

June 30, 1893
To the Wen patriarch, honored Wen Feng Jin:
    *Please accept this small token of my esteem. I
have such happiness in my heart from my be-
trothal that I cannot resist sharing my bounty with
others.*

> *With much joy,*
> *Wen Ken Jin*

*(Attached, three sacks of rice, three of flour, three
bolts of silk, and three lacquered chests, each
containing three ingots of gold.)*

Heavenly Pond (P1):
Location: One thumb-width outside the nipple
Benefits: Holding this point nurtures the spirit in the heart, increases sexual intimacy and cultivates the expression of love.
Acupressure for Lovers, Michael Reed Gach, Ph.D.

Chapter Eleven

The first thing she would do was strip naked. The heat was unbearable. Her shift chafed, and her drawers were wet with . . . They were wet. Charlotte clamped her jaw shut rather than release a moan of frustration.

"Why did you go there?" Ken Jin's voice started a shiver in her belly—not strong enough to be satisfying, and yet delicious nonetheless. She closed her eyes to better appreciate the sensation.

"Charlotte," he repeated, louder this time. "Why did you go to the school?"

The low tremor continued, but she could tell Ken Jin would insist on an answer. She sighed. "I wanted to understand."

"What?"

She'd known he would ask that, but she was plying for time. She needed to understand herself before she tried to explain it to him. "Why does Little Pearl hate you so much?"

They arrived at a stable that served Ken Jin's nearby apartments. He dismounted and quickly tossed the reins and a coin to a stable boy. Then he turned and grabbed her waist to lift her down. She went willingly, anxious to get inside, happy to experience his large hands around her waist and the slide of his body against hers as she leaned into him.

"Keep your head down," he said.

She knew without being told. It was broad daylight, and she had no wish to be seen alone with him in such a manner. The gossip could be easily turned aside, of course; he was her family's First Boy and well known as her companion on a variety of shopping trips. Plus, they were in that rare area of Shanghai that housed both Chinese and white. But this was no marketplace, so the fewer people who saw her, the better.

He clearly understood the danger, because he grabbed a cloak off a nearby peg and surrounded her with it. The fabric was coarse and smelled of horse, but it covered her from head to toe. She held the hood close to her face for all that it made her sneeze and her skin itch, and soon they were walking quickly down the back alley and to a block-like building.

"Third floor," he said as he pushed her inside.

She went quickly, her teeth clenched against the tingles that sparked all over her body as she moved. No one was about as they climbed the stairs, so she threw off her hood and began unfastening the cloak. He had the door open and pushed her inside before she had it completely off. Then she was finally able to strip off the heaviest of her clothing. Her hands were shaking, but no less efficient as she dropped cloak and tunic with desperate speed. Ken Jin shut and locked the door, then crossed to a nearby table. Tepid water splashed into two teacups as she released her sweaty hair from its pins and shook it out.

"Drink," he ordered.

Charlotte swallowed it without tasting, then waited impatiently as he passed her the second cup. When had she gotten so thirsty? And why was it still so hot?

He opened a window—the only one in the flat—and a soft breeze stirred the air. But it wasn't enough, so she set down her empty teacup and stripped off her shift. He had already seen everything; modesty now would be ridiculous.

She sighed in delight as a cool breeze caressed her skin. Her nipples puckered, and she barely restrained herself from stepping up to the window to feel its full effect. Instead, she distracted herself by looking about his apartment. It was smaller than she expected, given his position. Most First Boys had lavish homes separate from their employers. They lived like kings in huge mansions. Ken Jin lived in a tiny third-floor apartment.

It was extremely clean, sparse. The sitting room sported large cushions on the floor beside a washstand, and another table with a lamp. A very large and strange piece of art occupied the rest of the room. It looked like two rounded mountains, one much shorter than the other. The piece was only about a foot deep, and the top had a flat surface completely covered by a long silk cushion. Tilting her head, she decided the mountain image did not fit. It was more like a large letter B lying flat on its back, though the top mound was half the size of the bottom. She stared a moment longer, still puzzling, when she heard Ken Jin in the other room. It was his bedroom, she knew, his private place, but she could not resist following him into it to see.

It was as bare as the sitting room, with a bed and a wash area next to an open trunk. Inside the chest lay clothing, books, and letters. Personal letters, it looked like. Was that an imperial seal? She stepped closer, but Ken Jin was before her, kicking the lid closed with a quick snap of his foot.

Beyond those items and a few pairs of shoes, a large, low flat bed dominated the room. Clearly, this was where Ken Jin had spent his money. Stunning silk pillows were settled atop a silk-embroidered blanket. The fabric was green, the stitching quite detailed. It showed a mountain scene with waterfalls and mists and trees. Throughout the landscape, people wandered or reclined. She narrowed her eyes. No, they weren't reclining. They were . . .

Her eyes widened. They were coupling. In a great variety of ways. And the groups were not limited to couples. Charlotte leaned down. She even went to her knees to look closer. This was as educational as the sacred scrolls. Perhaps even more so.

She heard Ken Jin behind her. He was stripping off his own shirt and washing his upper body. She heard the splash of water and the muted violence in his movements. He was still very angry, and she was still very warm just thinking of his rescue. What would have happened if he hadn't come looking for her?

She closed her eyes and straightened from the bed. She didn't want to look at other couples right then. It was making her belly jump, and she felt agitated enough. Searching for some way to distract herself from her erotic thoughts, she returned to the one question that could hold her attention.

"Why does Little Pearl hate you?"

He was naked to the waist—just like her—and water glistened across his flat torso from his ablutions. She stared at a sparkling droplet that trembled on his nipple. She couldn't stop herself; she reached out and touched it, spreading it around in a circle across the hard pebble of his flesh. He didn't respond, didn't even move, but she felt a change in the air, a sudden tension that deepened the color of his eyes.

"I wasn't careful with her," he finally ground out, and it took a moment for Charlotte to remember they were talking about Little Pearl.

"She was your partner? In the practice?"

"Yes."

Charlotte had stepped closer to him. Now she grabbed his abandoned washcloth with one hand and wet it in the basin before returning it to his chest. He didn't flinch as the wet cotton dripped across his right shoulder, but he put a hand out to steady her hip. Or to steady himself. Either way, he made no objection as she trailed the cloth across his collarbone, then lower, across and around each hard nipple.

"Are you careful with me?" she asked as she worked.

"Always," he replied, his voice a low croak.

Her hand stilled and she looked into his eyes. "Am I so fragile?" Her recent experience had left her feeling small and powerless. She couldn't bear it if he thought her weak as well.

He reached out and caught the washcloth, his fingers entwining with hers, his heat flowing into her. "You are worth a thousand Little Pearls. She is nothing compared to you."

"But am I weak?" After all, she had nothing to show for her life. She did not study great thinkers like Joanna; she had not captured a husband like many of her friends. She was constantly getting into scrapes, saying the wrong things, *doing* the wrong things. Everyone said so.

Did that mean she was feebleminded like her brother? That her character was lacking in some essential quality? Perhaps she simply did not have the intelligence to navigate her world without disaster.

He shifted her hand, moving the washcloth to her body, to her breasts. He began with her nipples, moving in the soothing, dispersing circles they'd used before. He spiraled around her flesh in larger and larger movements while she kept herself still by an act of will.

She knew he meant to throw off her bad energy, to release that which was disharmonious to her qi, but his actions did nothing of the sort. The cool slide of water, the rough brush of coarse cotton, and the steady pressure of her inhalations against his hand set her belly to quivering again. It should have been delightful. It *was* delightful; but the silence that stretched between them was an answer that brought tears to her eyes.

"So I am stupid," she said, turning away. "I went to that school when I shouldn't have. I let her give me tea and take me into that room. I—"

"Do not be a fool!" he snapped, and jerked her back to him. She blinked in surprise, stunned by the fury in his voice. "What Little Pearl did was wrong. It was an abuse and a perversion that would be severely punished were the Tigress Shi Po still here."

Charlotte shook her head, her throat too clogged to speak. Didn't he understand? Didn't he realize that she couldn't care less about what Little Pearl had done? What mattered was that Charlotte had ventured there in the first place. That she had not seen the danger and saved herself. That she had drunk the tea and walked of her own accord into that terrible room. How could she be so idiotic?

"Little Pearl has a darkness inside her," Ken Jin continued. "Without Shi Po to restrain it, she has already left the Tao, the Middle Path."

Charlotte shook her head. He didn't understand, and she couldn't explain. So she broke away from him and quickly moved back into the main room. She had no purpose except to avoid hearing more about Little Pearl.

He followed, and she stopped running. There was nowhere for her to go with her breasts bare and her hair wild. Her head was pounding, and she needed air. She needed the breeze that was stronger here. She needed . . .

He stopped her before she went blindly to the window. He drew her backward against him, his hands strong around her upper arms, his chest hard and still slick with water. He rubbed her arms with his thumbs, and then he slid his hands around to cup her breasts. She pushed him away despite the hunger still simmering in her blood.

"Don't, Ken Jin, just don't. You don't understand."

He spun her around, and her knees buckled from the force of his pull. He caught her, of course. He was strong enough to support her as she stumbled, to lift her slightly and set her down so she sat in the dip between mountains on his strange piece of art. Except, it didn't feel like art. It was more like a chair right then, one with uneven armrests.

"What don't I understand?" he pressed.

She blinked back her tears. She didn't want to cry in front of him, didn't want to speak of something that he couldn't change. She shouldn't have brought it up, but she couldn't stop herself. She needed to know.

"Am I feebleminded?" she asked.

He blinked. "What?"

"William doesn't know. He . . . he's happy. I think he knows he's different, but he doesn't seem to understand how . . ." She swallowed. "How slow he is. We protect him. He doesn't go out; he plays with servant children. If people talk, he doesn't hear it." She gripped Ken Jin's arm. "He doesn't know."

He stared at her, but she couldn't read his expression or guess at his thoughts. Finally he spoke, but only after he had settled onto his heels before her. Only after he had brushed her hair from her face and took her hands in his.

"The Chinese value different things in a woman than the English." He frowned, as if struggling with the words. "We call you 'ghost people' because you are white, yes, but also because you value things of little substance—gold and pleasure, the things of appetite. In your women, you want soft, full flesh to lie upon and an oxlike obedience."

She nodded. It was true. The Englishmen she knew wanted a woman who would bear their children and not interfere in their pursuits, be they fame, fortune, or any known vice.

"The Chinese look for different things," he continued. He switched languages to Shanghai dialect, using idealized words that she recognized from Joanna. They came from the Confucian classics and were poetry as much as instruction. "A Chinese woman must be beautiful in form and heart. She is humble, yielding, respectful, and frugal."

Charlotte winced. She did not recognize herself in that list. He continued, unaware of her anxiety.

"If the English wish for an ox, the Chinese look for a delicate bird with beautiful plumage, sparing demands, and a lilting voice that raises a man's heart whenever she speaks." He sighed and looked down at his hands. "Such a woman is married and promptly caged."

"Caged?" she asked in surprise.

"Women do not have public affairs. They would stop their weaving," he quoted. He shrugged. "That is what we are taught. That our women should stay in their homes, away from all eyes, so that they may work untouched by anyone else."

She looked away. It would seem she was fit to be neither a Chinese nor an English wife. "Ken Jin," she began.

"A Dragon has different needs. A Dragon looks to a Tigress for his fulfillment. The Tigress must be strong of character or the Dragon will eat her. The Tigress must be pure . . ."

She flinched, but he corrected himself.

"Not pure of body, but pure of purpose. Only single-minded devotion clarifies the qi." He paused and waited until she looked into his eyes. "It goes without saying that a Tigress must be intelligent. How else would she hunt with any success? And only the wisest can ascend to Heaven."

She swallowed, at last understanding what he was headed. "But I am not a Tigress."

He caressed her: a long single stroke that started with her cheek, trailed down her neck and over her collarbone, until he finally circled her breast to thumb her nipple. She inhaled deeply at his touch, and her eyes slipped closed to savor the sensations. Little Pearl's drug was wearing off, the fires across her body fading, and yet his single caress set off a low roar in her ears.

"Neither the Chinese nor the English wish their wives to be intelligent. Only Dragons prize such a thing." His hand stilled, and she opened her eyes. His gaze was dark with meaning, but it took a moment for her to understand.

"You are a jade Dragon," she whispered.

"Yes." Then, when she said nothing, he pushed himself forward to capture her nipple in his mouth. She gasped even as she arched into his kiss. He sucked her nipple deep inside his mouth, using tongue and teeth to shape its form. She murmured her appreciation at the wet flick of his tongue, the harsh nip of teeth, and the long pull that came with being sucked deep into another soul.

He pressed her backward and to one side. Soon she was leaning against the slope of the larger mountain. Indeed, she straightened her legs, rising up so that her head fell across the rounded peak and her breasts were offered up to the Dragon above her.

Then he stopped. He stood, looking down at her with a stunning fierceness. He did indeed look like a towering dragon poised in the clouds above her. "Do you understand, Miss Charlotte?"

"You are a Dragon," she repeated though her mouth was dry.

"And I have found my Tigress, one whose yin qi is strong and pure. One who is wise enough to reach the antechamber to Heaven and brave enough to hunt in a forbidden Chinese school."

"I wasn't hunting when I went to the school."

"Of course you were. You hunted enlightenment."

"But it wasn't there. They didn't teach me anything."

He smiled slowly, a challenge sparking in his eyes. "So where then, my Tigress, will you find your answers?"

A flash of power burned through her body when he claimed her as his Tigress. "With a Dragon," she answered. "With a wise and powerful jade—"

He claimed her mouth with a deep and penetrating kiss, using the same skill he had used on her nipple. Then he pulled back. His hands framed her face while his thumbs stroked the curve of her cheeks and the wet outline of her lips. "I am a jade Dragon," he said loudly—firmly. "I choose you as my Tigress. I will stalk you. I will eat you. I will take your yin into myself, and I will use it to fly into the heavens." He paused as his hands slid down her torso. Up and over her breasts he moved, past the flat of her stomach, down until he grasped the tie of her pants. Her belly flattened as he moved so he had ample room to rip the fastening, exposing her sex to his probing fingers.

"Do you understand, Charlotte?"

She swallowed, even as her hips tilted and opened for his touch. He stepped between her legs as she spoke. "A Tigress must be very clever with her Dragon."

"Or I will devour you," he replied and thrust a finger deep inside her.

She tensed at the invasion, her stomach tightening. Without clear thought, she lifted her legs and wrapped them around him, capturing his hips with her calves and pulling him tight. His hand was trapped against her, inside her. "You want me to be smart?" she challenged. It was as much a statement as a question. "To toy with you as a cat does a mouse?"

He began to wiggle his finger, stretching her. "I *demand* it." He leaned forward. "That is why I chose you." Then he grinned as he pushed his hips hard against her. His finger probed deep and his thumb slid high through her pleasure grotto. "And so the Dragon plays in the Tigress's cave," he murmured.

She exploded around his hand. She had not expected it; it came upon her so fast. Her belly convulsed, her yin cave compressed, and then wave upon wave of pleasure roared through her.

He did not waste a moment. Shoving hard, he pushed her backward across the larger mountain. Her legs dangled open as he sat in the valley and pulled his hand from her. Bracing her at the tops of her thighs, he put his lips to her yin pearl and began to suck. The power flowed straight into him. She knew it. She felt it, a hot rush of energy that poured from her abdomen into his mouth. It brought tingling heat with it, burned across her yin pearl, and kept the shuddering waves of pleasure going on and on.

She didn't even mind that he absorbed her power. She knew she would feel drained and exhausted when it was done, but since her yin went to Ken Jin, she opened herself even more and let him drink. She owed him that. And even if she didn't, she wanted to gift him with it.

In time, he stopped. He fell backward with a gasp, his head and shoulders dropping against the shorter mountain as he struggled for breath. Without his support, she slipped back down the large mountain until she sat across his knees, her sex exposed to the cooling air, her torn pants slipping away.

"So much," he breathed. "You have so much yin, I cannot take it all in."

She would have grinned at the awe in his voice, but she

had no strength anywhere in her body. Her legs would not support her. She couldn't even lift her head. All she could do was lie against the larger slope and wait while her heartbeat steadied and the tingling gradually faded from her blood but not her mind. Her consciousness still shimmered; her joy continued to sparkle in her thoughts. "I think I shall enjoy being a Tigress," she murmured. Then she laughed at the silliness of her statement. She obviously enjoyed it.

"I am using you."

Ken Jin's heavy tones dimmed her sparkling thoughts. She blinked and lifted her head. Apparently she had enough strength to stare at him. "What?"

"What we did . . . this . . ." He gestured to her belly and her cinnabar cave. "I am stealing your yin. I am taking your power to strengthen my own."

"I know."

He shook his head. "No, you do not understand. I am stealing what you need. You should be keeping your yin power. A Tigress takes a man's yang power, adds it to her own, and then finds someone like me to stimulate her. The two energies combine and take her to Heaven."

She nodded. "That's what happened last time."

He sighed, straightening in his seat. But his motion shifted her weight on his knees and she slid farther down the mountain, which dropped her higher upon his body and against his jutting dragon. He hissed in pleasure as her weight pressed against him. Out of curiosity, she rotated her hips. She pushed hard against him, then pulled away. Push, pull. Push—

He grabbed her hips and set her away from him. "Listen to me!" he ordered, frustration growing in his tone. "I lied to you. I am stealing your power. I promised to teach you, but I am not. That is why my dragon is as strong as it is now: because I stole from you."

She leaned forward, but he held her hips still, so she settled for dropping a kiss on his nose. "You cannot steal what is given freely." Then, because he would not allow her to do more, she disentangled and moved away from him. Her legs still trembled, but they had enough strength to bear her up while she discarded her torn pants. Then she was gloriously naked. How freeing it was to stand without shame while the afternoon breeze whispered across her skin.

"You understand?" His tone held awe and confusion.

"Of course I do."

"But . . . aren't you angry?"

She shrugged. "I stole your yang. It's only fair I replenish you."

She heard him shift on the chair and twisted slightly to see him settle in the valley between the two mounds. "But what you did was unintentional. What I do—"

"I give it to you, Ken Jin. You have already given me so much." She didn't have the words to explain how she felt when she was with him: daring, vital, and so free. She extended her arms and threw back her head. Without even knowing why, she spun around in a circle, laughing as the world twisted about her. She moved faster and faster, loving the way her hair flew out behind her, how the air blew through the wet tendrils. She was alive. She was happy, and she felt fabulous. With Ken Jin beside her, her earlier fears seemed like nothing: a dark smoke cloud easily blown away by her Dragon lover. Her laughter spun out from her, on and on and on until she could no longer stand. She fell. Without grace, without beauty, she simply collapsed in an ungainly heap upon the floor; and still she laughed.

It took a while to catch her breath. A long while, because she still giggled. Her entire body shivered with sheer joy at being free. But eventually her heartbeat steadied, her breath slowed, and silence returned. In the street, she could hear the distant market: cries of hawkers, the chatter of Chinese women bargaining. She heard the laughter of a child, the sharp bark of a dog, and somewhere the low drone of the coolie *ah-ho* chant. But inside, there was silence and peace, until Ken Jin spoke.

"I was wrong."

She opened her eyes, then twisted around to find him. When she did, she stilled. His eyes were dark, his body tense, and a strange energy filled the air as he stared at her.

"Ken Jin?"

"You are not beautiful," he said. "You are . . . *celestial*." He said the last word in Chinese, and she had to struggle to remember its meaning.

"Ken Jin—"

"You are a goddess come to Earth. That is why you ascended so easily. That is why—"

Her laughter filled the room. It rolled out of her. She could not stop it; she couldn't even try. She looked away and held her sides. She tried to recover her breath, but whenever she opened her eyes and saw him staring at her with such bewilderment, she began to chortle again.

"Goddess . . ." he began again, then dropped to the floor beside her, his expression so earnest. "Goddess, please—"

"No, Ken Jin. Oh, stop, please." Her laughter rekindled, but this time she had better control of it. She bit her lip and kept the joy inside until she could breathe, until she could roll on her side and look at him. "Ken Jin, you are the only man I know who could look at a naked wanton on the floor and think she's a goddess." Then the meaning of what she'd just said sank in, and the joy faded.

Was she a slut? She knew the answer, and she shied away from it.

Ken Jin had captured her hand. "The Chinese believe in goddesses, Miss Charlotte. You might call them angels."

"I'm no angel."

"They come to Earth to bring enlightenment to mortal men—"

"I haven't brought anything to anyone—"

"And they must, of course, deny their identity for fear of capture."

"No one wants me, Ken Jin. Men come close, but then they disappear again. I let them go because of William. He needs me more than I need a husband, and besides, most of them are idiots anyway. But the truth is that no one has ever pursued me. Why else would I . . ." She stopped speaking, but her thoughts continued. Why else would she become a slut? True, she still had the idea of helping William. She still wanted to speak with his angelic soul. She still intended a lot of things, but deep down, she knew the truth.

She acted the slut because she was lonely, because no one other than a forced First Boy wanted her. And because she'd found she liked acting this way. She sighed, her joy completely gone, buried by shame. She knew she'd chosen this path. She had been aware every step of the way, and in truth, she didn't regret what she'd done.

And yet, shame still crept inside. Shame and guilt. After all, she wasn't at home teaching William, was she? She wasn't writing out menus or counting linens or even settling household accounts. She was here, in Ken Jin's apartments, indulging in her own pleasures while hoping—pretending?—that it would help her brother in the end.

Grimacing in distaste, she pushed herself upright and sat before Ken Jin. They were eye to eye, but her gaze sank lower to his thick, erect dragon. Here, at least, was something she could think about, something she *wanted* to think about.

"Do you have enough yang yet?" she asked. He didn't move, and she could sense his puzzlement. She rephrased her question. "Have we replenished your stores? Do you have enough to go to Heaven like I did?"

He shook his head slowly. "I spent many years purifying my qi. It does not come back in a single day."

She nodded. That made sense. "Which means," she said as she reached out to him. "That we had better get back to it."

He stopped her halfway, gripping her wrist with a firm hand, though his gaze was gentle. "What do you want, Miss Charlotte?"

"First of all? For you to call me Char."

He nodded. "What is it that you want, Char?"

She looked into his eyes. He still thought her a goddess, she realized with shock. He actually believed it. And in his confused Chinese mind, he was actually asking her what her mission was on Earth. She shook her head at his bizarre culture. Imagine, thinking angels could be on Earth! To believe that divine creatures would come down to have sex with mortals for some celestial purpose, that . . .

She smiled. Why not? Why couldn't it be true? Especially if sexual power was the fuel that launched one to Heaven, then how else would enlightenment come except through sex with a heavenly creature? Not that she believed she was an angel. Far from it. But that he could think it made her cherish him even more.

"I want to help you," she said. "But you must tell me how."

She watched him swallow as he thought. Then, with a slight nod to her, he released her wrist and stood. She followed him, gaining her feet as he stripped away the last of his clothing. Soon he stood before her completely naked.

She had seen William naked, of course. Her brother was often completely unaware of his state of dress when he dashed about the house. But Ken Jin was different. He knew she was looking at him. He knew she was filling her mind with the sight of his lean frame, his broad shoulders as they flowed into the smooth contours of a muscular chest. His waist was narrow, his hips jutting only slightly above corded thighs. And as she looked, his dragon flushed a darker red and pushed out of its sheath.

She extended her hand to brush the side of her index finger along the dragon's back—the tight skin closest to her. It was cooler than she'd expected, and the skin felt soft, moving slightly with her as she drew her finger up toward the dragon's mouth.

She glanced at Ken Jin's face, wanting to know what he thought when she touched him. How did it feel? Was his heart beating as fast as hers? Was his breath shallow with heat? There was no expression on his face, only a studied blankness though his gaze flickered when she met it.

"Tell me how this feels to you," she whispered.

She watched him nod. Then he spoke, his voice thick and low. "My dragon strains for you. It pulses with my blood." True to his words, his dragon surged upward, rearing toward her before dropping back against her finger. She raised her other hand and placed it on his chest. Closing her eyes, she felt the taut muscles beneath her fingers, but also the deeper rise and fall of his breath and the hard beat of his heart.

Farther down, she extended her finger to caress from the base of his dragon to the wrinkled pouch of skin below. She cupped the two round shapes inside, feeling their weight and size. Then she rolled them around a bit, ending with a slight squeeze just to see his reaction. He said nothing, but his heartbeat accelerated.

"Those are the dragon pearls," he said, his voice a low rumble by her ear.

She looked up at him, drawing back just enough to see his eyes. She could hear that his breath was shallow, but she wanted to know if his eyes still looked at her with awe. They did, but there was something else as well—an intense hunger that caught the breath in her lungs and quickened the beat of her own heart.

"You look like a Dragon," she said.

"And you are holding me as a Tigress."

She grinned at his statement and grew bolder. Opening her hand slightly, she abandoned his pearls with a caress. Then she drew upward, sliding her grip along his jade stem. She watched his nostrils flare, but she heard nothing over the roar of her own blood. She had not realized touching him would be so exciting.

Her hand flowed upward. Her palm skimmed the underside of his dragon, and she watched as he closed his eyes, his breath suffering its first hitch. "That is the dragon's belly," he murmured. "It is sensitive to the lightest touch."

She paused to play there a moment. Twisting her hand, she felt the ridges of his dragon's skin, even lifted it slightly and felt an answering pulse in his dragon.

"The yang grows stronger," he said. "Can you feel it?"

She closed her eyes, trying to focus on his dragon. Not just the shape, but the temperature, the texture, and his qi energy. "I feel your heat." It wasn't a physical thing. In truth, his skin was still cool. But there was a power that enveloped her hand—the back as well as the front—and seemed to surround all of Ken Jin, not just his dragon.

She pressed her lips to his neck without even realizing she had leaned in so close. The sensation against her mouth echoed what she felt with her hand: smooth skin, a trembling heartbeat, and the tingle of power against her lips. She smiled. With her face pressed against him, she could add two more delights: the musky scent of his body and the tangy taste of his skin.

She drew her hand up to the very top of his sex.

"That is my dragon's head," he said, and this time his voice trembled. "It has ridges, a crown, and a mouth that weeps with desire."

She felt it all. She traced the ridge, even pulled the sheath back to better explore. Then she followed the center line up to his dragon's mouth. "It's so smooth," she murmured, surprised by the silky feel of taut skin.

"That is so the attention centers on the mouth."

She had found it: the tip that she could open and close with the lightest of pressure. Moisture leaked out, and she smoothed it around. "I saw pictures in the scrolls," she said. "Of women—of Tigresses—tasting the dragon. It's what I wanted to learn from the very beginning."

He nodded. "There is a position on the dragon chair that would make it more comfortable for us both."

She straightened, intrigued. "Show me."

He moved slowly, almost stiffly, and she flashed on an image of a dragon moving awkwardly over land. His natural habitat was the air. The image fled as Ken Jin lay down on the chair, his head supported by the smaller mountain, his legs spread to either side of the larger, and in the middle, his dragon pushed high and proud. Charlotte went to his side, kneeling down beside him, but he extended his hand to stop her.

"The Tigress crouches above. The Dragon flies from below," he said.

She didn't understand, so he gestured to the area above his face.

"You must mount here, as if you were climbing upon a horse."

"There?" But that would mean her pleasure grotto would be just above his face. She gasped as she understood. "Of course. Then my hands are down there." By his hips and his dragon.

He said nothing, merely waited for her decision. There

was no question. She wanted to do this, but the position seemed so very open. Then she envisioned how she would be crouching, and felt a surge of power. There was a dominance in the position, a kind of primitive strength.

"I am a Tigress," she said out loud.

"You are much, much more," he answered.

She didn't wait for him to explain. She quickly mounted. With her legs straight, even straddled as they were, she could stand well above his mouth. Then, when she leaned over, she felt almost as if she were flicking a tail in the air. It was exciting, this role as a Tigress. She felt invigorated.

He put his hands on her upper thighs to brace her. She trembled. He was a strong man; she knew he could easily support her weight. But she didn't want to press down on him, so she leaned forward. The very tip of her nipples flowed across his belly, and she gasped as the familiar sparks of yin fire warmed her blood.

Then she was directly in front of it: his dragon. It stretched out for her. There was a scent to it—male, musky—and a taste of smooth salt. She felt his hands quiver as she explored his tip with her tongue. There wasn't enough width to the mountain chair for her to rest her hands anywhere but on him. So as her back began to ache, she shaped his hips with her palms, then began to slide forward. She bent her elbows and let her breasts press into his heated flesh. Her hands slid to the base of his dragon, her forearms slipped across his thighs, opening them wider. And while she slid her tongue past his tip, around the dragon's head, her legs relaxed even more and he began to kiss her cinnabar cave.

She felt his hands slide inward to the inside of her thighs, and he opened her even wider. Then he let his mouth explore. She mimicked his actions, swirling her tongue when he did, sucking too. And when he began pressing his fingers deep into points between leg and pleasure grotto, she began fondling his dragon pearls. Bit by bit, she lost herself in the sensations.

She felt the yin flow pouring into him from his first taste. She opened herself willingly, giving him all she had. But as she opened herself to give, she was shocked to feel the tangy burn of his yang. It began as a prickle of energy at the roof of her mouth, but the more she let her yin pour down to him, the more his yang energy flowed upward into her.

She felt it as a fire in her mind, like a lava fountain that saturated her brain and made her dizzy. She knew it was not her own yin fire. His was a darker power, essentially alien to herself, and yet a perfect complement. She began to suck harder, using hand and tongue to accentuate his power. She heard him growl, a low vibration of hunger that trembled through his mouth to her yin source.

The contractions began immediately. Her yin loved everything he did. His dragon seemed to agree, for his buttocks began to flex in time with her. His dragon pressed rhythmically forward, deeper into her mouth, and as he moved, his yang did as well. It penetrated her mind, mixed with her yin, and pushed them ever higher. She felt Ken Jin with her as well, not just in body, but also in spirit. They were rising together.

They were climbing to Heaven. With every push of their hips, with every amazing wave of power, they were ascending to the Immortal Realm.

"My God! Oh my God!"

The words barely penetrated her consciousness. Her breath was so fast; the roaring in her ears so loud. But a movement from the corner of her eyes continued the disruption. A movement that should not have been there, a presence that violated this holy space.

She lifted her eyes. She didn't stop what she was doing, she couldn't. She didn't want to, but she raised her gaze to see . . .

A woman she didn't know. She was older, overly painted, and in a cheap gown that was too small for her ample breasts. And she was giggling even as she clutched the arm of . . .

Charlotte's father.

❧

Jan 4, 1895
To Wen family patriarch Wen Feng Jin:
  Happiness and much luck this new year! I know my monthly package comes early, but I am especially excited for the imminent celebration. I shall be in Peking for the holiday and cannot wait to meet my fiancée at last.

  In much anticipation,
  Wen Ken Jin

(Attached, seven bolts of red silk, richly embroidered for the New Year's celebration, four sacks of rice, and another three of flour. Five baskets of fresh fruits and vegetables make the full offering of twelve. All is delivered by an armed escort.)

January 9, 1895
Dear Sir, Wen Ken Jin:
  Woe has befallen our household! Dearest Jan Wan has fallen ill. Such was the excitement of your gift and the anticipation of your arrival that she overset her delicate constitution. The entire household is in fear that any excitement will end her tenuous hold on this life altogether. Pray do not come this holiday. We cannot risk the joy your visit would bring.

  In desperate fear,
  Wen Feng Jin

January 13, 1895
Dear Wen patriarch Wen Feng Jin:
   I cannot have a wife who falls ill every time I come home. Perhaps she would be better pleased with a different husband.

Regretfully,
Wen Ken Jin

January 20, 1895
Dearest Wen Ken Jin,
   Congratulations on an excellent new year! Jan Wan has graciously accepted your suit! She wishes most anxiously to see you this holiday.
   We are, of course, worried about the excitement, but feel that you should see the glorious beauty off your wife-to-be. Pray come on the fourth day of New Year's celebration, as is appropriate for a distant friend of the family. She will see you from two to three in the afternoon.

In great joy,
Wen Feng Jin

Dizziness or light-headedness can result when the energy bound up inside a point is released and then circulates throughout your body. The circulation of this vital energy can refresh your whole body, clear your mind, and make you feel new again.
Acupressure for Lovers, Michael Gach, Ph.D.

Chapter Twelve

It was working. Ken Jin could feel the power—so alive, so filled with light—as it circled between them. They were flying to Heaven. Soon he would be whole again.

Then something changed. He felt Charlotte stiffen, her energy cooling, her power waning. Ken Jin increased his efforts, straining with tongue and lips, but something was very wrong. He opened his eyes, but there was little to see beyond her thighs, her pleasure grotto, her beautiful yin power.

A roar echoed through the room. It was loud and brutal and virtually incoherent, but Ken Jin understood the tone if not the meaning. "I will kill you!"

Ken Jin pushed upward at the same moment Charlotte leapt. He was pushing her behind him, and she was jumping in front, so she went straight up while he scrambled out from beneath. Then he was forced to catch her, though his still swollen dragon made his legs weak. It was a painful distraction that took his attention away from his employer's advance. Except, this couldn't possibly be Charlotte's father. Mr. Wicks was staying in Canton for three more days. He had plans with his mistress; he couldn't be here.

Except, his employer sometimes came back early from his trips. The man delighted in introducing his women to the Dragon chair. Up until now, Ken Jin had not minded. Mr. Wicks was easier to control when he had ready access to a variety of toys. And besides, his employer was the one who had paid for the expensive piece of furniture, on the condition that he could "store it" in Ken Jin's apartment.

And now Mr. Wicks was here, his latest mistress beside him, her mouth open in shock. "How dare you!" he bellowed, advancing with his meaty fists curled into weapons.

"Father, don't!" Charlotte rushed forward despite her nakedness, despite the fact that Ken Jin tried to push her behind him.

"Dead! Dead!" Mr. Wicks bellowed, his hatred pouring out at Ken Jin.

"We're married!" Charlotte cried.

Ken Jin jolted, shocked by her preposterous claim. Chinese and white did not marry. Servant and master did not mix. And yet . . .

"Father!" she cried against as she reached for the man's fists. He pushed her aside. Unfortunately, she had never been one to leave well enough alone. Instead of staying to one side, she leapt forward and grabbed hold of her father's massive upper arm. "He's my husband!"

"The devil he is!" the man snapped. Then when she didn't release him, he slammed his opposite fist down straight at her face.

The blow never landed. Ken Jin was there, catching his employer's arm well away from Charlotte. Mr. Wicks answered with another roar, and then the battle was joined. He lunged, dragging Charlotte with him as she tried to restrain him. Ken Jin did his best to protect her, but there was little he could do when she was so determined to place herself in the middle of it all.

In the end, he was the one who set her aside. He grabbed hold of her waist and lifted her bodily away, paying for the choice with a blow to his shoulder and another to his skull. But he had received much worse in his life. It was a small price for her safety.

"Get out," he said. "Get safe." At least, that was what he thought he said. He couldn't hear himself over the ringing in his ears.

"Get dressed!" her father bellowed, lunging again at Ken Jin.

Then the fight began in earnest. Ken Jin did not raise a hand. No Chinese man could raise a finger to a white and live, not in foreign-dominated Shanghai, and certainly not after debauching the white man's daughter. So Ken Jin fought in the way he had learned as a boy: by avoidance.

When Mr. Wicks attacked, he sidestepped. Mr. Wicks punched; he ducked. Every lunge was slipped around, every grab was misplaced until the white man lost all sense of reason and began a wanton destruction of whatever he could find. Teapot and cups were smashed, cushions were torn to threads, and the Dragon chair was attacked. Fortunately, the piece of furniture was too strong to be demolished by Mr. Wicks's massive fists, but the sight of someone beating it hurt Ken Jin nonetheless.

And yet, he could only watch and silently thank the goddess Kwan Yin for sparing the sacred scrolls. The door to his bedroom was ajar, but Mr. Wicks was not rational enough to push through to the other room. He was too animalistic to do more than destroy the things in sight.

"Father, stop this!" Charlotte's voice was high and angry. "It's very common to marry a Chinaman," she pressed. "Joanna did it. I've done it. Everyone's done it."

"Hush!" Ken Jin hissed at her. She could not possibly

expect her father to believe such nonsense. It did nothing
but draw her father's fury to her.

As expected, Mr. Wicks spun, his fists already raised to
strike. Charlotte stood tall and defiant, daring her father to
hit her. Ken Jin stepped into the breach. He had done
everything he could to draw the fight away from her, but
this was a small room and neither Charlotte nor the other
woman would leave. So he had no choice but to take the
brunt of her father's attack straight on.

Ken Jin allowed the bearlike man to grab him. Then, at
the last moment possible, Ken Jin shifted his weight and
knocked Mr. Wicks's feet out from under him. The man
went down with another bellow. Ken Jin shifted and
pressed his knee deep between his employer's shoulder
blades. Mr. Wicks could not rise until Ken Jin released
him.

"Father—" Charlotte began.

"You are no daughter to me!" The raw pain in the man's
voice made Ken Jin grit his teeth against guilt. Mr. Wicks
had every right to be furious.

"That's right," Charlotte said, her voice commanding
and calm. "I am married, Father. I am a wife now—"

"Enough!" snapped Ken Jin. "Lying will not help matters." Though he was tempted. Sweet Heaven, how he
wished it were possible.

Charlotte stared at him in shock, and the agony in her
face cut at his resolve. But one look at his employer told
him it was too late. Even if the lie were possible, Mr. Wicks
would never allow it. So he forced himself to turn away
from Charlotte. His job and his future were gone. That was
inevitable from the first moment she had stepped into his
bedroom four days ago. All he could do now was make it
easier on her. And that meant mollifying her father.

Ken Jin dropped to his knees and pressed his forehead to
the floor directly in front of Mr. Wicks's face. "She is still

a virgin and can marry respectably," he said to the floor-boards. "I accept your punishment."

Mr. Wicks straightened slowly. His breath huffed like the great bellows of an ox, but he said nothing. Charlotte, on the other hand, was scrambling to her father's side, her words rushing about in the small room.

"Don't be ridiculous, Father. I chose him. I married him. It was a quiet little Chinese ceremony. I knew how you would react, so I didn't tell—"

A single blow across her mouth silenced Charlotte. Ken Jin heard it fall and had to force himself to stay still. It was a father's right to punish his daughter. Worse, if Ken Jin interfered now, it would likely make life harder for Charlotte later. So he remained in his kowtow and waited, though he tilted his head slightly to watch his employer.

"Come along, ducks," said the other woman. "We'll just go have a spot of tea somewhere. Leave your father to his business."

Ken Jin watched as Charlotte straightened. Her father's handprint burned bright red on her cheek, but it was nothing compared to the blaze in her eyes. "Who are you?" she asked, her voice tight.

"Me?" trilled the woman. "Why, I'm Maggie. I'm a friend of your father's, is all. A—"

"A strumpet," interrupted Charlotte as she rounded on her father. "You brought *her* into this house and you dare hit me? You're an adulterer!"

Mr. Wicks bellowed again, but his fist never fell; Ken Jin had hold of it again, though he had to launch himself up from the floor.

"Please, Charlotte," Ken Jin hissed as he steadied both himself and Mr. Wicks. "Leave. Let us discuss this."

"No!" she snapped, as he'd known she would.

"Then at least get dressed," he begged.

She looked down at herself, and color rose in her cheeks

when she realized she was still naked. Maggie came to the rescue, handing over pants and tunic. Unfortunately, the woman didn't think to remain silent as everyone watched Charlotte hastily dress.

"I understand the lure, ducks, truly I do. But he is a Chinaman, and not a very rich one by the looks of things."

"We are married," Charlotte insisted as she pulled on her shirt. Then, when her head finally emerged, she looked hard at Ken Jin. "Tell them we're married, then make them leave."

He didn't answer her. Mr. Wicks radiated fury, but his violent impulses had been stopped. For the moment. So Ken Jin slowly released the man before donning his own pants. His employer's eyes followed his every move. Mr. Wicks's shoulders hunched and his face pushed forward. He looked very much like a mongoose squaring off with a snake.

"I can ruin you," Mr. Wicks suddenly said. "I *will* ruin you."

"You will not!" cried Charlotte, but her father ignored her.

"I know you have invested your money as if it were mine, all under my name. I will keep it. All of it. You will have nothing."

Ken Jin swallowed and wondered why there was so little pain. All his money, all his plans would be gone. He'd be destitute once again. Why wasn't there more pain? The first time had cut him so deeply that he screamed for days. But now? Nothing. Nothing except the sight of Charlotte's steady, silent tears.

"Do you understand?" Mr. Wicks suddenly screamed. "You will have nothing!"

Ken Jin bowed. It was what servants did. They bowed. "Will you consider that adequate recompense?"

Mr. Wicks's eyes narrowed. His lip curled as he looked down at his daughter. "She is still a virgin?"

"No!" she cried, but Ken Jin's voice was lower and clearer.

"Yes," he answered. "There are doctors who can verify it."

"I will expect a clear accounting," her father continued, "down to every last groat. Then you will leave Shanghai. I never want to see your miserable face again."

"Of course." He would be left with nothing but the clothes on his back. Again.

"No!" Charlotte pushed forward, her eyes shimmering with tears, but her stance firm with her own fury. "We are marr—"

"Charlotte!" Ken Jin would not support the lie.

She rounded on him. "Fine! Then we *will* marry. You will get every last penny of your money plus a great deal more as a wedding gift. We will live together in . . ." She looked around at the destruction her father had caused and shrugged. "In a house. And no one . . ." She glared at her father and his mistress. "No will say a thing to Mother about this, about today. We will be a happy bride and groom." Her voice shook when she spoke, and he knew she understood a small bit of the lunacy she proposed.

"I will disown you, you disgraceful slut!"

Charlotte reared back as if struck, but she was not silent. "I'm a slut? I'm not married to someone else. Mother loves you! Were you ever faithful to her? Ever?"

"Aye, ducks," drawled Maggie sadly from where she was inspecting the Dragon chair. "That's the way of it, all right."

"Do not think to speak to me in that tone of voice!" bellowed Mr. Wicks at his daughter. "You have behaved like a common tart. Worse!"

"I've been following my father's example!"

Ken Jin felt his chest tighten and his belly grow cold. The screeching, the threats, even the debris beneath his feet felt familiar to the point of dizziness. But he wasn't a child anymore, and his home would not descend into mindless violence. So he stepped into the space between father and daughter. There was little room between them, but he slid in nevertheless, holding back the father's blows and pushing the daughter backward, away from harm.

"Ken Jin!" the father cursed.

"Ken Jin!" the daughter pleaded.

He answered neither of them until there was room to breathe and space to listen. Only then did he speak. "Do you know what it is to be a Chinese wife?" he asked.

It took a moment for Charlotte to process his words. He saw her glare shift from her father to him, then back again, before finally returning to his eyes. "You said something about a cage."

He nodded, hating that he had to disillusion her. Hating himself for the pain he had to inflict. "You would be a servant to the entire household. You would be insulted twice for every grain of rice in your bowl. Tears would be your tea, and bruises your mattress."

"But you wouldn't do that to—"

"I would have nothing to do with it," he answered. "It would come from my mother when I am away."

She lifted her chin. "I wouldn't live with such a shrew."

He paused, not wanting to say his next words. But she had to understand that her beautiful dream was impossible; they could never marry. "The abuse would come from my first wife."

She gasped. Even Mr. Wicks drew back in shock. "You're married?"

He shook his head, but kept his gaze steady. He owed it to Charlotte to look her in the eye when he delivered the news. "I am engaged. As she is Chinese and our arrangement is long-standing, she would be my first wife. You could only be a concubine."

"The devil you say," growled Mr. Wicks. Ken Jin ignored him, his attention riveted to Charlotte's stricken expression.

"You would have to break that engagement, Ken Jin. I will be your only wife."

He shook his head. "That is not the Chinese way."

"It is the English way!"

He nodded. The English married one woman, then slept with many without responsibility or interest in their care once the liaison was finished. He found it appalling and would not be party to it.

Instead, he stood immobile while Charlotte crumpled before him. She did not sink to her knees; she had too much power for that. But her face lost all heat and her eyes became vague with fear. "You said I was your Tigress," she whispered.

At last he felt the pain. Simple and deep, it cut into the lowest recesses of his belly. "You are my Tigress," he said, not because it would help her understand, but because the words would not be denied. "There will be no other." Her knew that without doubt. Theirs had been a synergy unlike any other. Most spent their lives searching for such a thing to no avail. He had found it and now must throw it away. "As my wife, you would have to leave William. He would be miserable with my family, as would you."

She gasped, her greatest fear voiced aloud. But then, to her credit, she straightened her spine and fought—for him, for a life together. "We will live in a house in Shanghai," she said. "You, me, and William. No other relatives. Just us."

The pain burrowed deeper this time, in a long line starting from his heart all the way down to his yang seat as he shook his head. "I cannot afford such a life."

"But there's a way. There has to be a way."

He stepped forward, but he did not touch her. He no

longer had the right. In truth, he'd never had the right. "You wish there was a way. You dream of possibilities, but in your heart you know it is impossible." He looked down at his hands as they fell uselessly to his side. "We knew this would happen if we were discovered; be grateful that it is not worse. Joanna and her monk are likely dead."

"No!" She spoke in defiance, but he saw the way her hands trembled. She knew she was defeated.

Ken Jin said nothing. He had no more words, only the silent plea that she understand. She would hate being a Chinese wife, and he could never become English for her. Her friends would never accept either of them, and without money, he could not give her the life she wanted. But she didn't see it even when her father explained.

"Don't be stupid, girl," the man spat from where he stood behind Ken Jin. "No one would accept you; neither his kind nor ours."

"I don't care." Brave words, but her voice wobbled and her shoulders were beginning to slump.

"Our children would," Ken Jin whispered. "I have no wish to give you up, Miss Charlotte." No truer words had ever been spoken.

"Then don't!"

"You cannot live without wealth, Charlotte, and I cannot afford you."

Her head snapped up, and her eyes flashed with fury. "You don't know what I can and can't do."

He dipped his head in acknowledgment—not of her words, but of her pain. "And William? How would he live in a poor man's house?" When she didn't speak, he stepped forward to press his point. "You could not manage as a Chinese wife; I cannot be an English husband. Without money . . ." They both knew he would never work as a white man's First Boy again. Her father would see to that. "I must return to my family." And their charity. The very thought made his legs go numb. Could he face that? He didn't know. But he certainly wouldn't bring Charlotte into such a situation.

"There must be a way!"

Her anguish touched him. He felt it in his chest as a deep burning ache. How strange, that he would feel her pain when his own body was slipping away from him, growing more and more numb as each moment passed. Unable to stop himself, he reached out for her face. His fingertips brushed away her tears: hot, wet, each drop a yin blade that cut at his spirit.

He made his decision. "Unless we can find another way, I will make my bargain with your father."

She straightened, and he felt her withdrawal like ice on his skin. "I will not be bartered like a cheap toy."

"An' what would ye be instead, ducks?" asked Maggie in a surprisingly tender voice. "Ye're not married, and ye can't work. Ye're trained to care fer a rich home. He ain't rich. Ye'd just be a burden." She stepped forward and gently tugged on Charlotte's arm. "Let's get you home and into some decent clothes. Let the men find a way out o' this coil."

"No." Charlotte said the word, but there was little fire in it.

Mr. Wicks moved around Ken Jin, the gleam of greed clear in his face. "Every groat, Chinaman."

Ken Jin bowed. "And she will be cared for? As if this never happened?"

"She's my daughter," the white man growled in response. "I look after my own."

"I will get all in order and give it to you in the morning."

"But it *did* happen!" Charlotte bellowed. The words beat at Ken Jin's temples and trembled through his chest, but there was nothing more he could say. Even her father ignored her except to grab her arm.

Maggie patted Charlotte's left hand. "You'll grow up, ducks. We all do, one way or another."

Charlotte stared at the woman. Ken Jin could see the war inside his fierce Tigress. He recognized the hot denial, the boiling anger, and underneath it all, a churning confusion. How barbarian of her father to have raised her with the illusion of choice. She'd had the responsibility of her brother and their household from a very young age. It had made her believe she could manage her own destiny.

Her glare slid to her father, who matched it with equal determination and fury. Then her eyes cut to him. Ken Jin did not bow; his body was too numb to move. "We would have gone to Heaven together," he said. He didn't know where the words came from, only that they were true.

Her eyes widened. He saw surprise and anger there, plus more besides. He knew she felt too much to express, while he felt nothing. Even her pain could not reach him anymore.

He was empty.

"I hate you," she hissed. Then she jerked away from the other two, breaking their hold as she ran out the door. Mr. Wicks cursed then and followed. Maggie remained, sighing as she jingled the coins in her purse.

"I guess they won't be needing me, then." She glanced his way. "Tough luck for you though, ducks. 'At's why me mum told me never to fall for the rich ones. They don't understand the basics o' life. An' who pays? It's us." She slanted him a look. "You do have something hidden away—right, ducks? Just in case?"

He looked down at the floor, still too numb to even kick at the debris.

"You don't, do ye?" she realized. "Ye're really giving it all up. The girl, yer job, and all yer money." She shook her head at his folly. "Guess the Chinese can fall in love."

His gaze cut sharply back to her, but the woman didn't notice. She was carefully counting out English coins. Two pounds, one shilling, and four pence. She pressed it into his hand. "Take this. It'll hold you until you get back to yer family." Then she carefully tucked her purse into her bodice. Patting him lightly on the cheek, she turned to leave, chuckling all the way. "A Chinaman in love. With a rich chit, no less. Ah," she added as she winked at him. "Ye've given me a story for me grandchildren. Ta, love!"

She left. Ken Jin stood without thought, without sensation, Maggie's laughter echoing in his head. A Chinaman in love, she'd said. Was that what had happened? Had he lost everything for love? Or was he merely cursed, his fortune perpetually given to the whites? Wasn't that the curse of a man who thwarted the natural order of things, that all his endeavors would turn perverse? Money to the barbarians, love to hate, fullness to nothingness.

Did he love her?

Yes. With her, he could go to Heaven. With her, his yang ran thick and strong. With her, he felt all things as a whole man should. Of course, he loved her.

But in China, such feelings meant less than nothing. Family, responsibility, honor—all these things superseded love. And he could not regain them by embracing a perverted love—a love for a barbarian woman—no matter how his body trembled in her presence. No matter how strong their yin and yang combined, such a relationship was doomed from the beginning. His entire life from his eighth birthday had been doomed.

It was time for him to return, to begin again where he had left his life's proper path. It was time for him to do what he should have done as a child.

He would be of value to the Emperor, he realized, broken vessel that he was. He spoke English well. He understood how the barbarians thought and what they wanted.

He would likely rise quickly to some form of power, and his last two decades would not be a total waste if he aided his troubled country.

His family would honor him again, and his name would once again be written on the family altar. He might even still marry Jan Wan, assuming she would accept her status as an honorary wife. Plus his dragon and its power would no longer consume his thoughts. Neither would a barbarian woman with yin that burned as bright as her golden red hair.

It was decided, then. He knelt to gather up the scattered threads of the Dragon cushion. Tomorrow he would leave for Peking and enter the ranks of the Emperor's most esteemed servants.

He would become a eunuch.

❦

Triple happiness! Heaven's fortune!
The dowager Emperess Cixi blesses her most faithful servant Wen Gao Jin.
The most honored Sung Ling Yi requests your presence at the wedding of his most precious daughter Mei Bing to Wen Gao Jin.
The divine Empress blesses the union with her presence at the Forbidden City on April 13, 1895.
Triple happiness! Great fortune!

February 26, 1895
Dearest brother, Ken Jin:
I am to be married! The Empress blesses me for great service. Though the deaths of the barbarian missionaries no doubt cause you great distress, I have worked tirelessly to bring such news to the Dragon throne. And at last the Empress recognizes my great devotion.

I am to be wed! To an imperial relative no less! The honor sets my heart to leaping!

Only one darkness shadows my perfect joy. My bride is an older woman of delicate constitution. At twenty-four, she trembles in fear at the child-less future. She is understandably nervous at mar-rying a eunuch and mourns the babes that could have been hers. But again, the Empress has smiled upon my diligent service. She has allowed me a wedding night.

I implore you, dearest brother, to come to my wedding. You will be most honored.

In ecstatic joy,
Your dearest brother,
Wen Gao Jin

*ANGINA—Pc 6, Inner Gate. This point is located on
your wrist at the palm side. It is located two thumb
widths above the wrist crease in the center of the arm. According to oriental medicine, the inner point (Pc 6) regu-
lates ch'i as well as blood in the chest. Hence, it is the
point of choice for any pain or discomfort of the chest.
Start with applying medium pressure. Build it up gradually. Hold about a minute, and gradually release the pressure. Do it on both wrists.*
http://www.holistic-online.com, Dr. George Jacob

Chapter Thirteen

Charlotte ran. She had no thought except escape, no feelings except hatred and anger. But once outside, reality in-
truded. She had nowhere to go. She didn't even have shoes
and held her torn pants together with one hand. She didn't
have money or a clear thought.

The mews. Ken Jin's horse was there. She could ride
it . . . where? Not home. Not yet. But she wasn't dressed
decently. Where else could she go?

She hurried to the stable, but her father caught up. He
didn't even speak to her, simply wrapped her in a cloak before helping the stable boy with saddle and tack. She stood
in silence, stewing. She toyed with the idea of escape, but
once again, where would she go? Her father would catch
her anyway. So she stared at her dirty toes and tried not to
cry.

Ken Jin had betrayed her. He didn't want her. After
everything they'd done, everything that had happened between them, he didn't want her. She sniffed back tears. She
wouldn't cry for him or for what they might have done together, though his words echoed in her head.

We would have gone to Heaven together.

She wanted to scream at him. She wanted to stomp right back into his tiny flat and rail at Ken Jin until he saw reason. Some part of her knew she was acting the shrew. Some part of her knew that Ken Jin saw reason whereas she was all emotions. And yet, they could have had so much. They could have gone to Heaven together.

"Come on," her father snapped from above her. He had already mounted and now waved an impatient hand in her direction. She was supposed to sit in front of him, just as she'd sat before Ken Jin just a few hours before. Right after he'd rescued her from . . . She gritted her teeth against a sob. She would not cry for him. She would not.

"Now!" bellowed her father.

"What about your whore?" Charlotte challenged and had the satisfaction of hearing her father curse.

He dug into his pocket and pulled out a couple shillings, then tossed them to Maggie, who had been waiting near the door. "You'll be at the usual place?" he asked.

The woman grinned, quickly pocketing the coins. "Of course, ducks!" Then with a wink and a sympathetic wave to Charlotte, Maggie turned on her heel and sauntered away. Which left Charlotte once again facing her father.

"Now come," he repeated, his voice filled with a low threat.

She knew better than to disobey, so she mounted and tried to sit in stoic silence. She failed. Despite her earlier resolve, she cried the entire ride home, while her father glared daggers at the scenery and did his best not to notice. He held her arm on the walk into the house only to shove her away the moment the door shut behind them.

"Get dressed," he ordered, loud enough for his words to echo throughout the house. "I will await you in the library."

She nodded, too miserable to respond. But before she could mount the stairs, William came barreling out the parlor and wrapped her in his arms. "You're home!" he cried, his joy sparking a smile in her heart. "We've been waiting ever so long. Mama said we could go the park as soon as you got here, and I've been waiting and waiting and—"

"Good heavens, what are you wearing?" came her mother's voice. "And, Thomas! You're home early."

"—waiting. We played cards, and Mama said I was very clever and—"

"You didn't go out dressed like that, did you? You couldn't have!"

"—a bird flew at the window with a big thunk, which scared Mama and she spilled her tea and—"

"Charlotte? Thomas? What's going on?"

"—but I ran to the window. It just flopped around and flopped . . ." William released her long enough to imitate the dazed bird, but that gave Mrs. Wicks an unobstructed view of her daughter. The woman paled as her gaze slowly took in Charlotte's flyaway hair, torn pants, and bare, dirty feet.

"That will be enough, William!" Mama snapped. "Go to your room!"

Charlotte lifted her chin, diverting some of her misery into defense of her sibling. "You are angry with me, Mother, not William—"

"Don't talk back to me, young lady. I demand to know— where are you going, Thomas?"

Her husband didn't respond. He rarely did. But everyone watched him sidestep the three of them and stomp down the hallway into the library. Within moments, they would hear the clink of the scotch decanter.

"But you promised we could go to the park," William whined. Except his words were deeper than a whine, more like the rumbling prelude to a tantrum.

"I will take you later, love," Charlotte said, "but I am not suitably dressed."

William frowned. "Where are your shoes? Mama says I always have to wear shoes, even when I don't want to—"

"I know, dear, but they got lost."

"Lost?" snapped Mama. "Where? How? What exactly has occurred, Charlotte? Why do you look so . . . so . . . disreputable?"

"Because I am disreputable," Charlotte snapped, then immediately regretted it. She was in no position to antagonize her parent. "I am going upstairs. William, why don't you and Nanny decide what toys to bring to the park?" That ought to keep him happily occupied for ten minutes at least.

But he didn't immediately leave, so the three of them stood in the front hallway and waited to see if he would cooperate or not. Until Charlotte remembered something.

"Didn't Ken Jin buy you a new kite?" She was pleased her voice didn't quaver on his name. "Perhaps Nanny could help you put it together. . . ." The ploy worked; William was already moving, his feet thundering up the stairs.

Her mother turned to her. "Charlotte Anne Wicks, what exactly is the meaning of this?"

Charlotte didn't answer. Wearily, she climbed the stairs. With luck, her mother would simply quiz her father.

"You have been running much too wild, of late," Mama continued as she mounted the stairs in pursuit of her daughter. "I begin to believe you have fallen into disreputable company."

"I have been with Ken Jin, Mama." This time she couldn't stop the pain, and she winced at his name.

Her mother shrugged. "Well, I know he is a servant and all, but standards must be maintained. No one should see you dressed—"

"He saw me—" She bit off her words. She pressed her teeth deep into her lip to keep from spilling out all the misery that might very well drown her. Instead, she forced her thoughts back to her mother. "You are back early from the mission."

Her mother's face tightened into a disapproving scowl. "I'm not at all sure I like the new priest. He was very tart to me yesterday."

Charlotte nodded, barely listening. "But you came home and played with William. That must have been very nice."

"Well, what was I supposed to do with you gone and Nanny complaining of a headache?"

"I know he can be difficult, but if you perhaps stopped trying to correct him—"

"William is maturing quite nicely, young lady. I have no wish to discuss *him* right now."

They made it to her bedroom, and Charlotte ducked gratefully inside. It had been years since her mother had crossed this threshold, since the day Charlotte had first begun running the menus, in fact. So she had every expectation of privacy now. Except, her mother had apparently decided to be motherly. She not only crossed the threshold, she shut the door behind her and folded her arms across her chest.

"Tell me everything, Charlotte. From the very beginning."

The very idea was enough to freeze Charlotte's tongue to the roof of her mouth. She couldn't possibly begin to express everything. So she rushed behind her privacy screen and prayed that her mother would just go away. But her prayers were never answered, so her mother remained, still talking, still demanding answers Charlotte could never ever give.

"Don't think you can hide from me. I am most determined when my children's welfare is at stake. Why would you go out like that? What happened to your shoes?"

Charlotte reached out a slender arm to draw her washbowl and pitcher behind the screen. It was awkward. She had to place the bowl on the floor and squat down to wet the cloth. But then again, squatting was exactly what she needed to do if she wished to cleanse away every memory of what had happened.

"Make sure to clean your feet well, Charlotte," her mother called. "An infection of the toes can be quite hideous."

Charlotte felt a tear splash her arm. When had she started crying? She pressed her lips tight to hold them in, but it didn't work. She squeezed her eyes shut and vigorously scrubbed her face. It didn't help.

"And how is it that your father brought you home? He was supposed to be in Canton for another two days. At least, I think he was. He comes and goes so frequently these days."

The sobs would not be contained. Charlotte had no strength left in her legs, so she sat on the floor. She tried to get herself to stop. She told herself that she had to get dressed, that she couldn't just sit here naked. But in the end, all she managed was to pull on her stockings and drawers while her chest jerked and her breath came in short gasps.

"Are you quite dressed yet, Charlotte? You cannot avoid me, you know. I am not moving from this spot. Char?"

Then it happened. Her mother came around the screen. Charlotte tried to hide. She turned her back to her parent, fumbled with her shift. But the fabric was crumpled, incorrectly starched by the stupid maid, and the more she tried to smooth it out, the worse it became. The worse everything became as the sobs began to choke her.

"Charlotte? My heavens! Really, dear, get up off the floor. Oh my. Oh . . . dear." Her mother reached around and gently removed the shift from Charlotte's knotted fingers. "Raise your arms, dear."

Charlotte obeyed. What else could she do? She had to get dressed. The fabric settled down over her body, hot and heavy, like a layer of scratchy wool pulled over her soul. And yet it was comforting, somehow, as was her mother's fussing.

"Come out of there, Charlotte." The words were impatient, but also familiar. So she obeyed, stiffening her wobbly legs and dragging a hand across her wet cheeks. Then she was in her mother's arms, blubbering like the smallest child. She was loud and messy and completely out of control while her mother patted her back.

Thump. Thump. Thump. The steady rhythm of a mother. *Thump. Thump. Thump.*

And in time, her sobs eased.

"Well," her mother finally said, "that was quite a watershed."

Charlotte said nothing. How could she? Then they both heard William's heavy footfalls in the hallway.

"It's done!" he bellowed through the door. "We have the kite together, Charlotte! We can go to the park now. Charlotte!"

Charlotte sighed, the sound released from deep within her belly. William would not be put off. "Nanny is ill?" she asked.

"Nanny is overpaid for what little work she does."

Charlotte sighed. Her mother was being unfair. Nanny worked as hard as any of them. And she loved William. It was just that . . .

"Charlotte! Where are you? Charlotte?"

Heavy bangs sounded against the bedroom door. They had less than a second before the handle would turn and—

"Don't you dare open that door, William Christopher!" her mother snapped. "Charlotte is not dressed yet."

"But—"

"No, young man! You will go down to the library and wait until we are there."

"But, Charlotte—"

"Go!"

And miracle of miracles, William obeyed. They heard him stomp all the way down the hallway in a manner very much like his father.

"Mama," whispered Charlotte. "*Father* is in the library."

"I know," her mother answered, her voice light with mischief. "Perhaps they will share a spot of brandy and discuss horses." Then she looked down at her daughter just as Charlotte looked up. Then they both descended into giggles. It was ridiculous giggling, after such a scene and over the stupidest reason. And yet, it was a moment of perfect accord between them such as had not happened in years. But then that too faded, and Charlotte's gaze slid away from her mother.

"You have gotten yourself into a pickle, haven't you?"

Charlotte didn't answer. She honestly didn't know.

Her mother shook her head. "I'll never understand you, Charlotte. Why haven't you chosen some man and gotten married? It's well past time, you know. You're just rotting here at the house."

Charlotte stared, her body and soul pulling back from her mother. But one look at her parent's face, and she knew she would have to answer. Mother had a determined look about her. "W-well," she stammered as she pushed away thoughts of Ken Jin. "There is William to consider."

"Nonsense! We have Nanny. She's young and healthy—except for her unfortunate lip—so we know she'll never marry and leave us. Besides, they get along famously." Mama's expression softened at Charlotte's stricken expression, but her words were still clear. "Of course, William loves you here, but that hardly means you have to give up your life for him."

Charlotte blinked, her thoughts whirling. "I do quite a lot of work here, Mama. The menus, the staff—"

"Of course you do, dear. And it was very wrong of me to rely so heavily upon you. But I managed when you were younger, you know. I can manage again." Her mother grasped Charlotte's hands, pulling them tight to her heart. "So tell me the truth, dear. What is the real reason you have never married?"

How to answer? She'd wondered, of course. Every time one of her friends married, she thought about when she would take the same trip down the aisle. But the men she knew never interested her. They all seemed like younger versions of her father or . . . what?

Incompetent. They were, to a man, incapable of offering the least assistance with her life. She could never see her turning to one of them for help. They were too involved in their own pursuits, be it money or pleasure. She couldn't imagine asking them about the staff or a medical complaint, much less receiving help when any of her family became too difficult. She couldn't see turning to one of them to discuss religion or energy or any of the new ideas that had been bursting through her mind these days. No, the person she looked to for all these things was . . .

Ken Jin. From the moment he had entered the house with Charlotte's drunken father sprawled across his shoulders, Charlotte had known he was a man who accomplished things. He did it quietly, with an unobtrusive skill that she found all the more amazing for its silence.

Soon after he joined the household, the household supplies began to arrive smoothly. A small thing, but it made her management of the staff ten times easier. Next, her father started leaving the house for entertainment instead of bringing his parties home. And she never saw the opium traders again. Money began to flow, which meant she could hire more staff. And best of all, Ken Jin found Nanny, a truly wonderful girl in her early twenties, cursed with a hairlip but with infinite patience and skill when it came to handling William.

So the truth was, no man she ever met could measure up to Ken Jin. No man would be as capable, as tender, as perfect as . . . the man who had just flatly refused to marry her. To her shame, her lip began to tremble and once again she was sobbing in her mother's arms.

"Oh dear," her mother murmured. Then she kept repeating it for some time until Charlotte once again got a hold of herself. Then mother and daughter together straightened their clothing and patted their cheeks dry. "Don't worry, dear," added Mama as she tugged at her skirt. "Everything will be better in England."

Charlotte frowned. "England?"

Mama nodded and folded her hands serenely before her. "Yes, dear. England. You see, Father's brother has died."

Charlotte jerked backward. Of all the things she had expected her mother to say, this was the absolute last. "Uncle Phillip, Baron Wodesley? That Uncle Phillip? He's gone?" She had never met the man, and yet it felt unsurprising that someone had died this day.

"The letter arrived several days ago. Your father went to Canton to see about closing his affairs there."

Charlotte shied away from considering exactly which affairs he was closing. She focused instead on the news itself. "Several days ago? But I didn't know. You never said."

"No one knows except your father and me, and now you. We didn't want to upset William. And you know how superstitious the Chinese are about death. We can't let the servants know or they'll all quit. A house surrounded by death, and all that nonsense."

Charlotte blinked. "But Uncle Phillip was a baron. That means—"

"Yes, your father's inherited the title. He's a baron now. I'm a baroness." She leaned forward to touch her forehead to her daughter's. "And you, my dear, are the daughter of a baron."

Charlotte waited a moment. She allowed herself precious seconds to enjoy her mother's tender gesture, but eventually the woman pulled away. Meanwhile, Charlotte had to ask, she needed to know what the future would bring. "What does it all mean, Mama?"

"It means, my dear, that we must return to England. We can finally leave this heathen place and get you a real English husband. None of these foreign transplants, my dear, but a real, honest-to-goodness English gentleman—someone who's never heard of a rickshaw or seen chopsticks."

Charlotte blinked, her thoughts whirling. "But I like rickshaws and chopsticks."

Her mother patted her cheek. "Yes, I know. And that is all my fault for letting you take on so much. I should have insisted on returning home long ago. But everything will right itself once we're back on English soil, you'll see."

"But—"

"Elizabeth!" It was Father's bellow. William must have run through all of the man's patience.

"Tch," her mother said, rolling her eyes. "He must learn not to do that. He's a baron now." Then she pushed up from her seat on the bed. "Finish getting dressed, Charlotte. Fix your stockings, then take William to the park. You know he can't wait much longer."

"I know, Mama."

"There will be a great deal more to discuss tonight, but for now—"

"Elizabeth!" Another of Father's bellows.

"I must rescue your father. Hurry now. I'll make sure the carriage is waiting." Then she was gone, leaving Charlotte to mind her tasks.

She cleaned her face, dressed, and then took William to

the park. She helped her brother raise his dragon kite. She clapped when he got the streaming ribbons into the air. She even held it for him when he became bored and went off to play in the dirt. She did all the things she normally did as if nothing extraordinary had happened today. As if her entire world hadn't changed this morning only to return to exactly how it was by afternoon. How could the world feel completely disorienting and yet painfully familiar at the same time?

She didn't know and she couldn't think, so she didn't. She simply played with William as usual. She even planned next week's meals in her head. Then, when William grew hungry, she packed him back into the carriage and headed home.

He complained on the drive, just as he always did. Charlotte nodded her head and pretended to listen, just as she always did. Then she opened the carriage door and let him run ahead of her as they both always did. Until he stopped dead in the center of the front door, a strange frown on his face.

Charlotte speeded up, wondering what could possibly go wrong now. Then she reached the step and stopped as well. Looking around her brother's shoulder, she saw her trunk in the center of the hall, right in front of her parents.

"Father?" she asked, gently prodding William into the house.

"Say your good-byes," he answered coldly. "You're going to the convent."

Charlotte blinked, sure she could not have heard correctly. But one look at her mother's tearstained face, and she knew it was true. Her next words were out of her mouth before she could think. "You promised," she hissed. "You swore everything would be like it was."

"I most certainly did not!" he returned, his voice even harsher than before. "How could anything be the same af-

ter what you did? I promised to take care of you, and I am."
He motioned to a pair of footmen, who deftly lifted her
portmanteau over everyone's head and carried it out to the
carriage. "Your mother thinks this is best," he added
sternly.

"This isn't Mother!" Charlotte cried. "This is you, Father, unable to—"

"She feels a good dose of God will straighten you out."
He shrugged. "It could hardly hurt."

"Of all the hypocritical—"

"You are leaving, Charlotte, and let that be the end of it."

And right then, William began to understand what was
happening. He had been staring wide-eyed in the middle of
the hall, unable to follow the conversation. But his father's
words were clear enough for even him. "Leaving?" he
cried, his voice rising in pitch until it became a wail.
"Noooooo!"

"Stop it!" Father roared, as if yelling at the boy had ever
helped anything. "Stop it this instant!"

"Thomas!" cut in Mama. "You can't just scream at him.
He doesn't understand."

"Noooooooooo!" William threw himself onto Charlotte
and tried to climb up into her arms, but his size and weight
were too much for her and she stumbled backward. She
nearly tripped over the door frame, but managed to steady
herself on the front railing.

Her father continued to bellow. "Cease this instant! You
are a young man now! A future baron!"

"William, dear. William, come upstairs," called Nanny
from the top of the stairs. "Nanny has new game for you to
play."

"Nooooooo!" The boy didn't even know what he was
protesting anymore. His sobs were loud, his distress overwhelming, especially as Father reached over and grabbed
him. William screamed, of course. He hit and kicked and

fell down in a proper tantrum, but Father was still larger, especially with the assistance of the two returning footmen. Soon, William was dragged into the house while Mother hovered helplessly on the side.

"Do be careful!" she fluttered. "He's still a boy. He doesn't underst—"

The door slammed, with Charlotte on the outside.

"Forgive me, Father, for I have sinned. It's been eight days since my last confession." Charlotte frowned. Had it been so short a time? Barely more than a week for her whole life to change. And yet, she had been anxious for something to happen for so long now.

"And what is the nature of your sin?" Father Peter pressed when she remained silent.

"Yesterday, I lay with a man who was not my husband." How few words to encompass so much.

"Fornication is a grave—"

"We didn't—I mean, I'm still a virgin," she rushed to add. Then she stopped. Why exactly was that so important?

"That is excellent news," he intoned.

She frowned. "Why?" Father Peter remained silent, but she could feel his confusion. "I mean, why does it make a difference? If we've done everything else, why would the simple act of . . . Well, why does it matter?"

"That is an interesting question—"

"We've done everything, Father, and it was wonderful. He has this strange philosophy about energy. Yin and yang and qi. I don't—"

"That is a heathen religion." The priest's voice was hard.

Charlotte hadn't expected anything different, but she was still surprised by the hatred in his tone. She paused, then turned to the window and wished she could see better in the darkness.

"So you know about it?"

"I know that the devil has many forms of deception, of luring the unwary into the gravest of sins."

"But it wasn't the devil, Father. I even went to Heaven."

The priest released a snort. "I'm sure the experience felt most interesting."

She shook her head. "More than interesting, Father. It was spiritual. Holy."

"Only the Church is holy. Only God—"

"But I was there in Heaven." Her voice was gaining in volume. Why wouldn't he understand? "My spirit went up there, and I saw William."

"Your brother was with you?" Alarm vibrated through his voice.

"No, no, I saw William's spirit. Father, he was normal and beautiful and so perfect."

Father Peter sighed. The sound of his disappointment filled the small chamber. "Opium dreams cannot be—"

"There was no opium, Father. Some incense to clear the air, but—"

Father Peter cleared his throat. "Charlotte, you have been deceived. Opium was in the smoke. Try to think clearly, child. Our souls go to Heaven through Jesus Christ our savior, and only through—"

Her hands clenched in her lap. "It was *real*."

"Satan's deceptions *are* real, Charlotte."

"He is not the devil!" She knew she was losing control, but she couldn't help herself.

"Oh, Charlotte, it is good that you have come to me." His voice modulated softer, more filled with comfort. "I can see now that you are deep in the clutches of Lucifer. Tell me who this instrument of Satan is. Tell me who leads you astray."

She felt her eyes burn with tears, but she would not shed them. Charlotte had shed too many on her tiny cot last night. "He's not the devil just because he doesn't worship as we do."

"Who is it, Charlotte?"

"I'm not going to tell you," she snapped, "because he isn't evil."

"You must!" the priest ordered. "I cannot allow a lost soul to wander further into the wild. I must rescue you both, return you both to God's holy embrace. Do not leave a man to suffer in—"

"Stop it!" she cried. Father Peter's impassioned speeches were well known throughout Shanghai. He could fire the blood, stir the soul, and have a person believing anything just by the power of his voice. Charlotte didn't want that. She didn't want to believe that everything she'd done with Ken Jin was a devil's trap. "It's not true!" she cried. "It's just not true."

Father Peter fell silent. She knew the trick. Indeed, she'd seen it often enough when she'd accompanied her mother and the good Father on his clerical rounds. He waited in silence for the petitioner to see the error of his own ways. Eventually, guilt forced whomever into a confession. Rather than do that, Charlotte turned her thoughts a different direction. "Is it a sin to love, Father?"

"You think you love this man, Charlotte? This one who would indulge your most depraved fantasies of the flesh without offering marriage? This man who takes you from your family into a den of iniquity for his purposes? *This* is the man you love, Charlotte? This is the man—"

"No!" She swallowed. Put that way, Ken Jin did indeed appear heinous. He was well known for his relationships with white women. He had burned some sort of incense when they were together in the gardener's shed. And, worst of all, he had absolutely refused any suggestion that they be married. Weren't those the acts of a reprobate? Of a deceiver of innocents?

250

"But I'm not an innocent," she said firmly. "I pursued him. I insisted—"

"I never said you were innocent, my child."

She closed her mouth with a loud click. She raised her eyes to the crucifix and wondered exactly what was true and what was a lie. "I don't think I'd make a good nun, Father Peter. I know it's what my parents want, but I don't think—"

"Let God do the choosing, Charlotte. Our task is to follow."

She shook her head. Nothing made sense. Or perhaps it all made too much sense. They both seemed real: Ken Jin's Heaven, and Father Peter's Satan. But they both couldn't be true, could they? Ken Jin couldn't be both the devil's instrument and a man searching for enlightenment, could he? "I have to know, Father. I have to know which is the lie."

"Then pray, my child. Listen to what God—"

She groaned. "I've never heard anything when I pray."

"Sometimes God's voice is very quiet," he countered. "Perhaps you could try for just today. We will speak again tomorrow."

Charlotte nodded, even though she had no intention of doing as he asked. "I will take this day to find the truth, Father. And if you are right . . ." She took a deep breath. "Then I will come back here tomorrow and devote myself to God." She reached forward and touched the crucifix before her. She needed a physical connection with the God of her heritage. "I will become a nun."

"That is a wise decision, Char—" She heard Father Peter's voice stop as he caught her full meaning. "What do you mean, come back here? Where are you going?"

But Charlotte had already stepped out of the confessional and was heading out of the church.

March 9, 1895

Dearest brother Gao Jin:

What happiness flooded my spirit at the news of your marriage. Of course the Empress has realized your greatness. You were always the most clever, the most handsome, the most skilled of all of us. I never doubted that you would do the Wen family great honor in the Forbidden City.

Alas, but I cannot escape Shanghai in time for your wedding. My barbarian employer will allow me no absence despite the promise of Imperial favor.

Fortunately, we have another brother who, I am sure, will happily join you at the consummation of this most wondrous occasion. But please accept this most humble gift in celebration of your most excellent news.

In exceeding joy,
Wen Ken Jin

(Attached, two gold bars wrapped in red silk and delivered by an armed escort.)

B27–B34 Sacral Points—Located on the base of the spine, in the hollows of the bone, these are used for sexual reproduction problems, such as impotence, vaginal discharge, and genital pain.
Acupressure for Lovers, Michael Gach, Ph.D.

Chapter Fourteen

Ken Jin wasn't home. He was probably still giving over all his money to her father without even realizing that she'd been tossed out on her ear. Charlotte sat down at his door, prepared to wait all day if necessary. She had to see Ken Jin again. She had to know if it had all been a lie. Besides, where else did she have to go?

It was midafternoon before a familiar voice woke her out of a doze. "Miss Charlotte? What are you doing here?"

Ken Jin! Charlotte was on her feet and rushing toward him even before she'd fully opened her eyes. He caught her, of course; he always did. But he was slow to embrace her.

"Why are you here now, when you wouldn't see me at . . ." His voice trailed away. "You weren't at home this morning, were you?"

She shook her head and buried her face in his shoulder.

"Have they disowned you?"

She could feel the tension in his body. Joanna had once said that disowning a Chinese was worse than murder. No

253

greater insult, no worse punishment could occur than to be disowned.

"No. At least, I don't think so," she said. "They want me to be a nun." She couldn't keep the bitterness from her voice.

He frowned, then slowly pulled away from her. "Let us go inside." He unlocked the door and ushered her in. She moved quickly, fully aware of the differences between yesterday's entrance into his private home and today's. "You should not be here," he said. "Your father will be furious."

"I hardly care what my father thinks," she snapped. "He slammed the door on me, Ken Jin." She blinked away the tears. "No matter what happens now, I will never, ever go back to that house."

He didn't answer. He simply looked at her, his dark eyes giving nothing away.

"You were just there?" she asked.

He nodded.

"How was . . . how was William?"

"Sleeping. He had a very bad night."

She nodded, chastising herself for feeling a bit pleased by William's unhappiness. She should not be grateful that her brother gave her parents a hard time; but everything would have been fine if she'd been allowed to stay at home. "I've b-been thinking, Ken Jin," she stammered as she tried to clarify her thoughts. "I had a lot of time last night at the mission."

His eyes darkened. "I did not know. If I had, I would have . . ."

"What?" she pressed when he did not finish. "What would you have done?"

He sighed and rubbed a hand across his jaw. It was an unusual gesture for him. It made him look . . . lost? The thought was so disconcerting that Charlotte found herself sitting down. There was only one place to sit, of course; all else was bare after yesterday's fight. She sat in the valley of the Dragon chair and tried not to remember how she'd used it before.

"I don't know, Miss Charlotte. I don't know that I could do anything for you."

"Char," she snapped. "You once called me Char."

He merely shrugged, though she thought he looked sad.

"What are you going to do now?" she asked. "Will you look for another job?"

He shook his head. "I would not be hired. Not by anyone in Shanghai. Your father will see to it."

She knew it was true and felt guilt eat at her for what she had done. For what they had done together.

"What will you do?" he asked. "Will you become a nun?"

She looked down at her hands. "No." It wasn't a conscious decision, and yet she felt the truth of it deep within her. Maybe Ken Jin had lied to her, maybe he'd sought her yin essence to the exclusion of morality and ethics. But being with him now, she could not believe it. Nor could she imagine him as an instrument of evil. He was merely Ken Jin—servant, protector, brilliant financial assistant. Her Ken Jin.

She lifted her head. "I don't really know that much about you, do I?"

He frowned, clearly unable to follow her thoughts.

"I mean, I don't know anything about you as a person. Your family. Your history. Your plans or hopes. You know everything there is about me, but I . . . I never looked beyond the surface of you."

He stared at her. "I am your servant. One does not discuss family with servants."

She felt her lips curl in a soft smile. "But you're not my servant anymore. Can't we share that now? Like friends?"

Clearly, the idea confused him. But eventually he nodded and settled cross-legged on the floor before her. She watched him there, his head slightly bowed. He was still acting like her servant, and the sight irritated her no end. So with a huff, she pushed off the Dragon chair to sit on the floor directly before him. She saw his eyes widen in surprise, and she felt herself smile for the first time since . . . well, since she last used the chair.

"I want to talk to you as a friend, Ken Jin. Can we please try?"

He nodded, but she could see he didn't truly understand.

"Don't the Chinese have friends?"

"Of course we do."

"So, who is your best friend?" He already knew hers was Joanna. "Who do you tell your hopes and fears and thoughts to?"

He tilted his head slightly. "My mother used to talk with our neighbors over mah-jong. I remember the sound was deafening. It would keep me up at night. But when I left home, I missed it."

"The sound?" she pressed as he fell silent.

"The clack of the tiles hitting together between rounds. It was like thunder. And they would all be talking at once, laughing or hissing—"

"Hissing?"

He said something in Mandarin. She did not understand the dialect, but she could hear the large number of sibilant sounds. The words did indeed sound like a snake's hiss.

"My mother loved lychee nuts," he continued, and his hands lifted as he remembered. "She would eat the meat, then suck on the stones. Always she had one in her mouth, so she talked like this." He spoke again, but with a lisp that had her laughing in delight.

"How could you understand her?"

He shrugged. "I was her child—of course I would understand." Then he abruptly closed his mouth, and his expression shifted. He blanked his emotions out completely, and the sudden return to his servant persona was shocking.

"Ken Jin? Is your mother dead?"

"She died of a fever many years ago, along with my father and grandmother." He lifted his gaze and pinned her with a dark stare. "My brother blames the whites."

She pulled back. "For a fever?"

His gaze was uncompromising. "Whites have brought diseases to China."

"And opium, I know. But we brought ships, housing, and commerce, too."

He did not so much as blink. "I have worked for whites since I was twelve. You do not have to tell me what they have and have not done in my country."

She frowned. He clearly wanted her to understand something, but—

"You wanted to know about my family. Here is all you need to know: They despise the whites. I think one brother may have helped murder missionaries—" She gasped in horror, but he did not stop. "At best, they want you all gone. At worst . . ."

"Dead. They want us all dead."

He nodded, clearly thinking he'd shocked her. In truth, she was more annoyed than horrified. It wasn't as if the attitude was unusual. Anyone who actually looked would know exactly what the Chinese thought of the ghost barbarians.

"I asked if you had a best friend, Ken Jin."

He blinked. Then she thought he flushed. His skin turned more golden in the harsh afternoon light, but he didn't answer.

"Who do you talk to, Ken Jin? Do you have a confidant?"

He shook his head. "I have work, or I did. I have goals. Why would I invite disaster by telling anyone?"

"You must be very lonely," she murmured. "Even your room is bare."

"That is your father's fault," he said with marked irritation.

"No. It was spare even before."

He didn't answer. In the end, she dropped her head back against the higher slope of the Dragon chair and smiled at him. "Tell me about your fiancée."

He flinched.

"How did you meet her?"

"My younger brother engaged us. She is my cousin on my mother's uncle's side."

"Second cousin?"

He frowned, as he no doubt sorted through the English terms. "My great-uncle's great-granddaughter."

"You haven't met her, have you?"

He lifted his chin. "Once. A few years ago during New Year's celebration." He let his eyes drop slightly. "She has big feet."

Chralotte stiffened. "You don't actually find that attractive, do you—feet the size of a guinea? Ken Jin, that's—"

"Smallness in a female is prized, Miss . . . Char," he amended.

"But you . . ." She swallowed, suddenly aware of her large feet, her large breasts, her large . . . well, everything. She was not small-boned. But then again, neither was he. For a Chinese, Ken Jin was downright huge. "I cannot imagine you with a tiny wife. You would dwarf her—"

"I have no special liking for tiny things," he finally admitted. Indeed, it sounded as if he was ashamed. "I suppose I have spent so much time with whites, I appreciate curves."

She blinked. Was he looking at her breasts? He raised his gaze to hers and a smile tilted his mouth.

"I like your curves very well, Char. And your well-formed feet." He leaned forward. "Truthfully, I understand bound feet smell terrible!"

She giggled, as he obviously meant her to. But then she sobered as she set her intellect to work on what she'd just learned. "So, your fiancée is a distant cousin and she has large feet."

"Her mother died in childbirth. There was no one to bind them."

"Which means she can't be considered a marriage prize. Were your mother's feet bound?"

He nodded.

"And your grandmother's?"

"Yes."

"So that's a bit of a step down for you, isn't it? To marry a woman without bound feet. And for your brother to make the engagement . . . it's almost an insult." She paused to study his face. "Isn't it?"

His gaze dropped to his hands, which were neatly folded in his lap. Finally he spoke. "As I said, my family despises the whites."

"And you for working for them?"

He remained very still. Charlotte couldn't even tell if he was breathing. Then he spoke, his voice low and emotionless. "They despised me long before that. I was disowned before I came to Shanghai."

"Disowned?" She gaped at him. "But . . . before Shanghai? You must have been two years old!"

"I was eight."

"My God. How did you survive?"

His posture slumped—not significantly, but just enough for her to realize that these memories were painful for him. Which made her feel doubly honored that he shared them with her. "My grandmother sent me to the Tan family. My grandmother was a Tigress like Tan Shi Po. She begged her sister-in-the-practice to care for me. And Shi Po did."

"The Tans who are in jail now?"

He nodded, his misery obvious.

"I'm so sorry, Ken Jin. But I'm sure you can get them out."

He shook his head. "I am penniless now. The most I can do is pray for Imperial favor, but that will take a long time."

She took hold of his hands. They were cold, Asian smooth, and yet when she touched him, they opened to receive her. She felt the calluses along his fingers and palms, and she felt his strength as he gently gripped her.

"I have a plan," he finally said, his words low. "But I am afraid."

She leaned forward and tried to communicate her faith to him through their hands. "You won't fail," she murmured. "I know you, Ken Jin. You never fail at anything."

He released a short huff of humor. It wasn't a laugh as much as a groan, the creak of a tree when blown too far by the wind. "I fail," he said. "Indeed, I have failed at everything I intended from the day I was disowned." He looked into her eyes. "Charlotte, a Chinese man is nothing without his family, his every effort is doomed."

"Nonsense!" she snapped. "We whites value family as well, but there is much that a man all alone can accomplish. For example, such a man could travel alone from Peking to Shanghai. He could learn English and begin work on the docks. He could find a job as a First Boy and make lots of money doing so. He could . . . he could befriend his employer's daughter and . . . and . . ."

"And she would become his dearest friend."

She looked at him and tried hard to hide the surge of yin heat his words produced inside her. "I . . . I am?"

He drew her hands up to his lips in a very loverlike, very European manner. "I have not spoken of my past or my future with anyone since . . ." His voice faded away, but she guessed what he'd been about to say.

260

"Since Little Pearl?" she asked, hating to say that woman's name, but needing to know the truth.

He shook his head. This time his laugh was not so forced. "I told nothing to Little Pearl. Our focus was very different." His mouth curved in a smile. "I spoke for a while with Tan Kui Yu in the way a boy speaks with a teacher."

"Or a father."

He acknowledged her comment with a slight dip of his head. "But never a woman. Never until you."

"I am honored," she whispered. And she was, right down to the very bottom of her soul.

Ken Jin abruptly straightened. His shoulders slid back and his spine straightened, but he did not stand. He had the attitude of a man who had just come to a decision, especially as he withdrew his hands from hers. And when he spoke, it was directly at her, with barely a hitch to betray the great emotions he surely hid.

"I must tell you why I was disowned," he said.

She waited, her breath held in anticipation.

"There is a tradition in my family. I understand the English have something similar. The eldest son follows in the father's footsteps. My father was an acupuncturist. My oldest brother was to learn that path as well."

She nodded. "The English do something similar. The eldest son is the heir."

"Yes, exactly. But what do the other sons do?"

She shrugged. "Whatever they can, I suppose. One often goes into the military. Another the church. My father came here and started his tobacco and wine shops."

"So it was in my family as well. The eldest son learns at his father's knee, but the second son is given to the Emperor."

She frowned. "Given to the Emperor. You mean, becomes a soldier or takes the civil service examination?"

Ken Jin shook his head. "He is given to the Emperor as a eunuch."

Charlotte stared, at first unable to understand. She knew what a eunuch was. Indeed, everyone discussed the barbaric practices of mutilation in China: girls whose feet were kept at a horrifying three inches in length, boys who had their privates cut off—all off, dragon pearls, jade stalk, everything—just so they could live as servants to the Emperor. Horrible.

"But . . . but *you* are the second son, aren't you?" She couldn't stop herself from looking at his groin. He was no eunuch.

Ken Jin's gaze dropped to his hands. His long fingers were still, but she had learned that the quieter he became, the more disturbed he was. At the moment, Ken Jin was very upset. "Yes, I was the second son—the one to be given to the Emperor." His eyes became dark and filled with pain, and he didn't move except to speak. She didn't dare touch him, but she kept her hands palm up before her in case he reached for her.

"My uncle came when I was eight," he continued. "The uncle who is a eunuch."

"Did you know why?"

He nodded. "My mother told me the night before. She explained it to me so I wouldn't be afraid."

"But they were going to chop off . . . to cut off . . . Of course you were going to be afraid! Who wouldn't be terrified?"

"I was very young, but I was also clever." He didn't sound like that was a good thing, and at last she began to put the clues together.

"What did you do? Were you disowned because you refused?"

He shook his head. "There is no refusal in China, not for a child."

"But—"

"I tricked my older brother Gao Jin into going."

She frowned. Then she stared. "Your older brother—"

"My father's heir. He was given to the Emperor instead of me."

"And being a child, you probably thought that you would step into his position as heir."

He blanched. It was a subtle shift in color, but Charlotte was watching him very closely. Still, he did not hide from her statement. "I was very jealous of my brother," he said, his words flat and somewhat halting. "He had no interest in acupuncture. If anything, he had a cruel streak." His gaze flickered. "He enjoyed sticking the needles in. He especially loved twisting them." He flinched, apparently in memory. "It can be quite painful."

She leaned forward. "He practiced on you, didn't he?" Ken Jin's eyes widened in surprise, and she almost laughed. "It's not a large leap. Many people are jealous of their siblings. Was he much older than you?"

"Barely a year."

"So, he was the great heir. He got to stab his brother over and over and claim he was practicing for his future career."

Ken Jin nodded. "He would have made a poor acupuncturist. I was the younger, but I understood the art. I memorized the qi lines."

"You wanted his place. It's only natural."

"Yes!" But then his eyes clouded, and his body slowly drew in on itself. His chin dipped, his spine curved, and his gaze dropped to the floor. "I was wrong." He sighed. "I was very, very wrong."

"But why?" She leaned forward, daring to touch his leg. "If you ask me, the system is at fault. Of course you were jealous of your brother—all second sons are. And if you had more aptitude, you should have inherited the shop, and your brother . . ."

"What?" he pressed when her voice faltered. "Did he deserve to have his dragon sliced off because I wanted to be an acupuncturist? Dragon, jade stalk, and dragon pearls—all gone in a single cut!"

She shook her head, startled by his vehemence. "N-no. Of course not. No one should have that happen to them."

He shook his head. "What would you know? You are a barbarian."

"Ken Jin!"

He pushed her hand off his leg. "We are in China, Charlotte, and I am Chinese. My family has always given the second son to the Emperor. And I—in my arrogance— chose to subvert that order."

"You were eight years old!"

"I was a cheat! And everything I have done since that moment has been a lie." He spoke firmly, his voice loud and true. Charlotte could see that he believed what he said, and yet she couldn't understand a word of it.

Pushing to her feet in frustration, she began to pace the room. How odd that she was the one stomping about his room when he sat with complete composure. "How can you be so calm? You were a child who didn't want to be mutilated. That doesn't make you a cheat."

"It was my path whether I knew it or not."

She let her head drop backward and stared at the ceiling. There was no talking to the man. "So, what happened when your family found out?"

"I had a younger brother. He was healthy and more sweet-tempered than either me or my older brother."

She straightened to look at him. "They made him the heir?" she guessed.

He nodded. "I was disowned and thrown out of the house. They hoped I would run to Peking to embrace my true path."

"Well, thank God you didn't."

He shrugged. "My grandmother interfered. She gave me money and directions. She sent me to the Tigress Shi Po."

"At least someone in your family had sense."

He sighed. "She was a foolish old woman. She was wrong, but she erred out of love. I cannot hate her for that."

Charlotte blinked. She couldn't possibly have heard him correctly.

He saw her gaping at him and stood, crossing to her side. "My path has always been in service to the Emperor. It was so ordered the moment I was born a second son."

"But you escaped. You shouldn't—"

"There is no escaping the will of Heaven. Do you not understand that?"

"What 'will'? Tradition isn't the same as a heavenly decree."

He shook his head. "Everything I have done since that moment has been a failure."

She felt a panic begin deep in her belly. "You can't mean that. You've done well for yourself."

"I have done well for the barbarians invading my country."

"We're not invading!" she snapped. "And we're not barbarians! Stop saying that."

"You are unwanted. You use gunboats to enforce your presence, and opium to weaken our will."

She bit her lip. It was true. As much as she pretended otherwise, the Chinese had a legitimate grievance against the whites. Still, she felt her eyes burn with unshed tears. "You can't think that I—"

He touched his finger to her lips, stopping her words. "I think you are the sun in the sky, Miss Charlotte—"

"Char."

"*Miss Charlotte*," he repeated. "And I believe you are my closest friend."

Moved, she pressed a kiss to his finger. She tried to lean into him. She wanted to kiss him, but he held her away.

"That is why I need you to come with me."

She frowned. "Come with you where?"

"I am going to Peking. I am going to return to the place where I left the Tao—the true path."

She shook her head, horror rising to choke off her breath.

"Yes. Yes, Miss Charlotte, I am going to dedicate myself to the Emperor." She heard the ring of passion in his voice. Determination, but also joy.

"No, Ken Jin. You can't!"

"Yes, Miss Charlotte, I will." His eyes begged her to understand. "It is the only way I can regain what I lost."

"You're going to lose a great deal more!"

He shook his head. "No, I will regain everything. Can't you see that?"

"You're doing penance for something that happened when you were eight!" She was screaming now. She had lost all control, but he was talking about mutilating himself!

He frowned. "What is penance?"

"Hurting yourself. Punishment. Because of what happened—"

"It did not just 'happen,'" he snapped. "I *did* it. I did it to my brother."

"But he's not going to get his dragon back," she countered. "Doing this won't help him at all."

He growled. He actually growled at her, and his hands gripped her arms tighter. "This is not for my brother's forgiveness. I have already received that."

She pulled up short, surprised. A brother with a mean streak would not easily forgive Ken Jin's crime. After all, Gao Jin had lost his birthright along with the rest. She narrowed her eyes. "What did you do?"

"What?"

"What did you do to gain his forgiveness?"

Ken Jin sighed. It seemed as if the breath came from the depths of his soul, from his very roots. "Please listen to me, Char."

She bit her lip. It was obvious that this meant a great deal to him. She would do her best to understand, if only to ease his pain. "I'm listening," she finally managed.

"I return now to my preordained path. It is not punishment. It is not to seek forgiveness. In order for my life to have meaning, I must walk the right path."

"And that path means . . . castration?"

"Yes." There was no compromise in his tone, only absolute determination and a kind of weary knowledge. He had not come to this decision lightly; that much was clear.

"What about your fiancée?" she asked, knowing she was clutching at straws. "Won't she be upset?"

He shrugged. "I have already given her and her family all my money. That is what they truly wanted."

She felt pieces of the puzzle click into place. "That's why you never have any money. That's why you live in this tiny little place." Other men in his position built grand palaces for themselves. "You've been giving it all to your bride's family."

He nodded. "I was trying to buy my way back to the right path, but that is not possible. I cannot buy—"

"So you're going to become a eunuch? Ken Jin, you just can't!"

"I can," he answered firmly. "I can help the Emperor. I have a great deal of knowledge about the whites. I speak English. They will be most grateful to have me."

"Of course they would," she snapped. "You're a brilliant man."

"I will be a brilliant eunuch."

She twisted out of his arms, then immediately missed

his warmth. "But you could die!" She spun around to look at him. "I mean, don't they do this to boys? For men—"

"It will be extremely painful."

She thought it would be a great deal more. "But—"

"Adult men dedicate themselves to the Emperor. The surgeons are quite skilled with the process. Few die."

"Few!"

He shrugged. "Very few."

She felt her knees go weak and kept herself standing by sheer force of will. "No, Ken Jin, you can't." But there was no arguing the point with him. She could see it in his eyes; he was absolutely determined. He truly believed it was the only way to regain his soul. "There has to be another way."

He embraced her then. He held her arms and pressed his lips to her mouth. She tried to deepen the kiss. She tried desperately to reach him in the way they had always related—at least lately—but it didn't work. After a moment, he set her away from him. "I am going to Peking. I would have left already if you had not come."

"But—"

"I am going," he stressed. "And I wish you to go with me."

"What?"

"It will be difficult and unusual," he admitted. A ghost of a smile skated across his lips. "But the surgeons allow a companion during the process, a man's best friend."

She was gaping at him, but pulled herself together enough to try to understand. "You want me to go with you?"

"We will dress you as a coolie and cover your hair. There are ways to keep your identity hidden."

"You mean hide my white skin?"

He nodded. "Yes. There is always money paid to the family. It would be enough for your passage back here, should you choose. I will send a message to Captain Jonas. He often has business in Peking. He could come for you in a few weeks. Or I could introduce you to some whites I know in the capital."

She shook her head. "I don't care about that."

He let his hands slip to hers. "But you should care. You also need to decide your future. I can help you decide it as we travel. And after I am dedicated, there will be money to pay for whatever you wish."

She closed her eyes. This was so bizarre. "You want me to be with you, to hold your hand as they cut off your . . . As they . . ." She couldn't even say the words.

"Is that not what best friends do for one another?"

"Maybe best friends talk a person out of his idiocies," she shot back.

"This is no idiocy. It is my true path. I am sure of it."

He believed it. God help her, but he clearly did. And the knowledge brought him peace. She could see that as well.

"I . . ." What could she say with him looking so earnestly at her? What a great leap forward they had taken today. He'd called her his best friend. He'd shared with her today more than he had shared with anyone ever; she was sure of that. And now, as a reward, she got to sit beside him. She got to hold his hand while some Chinese doctor sliced off his manhood. And she got to sit by his bedside and pray that he survived. What did she say to that?

"Are you sure?" she whispered, already knowing the answer. "Absolutely sure?"

"I have never been more certain of anything." Passion and truth rang in his words. Then his expression softened, and he looked as if he were begging her. "Will you come, Char? Will you help me?"

What could she say except . . . "Yes."

March 15, 1895
Brother Ken Jin:

You must attend my wedding. Kill your employer, steal his ill-gotten gains, and come prostrate yourself before the Empress as you beg my forgiveness.

You were the clever child, the unfilial one devoid of honor or loyalty. You stole my children and my future. Only you may give it back.

Wen Gao Jin

THE HEART—The heart reflex is found only on the left foot. Supporting the left foot with your right hand, use your left thumb to work the area in horizontal lines. [Work on the ball of the foot from the base of the big toe inward to the base of the fourth toe.]
The Joy of Reflexology, Ann Gillanders

Chapter Fifteen

"What about your Dragon practice?"

Ken Jin glanced to the side of the small donkey cart and smiled at Charlotte. The late afternoon sun turned her hair to copper, making her look, for a moment, like a bright new coin. Surely that was an omen of success.

He still could not believe she had joined him on this journey—without complaint, without question. It had taken him barely an hour to arrange the last details. Most had been accomplished that morning when he bought this cart and donkey for the journey. It had been a simple matter to spend his last coins on food and coolie clothing for Charlotte. Unfortunately, it soon became clear that she intended to spend the entire journey trying to talk him out of his decision. He didn't mind, though. He liked listening to her voice.

"You have spent years practicing as a Dragon," she pressed. "Do you really want to abandon that completely?"

He shrugged. "A eunuch cannot store or refine his yang. I suppose I could still gather yin in the usual manner, but without my Dragon seat . . ." He shook his head. "I cannot see a reason."

"But . . . but . . ." Her voice sounded tight as she bounced in her seat. Amazing, that after seven hours on this hard board, she could move at all. He himself ached everywhere, from his knees through his arms, and most especially his behind.

"But?" he prompted when she fell silent.

"But we almost made it to Heaven. You have worked so hard. And that last time, I felt it. I felt . . . you know, everything."

He was silent for a long moment, the twisting of his heart making him hunch in his seat. He didn't want to make his next offer. The very thought was repellent, and yet he would not stop her just because he had chosen another path. "You may have it," he finally said.

"What?"

"My bed, the Dragon chair, all the things I have left in my rooms for practice. They are yours." He forced himself to look her in the eyes. "I sent a message to Captain Jonas before we left. He will meet you in Peking after my dedication. He will take you back to Shanghai if you wish. Then you can collect the bed and my other things. You could continue to practice."

Her mouth opened, but no sound came out. Then she snapped it shut again only to fiddle with her coolie hat and at the slow donkey. Finally she sighed, her entire body drooping. "I don't want to keep practicing. Not without you."

He felt a surge of happiness at her words, selfish though that was. The idea of her with anyone else infuriated him, but he had no claims to her—as a partner or a friend. The moment the surgery was complete, he would live within the Forbidden City. The outside world would cease to exist for him unless the Emperor decreed otherwise. He and Charlotte would be, in practical terms, dead to one another. And that thought pained him more than any other.

He had not realized how alone he felt until she'd sat on his floor and demanded that he talk to her as a friend. Was it a measure of his deviance that his closest companion was a white woman?

Without a full understanding of why, he reached out for her hand. He did not shift his eyes from the road, but all his attention was centered on her—on the smoothness of her skin, on the way she seemed to grip all of him with just her fingers, and how perfect her qi meshed with his. There was no dissonance in their touch, only a simple press of palm to palm, heart to heart.

"I will miss you," he said, startling himself with his words.

"You don't have to, Ken Jin," she urged as her fingers intertwined with his. "Don't—"

"I have made my decision. Do not spend the last of our time together in argument." His voice was toneless, but inside, his heart pounded in his throat and temples. Clearly his qi was vastly out of alignment. "Will you help me tonight?" he asked, once again surprising himself with his question.

She started as well. He felt the slight jerk in her body through her hand. "Of course," she answered. "What . . . what do you need—"

"I would like you to help me insert the needles."

She flinched again, but he was holding her tightly. He did not release her hand even as she straightened on the hard seat. "Needles?" she asked. "As in acupuncture?"

"Yes. I cannot reach the places on my back. I will need you to—"

"I won't know where to put them," she rushed. "I . . . I don't want to hurt you."

"There is very little pain, and I can tell you what to do."

She fell silent for a long while. They would have to stop for the night soon, and he kept an eye out for the most likely place. At least the weather remained mild. The cool northern air was a welcome.

"Do all Chinese enjoy pain, or is it just you?"

Her statement was so odd that he thought he hadn't understood. But as he replayed her English words in his head, he knew her statement was exactly as it first appeared—completely bizarre and rather insulting as well.

He stared at her. She stared back. And so they sat for a long, long moment. Normally, she would break first; Charlotte never could remain silent for long. She would make a terrible servant in that regard. But in this case, she simply continued to look, her head tilted to one side as if she were inspecting a rare form of plant or insect. In the end, he was the one who felt compelled to speak, and he did so with a tone of great offense.

"I take no enjoyment in giving pain."

She rolled her eyes. "Not other people's pain. Your own."

"What are you talking about?"

"You stick needles into your belly. You want to cut off your dragon. You . . ." Her gaze abruptly dropped to his lap before jumping back to his eyes. "Maybe it's just your dragon you hate." She leaned forward. "Think about it. You have spent more than a decade denying its release."

"That is a Dragon's training," he snapped.

She shrugged. "Maybe so. But don't most men want to release their seed? I mean, doesn't it feel good?"

"I am not most men," he replied stiffly. "I have already explained the reason for this."

"Yes, yes, I know all of that. But still, most men would find it really hard to restrain themselves. Did you ever break? I mean, when you were with other women, did you ever—"

"No!" The word leapt from his strangled throat. "Not until you."

"Exactly. And you stick needles into—"

"Not into the *dragon*," he said, switching to Chinese. The words came out as a kind of hiss, but she was undeterred.

"No, not exactly, I suppose. But close enough. Who wants to put sharp things right there?"

"It was a treatment."

She twisted on the seat to stare at him more fully. "A treatment? For what?"

"For impotence!" he shot back.

She frowned, obviously not understanding his word even though he said it in English. To make matters worse, the Chinese word for such a condition was "eunuch," which would further confuse matters. That meant he had to explain the condition.

"For a weak and limp dragon."

She frowned. "But isn't it usually limp? I mean, you can't always have—"

"Always," he ground out. "An always weak dragon."

"Well, yes. Always whenever you're not—"

"Always!" he ground out. "That is the problem. It is always weak, always limp! It began long ago with less power, less strength every day. And in the last year . . ." He shook his head. "It was a dead thing. No life at all."

She stared at him, her mouth open and her eyes wide as she at last understood. He turned away and his face burned with shame. But then she laughed. She didn't only laugh; she held her sides and guffawed. She startled birds. She nearly fell off the cart. Even their placidly slow donkey snorted and flicked his tail in irritation.

"I do not see the cause for humor!" he growled as she paused for breath. But that only made her laugh harder, until she finally could laugh no more. He shot her another glare just as she was wiping the tears from her eyes.

"Oh, don't get snooty on me," she said between giggles. "You're the one who started it."

"Started what? I merely explained a procedure—"

"You merely lied through your teeth and think I'm stupid enough to—"

"That was no lie!"

She stared at him a moment, then descended into another long peal of laughter. It was a long while before she finally contained herself. "And here I was thinking you had no sense of humor."

"Of course I do," he grumbled. "But I was your servant. Servants do not make jokes."

"Well, you're not my servant now, and you definitely made a joke."

"It was no joke!" he snapped.

She grinned at him. "Ken Jin, you're not impotent. I know that from personal experience. And even if I didn't, your . . . um . . . size and girth is well known among the ladies you have visited."

He turned and stared at her, unsure what to say.

"Yes," she returned, and her eyes seemed to sparkle in the fading sunlight. "Legendary. My God, Ken Jin, you have a large and healthy dragon. Whatever made you think you were . . . whatever that word is? Impotent?"

His mind worked very slowly. "Legendary?"

"I have told you and told you that you have a reputation."

She had, but his reputation was because he pleased women as he gathered their yin, not for the use of his dragon. He lifted his chin, his words and spine stiff. "Surely I am known more for my restraint." He turned away. "That was a product of my condition."

"Your condition was described as bulging, muscular, and astonishing," she shot back.

He frowned. "Muscular?" He shook his head. "White women exaggerate."

"No," she retorted. "No, they didn't. Remember, I know the truth."

"But . . . with you it was different," he huffed. "Why else do you think I allowed myself to practice with my employer's daughter?"

She abruptly fell silent. After a moment, he realized that her laughter had been replaced by hurt. He turned to look at her, only to see that she'd turned from him. He could glimpse only the smallest portion of one cheek.

"Char?"

"Is that why you came to my bedroom? Is that why . . . ? You know. Because I made your dragon stiff?"

Up ahead, he finally saw a place to stop for the night. He clucked to the donkey, his attention split between maneuvering the cart and his companion. "You were my employer's daughter. You know what I risked being with you."

"I know," she answered in a small voice. "I know what you *lost* because of me. What I want to know is why." He heard her shift her body back toward him. "Why, Ken Jin? Why did you take such a risk?"

He frowned at the stubborn donkey who would not move according to direction. "Because you stiffened my dragon, Char, in a way that no one had done in a very long time. I was beginning to fear it had died."

Finally, the donkey obeyed, and Ken Jin could direct his full attention to Charlotte. He turned to see her face compressed in thought, her eyes distant in memory.

"I don't understand," she said. "All those women. All that yin you gathered for years. They all said—"

He grunted and set down the reins. "I do not know what they said, nor do I care. I know the truth, Char. My dragon was a withered pole until you." He shook his head. "At first, I thought my renewed strength was because of the treatments."

"Treatments?" she echoed. "The acupuncture?"

"Yes. But I soon realized it had nothing to do with my qi.

It was yours. Your power is such that even my lost yang responded to it."

"My qi?"

"Your . . . *You.*"

"And all those other women, they couldn't get you to . . . Your dragon didn't respond to them, so you thought you were impotent."

"I *was* impotent. I wouldn't even undress before them. Then you touched me and everything changed."

"It can't be true."

He threw up his hands in frustration, then hid the reaction by climbing out of the cart. "No man wishes to discuss this, Char." He grumbled low curses beneath his breath as he released the harness on the donkey. Meanwhile, Charlotte climbed out of the cart, moving with the kind of care induced by hours seated on a hard bench.

"I just can't believe it's true," she continued as she grabbed the beast's brushes and bucket. Ken Jin had spent the last of his coins on this trip. Looking at her, he felt his heart swelling with joy that she didn't mind helping with the poor creature's care.

He tethered the donkey to a nearby tree and let her work. Meanwhile, he spread blankets in the back of the cart for a bed. He knew she might refuse to share the space. He was fully prepared to sleep on the ground, but he hoped differently. He hoped—

Suddenly, she stood before him. He could smell the work she had been doing. He noticed the dust in her hair and on her skin. He even saw the pull of fatigue on her face. But mostly he saw her: the last caress of sunlight sparkling in her wide blue eyes, the slight moisture on her red lips, and the simple honesty in her spirit.

"You are not impotent," she said. Then she pressed her hand to his dragon. Neither of them moved. She gave no

caresses, no stimulation. And yet his dragon steadily thickened. "You are *not* impotent," she repeated.

"Only with you," he stressed.

"Then it was your choice in partners that was at fault.
Not your . . . not your biology."

He smiled. "Whatever the fault, you have cured it." And
then he could not stop himself; he reached up and caressed
her cheek. How beautiful she was. Even with her covered
in dust and dressed as the poorest laborer, he could not take
his eyes from her.

"Kiss me, Ken Jin."

He could not refuse. Pressing his lips to hers, he felt the
burn of her powerful yin the moment they touched. His
yang was already rising. It always did when they were together. And yet, something was different. Something felt
more pure than before, or perhaps simply less cluttered.
Was it her? He couldn't tell. Perhaps it was them both, because they had left their lives in Shanghai.

Whatever the truth, he could not turn from the power.
His hands found her hips and drew her closer. With all his
skill, his lips and tongue stroked, teased, and suckled her.
She more than matched him, and soon he was lost to all but
the pulsing beat of their combined qi.

When she pulled back to draw breath, she glanced nervously about them. "We're out in the open. Anybody could
walk by."

"It will be full dark soon. No one will come by."

"But—"

"Trust me."

She looked back at him, her eyes full of yin power and
her expression completely open. "I do."

The two words rippled through his spirit. He stepped
back and stared at her, seeing her for the first time.

Sweet Buddha, she was a Tao master!

How could this be? She had no Buddhist education beyond the little he had taught her. She was a barbarian female! And yet she stood before him, fully centered in the Tao. He knew that without question; he felt it in her every gesture and word. She trusted completely and loved openly. Wasn't that the key to all Taoism?

She smiled sweetly at him and took a deep breath. "The air is so clean here," she said. Then she let her head fall back to look at the sky. "And so beautiful."

He watched the long white expanse of her neck and tried to focus his thoughts. Was this why her qi was so strong? Because she openly embraced everything and everyone that surrounded her?

It wasn't that she was an untried innocent. Far from it. She had raised William almost from infancy. She understood the difficulties of an adolescent boy without the brain to restrain his baser instincts. And if she didn't comprehend the bestial from her brother, there was always her father. She'd seen her father's character. She knew of his mistresses and his dealings with opium. After all, the man had brought his partners into their home on several occasions.

She knew about carnality in most of its forms, and yet whenever Ken Jin touched her, she felt open and innocent. She had experienced cruelty on behalf of her brother, felt betrayal from her father and casual neglect from her mother, and yet she could trust him openly with her well-being. These were all marks of a true master. His own abilities paled in comparison. He had never been that trusting, not in a household with three sons competing daily for food and attention. He wondered if he ever could.

He reached out and stroked her cheek. "I want to practice with you." That wasn't what he had intended to say. In fact, he had resolved not to be with her again in any way. And yet, she was smiling at him in a way that made him feel strong and alive. "With you," he murmured, "my yang expands and I become whole again."

She straightened. "I promise you, Ken Jin, you have no missing parts."

He traced his finger across her lips. "You bring all my scattered pieces together."

Charlotte sucked his finger into her mouth, and his yang surged so hard that his whole body trembled. Then she spoke around his finger.

"Teach me, Ken Jin. I want to learn everything."

He should be saying that to her. He should be begging her to show him how to be so innocent, how to hold to joy even when one was penniless and disowned. But he kept silent, his spirit too small to embrace her largeness, and in his shame, he looked away.

"Ken Jin? What's wrong?"

"Nothing," he lied. "We must make ready before dark. I have food and bedding."

In truth, it took very little time to arrange themselves. The weather was warm enough without a fire and clear enough to show the stars. There was grass enough for the donkey to eat, and privacy on the deserted track.

They shared a pair of dumplings; and though he worried at the meager fare, she never complained. Indeed, she seemed happy with his Chinese food. She sat on the back of the cart, kicked her feet as she ate, and stared at the stars. "I wish this night would never end," she said.

"You lie." He spoke without accusation, but she flinched nevertheless. "You are thinking of your home," he guessed. "You wish you were with William."

She shook her head. "I am worried about William, but the only one I want to be with is you."

He couldn't accept her honesty, and it made him all the more surly. "You have never slept on a hard floor, much less an open cart. You are used to five times this much dinner. Your clothes must itch and your bottom ache. You cannot want to be here; you must be wishing for a hot bath, your own clothes, your—"

"My family?" she interrupted. "My father? For all the things of my life that are now gone?"

"Of course."

She sighed, and he expected to see the shimmer of tears in her eyes. He didn't. He saw only starlight and a strange quiet. "I do miss them, and I am worried about the future. What will happen to me? What will happen to William?" Her voice trailed away as she lifted her face back to the sky. "But I'm not afraid, Ken Jin, not when I'm with you. And not here, where everything is at peace."

She slowly straightened. Her gaze left the heavens reluctantly to land upon him. "It's not me who lies, Ken Jin, but you. You say you want to practice, but you don't touch me. You say you want to travel to Peking, but you bought the slowest donkey in China. You are surrounded by peace and beauty, and yet you try to pick a fight with me. Why?"

He stared at her, his mouth open in shock. He tried to shut it, only to have harsh words tumble out in accusation. "You make me feel too much!"

She didn't move; she didn't even blink. She just stared at him as one would stare at a lunatic. And he stared back, wondering if he had truly lost his mind.

"Is that possible?" she finally asked. "To feel too much? I can't imagine it."

"Can't you?" he challenged. "Wasn't Heaven too much?" He'd been overwhelmed when they'd begun to ascend yesterday, and they hadn't even made it to the first chamber.

"It was incredible," she whispered, and he could almost see the lantern antechamber in her eyes. "I cannot wait to go back."

"What about how you felt when William threw his tantrum in church? Or when he cut your clothing with scissors?"

She smiled in memory. "I was embarrassed, yes, and angry. But William would not be William if those things were changed. The only way to feel less embarrassment or anger or frustration would be to love him less, and I won't do that."

Ken Jin nodded, knowing she was right. "But what about when your father threw you out? When he sent you to the mission in disgrace? There must be pain. You must feel—"

"Of course there is," she snapped. But then she continued, her words slow and careful. "But I think . . . there is relief, too." She took a deep breath and set her feet to swinging again. "I never realized how freeing disgrace could be." She flashed him a weak smile. "I'm a fallen woman now. I could have saved myself in the mission, but not now—not here alone with you."

Her smile faded, and he could see the reality of her situation slowly sink into her consciousness. Even though he had brought these thoughts to the fore, even knowing he had made her see the truth, her sudden cloak of sadness brought tears to his eyes.

"I'm a fallen woman," she murmured. "No respectable man will want me, and no dignified woman will accept me. Good little girls will be told to curse and spit at me; little boys will be free to tug on my hair or clothing and their parents will just laugh." She shuddered. "How cruel the righteous can be."

"You can still go back. I will take you to the mission. You can—"

"Become one of them? Forswear everything I feel to become a nun?" She turned to him, and he was stunned by the fury in her eyes. "I will have to swear that you are an evil man, Ken Jin. I will have to confess that what we did together was an act of depravity. You will be vilified. I will be castigated."

"Don't think about me. I will be—"

"I know where you'll be!" she snapped. "You're going to have your dragon cut off in some insane act of self-destruction, and so you think I should too. That I should become a nun, deny everything we did, and make it into something heinous."

"No!" How quickly his temper rose to match hers. "What I plan has nothing to do with you!"

"Are you so sure?"

"Of course!" But then he fell silent, wondering if he spoke the truth.

She must have sensed his weakness. Or perhaps, as a Tao master, she saw when he left the path of truth. "It all works together, Ken Jin. You cannot pretend one action doesn't touch another, that one part of you isn't a piece of the whole."

He looked away. Or, more accurately, he looked down. He did not want to think too deeply about what he intended. He did not want to dwell on the slice of the knife or the painful three days afterward. Three days when he would not be allowed to eat or drink or urinate. Would his dragon still be part of him then? Would . . .

"I'm not talking about your castration." Her voice trembled on that last word, but she did not stop. "I'm talking about everything. Your family threw you out."

"I survived. Tan Shi Po took me in."

"Until she and Kui Yu were taken to prison."

He closed his eyes, feeling the weight of yet another failure.

"Your employer's daughter pursued you, and you lost everything. Again."

"It was my choice as well."

"So, we are both at fault. Both—"

"Disowned. We are both disowned." He lifted his gaze to hers, regardless of the hot burn of humiliation in his face. "Why do you press this? What do you want, Char?"

She shook her head, obviously struggling with her answer. "I want you to be whole, Ken Jin. I want—"

"There is no whole for a disowned man! Do you not understand that? Without my family, I am a broken piece of an altar decoration, a thread cut off and discarded from the full tapestry. I am nothing!"

"But don't you see?" she countered, grabbing his hands and holding him to her. "You aren't broken, and you aren't discarded. Not unless you want to be."

He stared at her, and he could see she didn't understand. "A Chinese man is not just himself alone. His ancestors watch over him; his descendants care for him."

"So, since you don't have one you will cut off the other?"

"Yes!" he snapped. "It was my destiny thirty years ago, and I used treachery to avoid it. I told my brother that I was going to a fair without him. I pretended to brag, saying I would eat sweets and see a great magician. Then I let him sneak in the cart in my place and pretend to be me. I let him walk into the surgeon's tent expecting a show instead of the knife."

"You were eight years old!"

He shook his head. "I knew better." He straightened. "And now I return to the path I should have walked."

"You can't," she pressed.

"I can."

"You can't!" she repeated with more force than he'd ever heard from her before. "You can't become an eight-year-old boy again. You can't ignore what you have learned and done and been these last twenty years."

He meant to argue. He meant to claim that he could indeed be what he once was, but she was right. He was changed, and not even castration could erase the last two decades. He sighed. "I must return to the middle path. I must find peace."

She reached for him, stroking his arm. "Perhaps to be whole, you must look ahead instead of behind. Forget the past. Forge ahead to a new future. Create your own clan and your own ancestors."

He almost laughed at her silliness, but refrained because she would be insulted. "I cannot simply make up new ancestors."

She smiled. "Of course not. But you can create your own family altar. Write down the names of the people who still love you."

He snorted. "Ancestors are not so easily accepted or discarded."

"Then neither would their descendants be. Surely someone loved you. Someone would still claim you."

His grandmother. He knew this but did not admit it. Charlotte must have seen the thought inside him, though, must have sensed the softening in his heart at the memory of his father's mother.

"There *is* someone, isn't there?" she pressed.

"A woman does not go on a family altar."

"Says who?"

"Says me." And all the ancestors before him.

"Well, you're wrong."

This time, he did laugh. It was a clean sound, bursting from him. It brought lightness in its wake, and peace—a small, beautiful measure of peace. Then his laugh faded and they sat once again, side by side in silence.

Finally she sighed. "You're still going to Peking, aren't you?"

He nodded. "Unless you wish to go back to the mission."

"No. You'd just go on to the Forbidden City without me, and then we'd both be miserable."

He felt a smile tug at his lips. "I have no desire to see you miserable."

"I have no desire to see you castrated."

He laughed. "You need not watch."

"You need not do it at all."

Silence again settled between them, but it was not so heavy this time. Especially when he turned his hand palm-side up and her hand slipped into his. As always, their qi quickly harmonized.

"Will you still teach me?" she asked.

He smiled. How could he deny her anything? "If you still wish it."

"I do."

He was silent a moment. "How much do you wish to practice? Do you want me to take your virginity?"

She hesitated. "I've lost my reputation now. Everyone will expect that I'm . . . that I'm not . . ."

"But what do *you* want, Char?"

She sighed. It was a quiet exhale, a breath that he felt rather than heard. "I want to keep that part of me pure right now."

"Very well," he said. Then he gently disentangled their hands and drew his fingers up her arm.

Her body was exquisite, her trust in him divine. The moonlight made her skin glow like the finest pearl, the stars sparkled in her eyes, and the evening air became perfumed with her sweet scent. She was the evening: the moon, the stars, even the sweet water that trickled nearby. When he touched her, he touched the world. When he kissed her, he kissed eternity. And when she began to vibrate with yin power, he knew he could bring her to Heaven.

And with every caress, every kiss, and every gasping moment, he felt eternally blessed.

In this fashion, they passed every day and night until they arrived in Peking.

❦

Triple Happiness! Great fortune!
A son is born to Wen Gao Jin!
Joyous celebration! Heaven's blessing!

(Attached, a bill for expenses dated November 19, 1895. It includes expenses for the midwife, child's clothing, and the fourteen-day birth celebration, already completed one week before.)

Acupressure can be used as an adjunct therapy in the treatment of migraine pain and the underlying cause of this physical disturbance. First, massage your head as if shampooing your hair. Second, place your thumbs underneath the base of the skull on either side of the spinal column. Tilt your head back slightly and press upward for two minutes while breathing deeply.
http://www.holistic-online.com, ICBS, Inc.

Chapter Sixteen

Charlotte had never been in Peking. She'd never seen the dragon tiles that decorated the Forbidden City, never even conceived of the huge pagoda temples that punctured the landscape, but she recognized wealth when she saw it. And she knew the neighborhood they drove through had to be one of the very best.

"Who lives here, Ken Jin?" she whispered from beneath her coolie hat.

"Wen family son number one," he answered in the Chinese style. When she frowned, he elaborated. "My older brother, Gao Jin. Not the acupuncturist."

The eunuch, then. "But I thought they all lived inside the Forbidden City serving the Emperor."

"Most do. My brother was honored for exceptional service."

She remembered. "For killing those missionaries—"

"No," he corrected, though his tone remained cold. "For bringing the news."

She rolled her eyes. As if any simple messenger would be so honored. "Is he a Boxer?" She had heard stories of those revolutionaries. Joanna saw them as the Chinese form of freedom fighters, but Charlotte wasn't so sure. They seemed to have a great deal of antiwhite sentiment. It could be dangerous for her to—

"I will keep you safe." His quiet words soothed her even before she realized she was worried.

She smiled and took his hand. He returned her grip, and they continued riding behind the slowest donkey in China. "So, your brother was given permission to live outside the Forbidden City," she said after a few minutes.

"He was given an honorary bride and a son."

She started. "A son? But how? If he's a eunuch . . ."

"A member of the family assisted on his wedding night."

She twisted to stare at him. "Assisted? As in . . . as in took over the marital rights?"

"Yes." His voice was very stiff.

It took her a moment. They had spent the entire trip learning about one another, and she had done all but surrender her virginity as they explored every detail of each other's bodies and souls. But even so, Ken Jin was still a hard man to read. It was harder still for Charlotte to accept this new truth.

"*You* did it. My God," she breathed. "You have a son."

"My brother has a son. I merely . . ."

"Assisted." She didn't know how she felt about that. She'd known Ken Jin for a decade, and yet every day she discovered something new. A son! Despite the discomfort, some part of her softened at the thought of a baby Ken Jin with bright eyes and those cute, chubby little fists. "I bet he's wonderful," she said. "And you have an heir."

He turned to stare at her, his expression cold. "My brother has an heir, as is appropriate. He should have—"

"Enough with the should haves." She couldn't help rolling her eyes. "You can't spend your life making amends for something that happened when you were eight."

"In China, generations can pay for the actions of a single man."

She let out an exasperated sigh. "And I felt burdened by caring for William every day," she muttered. "You bear the weight of generations. No wonder you never smile."

He was busy turning the donkey down another lane, but still managed to shoot her a hard look. A month ago, she would have thought his stare disapproving, but now she saw the sparkle in his eye and the slightest curve to his lips. He wasn't annoyed with her, he was amused but too restrained to show it. "I never smiled because I didn't know you," he said.

"La, sir," she trilled to cover her surprise, "are you flirting with me?"

He squeezed her hand as his smile broadened and his gaze intensified. "I am saying that I feel richly blessed. These last days, Char . . ." His voice faded as he struggled for the words. "I will remember them for the rest of my life."

She swallowed, instinctively flinching away from any thought of the future. So she focused on the present—on the sunlight as it lit the black velvet of his hair, on the crinkles at the corner of his eyes when he smiled at her, and on the curve of his lips, the strength of his hands, and the joy she felt when they were together.

"I love you, Ken Jin." The words were out before she truly understood their meaning, before she even labeled the emotion swelling inside her. But once said, she did not regret them. If nothing else, they would both know what she felt.

She waited in silence, aware that he was shocked. His hands went slack. His eyes were dark, his gaze steady. So steady that he couldn't be breathing.

"It's not because of . . . because of what we've been doing," she stammered, to fill the silence. "I love it, but I don't love you because of that. It's because of you, of who you are and how I feel when I'm with you."

He blinked. Then he took a sudden, deep breath. "I understand, Miss Charlotte."

"Miss Charlotte?" Disappointment blew through her body. "What happened to Char?"

He turned to look at her. "Char, then," he whispered. There was a wealth of meaning behind his tone, but she didn't understand it.

"Ken Jin—"

He kissed her then, swift and hard, right there on the street for all to see. She softened into it immediately. Her lips clung to his and her mouth slipped open, but he was already drawing away. She was left touching empty air, and she flushed in embarrassment.

"You do me a great honor," he said, his words obviously heartfelt; and yet she felt flat. Crushed, even.

"'A great honor,'" she echoed weakly. No words of love. No . . .

"You are upset," he said. Now his voice was unsteady; now he showed an emotion other than shock. He'd moved on to confused.

"Men usually say they love you back." She sighed. "Even if they don't mean it."

Ken Jin drew the donkey cart to a stop before a grand building. When he spoke, it was to the space between the donkey's ears. "A eunuch loves no one but the Emperor. To say otherwise is blasphemy."

"You're not a eunuch yet," she snapped. She knew she was covering her hurt with anger, but she couldn't stop herself.

Then he turned, and she saw the torment in his eyes. "I am already sterilized, Miss Charlotte. In my mind, I have already committed myself to this act." He waited a moment longer. She thought he had more to say, that he had something important to tell her. But he looked away. "We have arrived at last," he said to the donkey.

She looked up to see a grand gate entrance with thick red doors flanked by drum stones topped by dragon heads. Old men played Go and smoked across the street, but here all had an imposing silence. Even the trees didn't rustle and they barely provided shade from the glaring afternoon light.

Ken Jin tended the donkey, setting up food and water for it right in the street, while Charlotte did her best to fluff her hair. There was no appearing respectable, not when she wore creased pants and a threadbare tunic, but she didn't want to frighten Ken Jin's son. Then she heard the old men hiss and curse behind her. She turned, wondering what was wrong, only to watch them making signs of protection as they glared at her.

She understood immediately, and covered her hair. Her white skin had darkened after days in the sunlight, but not enough to appear anything but what she was: a ghost woman in Chinese Peking.

The old men's rancor gained in ferocity. Ken Jin was at her side in a moment. He stood between her and the men, even while aiming her inside. The gate was open— probably to catch what minimal breeze whispered down this ancient lane—and so she easily climbed the three steps up and slipped through, skirting around the screen designed to deflect wandering spirits. Ken Jin joined her a moment later, his face set in a tight frown.

"Will Yi-tou be all right?" she whispered, using her pet name for the donkey.

He nodded. "I have told those men we are on the Emperor's business."

She gestured to his ragged pants and dirty shirt. "Did they believe you?"

He shook his head. "No, but they will not take the chance of being wrong."

She would have said more, but household servants had appeared. Only one was supposed to greet them—a rather large and imposing butler—but a kitchen maid and an upstairs maid peered goggle-eyed around the corner as well. Ken Jin did not give any of them the time to speak.

"Tell my brother that Ken Jin is here to see him."

The butler paused, and Charlotte got to watch a Chinese butler show disdain. The English sniff and step haughtily away; the Chinese spit. And if they cannot—as this man obviously could not do to his master's brother—then they act as if they would spit. He pursed his lips and scrunched his face. He paused, as if deciding what to do.

"Now, dog, or I shall have you whipped!" Ken Jin's low voice carried clearly through the courtyard. Everyone scurried away, even the maids. Then Ken Jin turned to Charlotte. She saw a note of warning in his eyes, but again there was no time to speak as a young boy came bellowing into the courtyard from the inner quarters.

"Aie-yi-yi-yi-yi!" He punctuated each of his squeals with a tiny jump over the courtyard steps. Following behind him in a breathless flurry of skirts came one woman and two maids, obviously playing Follow the Leader.

"Aie-yi-yi," one of them gasped. As she was dressed better than the other ladies and had tiny bound feet, Charlotte guessed her to be the boy's mother. The others were just pretending to hop. Though they had natural feet, they appeared too tired to play earnestly.

The boy spun around and aimed a colored toy stick at the women. "You didn't make the call!"

"Aie-yi-yi-yi," they responded in the dullest voices possible.

He nodded with the confidence of a born tyrant. "Keep doing so! And remember to hop."

"But, little master," his mother gasped, "it is very hard

on my tiny feet." Indeed she clearly struggled, one hand on the wall as she descended the steps into the courtyard. She also glanced nervously at Charlotte and Ken Jin, but her words were for her son. "Let your mother—"

"Am I not the master here?" he bellowed. "You will obey! Obey! Obey! Obey!"

Charlotte drew back in surprise, especially as the child screwed up his face in preparation of a first-class tantrum. Obviously this was the number-one son—Ken Jin's son— but she'd never seen so ill-behaved a boy in all Shanghai. Certainly not one who disrespected his mother with such ferocity.

To her shock, the mother and the maids prostrated themselves before the boy. "Little master, little master!" they cried. "Do not upset yourself. You will do yourself harm. Little master!"

"That is enough!" Ken Jin snapped in a tone Charlotte had never heard him use before. She whipped her head around and nearly jumped when she saw the dark red flush to his features. "You will present yourself as an obedient young man!" His voice rang through the courtyard and cut off the child's tantrum midwail. All eyes flew to Ken Jin as he strode forward to glare down at the boy. His fists were planted firmly on his hips, and he stood as only a truly powerful man could.

The boy's jaw went slack, and he clearly had no idea what to do. He looked to his mother and her maids, but they were of no help. As they were already on their knees, the women remained there in silence, waiting for the boy's cue—an odd state of affairs given that the child couldn't be more than five years old.

In the end, Ken Jin took pity. "I am Wen Ken Jin, and I am your father's brother." His voice had softened for the introduction, and Charlotte saw that he had tender feelings for the child though they'd obviously never met.

Charlotte watched understanding slide through the boy's frame. His gaze fell on her and he straightened; but not to bow. Instead, he screwed up his tiny face and screeched, "Bastard Ken Jin and his white whore!" Then he spat— twice—once at each of their feet before dashing away, around the guest hall, presumably toward the children's chambers. With another quick flutter of skirts, the three women rushed after him.

Ken Jin didn't move. He stood frozen to the spot, but not Charlotte. She was already rushing forward—right after the twittering maids—to stop the child. No one, not even a spoiled first son, should ever act so horrid to his own father, and certainly not in China where family was everything. But she was stopped by a booming laugh from the center doorway of the guest hall. It wasn't deep, simply loud in the silence left by the rude boy, and Charlotte turned to face her first eunuch-turned-mandarin.

He was large, not in height but because of his voluminous clothing and fatty body. He had a round face, round hands, and a round body all draped in richly embroidered silks. He was laughing in cheerful good humor, though true joy never reached his deep-set black eyes. "Children play such funny tricks, and Hong Fa has such a quick mind. He has become quite sure of himself."

"He is rude and must be whipped," Ken Jin replied. "How can you allow—"

"I will see to the discipline of my son," the mandarin shot back. Anger quickly overwhelmed his false humor. "And no beggar will ever instruct me."

Ken Jin didn't flinch; Charlotte was watching the two men closely, so she would have seen it. Then she saw her lover grow taller and colder—more authoritative—even as his voice grew softer. "My godson would never act so dishonorably to a guest."

"You don't look like a guest, and he is only a boy."

"Any man, woman, or child who enters this house peaceably—"

"Pah!" The mandarin spat in the courtyard, a few inches away from Ken Jin's feet. "You even speak like a ghost devil. 'Man, woman, or child,'" he mocked. "Why are you here—and with that?"

If he spat at Charlotte, she was ready to leap on his fat, girlish face and claw his piggy eyes out. But he didn't. Clearly she wasn't worth even that much disdain. He didn't even gesture at her.

"I come seeking lodging for the night, brother," Ken Jin ground out. "Before tomorrow's dedication to the Emperor."

The news had palpable impact. Even knowing it already, Charlotte couldn't stop herself from flinching. Gao Jin had a much greater response. His body jerked, and his eyes widened. His mouth even fell open in shock as he stared first at Ken Jin's crotch. Some moments later, the man's thoughts began to churn. Charlotte could see it in the slow shifting expression as his gaze roved over Ken Jin's tattered clothing, lean face, and dirty hands.

"So, the foreign devils have brought you to this. How much money do you owe?" He glanced at the front gate. "Do we bar the door against your creditors?"

"No one chases me, brother, and I have no need of money." Ken Jin's gaze was equally pointed as it wandered over the gold embroidery that adorned his brother's robe. "Indeed, you well know the money I have at my disposal."

Charlotte straightened in surprise. She already knew Ken Jin supported his fiancée's family. Did he support his brother as well? Then she nearly hit herself for her stupidity. Of course Ken Jin supported his brother! Or, more accurately, Ken Jin supported his son, even if the child was a rude little brat.

"We traveled in disguise," continued Ken Jin. "For

safety." So forceful was his statement that Charlotte believed him, even knowing that it was a lie.

"Foreign thinking," the brother spat. "Honest Chinese have no need to hide themselves—"

"Are we to stand out here like strangers speaking politics? Or do you invite us in as family?"

Again, Gao Jin pulled back. Apparently he wasn't used to being reprimanded. "Your associations do you no credit," he snarled. Then he frowned. "What is she? A gift to the Emperor? I can tell you that Heaven's son has no perversions such as yours. He will as likely have her killed as—"

"She is no gift!" Finally Ken Jin's temper showed. He even advanced a furious step toward his brother, far enough that Charlotte put out a restraining hand. She had no wish for fisticuffs here.

"Perhaps I should go," she began, though she had no idea where she could possibly go in Peking dressed like this and without money.

"You will stay, Miss Charlotte," Ken Jin said firmly as he stared at his brother. "Stay and be treated as the honored guests we are." Then he let his gaze travel across the expensive carvings adorning the outer courtyard, the ornamental lanterns painted in red and gold, and the hanging tai shan plaque to repel bad fortune. All of it added up to money that no doubt had come from Ken Jin. She sincerely doubted a eunuch had managed to accumulate so much wealth. "Unless my godson wishes to end his relationship with me," Ken Jin drawled. "You have only to say the word—"

"Nonsense! Nonsense!" returned Gao Jin. "Don't be so polite. My son adores you! He was only taken by surprise, is all. Understandable, given your appearance. He is but a child, of course. Come in, come in."

Then he draped one fleshy arm across Ken Jin and steered him up the stairs to the guests' entrance hall. Charlotte had no choice but to trail behind. It felt a little like walking open-eyed into a den of thieves. She half expected some servant to leap out of the shadows and plunge a dagger into Ken Jin's heart—or her own, which was much more likely.

But her only concern was to protect Ken Jin. It was a ridiculous thought. He was more than capable of handling a greedy sycophant. Wealthy First Boys often had to push away hangers-on, women after their money, or simple beggars looking for a handout. She'd seen him gently push aside a dozen or more on any given outing.

Except, of course, Gao Jin was no simple leech. He was a brother. Worse, he was the brother tricked into becoming a eunuch. If Ken Jin had an Achilles' heel, it was right here in this fat, bigoted, pudding-faced devil of a brother. And so Charlotte had no intention of leaving Ken Jin's side, no matter how many social niceties she trampled.

She trailed behind the two men as they crossed into the inner courtyard. She had a quick impression of a rather sad locus tree lost amid a dozen toys. Then Gao Jin snapped his fingers at a maid and spoke in rapid Mandarin, the words flowing much too fast for her to follow. Soon he was bellowing again to his wife and son, snapping his fingers while people scampered all around. Within moments, his son was bowing before Ken Jin, his mulish attitude cowed by his father's fist. The wife hung behind, anxiously fluttering about her child. And then Charlotte felt a nervous tug at her sleeve. She turned to see a frightened maid bowing before her.

"Please come," the girl said in very slow Chinese.

Charlotte smiled and shook her head, trying her best to refuse politely. She wasn't going anywhere without Ken Jin. The maid nodded and bowed more vigorously. Her smile widened with obvious urgency as she gestured to the side. "Please come."

"No, I'm fine here," she said in Chinese.

The woman's eyes widened in shock. Clearly she hadn't thought Charlotte spoke Mandarin, but Ken Jin had been teaching her the dialect along the road. Given her base in Shanghai dialect, Charlotte had become almost fluent.

"I will stay here—" she began, but the maid cut her off.

"Bath. Clothes. Come see." She spoke as if she were tempting a child with treats, but Charlotte just shook her head. As much as she wanted those things, she wasn't about to let them separate her from Ken Jin.

"Yes, you come."

"No, I stay."

"Bath very good."

"I will stay here—"

Ken Jin's voice interrupted her. "Is there a problem, Miss Charlotte?"

Charlotte started, instinctively feeling guilty for drawing attention to the little argument. She opened her mouth to respond, but Gao Jin answered for her.

"She's just feeling anxious about a bath. You know how the ghosts fear water."

"I am not afraid of water," Charlotte snapped, then immediately regretted her unruly tongue. Women did not speak in this culture. Certainly not with that tone, and not to the master of the household.

Fortunately, Ken Jin smiled as if she had just discovered gold. "An excellent suggestion. It has been a long trip. Baths with oil, fresh clothing, and sweet melons while we wait." He grinned at his brother. "You are the most excellent of hosts."

He extended his arm to her in the most courtly of manners. "Please allow me to escort you to our chambers, Miss Charlotte." He glanced at his brother. "You have a most efficient staff. I am sure we will be excellently pleased by our service."

Gao Jin looked like he was not in the least bit pleased, but he forced a smile nonetheless. "You are too polite. Go rest. I will see to everything."

So Ken Jin and Charlotte strolled off to the guest quarters, while behind them Gao Jin started bellowing orders to a frantic and obviously inefficient staff.

Chapter Seventeen

"Well that was excruciating."

Ken Jin heard Charlotte's muttered words even though her voice was low and muffled. Odd, that he could, especially since he stood in her bedroom doorway and she had dropped facedown onto her small bed. But then again, he now was so tuned to her that he heard everything about her.

He'd heard her argue with the maid who wanted to take her off to the servants' quarters. He'd listened to the splash of her bathwater and her hiss of disgust at the cheap clothing his brother had given her to wear. And he'd noticed her every shift and stifled curse as she'd held her tongue all through dinner and evening chatter.

In truth, he was quite proud of her restraint. He doubted his brother realized the depths of her hatred of him and his family. Gao Jin likely dismissed her as a ghost barbarian too stupid to understand the petty slights he had inflicted upon her all evening. But she had known. And she'd held her tongue, though it cost her three broken nails and his brother two pairs of chopsticks that she'd snapped in fury.

He stepped into her room. How he cherished her for her self-control. "I am sorry you were subjected to that," he said.

She lifted her head to stare at him. "Me? Pfff." Her hair lifted off her face with the force of her exhalation. "But you, Ken Jin—how can you stand it? He's terrible to you."

She pushed up to a sitting position, and he crossed to her side. "He is a eunuch, Char. I have cost him everything a man wants."

"Horseshit. He's got a wife. He's got a son. You're supporting them. He's got everything, and they don't even have the decency to say thank you." She leaned toward him.

"He is a *eunuch*. Do you not understand—"

She cursed and rolled her eyes. He was startled enough by her expletive, but then she continued with no restraint at all. "He's got everything, Ken Jin, and you have nothing!"

"He deserved—"

"Nothing! Bloody hell, no one should become a eunuch. No one! But *you* can't keep paying. You can't . . ." Her voice trailed off. Then, "Ken Jin?"

He opened his eyes. He hadn't even realized he'd shut them. And once he looked at her, he noticed that she gripped his hands and yet he barely even felt it. His entire body was numb. "Yes, Char?" he asked.

She sighed, her entire body drooping. "At least you didn't call me Miss Charlotte."

He frowned, and she groaned.

"You've gone all formal on me again. It's what you do when you don't want to deal with me. You think I don't know it, but I do. You're tired of this argument and want me to just shut up."

It wasn't a question, but he answered it anyway. "You are my dearest friend." Odd, how the words flowed easily now when a few short weeks ago he couldn't have imagined thinking it, much less saying it aloud.

She moved her hands, but he had to look down to see that she caressed his arm. "I want to help, Ken Jin. I can't stand seeing you like this."

He tilted his head. "I don't understand."

She laughed—a short explosion of sound that had nothing to do with humor. "You *do* understand, but you've cut yourself off. I watched it happen, you know. I watched all evening while Gao Jin picked at you and insulted you. He offered you the best food like a guest, then pitied your lost years toiling for the barbarians. He waved his finery in front of your nose without acknowledging that you paid for it. I wouldn't be surprised if he spit in the wine he gave you. I know he did mine."

He flinched. "What?"

She waved it away. "I didn't drink it. Didn't eat much either, because I'm sure it was dog meat."

He'd noticed that she hadn't eaten, but thought she was bowing to the custom of women not eating with men. "You saw this?"

She sighed as she stared at him. Never had she appeared more defeated. "I saw. I felt. I cried . . . for you. Ken Jin, how can you think you owe that man anything? His son spit at you. No, wait. He's *your* son."

"No, he's not."

"Yes, yes," she said as she pushed to her feet and paced about the small chamber. "I know that legally he's your brother's, but you . . ." She swallowed, clearly struggling with the concept. "You did the deed on the wedding night."

He shook his head. "No, Char, I didn't."

She stopped moving and stared. "What do you mean? *He* couldn't have. I mean, if you didn't . . ."

"She was already pregnant. How do you think such a no-ble woman could be married to a eunuch anyway? No man would have her. Only a eunuch who wanted a family any way he could. They only needed . . ."

"A pigeon to pretend to be the natural father. A rich fool who would pay for the boy's food and clothing and anything else the brat wants." She closed her eyes with a groan. "Why do you stand for it? You're the strongest, smartest person I know, and yet you're letting them destroy you. Why?"

He looked at his own hands and tried once again to explain what it meant to be Chinese. "I would not have been accepted back into my family otherwise. They offered me a wife, but she is a child. Even if I married her, she would become part of *my* family."

"But they disowned you."

He nodded. "Exactly. The girl becomes disowned as well. My name would *not* be written on the family altar. It is only in return for this act—"

"For pretending to father Gao Jin's son?"

"Yes. Because of that, my name was written on the plaque."

She slowly sank back onto the bed. "So, your name is painted on a piece of wood on an altar somewhere you never go. Is that worth everything you've done? Everything you're giving up?"

"Yes." He said it with total conviction. He said it with the force of an orphan who longs for a family. He said it, and he believed it—except, the word sounded hollow to his ears now.

"If you're going to buy your way into a family, Ken Jin, couldn't you have picked a better one?"

Ken Jin laughed. He couldn't help it. In fact, for the first time since coming to Peking, he felt connected to himself. His entire body and spirit shook with laughter. She joined him, of course. Not at first, but when the tears rolled from his eyes, her giggles began. Soon they both fell backward on the bed and belly laughs echoed through the room.

But eventually the laughter faded. In time, they lay face-to-face on the narrow pallet and felt the slow return to reality.

"I will always love you, Ken Jin," she whispered. "No matter what happens, remember that."

He touched her face. He could feel her now that the numbness was fading. She'd done that for him. She'd recalled him to himself, body and spirit. But did he dare say it?

"I love you as well, Miss Charlotte."

She rolled her eyes, and he laughed again.

"I love you, Char."

"Then, don't do this. Don't go to the Forbidden City tomorrow. We'll find a way to get through. We'll—"

"What?" he interrupted. "An impoverished Chinese and a destitute white woman? What would we do?"

"Love each other?" Her words were barely audible, but hope shone in her eyes. Everything inside him pushed him to agree, to throw aside logic and sense and everything he knew of the world to embrace . . . what? To embrace her: her goodness, her openness, her light and life and love. What he would give to have her at his side for the rest of his life.

He heard her sigh and felt the heat of her breath burn across his temple. "You're not going to change your mind, are you?" she realized.

He swallowed, barely able to force the words from his throat. "I go to the palace for balance, Char, to return to what should have been."

"Make a new path, Ken Jin. It has been done before. In fact, the Americans created an entire country out of the idea."

He shook his head. "I am not so forward-thinking. I am Chinese, and to a Chinese, family is everything."

She pushed him back. He did not see it coming; all he knew was that one moment they were lying face-to-face on the bed, and the next second he lay flat on his back while she mounted him. Her skirt was too tight to easily accomplish such a thing. The cheap silk scrunched up her legs, then tore as she forced it even farther. In moments, she pressed her naked flesh to the fabric above his straining dragon.

"*I* will be your family, Ken Jin. We will create a new—"

He silenced her with a kiss. She pressed down as he surged up toward her. But when the kiss was done, when he could no longer sustain the lift of his head or the thrust of his tongue, he reluctantly dropped backward. She knew what he was about to say. He could see the weary acceptance in her eyes, but he had to say it anyway.

"I cannot be free of my family until my brother is no longer a eunuch."

She bit her lip. "It can't be reattached, Ken Jin. You'll owe him for the rest of your life. And he'll suck you dry."

Ken Jin nodded. He knew this, had long since accepted it. "Such is the payment for my crime."

He watched in awe as her eyes began to tear, but she blinked them back. And when she spoke, her voice was strong with determination. "I want us to make love, Ken Jin. I want to have your child."

He gaped. He heard her words, but he could not believe she would offer such a thing. He opened his mouth to argue, but no words came out. All he managed was an incoherent sound of pain and longing.

"Don't even try to talk to me out of it," she warned. "I know what I'm saying." But she couldn't; she never had. Worse, she would regret it in the morning. And yet, such was the desire in his heart that he could not manage the words.

"I know, I know," she continued. "White virgin. Chinese man. They'll think you raped me. But what can they do to you? You'll already be castrated." Her words ended in a hysterical laugh, but she quickly recovered. "No, no, don't argue. I take the risk seriously. To you, to me, to the baby." Her voice broke on the word at the same moment his heart lurched.

A baby. A child from the two of them. How wonderful that would be.

"Think of it, Ken Jin," she continued. "You'd have a family even after . . . well, even after tomorrow. No one has to know but us. And you'll have a family." She bit her lip as tears dripped one by one on his face. "We'll be your real family, and we'll love you. I'll raise him that way."

He closed his eyes. He couldn't watch the love shining through her, or the hope that made her skin seem to glow. Her entire body pulsed with love for him. He couldn't watch, and yet, he couldn't stop himself. He opened his eyes. He opened all his senses to her. He smelled her scent, touched her heated body, and trembled to the sound of her breath. He wanted her more than he wanted honor, more than he wanted to walk the middle path of the Tao, more, even, than the qi that sustained him. He wanted her and the family she offered. And yet, he could not give her false hope.

"It will change nothing, Char. I must still dedicate myself in the morning."

She nodded, and he felt her tears drop onto his face. "I know," she whispered.

"And a child . . ." He swallowed. How he wanted such a thing! "You are a lone woman—"

She shook her head. "I'll say I'm a widow. I'm old enough. That my husband was killed by the Boxers." She rolled her eyes. "That's common enough these days."

"But—"

"There are ways, Ken Jin. You don't think it's never happened before, do you? That a single woman got pregnant." She released a soft laugh. "If nothing else, I'll work at the mission. Someone will help me."

"You would have all my money."

"I don't need—"

"You would." He grinned. "And we'll steal something from my brother. He has imperial jade. He showed it to me."

"You probably paid for it anyway." She began untying his tunic, stripping it away with impatient hands.

"This is madness. You cannot—"

"I can. I want to." His tunic was thrown wide and she ran her fingers over his chest. Then she leaned down to kiss his nipples, sucking just hard enough to make his entire body thrust upward. A son. A family. Of all the things anyone had ever offered, this was the most precious. This was what he had always wanted.

"You will be alone," he said. "Once I am in the Forbidden City, I cannot leave. I cannot help you."

"I don't care," she said to his belly. Her lips were kissing lower down his body. Her hands tugged at his pants.

"Char," he groaned. "What of William? What of your family? They will never accept a bastard child. And they will know he is mine."

In his mind, it was already done. He already had a son with dark black hair, a quick mind, and a ready laugh. A child that ran like the wind and loved like the sun. A child like his mother. How he wanted it.

She pulled opened his trousers and his dragon sprang free. She had learned a great deal about kissing in the last few days. She knew how to stroke his mouth with her tongue, how to caress his chest with her hands. She did so now, pressing her fingers into the points he had shown her, stroking her tongue across places she had discovered on her own. He knew she was placing herself, drawing herself higher on his body. And while he struggled with his conscience, before he found the strength to set her away, she dropped herself down upon him.

Her yin rain was plentiful, so his dragon slid quickly into her tight cinnabar cave. She gasped in shock and froze. He grabbed her arms to lift her away, but he hadn't the strength, and she hadn't the will.

"You're very large," she said, her voice high.

"Lift off," he said. "We must stop."

"No. *No*." She tightened her legs to grip him with force. He bit back a groan. He could move. He should move—away—but nothing had ever felt so excellent.

"Char," he growled as he forced himself to deny them both. "Think about the future. Think what it means . . ."

"No. No." She gasped out the words, but with each breath, she seemed to grow stronger. Her eyes focused on him. Her lips curved in a radiant smile. And as she spoke, yang surged through his blood. His mind fogged with her yin power. She was radiant with it.

She leaned down. He didn't know when she'd swept off the last of her ripped gown, but it was gone now. She was naked as she leaned forward, and her breasts dangled enticingly above him.

He helped her move, thinking she meant to lift away. But she didn't. Instead, she shifted his grip. She took hold of his wrists and moved his hands to her breasts. "Touch me, Ken Jin." How soft her skin was. How powerful the yin pulse beneath his fingertips. "Carry me away," she added as she moved his hands over her. "Take me to Heaven."

He shook his head. "I can't." He couldn't think. He couldn't focus.

She extended forward, drawing herself up high enough

to kiss his lips. He let her go, but not far enough to lose her all together. He was not man enough to draw completely out. Not yet. Not . . .

"You can," she whispered. She leaned down. She trailed her lips across his cheek, the heat of her caress nothing compared to the lick of her yin power across his face and body. It engulfed him. "You just have to want it."

He did. He wanted it more than life itself. And yet . . .

"Love me, Ken Jin."

"I do," he swore. "I always have."

He thrust.

Charlotte felt his driving energy and knew why the Chinese called it a dragon. Ken Jin was so very large inside her. Thick and full, his power pushed at her, filled her, expanded her. She was growing along with him, this heat in her belly. With his every thrust, she felt a quickening, a surging, a . . . something.

Her yin tide was rising. His hands were so skilled upon her breasts. His mouth nipped and stroked and suckled, one after the other, and she arched into the glorious tide. After all, she'd felt the yin rush numerous times before. She'd been overwhelmed by it, carried by it, even drowned in it; but this was different. This was . . .

Love.

She looked into his eyes and finally understood the truth. He loved her. He'd always loved her. That was why his touch sent her flying. That was why she craved him beyond reason, beyond logic. Because he loved her and always had. Only this time, he admitted it. And this time, he showed her without restraint. How else could his yang lift and push and expand her soul until she felt larger than her own body? How else could her yin draw him with her, combining together in the glorious cauldron of her sex, until together they became fire and air and more?

She slid to his lips, needing to fuse with his mouth while giving him more room to move below. He was saying something: whispered Chinese words that she couldn't hear. But she felt them. Each word brushed across her lips, each breath heated the dark recesses of her mouth. She arched in glorious response. How could simple words feel so wonderful?

His hands shifted off her breasts to slide down to her hips. But she remained poised above him, her nipples stroking across his contoured chest. Larger circles, then smaller, tighter circles. The yin fire sizzled in her breasts.

His hands were large on her hips, and he stabilized her against his thrusts. His power was growing, and his yang became a pounding beat that had her thighs opening wider to accommodate his greater strength. He was still speaking, his mouth teasing her neck, his breath hot and wet across her quivering pulse. Only this time, she wanted to know his words, know what beat in his mind and heart, so she reined in her senses and listened.

"All of you. All of you," he said.

She smiled. "All of us. All of *us*."

He blinked and, like her, had to shift focus. But when he finally heard her, the change was stunning. His face lit. His eyes became brighter, clearer, and his entire body opened. She had no other words for it. His energy gates were fully, gloriously open.

She thought his yang had been strong before; now it became a force of nature. What had been a steady push of energy became a deluge of fire. What had been powerful, now infused her with a joy so profound it could only be . . .

Heaven. On Earth. He was launching them to Heaven!

"I love you," she whispered again; then she poured all

312

she was into him. Just as he enveloped her with all that was him.

Their energies merged—yin and yang boiling together—but there were pinpoints of heat, nexuses where they joined more than others: his dragon, thick and hard inside her, as it churned her yin. The heat there felt like a tiny sun. Her breasts, as they brushed against his chest, trailing fire across his skin and pouring her power into his heart.

Those two places—chest and groin—were the top and bottom of the circle, yin and yang coiling and combining in ecstasy. That was the physical joy, and the electric burn of power. But they had something more. It came from his eyes, and it sang in her own—a vibration, a joy, a love that grew in beauty the longer they looked at one another.

Below was power, above was love. Both were expanding.

Their breaths quickened. Their hearts trembled.

Charlotte arched into him. Ken Jin rammed into her. And their gazes held.

"We . . ." she gasped.

"Whole . . ." he mouthed.

The energies touched and ignited.

His seed roared through her. Her womb opened to receive. And the power took them to Heaven.

"I am here. I am finally here!"

Charlotte turned to smile at Ken Jin's spirit. It was distant to her—a shadowy outline—but she could hear his voice and feel his joy. If she had to guess, she would say he was dancing.

They stood in the Chamber of a Thousand Swinging Lanterns. According to Ken Jin, it wasn't Heaven proper, but the antechamber to those glorious gates. And yet, how could anything be more wonderful? Black velvet dotted with swinging lights. A song of love felt more than heard. A joy that enveloped and permeated all that she was.

All that *they* were, for Ken Jin was here with her.

"Charlotte? Can you hear me?" he called.

"I am here!" she replied with a giggle. She doubted they were actually speaking. The words came as thoughts carried on emotions: felt, experienced, but not spoken aloud. They were so intertwined that she knew what he knew, and he felt what she felt.

Love. In all its myriad forms. For one another. For family. For animals and plants and birds. For the world. And for William, who glided closer.

Just as before, the radiant form of her brother appeared, with a great smile and wide-open arms. Charlotte felt her heart sing in joy as they embraced. Beside her, Ken Jin bowed deeply and with awe.

"Master William."

"Ken Jin and Charlotte. How pleased I am that you are here."

Charlotte felt his pleasure warm her soul. She had so much she wanted to say, so much to ask, but the words clogged in her mind and refused to step forth. It was ridiculous to feel intimidated by her little brother, but this being of light and love was beyond the boy she'd chased through the house to make him take his baths. This was William—an angel.

"Not an angel," he corrected, clearly hearing her thoughts. "I am William—the part you do not see in my body."

"His soul?" And her old fear returned. "You're not dead, are you? You're not—"

He laughed, not in mockery but with simple pleasure.

"Do you believe that I am so small as to be contained in a single biological form? That any of us are?"

She hesitated, unsure what she thought.

"I am so much more than what you see on Earth. All of us are." He paused and turned saddened eyes to Ken Jin. "Or all of us can be."

She followed her brother's gaze, automatically extending her hand to her love. But Ken Jin was too far away to grasp, too indistinct to clearly see more than just his outline. Except . . . She narrowed her eyes. He was here beside her. She could touch him. She could feel him, but his light was so dark, his power so cold.

"Ken Jin!" she cried. "What has happened?"

Her lover dropped his eyes, his shame a palpable weight dragging him away from her. "I am not worthy," he said.

Again William laughed, and again there was no malice in the sound, only the gentle humor of a parent to a child. "All are worthy, Ken Jin. It is you who have chosen this form. Do you wish to change it now?"

She felt Ken Jin's confusion, felt his pain in her own heart. But mostly she felt fear. Ken Jin was growing heavier by the second.

"William!" she cried. "Help us!"

So her brother bent down and kissed her cheek. She felt his caress and the joy it brought her. And then she heard one last message. "Thank you for lifting your shadow, big sister. Now I can grow stronger on my own."

She jerked her attention upward. They were plunging out of Heaven at a dizzying rate. And yet, there was no mistaking his words. But what did the mean? What shadow?

Then she saw. He was so bright that she hadn't noticed before. His radiance, his power . . . But with distance, she also saw a shadow, an outline that darkened his features and obscured his lines. Then, as she watched, it began to fade. She saw it clearly, how he was growing brighter as the darkness began to lift away.

Her shadow? But . . .

She plunged back into her body—heavy, dark, exhausted.

And alone. No one shared the thin pallet. No other presence filled the room.

Where was Ken Jin?

Five-Minutes Acupressure Wellness Exercise. Step 1,
Briskly rub your lower back along both sides of the spine.
Rub these Sea of Vitality points (B23 and B47) briksly up
and down for one minute, crating warmth from the fric-
tion. Step 2, Hold the base of the skull and the Third Eye
point. Step 3, Hold the Sea of energy (CV 6) three finger
widths below your belly button in your lower abdomen.
Acupressure's Potent Points, Michael Reed Gach

Chapter Eighteen

Cold. He had never felt so cold in all his life.

Ken Jin looked down at his hands, able to see but not feel them. He had spent much of his life in some level of numbness, but the lack of sensation now was particularly glaring. After feeling everything a few hours ago in Heaven, after being whole for a short time, he was completely disconnected now. Why was it so cold even in sunlight?

"Ken Jin?"

He lifted his head, though the motion was stiff and slow. Charlotte stood in the doorway to his room. She was completely naked, amazingly beautiful, and even his unworthy eyes could see the tendrils of Heaven that still made her skin glow.

"You have returned," he said, his voice rusty from the night's silence.

"Was I . . . ? How long . . . ?" She licked her lips as she struggled with her surroundings. He understood her confusion. He, too, had been disoriented for an hour or more.

"It is just past sunrise. You stayed in Heaven longer than

I." He'd woken beside her, and felt her body still entwined with his. He knew she remained in Heaven while he had been cast out. So he lay beside her, thinking of his life and basking in her heat. But he had never been able to think clearly when enveloped in her yin. Eventually, he forced himself to separate from her. He left her side and came to his room to kneel before the east-facing window and pray.

"No . . ." she said. She shook her head, her expression fierce. "We fell at the same time. I tried to hold on, but . . ."

"But I was too heavy," he answered for her. "I was unworthy of—"

"Don't say it!" she snapped. Then she stomped into the room, her breasts bobbing with her fierce movements. "You most certainly are worthy! Nobody is more worthy. You've given everything to the family that has treated you like dirt! You've—"

"I've cut myself into tiny pieces for them. I've given them all that I can, and now that it is morning, I am to cut my body as my spirit has been sectioned."

She gaped at him. Clearly she had not expected such clarity of thought from him. He almost smiled. "I have had many hours to meditate, and Heaven gives a man much to contemplate."

She shut her mouth with a snap. Then she crossed the last distance between them to kneel beside him. She moved so quickly, whereas he still felt the sluggishness of Earth dragging at his limbs. Before he could say anything, her arms wrapped about him, her chest caressed his back, and her sweet lips pressed to his cheeks. So hot was her presence, her kiss seared him like a brand; but he welcomed it nonetheless. A man in pieces needed the power of a woman's qi. Of this woman's qi.

"And what have you decided?" she asked.

He closed his eyes to better absorb her strength. Odd, that he had spent so many years searching for ways to take a woman's yin. He had spent nights stimulating one woman after another only to end up feeling weaker. And yet, all that time Charlotte had been nearby. The answer had been with him the whole time.

Perhaps that was why he'd always drawn yin from white women: because he was searching for Charlotte. And now, when he felt most confused, most alone, she gave him such power with no effort. Such was the generosity of her spirit that he had only to think of her and his qi strengthened. His dragon too, he realized, looking down. Hard and proud, it jutted eagerly upward against his pants, seeking her again.

"Ken Jin?" she pressed, her tone anxious. "What have you decided?"

"That I am whole with you." He reached up and drew her down onto the floor before him. He had come to this room seeking warmth in the sunlight. His was the only room with a window, but now he realized how wrong he had been. The warmth he needed came from her. It came from being a whole man. It came from having a unity of purpose and mind—which is exactly what she gave him.

"I want to remain with you," he stated firmly. She smiled at him and his blood heated. It was so wondrous a sensation that he nearly missed her next words.

"But what about returning to the Tao? Are you giving up on that?"

"I did abandon the middle path so many years ago when I tricked my brother, but not because of my foolishness. I wandered off the middle path when I left home."

"I thought they sent you away."

He nodded again. "I left part of my heart with my family while the rest of me traveled to Shanghai."

"That's why you've always wanted to return home."

He nodded. "And so I gave more of myself to my fiancée and her family. And then—"

"More to your brother and his wife and their son."

Ken Jin sighed. "Shi Po often said that a man of divided heart cannot find the Tao." He lifted his gaze to Charlotte. "Since I was eight years old, I have split my efforts, cut off pieces of my heart and my life. Only one thing has ever unified my heart and spirt and body."

Her eyes softened, and she reached for his hand. He gripped her tightly in return, and the numbness in his fingers began to fade.

"You have been my one purpose. When I am with you, I wish with one heart, I act with one body, and—"

"You love completely." She smiled. "I feel the same way, Ken Jin. You quiet the frustration in my heart; you give me a sense of direction and purpose." She grinned. "You give me Heaven."

He shook his head. "We gained it together. Because we worked for it."

"We worked together as one."

She understood. And now, with her, he did as well. "We will get married," he said firmly.

"You will not dedicate yourself to the Emperor?"

"We will find a way to survive." There would be many difficulties. They had nothing. But for the first time ever, he felt powerful. He was a whole man, and the energy that flooded his body gave him what he needed to face the future.

He straightened to his feet, pulling her up with him. "Come. We will begin our new life today." He grinned. "I already have an idea—"

"Yes!" bellowed a voice from the hallway. "Yes, today a new life begins."

They turned as one to face Gao Jin. Then Ken Jin dashed to the side to grab a tunic for Charlotte. It felt like blasphemy to cover her nakedness while the beauty of Heaven clung to her skin, but he would not have his brother defile her with his gaze. She pulled the garment on quickly, but not before his brother entered. Ken Jin felt his fists clench in fury at the sneer that crossed on his brother's fleshy face.

"We are not dressed," he said stiffly. "Please wait outside while we—"

"Don't be ridiculous, brother," Gao Jin said with a cackle. "Do you not recall that we share all things equally? As you enjoyed my wedding night, I shall enjoy that which you are now abandoning."

Ken Jin felt hot fury boil in his blood. And because Charlotte was with him, the power not only churned in his chest, but extended to his hands and feet as well. "Can you not see what has happened here, brother?" he asked. He kept his voice low, the threat implicit.

His brother laughed through his nose, and the sound was bestial. "All can see, Ken Jin. It is—"

"We went to Heaven's antechamber last night. We danced in the Hall of a Thousand Swinging Lanterns."

Gao Jin's eyes narrowed, and he released a girlish giggle. "Of course you did. And I don't blame you. A man's last night should be enjoyed." He reached out to stroke Charlotte, but she jerked away. She needn't have worried; Ken Jin had already pushed between them, using his body to block his brother's movements.

"I will not go to the Forbidden City, Gao Jin." He reached for the easiest explanation, one his brother could understand. "We are close to becoming Immortals. I will not throw that away."

His brother's giggles faded, and his mouth drew into a pout. "You disappoint me. I had thought you stronger than this." He sighed. "But you have never been consistent in anything but trickery."

Ken Jin reared back, pain at his brother's continued hatred searing through him. The pain was sharp enough to bring tears to his eyes, and yet it . . . it replaced the numbness that had surrounded him for years. It was a *good* pain.

"*I* am the trickster?" he asked, his voice gaining strength as he reclaimed the part of his spirt that he'd given to his brother. "I did not sneak into a cart to steal my brother's treat."

"It was not a treat! I went to the surgeons!"

Ken Jin shrugged. "And you would be whole now if you had not tried to trick me."

Gao Jin reared forward, his fists poised to strike. Ken Jin did not even flinch. He knew he was faster than his brother. So he continued to speak, his voice growing stronger with each word. "I did not pretend my brother sired my wife's bastard. I did not take your money and your love to clothe and feed a boy who has been raised to hate you."

"And I cannot father a son on my own because of you!" Gao Jin screamed.

Ken Jin nodded, acknowledging the truth. "That crime is mine to bear. Yours are the crimes you have committed since." He took a deep breath, and when he released it, he knew he had reclaimed all that was lost to this bitter brother. "I have no more obligations to you, my brother." He straightened. "You are disowned."

Gao Jin reared back, fear mixing with hatred in every quivering inch of his body. But Ken Jin knew he could not weaken in purpose. He would have to do it all. Turning his back on his brother, he grabbed his rolled pack. He and Charlotte would leave without again looking upon Gao Jin's face. Then it would be done, and he would be free. Happiness began to bubble inside his heart.

"No!" Charlotte screamed.

Pain exploded in his head, and he knew no more.

Charlotte launched herself at Gao Jin. Finally, she could vent her feelings on this despicable man. She'd seen him raise his fist, knew exactly what he intended, but had been too far away to prevent it. The blow had landed with a sickening thud at the base of Ken Jin's skull.

She attacked. Throwing herself forward, Charlotte dragged the eunuch off Ken Jin, who was already crumpling to the floor. Then she hit, she kicked, she even bit and tore with her nails. And Gao Jin went down under her assault. He was strong, but like Ken Jin, he'd been unprepared.

She avoided most of his blows and kept him too off balance to put much strength into those that did connect. Unfortunately, he did not live alone.

Within moments of her attack, Gao Jin began bellowing. She barely noticed until meaty hands grabbed her hair and arms. She was bodily dragged away despite her best efforts. Soon, pain exploded across her left temple and darkness edged her vision. She felt herself slip to her knees, the strength gone from her limbs.

Meanwhile, Gao Jin was giving instructions. "My brother has weak nerves. He wished to be unconscious during the cutting."

"Liar!" she screeched, but no one paid the least attention to her. Not Gao Jin, not the three eunuchs who had dragged her off to one side, and certainly not the scrawny Chinese man with the large knife who entered the room. She blinked to clear her blurry vision. Oh Lord, they were going to do the surgery right here. And Ken Jin was still unconscious on the floor.

She tried to struggle to her feet. Her vision stabilized, but her body was still weak. Worse, one of the eunuchs held her down with a single massive hand on the back of her neck. One squeeze, and he might very well snap her neck.

"Just as well," the scrawny man was saying. "Just as well in one so old."

"Stop!" she bellowed. "Stop! Stop! Stop!" She said it in

all the languages she knew. English, Shanghai dialect, Mandarin—none had the least effect except to draw Gao Jin's attention. He stepped over to her, his disdain obvious in the curl of his lip and the cruelty in his voice.

"I intended to kill you, ghost whore, but Heaven smiled upon me. A man came to me this morning, one of your own kind, who wished to buy you."

Charlotte tried to leap to her feet, only to be kept in place by the man holding her neck. "How can you do this to him? After all he's done for you. He's your brother!" She was allowed to lift her head enough to see a sick smile push his fleshy cheeks wide.

"But you heard him. He's not my brother anymore."

"Bastard!"

Gao Jin paused and stared down at her in mock sadness. "Barbarians," he spat. "They understand nothing." Then he turned to watch the surgeon.

Charlotte tried to see, but it was difficult. Ken Jin had been lifted onto the bed, and two of the eunuchs were undressing him. To one side, the surgeon had begun sharpening his knife, and the steady *shir, shir* of blade against strop set Charlotte's teeth on edge.

"Ken Jin!" she cried. "Wake up! Ken Jin!"

"Shut up!" snarled Gao Jin. Then he snapped a finger and both of the eunuchs holding Ken Jin straightened. They had finished their work. Ken Jin lay naked and exposed. And yet . . .

Charlotte narrowed her eyes. Could it be? His dragon was not a small thing. It was . . . moving? Could he be awake? Pretending? But it was four against one. He couldn't fight them all. She had to distract them somehow.

She surged forward, she screamed, and she fought like a demon. It accomplished absolutely nothing except a searing pain in her neck as the eunuch pushed her down to the floor.

"You!" Gao Jin pointed to the eunuch by the door. "Go get the barbarian Captain!"

The man hesitated, obviously afraid. Apparently they had no problem fighting a white woman, but facing a white captain alone was a little too intimidating. The superstitions that surrounded white sailors was legendary.

Gao Jin cursed. "Both of you go." He threw a scathing look at Ken Jin. "There won't be any problem here."

The two eunuchs scurried away. The surgeon stopped sharpening his blade. Only one eunuch remained, his hand hard and heavy on the back of Charlotte's neck. It was now or never. She tensed and her captor's hand tightened enough to draw a whimper of pain from her lips. She couldn't move. She couldn't do anything. It was up to Ken Jin. If he was awake, he had to act. *Now*. She silently willed him to move.

Nothing.

And the surgeon leaned forward and positioned his knife.

"Where is she?" a man's voice bellowed in accented Mandarin. "Get out of my way!"

Everyone turned to the doorway. Everyone but Charlotte, who wasn't allowed to move her head. But she trembled at the sound. The voice was hard, the accent rough. She had seen white ship captains and knew some of the traffic they carried. Flesh-peddling was a thriving trade in the Orient.

Ken Jin exploded off the bed. Charlotte hadn't even realized it was happening until the surgeon squealed in terror. She blinked and saw Ken Jin standing on the bed, using his superior position to grab the man's neck. Then he chopped at the surgeon's wrist and caught the knife as it fell.

Gao Jin spun back to the bed, but before he could do more, Ken Jin threw the surgeon against the wall and raised the knife toward the eunuch who held her down. Charlotte heard the thud of a fist meeting flesh, but she couldn't see who had hit whom. Then came another thud, a squeal, and she was abruptly released. Suddenly, Ken Jin was pulling her upright, his voice urgent in her ear.

"Are you hurt? Are you—"

"I'm fine. Are you—"

"Whoreson!" Gao Jin screeched, and then Charlotte was pushed back down, but this time by Ken Jin. He stepped in front of her.

"No!" she cried, but it was too late. Brother fought brother, and it was all she could do to scramble out of the way. She would have helped if she could; she stood and faced the combatants, but within moments she saw that Ken Jin had the upper hand. His brother attacked with fury but no skill, whereas Ken Jin was precise and coldly determined.

So she turned to face the newest threat—an angry bear of a white man who stormed into the room. He'd been delayed by the fleeing surgeon and eunuch, but now he burst into the room with a dark menace. Charlotte crouched to meet him, only marginally surprised to see Little Pearl rush in behind him. Leave it to that woman to take up sides with a flesh peddler.

Charlotte blinked, her mind scrambling to catch up. She knew the Captain. She'd met him before. . . .

Beside her, Ken Jin threw his brother to the floor and dropped one knee onto the man's back. Gao Jin was defeated. Even his curses were choked off, for Ken Jen pressed his other knee into the man's throat. Then Ken Jin looked up—first to Charlotte, then to the man poised in the doorway.

"Captain Jonas?" he said in English, his voice completely steady. "It is an honor to see you again, sir."

Charlotte gasped as a memory finally slid into place.

This was the Captain she'd seen at the Tigress school. The one who ran across the inner garden right after Little Pearl . . .

The bear straightened and visibly relaxed. "Are you all right, Ken Jin?" He turned to scan Charlotte. "Miss Wicks?"

Ken Jin glanced to her and waited for her nod before speaking. "We're both fine, but . . ." His voice trailed away as Little Pearl stepped out from behind the Captain. He hadn't been able to see her before. "What brings you here?"

The Captain didn't answer. Instead, he stepped aside as Little Pearl slipped forward. She was obviously uncertain, though she shot an angry glance at the Captain beside her. But then she bowed deeply to Kin Jin first and then to Charlotte. "We came searching for you. Much has been said about your departure." She glanced at Charlotte. "And yours."

"Why would you care?" snapped Charlotte. She immediately regretted her hasty words. Ken Jin obviously knew and trusted these people; she would be wise to remain silent until she understood things better. Unfortunately, she'd never been good at holding her tongue. "Gao Jin said you bought me from him."

"That was a ruse," Captain Jonas explained quietly. "Ken Jin and I have known each other for years. I am Tan Kui Yu's business partner," he added by way of explanation. It didn't help. At the moment, Charlotte couldn't even remember who Tan Kui Yu was, but she could tell that Ken Jin was perfectly comfortable with the man, especially when the Captain walked over and casually put a heavy boot on Gao Jin's back. "So this is the eunuch brother, huh?" he said in English.

Ken Jin straightened, which allowed Gao Jin to take his first deep breath since he'd hit the floor. Two moments later, the eunuch began cursing in Mandarin. Charlotte didn't know the words, but Little Pearl did and her cackle of laughter split the air.

"Arrogant words," she said, "for a man with his nose in the dirt."

That caused another round of vehement curses, until the Captain shifted his weight. When Gao Jin could no longer draw breath, his invective sputtered to silence.

Captain Jonas smiled at Ken Jin. "I know something of your past from Kui Yu. After I received your letter and heard about your disappearance . . ." He shrugged. "It wasn't hard to put two and two together. If nothing else, I knew you would come here to try and settle things with your brother." He glanced down at the purpling eunuch. "So, is it settled?"

Ken Jin didn't speak. He merely gazed down at the floor in mute misery. Charlotte knew she should stay out of it. She knew he had to decide on his own, but somehow she found herself moving anyway. Jaw firmly shut, she went to his side and touched his hand. His fingers immediately intertwined with hers. They were together, and that was enough. She trusted him to make the right decision.

He sighed and crouched down beside his brother. "We were brothers once, and I destroyed that. I thought we might be brothers again, but you have ended all hope of that. I am sorry, Gao Jin, for what I did to you. And I also grieve for what you did to me." He straightened. "We are done now. Pursue me or mine in any way at all, and even a white gunboat could not prevent the devastation I will visit upon your head."

At Ken Jin's cue, Captain Jonas eased his weight off Gao Jin. The eunuch lifted his head enough to spit at Ken Jin's feet. "You are a whoreson and no relative of mine."

Ken Jin nodded. "Then we are agreed."

It took few moments to dress and gather their belong-ings. Captain Jonas didn't release Gao Jin until all was ready. Then he leaned down and muttered something low into the man's ear. It was obviously a threat, because Gao Jin's quivering cheek paled to a sickly white, but Charlotte couldn't hear. Then Ken Jin, Charlotte, Little Pearl, and Captain Jonas all headed for the door. Charlotte glanced back long enough to see that Gao Jin hadn't moved. Even unrestrained, he remained on his belly in the dirt.

"My ship is waiting," Captain Jonas said. "We'll take you back to Shanghai."

"No!" Ken Jin said, his voice firm. "I must find a way to help the Tans." He grimaced as he looked behind him at his still-cowering brother. "But the only way into the Forbidden City is as a eunuch. And I—"

"There is news of Shi Po," Little Pearl interrupted, but then did not say more until they were out of the guest quarters and moving through the receiving hall. "A woman came to the school. General Kang's mistress. She told us of the Tans."

"Are they alive?" Ken Jin pressed.

Little Pearl nodded. "Yes. And safe for now." She glanced at Charlotte. "As is the Shaolin and his white woman."

Charlotte gasped. "Joanna? Joanna is all right?"

Little Pearl nodded her head, though there was confusion in her expression. "They build another temple in a place called Hong Kong."

"It's an island," said Captain Jonas. "South of Shanghai. I could take you there, if you like. Or . . ." He glanced significantly at Little Pearl.

The woman shot him a glare, but the anger quickly faded. Then she turned to Charlotte and bowed with all possible formality. "I offer you a home at the Tigress school. You can study there under my direction. I . . ." She swallowed and glanced at Ken Jin first, the Captain second. "I was in error when we last met. I beg your forgiveness."

Charlotte didn't know what to say. She didn't know how to take this humbled Little Pearl, especially since she didn't believe for one second that the woman was cowed. In any event, she already had her answer. He was still holding her hand even as they climbed into the Chinese carriage waiting by the front gate.

It was a tight fit—all four of them on one seat—but they managed. And Charlotte didn't mind curling tight to the man beside her. Neither did Little Pearl, apparently, as she settled tightly against Captain Jonas.

"Charlotte and I are to be married," Ken Jin said before she could speak. "We will have our own home, Little Pearl. I don't know where yet, but—"

"We can talk to Mr. Crane, Joanna's father," Charlotte put in. "Maybe he'll help—"

"No, no!" Captain Jonas said as he gathered the reins and set the carriage moving. "That's the other reason I came to find you. It's all a mess, Ken Jin. Mr. Wicks's accounts are a disaster throughout town. I can't keep Kui Yu's holdings together if you can't keep the Wicks partnerships from falling apart. We're in this together, and I can't do it alone." His voice was tight and angry, but the rest of his body appeared completely at ease.

Ken Jin shook his head. "I am no longer the Wickse's First Boy. My replacement—"

"*Aie-yah*," cried Little Pearl. "You still do not listen! The Wickses are gone. Your replacement cashed everything he could, then fled. All your partners—" She threw up her hands. "Disaster!"

"Gone?" Charlotte asked. "I don't understand."

Captain Jonas turned the carriage onto a busier street, but she could still hear him clearly over the city noise. "Your family boarded a ship for England some days ago.

They said you had dedicated yourself to the Church."

She jerked back slightly at the news, but then Ken Jin's arms tightened and his warmth braced her. "They're gone?" she asked, her voice gratifyingly steady.

"I'm afraid so."

They were gone. She was abandoned. Emotions blew threw her quickly, then faded. She wasn't alone—Ken Jin remained beside her, and a memory teased her mind. "That's what he meant," she breathed.

"What?" Ken Jin asked.

"William. The last thing he said to me. 'Thank you for removing your shadow.'" She looked at Ken Jin, her heart beating painfully in her throat. "He's out from under my shadow now. I can't protect him and so—"

"He can grow." Ken Jin nodded. "I remember. I heard it, too."

"But my mother . . ."

Ken Jin squeezed her hand. "They must sort out their power together."

She smiled, and though the act hurt, it was healing as well. "So . . . we're both disowned now."

He pressed his lips to hers. "No," he whispered. "We are both whole."

"Together."

He grinned. "And free to begin again."

AFTERGLOW—*After orgasm, hold the top and bottom of the spinal cord simultaneously to encourage cerebral spinal fluid to circulate through the spine, conducting energy throughout the central nervous system. It also increases the flow of the life force through the meridians, sending healing energy through the entire body.*
Acupressure for Lovers, Michael Reed Gach, Ph.D.

Chapter Nineteen

Feb 2, 1899

Dear Charlotte,
  I have never been happier to be on English soil. Proper tea, cold air, and not a coolie in sight—how could I have ever left? I work daily at the orphanage with the Pastor, and your father remains in London where his actions do not touch us in the least. I have no idea what he does there, and only care that he remain away and not interfere in the running of the baronetcy. So far, the arrangement has been perfect for us both.
  I know you left the mission. I have received two letters from Father Peter, the first telling me of your departure, the second informing me of your marriage to Ken Jin. I suppose if you were to marry a Chinaman, you could have picked far worse. At least he knows how to act properly in an

English home. Still, I cannot help but think we should have brought you back with us. You could have had the pick of the locals, and not a slanted eye among them. But your father insisted that China was best for you, and perhaps he was right. I understand that Ken Jin has been vital in managing the Chinese buildings your father still owns. At least I know you won't starve with him as your husband.

I am sure you are curious about William. He is deliriously happy in England. Indeed, he has gotten married—to Nanny, of all people. Without you on the passage home, he and Nanny became the closest of companions. At her age and looks, she had no hope of a decent marriage, of course, but she is a marvel at running the papers and whatnot of the baronetcy. Your father had no interest in it, of course, so he left it to me and I left it to her. Next thing I knew, she'd bound herself for life to your brother.

He adores her absolutely. And you know she is quite fond of him. Plus, now William has a proper outlet for his physical needs, which were becoming a bit of a problem. She seems quite content with her lot, especially since she will be a Baroness someday, and we no longer have to pay her that exorbitant wage. Indeed, they have even moved into the east wing of the manor so William could be closer to his cousins (Uncle Phillip's girls). The house is so large, we saw no reason to throw them out, and they do adore William.

Shocking as it all seems, I believe everything is exactly how it should be, praise God and His mys-

terious ways. I have enclosed our address in this letter, so you may now write me and tell me how your life proceeds.

Sincerely,
Your loving mother

Charlotte put down the letter with a sigh of relief. William and Nanny? Who would have believed it? Who would have thought any of it was possible? That she and Ken Jin would return after a shipboard wedding to live in her parents' home, the one where Charlotte had resided all her days. That Ken Jin and Captain Jonas could together repair the family fortune and build a successful business out of acupuncture shops, of all things. Or that she would find a surprising interest in learning herbs—from Little Pearl.

God did indeed work in mysterious ways.

"Are you reading the letter again?" Ken Jin asked.

Charlotte looked up as her husband walked into their bedroom. He looked tired and dusty from the day's work, but his smile was warm and full of promise.

She smiled. "I still cannot believe that William and Nanny . . ." Her words faded as her husband claimed her lips. The letter slipped from her hand as her thoughts shifted and her body heated. It was some time later before she had the breath to speak. "I like it when you come home early."

"I have thought of nothing else all day," he answered as he stood and stripped out of his jacket. A knock sounded on the door, and he turned to answer it. A maid stood respectfully at the door, lifting up a dinner tray. Ken Jin took it, then carefully shut the door.

Charlotte smiled. "Dinner in our bedroom? Scandalous!"

"A Tigress must keep up her strength. Especially when she carries a cub."

Her hand went reflexively to her growing belly. Who knew that pregnancy could feel so delightful? She hadn't suffered any of the usual complaints, and her husband found her condition endlessly attractive, not that she'd had any difficulties in that area before.

He pressed a hot dumpling into her mouth, and she closed her eyes to savor the sweet meat. Then she felt his hands on her shoulders and back as he gently pressed into energy points that soothed her aches.

"How do you feel today, my wife?" He never seemed to tire of calling her that. She grinned as she stretched closer to him.

"Well enough to practice," she responded. "Indeed, I have thought of nothing else all day."

"Are you sure—"

She cut off his words on a kiss. She had never been more sure of anything else in her life. They would reach Heaven tonight. Everything felt right. Even the weather was cooperating, giving them a balmy breeze that stirred the curtains and cleared the humidity from the room.

"Very well," Ken Jin responded as his hands shifted to her breasts. "Then let us begin."

Angel William opened his arms and Charlotte flew into them. Beside her, Ken Jin bowed with respect. They were in the Chamber of a Thousand Swinging Lanterns again, and this time all was different. It was also exactly the same. Like before, William was whole and so wondrous, Charlotte could not take her eyes from him. But this time, Ken Jin's form was equally stunning, filled with light and strength and love.

335

"William," Charlotte whispered, wishing she had the words to say more.

"Welcome," he said with a radiant smile. "Welcome to you both."

"Master William," Ken Jin said as he stepped forward. "I am greatly honored to be here."

"We are pleased to have you. You may visit at any time, but perhaps you would be more comfortable inside." So saying, he turned and gestured to the side where a light began to grow and expand. Soon Charlotte saw a gateway and a palace beyond where beings of such light and beauty walked.

"Heaven," whispered Ken Jin, awe suffusing his entire being.

"You are welcome here," William said as they stepped through the gate. "Whenever you choose to come. And here I can answer whatever questions you may have."

It was too much. The joy, the beauty, the truth was too much for her to handle, and Charlotte trembled before it. With her fear came weight. Her spirit grew heavy, and she began to slip away, falling back to Earth. "Help me!" she cried.

She thought that her brother would help her. He was the celestial being, the angel of power. But when she reached out, she found Ken Jin instead. His hand held hers, his love buoyed her up.

"Do not be afraid," Angel William said from beside her.

"I am here," said Ken Jin.

She took his hand and filled her soul with his love. With him beside her, she had the strength to face anything. Her spirit lightened again; then hand in hand, they followed William into Heaven.

They wouldn't stay long. She knew that. All too soon their combined qi would falter and their spirits would tumble back to their bodies on Earth. Such was the nature of life on Earth. But they would return; she knew that as well. With a love as strong as theirs, all of Heaven and Earth was open to them.

Desperate Tigress
JADE LEE

Shi Po has devoted her life to the Taoist ideal: enlightenment through ecstasy, through rigid control of the body and mind. The kiss, the caress, the bite, the scratch—these were the stairs to Immortality. But Heaven has been denied her. Shi Po, 19th-century Shanghai's most famous teacher and abbess, its greatest Tigress, has not been granted entrance into Heaven. And so it is time to die.

One man stands in her way: Tan Kui Yu. His fingers, his lips…his dragon. He swears he and Shi Po will attain Heaven even if he has to pleasure her every day—and night—for the rest of their lives. He has other ideas as well—ideas that have never occurred to the woman who has done it all. Perhaps, he says, it is not just about making love, but about feeling it.

Hungry Tigress

JADE LEE

Joanna Crane joined China's Boxer Rebellion because of the emptiness inside her. But when the rebels—anti-foreigner bandits with a taste for white flesh—turn out worse than their ruthless Qin enemies, her only hope is a Shaolin master with fists of steel and eyes like ice.

He has no wish to harm the meddling American, so, when she learns his secret, Joanna's captor determines to stash her at a Taoist temple. True, the sect is persecuted throughout the land, but he sees no harm in seeking divinity through love. What he does not see is that he and Joanna are already students, their hearts are on the path to Heaven, and salvation lies in a kiss, a touch, and sating the...*Hungry Tigress*.

----

reward *yourself* treat *yourself*

It's like getting **6 FREE ISSUES**

SEDUCED BY CRIMSON

JADE LEE

There exist those who oppose the Dark Ones, the demons from the underbelly of Crimson City: mystics attuned to the earth, the druids. They will send one of their mightiest to fight this battle—their Draige-Uisge. He can shape energy, twist it to harm or heal. But the requisite power can be summoned from one source: the beauty Xiao Fei, the Phoenix Tear. Her blood is the key, along with her ecstasy; her union with Patrick means salvation. Yet in a world of vampires, werewolves and evil untamed, even a kiss can be deadly. And both redemption and oblivion lie in one woman being…*Seduced by Crimson*.
